WICKED IS THE FLESH

OTHER BOOKS BY J. M. FAILDE

The Vampires of Malvania Series

The Crow Lord

The Sun Child

The Wicked Series

Wicked is the Flesh

A Not-Children's Book

A Krampus Story

For Teen Readers

Where Did the Wind Go?

WICKED IS THE FLESH

J. M. FAILDE

J. M. Failde

Atlanta, Georgia

ISBN: 978-1-967160-00-6 - Paperback
eISBN: 978-1-967160-01-3 - eBook

∞This paper meets the requirements of ANSI/NISO Z39.48-1992 (Permanence of Paper)

Cover by Anto Marr

Editing by @Slashers.Cauldron

041525

For Mayra,
I know you would've found this absolutely delicious

CONTENT WARNING

This book contains dark and mature language, themes, and content that may not be suitable for all readers, including violence, parental abuse, attempted sexual assault, religious trauma, and explicit sex. For a full trigger list, please visit my website, jmfailde.com. Reader discretion is advised.

1

MARCELO

Sticky heat clings to my forehead under the thick leather as sweat drips down. Fuck. It's no wonder I haven't been back home in over twelve years. It's way too fucking hot.

Sweet home Miami. Full of drugs, fake tits, and loud cars. People with no respect for anyone else's time but their own. Flashing lights, loud beats, and trips to Denny's at three in the morning after a night of sex-filled partying. It isn't a place I miss, but it still sings to my core whenever I hear the loud Spanish *abuelitas* and the old men sharing a *colada* at the corner bakery. It's large, yet still—somehow—everyone knows everyone, or knows someone who knows them.

But, right now, none of them know me. And I plan to keep it that way.

With the rich melting pot of Spanish culture that runs this city, religion—*my* religion—is fused into the humid air. There is a small hub of Roman Catholics from the diocese that reside here, and the handful of men who know what the Church is *really* doing here is even smaller.

And only one man knows what *I* am doing here—back in my home.

Father Rodrigo's voice grumbles in the ear piece I wear under the mask. "Well?"

I whistle back.

He sighs. "Just . . . make it quick."

Rodrigo hates nights like these. He hates when my . . . duty to the church goes beyond what the diocese accepts. But he has never once discouraged me from following my gut. I assume it was because he was *there*, but maybe it's more than that. Father Rodrigo has *seen* demons. He has known devils and Hell.

Yet, somehow, man is often worse.

I've been keeping to the shadows of the long street. Wynwood, the trendy party district, is just a few blocks away, and I can still hear the coagulated bass from the clubs through the soles of my boots, vibrating into my chest.

The poor hellion I'm currently stalking should know better than to wander into the dark alone, away from civilization. The streets around here are either lively and bumping, or dangerous and mute.

And we crossed the line into danger two blocks ago.

The target, Victor Samuel, is a devout Catholic and a tourist. He's here from some state up north where he left his wife and sixteen-year-old daughter at home to "finalize a business deal." Victor, the sinner that he is, hired a hooker his first night here. Then, on night two, he picked up another woman at the bar, gave her too much cocaine, and kicked her out of his room at four in the morning without her purse, phone, or wallet.

But cheating and lying aren't the sins I am following him for. No, I can leave those to God's judgment.

What I am following him for is damnation.

That prostitute from his first night hasn't been seen again. Since his hotel room the morning after had been filled with half-burnt candles and sigils painted in fresh blood, one can only assume the poor girl was used for more than a quick fuck.

I quicken my step, dropping my foot just a touch harder, loud enough for him to finally hear me. The moment he looks over his shoulder, I barrel at him. Victor's blue eyes widen in fear and shock—a deer caught in the headlights. I wonder briefly what I must look like to him as I dash through the night. A black mass? One of his demons?

It doesn't matter. As I near him, he finally comes to his senses and tries to run from me. He gets two steps before I tackle him to the ground. He's already whining and begging for his life, but I don't pay attention to any of it as I drag the metal rosary from my neck. Three little beads are scratched black, but the rest are as silver as the stars and they reflect the light of the lone streetlamp.

"Please, take my money. I'll give you whatever you want."

I wrap the beads around my knuckles, squeezing tight. The sharp crucifix dangles onto my wrist, lightly poking the exposed flesh there. I ignore Victor, instead mumbling a Hail Mary as I roll the bead closest to the last black one between my finger and thumb.

This is what causes Victor to finally meet my eyes. Well, I'm meeting *his* eyes. He's only meeting a black mask with a large white cross jaggedly painted in the center of it.

"Who are you?" he says, his words slurring together. "What do you want?"

I take my time finishing another Hail Mary. Two more.

I won't speak to Victor Samuel. I won't dignify him with an answer. He knows what he's done, and—more importantly—*I* know what he's done.

To kill an ant means nothing when the nest is still functioning, thriving, cultivating. But, damn, does it feel good.

I tighten my grip on the metal rosary as I say, "Pray for us sinners, now and at the hour of our death. Amen," and smash my fist into his face.

Victor screams, but the bastard doesn't give up. He manages to squirm from under me, clutching onto his bloody nose.

"You'll fucking regret that!" he screams.

Chuckling, I slowly rise. "Yeah? You sure about that?"

I know his next move before he even does, because I see it nearly every time I come face to face with one of these assholes. They're too weak to do anything, so they *always* need some muscle on their side.

Instead of answering, Victor starts speaking in Latin, using his own blood to draw sigils on the concrete. I let him.

Cracking my neck and knuckles, I wait for the prick to finish. I could use a little extra exercise tonight.

After *way* too long—what a fucking lousy cultist— Victor has a summoning circle painted on the ground. The Miami air gets uncharacteristically cool as a violent wind pushes through the empty street. A black mist swirls and thickens in mass the more he speaks, and soon a shadow figure stands between the fuckface and myself.

Faintly, I hear the nightlife. Sirens from cops, horns from late night drivers, and still that ever present base from the clubs just a few blocks away.

But now a high-pitched cackle breaks through the never ending beat—coming from the all-black figure. It's tall and thin, standing far too straight. But what I *should* find horrifying is its oversized eyes. Tiny black irises stare at me, revealing too much white. Slowly, it spreads its lips in a haunting smile, revealing teeth just as illuminating in the dark night.

It's horrifying. Truly.

I run at it.

"Nice try, Victor," I yell, smiling as wide as the demon. "But you're a shit Satanist if this is all you could summon."

The demon lunges at me, and all I have to do is raise my hand wrapped in the rosary for it to quiver back.

"Easy fuckin' pickings," I chuckle. "Our Father, Who art in Heaven, hallowed be Thy name." The demon screams, reeling back farther, farther, until it stands in the summoning circle once more. "Thy kingdom come; Thy will be done on earth as it is in Heaven. Give us this day our daily bread." It whines still, and Victor jumps back.

"What the fuck?" he screams.

With a smile on my lips, I continue, "And forgive us our trespasses as we forgive those who trespass against us; and lead us not into temptation, but deliver us from evil."

The demon returns to nothing but mist being sucked back through the summoning circle, through the ground, and straight back to Hell.

"Amen, fucker."

Victor's panicked eyes dart up to me, and he looks like a small rabbit about to flee for his life.

But I'm the motherfucking serpent already wrapped around him.

I lunge at the bastard, grabbing him by the collar. He screams and screams, but it doesn't phase me in the slightest.

"You killed that girl the other night all so you could summon *that*? *That* was the power you killed for?"

Victor continues to squirm. "Please, I have a child and wife. They're waiting for me at home!"

Fucking pathetic.

I pull my knife from my belt, flick it open, and slash through Victor's neck. As he bleeds out, I drop his body and straddle his chest. In a mirror of my own mask, I carefully carve a shallow cross over the bastard's face, starting from forehead down to his upper lip, then across his eyelids.

"And lead us not into temptation," I repeat, as I always do when *tainting* the cultists I kill. "But deliver us from evil. Amen."

I hop up the steps of the large wooden cathedral where I know Father Rodrigo is waiting for me. It may be close to four in the morning, but I know the man wouldn't have gone to sleep yet. He has always waited till I got home, even in the years where coming home was a possibility, not a probability.

I cringe a little, thinking of myself at nineteen. The drugs, the sex, the parties. That all changed in a quite literal "come to Jesus moment."

As I open the door to the church, the scent of frankincense punches into me, made even more pungent with Miami's constant humidity, even late into the night in the dead of October. It may sound odd but ninety-five degrees in fall in the middle of the night? Totally normal here.

As expected, Father Rodrigo is sitting in the front pew, facing the bloodied crucifix of Christ hanging in the sanctuary. The lights are off, but every candle is lit.

I clear my throat a little, just to announce myself, and Rodrigo immediately turns to face me. Not for the first time today, I realize how he's aged since I've last been home. The smile lines and crow's feet have only deepened, and his thick black hair has mixed with gray to make an authentic salt-and-pepper look. Not only that, but *el jefe* has grown a little belly he seems proud of.

"Marcelo, mi hijo, ¿qué haces?" He looks me up and down—probably looking for blood or the mask. But he won't find either. Though he knows of it, and even helps with tracking sometimes, I don't let him see that part of me. The mask is safely tucked into my bag in the car, and the blood was cleaned from the rosary the moment I finished with Victor.

"Nada, Padre. What are you still doing up?"

"Waiting for you, of course." He stands, bracing his hands on his knees, and making an over-exaggerated "oof" as he straightens. "It's done, I'm guessing?" I nod, not wanting to give the bloody details. "Good. That was the fifth cultist this month, *hijo.* Five. That's how many we had all of last year."

"Something's going on. None of them spill information, but it can't be a coincidence. And Miami isn't the only place the numbers are growing."

He walks to meet me in the center of the aisle, before wagging a finger for me to follow him into his office off to the right. "The Vatican has had increased numbers everywhere. Places where Catholicism isn't even the dominant religion. Georgia, Alabama, they too have seen increased numbers."

"What are they doing about it?" I ask, already knowing the answer. If the church is anything, it's slow and cautious. So cautious, things are rarely done about anything, which is why I started donning the mask.

Father Rodrigo shrugs. "You know them. It's all politics. But enough about that. I have your next case."

"Already? You begged me to come here, and now you're telling me to leave again?" I huff a laugh. "Father, if I didn't know you better, I'd think you were trying to get rid of me."

"*Ay, cállate*. You know we're short-handed."

"And I'm the best you've got." I smirk.

Now Rodrigo huffs a laugh. "*Cabrón*."

Besides being a bishop, my legal guardian from the time I was fourteen, and the greatest man I know, Father Rodrigo is also my boss. He runs the Office of Exorcists here on the East Coast—*real* exorcists. We travel to where he tells us, decipher if it truly is a demon terrorizing a place or the vanity of man, and then we exorcise.

I follow Rodrigo down another hall and into his office. Unlike most bishop offices, Rodrigo has personalized it. Pictures of me as a boy hang on the walls, along with my best friend and her brother, Willow and Rowan. The three of us at fourteen, arms around each other, smiles wide though so much had already happened by then.

I quickly look away from the photos and slump into the seat opposite his. "So, tell me of this job."

Rodrigo lands heavily in his seat. "Massachusetts."

"Boston?"

He shakes his head. "You wish, *mijo*. It's in West Massachusetts—middle of nowhere really. Small town, closer to New York state and Connecticut. Ever heard of Belmouth?"

I shake my head.

"Their priest claims his congregation is being possessed by the Devil."

"Of course he does. And the 'evidence'?" I make air

quotes around the words, my jaded work history making me ever the skeptic.

Rodrigo grins, and his teeth are dark from the cigarettes he's smoked his whole life. "Visions of violence and deviance have infected the congregation. If he is correct, exorcise the demon like usual. If he's not . . ."

My job entails deciphering hysterics from fact, and 80 percent of the time, hysteria wins. Most people who *believe* they are possessed by demons, are merely possessed by their own greed and cowardice to admit their faults. In those cases, we let the Vatican know, denounce priesthood if the priest is part of the problem, and quickly find a replacement. But, in the rare 20 percent, when a creature from Hell is involved, my brothers and I are needed.

Exorcists roam, from chapel to cathedral. We go where we are needed. And now, *Belmouth* seems to be calling.

"All right, I'll leave in the morning," I say, pulling out a cigarette and flicking the lighter on and off.

"It's another small town, Marcelo. You know people talk."

Chismosos, I think, rolling my eyes.

"Just . . . be wary. Don't be the *cause* of hysteria."

"Yo entiendo, Padre."

"And try to keep your . . . side job to a minimum. The Vatican is watching."

I take a drag of the cigarette. "You want me to keep the mask hidden? While in the center of exactly what it is I'm fighting?" I raise an eyebrow, flicking the loose ash.

Rodrigo sighs. "Look. I know you feel inclined because your parents—"

"It's not about them."

He ignores me. "And you know I agree with . . . your *work*. But there is a time and place, Marcelo. One of these days, you're going to get caught. And officers of the modern world won't accept you are killing men for God. They'll assume you're a sociopath and lock you up."

"Yeah? You think the sex worker Victor Samuels sacrificed to a demon two nights ago would agree? Or the three teenage girls in Georgia last month? They were kids, *Padre*. Children, getting murdered to summon these demons. These demons *I* exorcise."

I think back to the ant. To the colony. *Exterminate the nest and what do they have?*

"I am all for what you're doing. Killing cultists that are *actually* summoning evil into this world is helping man more than anyone realizes. And while the Vatican sits on their ass and does nothing, you're actually doing something. But they also have had a history with you. They know you're trouble and they are looking for any excuse to terminate your priesthood."

I sit back then shrug. "Truthfully, *Padre*? I don't think it would affect me."

"To lose your priesthood?" He leans his head closer. "Ay, Marcelo. You'll give me an aneurysm."

I chuckle. He's always been dramatic. "You know me, *Padre*. You know who I am outside the collar."

He sighs again and nods. "At least I know it isn't a question of faith."

"Never. I love God. But I love him *my* way. Not the way of the church."

Rodrigo doesn't say anything, he only nods. But I know. I know from the too many nights he's called me when he's had too much wine. I know from when he accepted and took in Rowan after he came out and his parents abandoned him, and more so when Rowan decided he, too, wanted to be a priest despite being a gay man. And most importantly, I know from when he took me in and raised me even when I was a little shit teen trying to rebel in any way possible. Including trying to summon the Devil in our church basement once.

It didn't work.

And he has the backing of the Pope, so he does as he pleases, much to the dislike of the diocese. He married gay couples before they were recognized by the church. He employed sex workers and the unhoused for events the church held, paying in wages *and* meals.

Rodrigo is a renowned man, and he, too, hates the politics of the Vatican, the laws of the Church. They are made by man. Not God.

So I don't listen to them.

I may be a bad priest, but I am a damned good exorcist.

Rodrigo continues to nod and then meets my gaze. "Fine. The cultists are up to something. If you see any-thing, investigate first. Then you report to me. I'll tell you if the mask is needed. That is the only way I can justify this, Marcelo. Tell me you agree."

Out of respect, I nod. "Okay. The mask stays hidden until further notice. Now, tell me about this church."

2

JUNE

F *at slut.*

The words are pounding between my ears like a heartbeat pumped full of adrenaline.

Fat. Slut.

That's what she called me. Even in my oversized sweaters and flowy skirts. Even though I'm a virgin and have never, ever, been with a boy in any way.

A huff of laughter escapes my nose—the irony of it all too plain to see.

But she's right. Mother is *right*. My boobs are large, and my butt is huge, so that makes men stare. I thought that was a good thing—to be admired. She always fought so hard to be admired. But, apparently, when I do it, it's bad.

It's because I'm a slut and eat too much.

I need to be better. I need to eat better. Maybe . . . maybe I'll just have one meal a day. Or just eat salad.

I scoff at myself. Yeah right. Salads are too expensive and we don't have that kind of money. Maybe if I lose weight, my butt will get small, maybe my boobs will shrink. Then I won't be a slut. Then *his* eyes won't be on me whenever I enter the room.

Fat slut.

Fat slut.

Fat slut.

Distantly, I hear a knock on the door.

I heave a breath, slowly exhaling as I push myself off the bathroom floor. The cold tile felt comforting on my tear-soaked cheeks, and it was all I could do to hold myself . . . together. In one piece.

To just *be*.

"Junia, hurry up, I need to get in there to do my hair," Mother shouts. We live in an old, small, manufactured home, with just two bedrooms and a shared bathroom. Before Daren moved in, it was comfortable. Now, it's *too* small.

Her voice jolts me into motion. Like the movements of a robot, I'm on autopilot whenever she's near, only taking the orders and commands set into place for me.

I get up, brush myself off, and rub my fingers under my eyes. My mousy brown hair is messy in its ponytail, sticking out in odd places, and because of the paleness of my dark blue eyes surrounded by pink, it's incredibly evident I've been crying—which I know will only upset her more.

Mother pounds on the door once more, and I quickly push my bangs further into my eyes before opening it. She stares at me, taking in my appearance. Her blond hair is in a perfect bun, her cheekbones are high and pronounced, her waist is as thin as a model's, and she once had the looks to be one too. Until age sagged her skin and thinned her lips.

"S—sorry." I try to brush past her, but she grabs my wrist.

"You've been crying?"

"No," I lie.

"Why? And don't lie to me, Junia Forester. You know what God does with liars." Her grip on my wrist tightens.

I nod. "I'm sorry. I—Yes. I was crying."

"From what I said earlier?" She turns me to face her in the tiny hallway.

I slowly nod.

"Oh, baby," she whispers softly. She pulls me closer to her and pets my hair down. "It's not your fault. It's the Devil that made you like food so much. He's forced upon you the sin of gluttony. He's the one that makes it all go straight to your curves." She pinches my stomach. "And this little belly you've got here."

I flinch back, and Mother grabs my upper arm, pressing her lips together. "We need to fight off his influence. You don't want to be his puppet, do you?"

I shake my head.

"So, we need to go against his demands. We'll pray about it. But it needed to be said, Junia. You're making Daren uncomfortable."

Daren. He proposed to my mom four weeks after they started dating. Which was a week longer than her last fiancé. And though he's been living here for three months—three months she's been having me call him "daddy"—I don't know anything about him. Not really. I know he's fifty-four, has no kids, and has sandy hair. I *assume* he works outside, because of what he wears when he gets home, and I *assume* he was maybe born closer to Boston, because his accent is thick compared to the muted inflections of the Belmouth natives.

Then there is what Daren *claims* to be. Things I should

know about him but only *assume* aren't fully true. The first is that he loves my mother. I've seen her engaged and married enough to know that her definition of love is definitely something I didn't see in the Disney and Barbie movies I watched — the *only* movies I was allowed to watch till I was fifteen. The second is Daren's claim of being a proper, God-fearing man. I know my mother can handle her own heart. I know she knows what's best. But something about him makes me feel like he doesn't have a single verse of the Bible threaded into his soul.

Maybe I'm jaded by her past loves. Maybe the last fiancé who stole her money and ran off with someone twenty years younger scared me. Maybe it was the Christmas we spent locked in her bedroom, as another fiancé pounded on the door, screaming bloody murder before the cops showed up, that changed my mind. Maybe the man she'd been married to — the only man she'd ever been married to — for two whole years when I was eleven, broke me.

But there were commonalities in all these men. They all claimed to be God-fearing.

And maybe it isn't my place to judge. Only God could judge, after all. Right?

"I'm sorry, Mother," I say, picking at the skin on my thumb.

"Don't apologize to me. Apologize to Daren." She lets me go, turns, and disappears into the bathroom.

Damn. I know she means *now.* I slowly hobble down the hall and into the living room, where Daren loudly watches TV. Some sports game. His sunburnt arm is thrown over the back of the couch as he sits slouched with his legs wide open.

I take a deep breath, picking at the skin on my thumb. *Just do it. Get it over with.*

"Uh-uhm, Dare—I mean . . . Daddy?"

His gaze turns to me, and a slow smile creeps onto his face. My stomach drops. He isn't a bad-looking man. He is tall, and has an okay face, if not a little sun damaged. But all in all, just fine. Normal. But something about him still sets me on edge, as though I'm looking into a dark closet, waiting for something else to look back.

"Hello, darlin'." He sits up a little.

"I want to apologize," I say fast, not meeting his eyes. "My mother said I should apologize."

He pats the couch, telling me to sit with him. Telling, not suggesting.

"What for?" he asks as I move across the room.

"For . . ." I hate that he's making me say it. "For making you uncomfortable."

As I sit next to him, his leg brushes against mine. His body is close. Too close.

"How would little Junia make *me* uncomfortable?"

I flinch. And though Daren notices, he doesn't back away.

Deep breath. I am alone with this man, for all intents and purposes. A man I barely know. A man I am supposed to pretend is my father.

I don't know my father, at all. My mother claims he was an awful man, a man she needed to run away from in the middle of the night, with me in her arms.

But I *do* know Daren is nothing like a father. He's . . .

"Why would I be uncomfortable, Junia?"

I hate the way he says my name. I hate the way he stares, the way he gets closer to me as he speaks. His breath is rancid with beer and Funions, but it would be rude to back away, and Mother doesn't like for me to be rude. She says it makes her parenting look bad, despite the fact I was already an adult myself.

"She said my . . . weight gain makes you uncomfortable."

He smirks, finally leaning back. "Not uncomfortable, just . . . distracted." His eyes lower to my breasts, and I feel . . . exposed, undressed, violated.

I stand up.

"Well, then—" I take another deep breath, hating that I have to apologize to this man. Have to apologize for my body. For something out of my control, something that I didn't do. "I'm sorry. I will work on it."

Daren raises an eyebrow and then turns back to the TV, dismissing me.

I hurry back to my room and close the door behind me until my heart realizes I'm finally safe, alone, hidden.

But it doesn't—because it knows the truth. In this house, I'm never safe. I'm never alone. Never hidden.

3

MARCELO

arcelo," *a soft, shaky voice whispers. I see my mother, lying on the white tile flooring, her dark hair spread around her like wilted petals. Her eyes are blank, staring at me—no, past me. I've lost count of the seconds since she stopped breathing.*

"Marcelo." I hear again. The voice is behind me, but . . . I don't want to turn from my mother. If I do, that'll be it. She'll really be gone with the Lord. I know she's in Heaven, in a better place next to God—there is no question she won't be there. But . . . but I'm a selfish creature. I want her here *with* me.

"Marcelo!" the voice says harshly, but still, I don't turn.

Instead, I feel something hot and wet spill on my toes. Wait—not spill but spread. I look down, breaking the one-sided eye contact between my mother and I. Below me is blood. It's so . . . vibrant, like the sangria my mother makes on Saturday mornings. Like guava in the pastries she picks up for me at the bodega. Like the color of her cheeks, when my father asks her to dance in the middle of our kitchen.

It's her blood.

I jolt awake to the sun creeping into the motel room, the ceiling fan spinning loose on its axis, and the covers fisted in my hand. It's six a.m., later than I wanted to wake up. I rub my tanned, dry palms together, warming them from the night, and reach for the rosary on the bedside table.

I left Miami yesterday morning, and drove all day—and most of all night—till I got out of Florida, through Georgia and the Carolinas, and stopped somewhere in the middle of Maryland.

I can't even remember how long I'd been in the car, but I didn't even shower when I arrived at this dump. I just flopped onto the bed and slept.

After morning prayers, I get up and strip my clothes as I near the bathroom. I need to wash the road from my skin before I do it all over again. The water is steaming hot, stinging the bruises and cuts all along my right knuckles, where the tattoo of a cross sits on my index finger, and where the metal rosary was wrapped two nights ago.

I stretch out my hand before shutting the water off and toweling myself dry. Then I adorn my collar and throw all my things in my duffle bag before heading out the door.

My prized possession, the gleaming cream 1967 Ford Mustang, sits as though she's waiting for me. Priests take an oath of poverty when becoming ordained, but I don't see my purchase of her as an "unnecessary extravagance." I'm a traveling exorcist after all, and I need a way to travel.

I hop in the car, her cold, white leather seats sending a chill up my spine, but the moment I hear the thrum of her engine, my blood sings.

Which I need right now. After twenty years, the dreams have never stopped. And each time they come for me, I'm not ready. They're still too much.

I whip out of the motel's parking lot and drive a little too fast for the back roads I'm on. But I need the thrill. It's also part of the reason I've taken up my work under the mask and my career as an exorcist. I *need* the thrill. So many of the stupid decisions I made as a teen stemmed from this need. Now, I know how to hone it. How to use it for the good of others.

It's been hours of being on the road. The day was bright and warm, turning into a cool, dark-blue night as I finally passed the sign for Belmouth. I call Father Rodrigo. Like always, he doesn't answer, but I know better than to toss my phone aside.

I know, in just three . . . two . . . one . . .

Ring.

Father Rodrigo *always* calls me back just after he doesn't answer. He's too busy to answer the first call but never too busy to call back. Especially for me.

"To what do I owe the pleasure, *mi hijo*?"

I put my phone on speaker and toss it onto the dash, driving with one hand on the wheel and the other scratching at my chin.

"I'm in Belmouth. It's smaller than I thought."

I hear him gruff on the other end. "And full of tradition. You need to be careful there."

"Careful? I hunt and exorcise demons, *Padre*. I think I'll be fine."

"Not you, *pendejo*. Your words. Your ways. Your beliefs. Not every priest is as open as you and I."

Don't I know it.

"Do you know anything about this . . . what's his name again?"

"Father Callum. And no, not much. He's been the sole priest in the parish for just over twenty years. Which is why I warn you to watch your tongue, Marcelo. Do not go spouting your distaste for the Church and the Word. You need to complain and vent, you call me. Remember what happened in Jersey."

Fuck Jersey.

I clench my fist around the leather steering wheel, just thinking of the politics of the Church and how much I detest them.

"You're lucky we don't revoke your priesthood, Marcelo."

The words still piss me off.

"I won't," I grit out. "Anything more you can tell me? About the demon or Belmouth in general?"

The town is . . . quiet as I drive through. Granted, it's a Tuesday night, but as I navigate through Main Street, most of the stores look like they are for lease or have only one or two people within.

Father Rodrigo's voice hums on the other end of the phone. "There was a convent there, but it burned down in the seventies."

"Natural fire or arson?"

"Reports say natural. But who knows what the truth is. Many of the Sisters went to work in other convents after that, but none had anything to report."

I drum my fingers on the wheel, taking it all in. Something about the convent doesn't feel right. And something about this *town* feels off. Dark. Watched.

"How far was the convent from where the cathedral sits today?"

"Across town. You think it's connected to the demon?"

I shrug, though he can't see me. "Not even saying there *is* a demon. But have Rowan send me the building and town schematics when he gets a chance. Both, for now—and one from before the fire."

Shortly after taking his vows, Rowan became Rodrigo's main assistant. Rodrigo's hope is that he one day takes the reins of not only his church, but of his duties over the exorcists as well. So now, Rowan's our everything man. Whatever we need out on the road, we call him.

It fills me with pride, to know how far he's come since Rodrigo took him under his wing. Rowan never let anyone tell him he wasn't a good Catholic just because of who he was attracted to, but he was afraid the Church wouldn't accept him as a priest. A gay priest, damned, they'd say—but he was the best damned priest I'd ever met. He was the one who encouraged me to take my vows after he and Willow saved me from the dark place I dug myself into after my parents.

Fuck. It's been a while since I've spoken to either of them. I need to call. I remind myself. She's going to be pissed at me.

"I'll have him do that," Rodrigo says on the other end, bringing me back to now, back to Belmouth. "He's going to be pissed you didn't see him when you were in town," he confirms, as though he read my thoughts. The bastard knows me too well.

"I can already imagine Willow's fury."

He chuckles. "In the meantime, remember you are representing me. Don't let the parish know what you're there for and call me if anything."

I grab the phone. "I will. *Gracias, Padre.*"

"*Vaya con dios, Marcelo.*"

"*Y tú también.*" I hang up and throw the phone into the passenger seat just as I pull up to a wooden chapel, calling itself a cathedral. St. Mary's Catholic Church sits surrounded by trees. It's larger than I thought a small-town church would be but not a standard cathedral by any means. A circular stained glass window sits high on the face of the building, illuminating the scene of Jesus holding a small lamb in his arms. It's stunning for a space that seems so small, so ordinary. The bright colors of the piece seem illuminated as the dark wood of the church dims into the darkness of the night.

I park my car in one of the parallel spots just outside the church, don my collar and a long black coat, and step outside into the crisp Massachusetts breeze.

It's only September, but already the air is biting and thick with the coming rain. The trees are already beginning to change to vibrant reds and yellows, but the deep greens are still sprinkled throughout.

I take a preliminary glance around the church before entering, seeing it for myself before Father what's-his-name gives me his own tour. Taking the small path up to the church, and then behind it, I check the windows for the scent of sulfur, for drafts that might weasel their way through to the cathedral, for the nearby street lamps that could create what some might consider light anomalies.

No sulfur but no drafts either.

The building is quiet within, and I can just barely make out the pews through the windows with the exit lights on.

As I step closer, I hear a scuttle directly beside me. It sounds like claws on concrete, and I immediately turn around.

I curse as a black mass dashes past, leaping onto the window's edge and then the massive green dumpster beside it, coming toward me at eye level. The mass hisses, and only then do I realize it isn't a demon, but an alley cat. It's larger in stature than most house cats, but sturdy—not fat. The little devil is all black, with golden eyes and a small tuft of white at his collar. My attention snags on his claws, spread wide and clinging to the dumpster, like a little lion ready to pounce. *El diablo* indeed.

The cat swipes at me, and I just barely dodge to escape it. Little fucker. I hiss back at the cat.

I round the building and stand once more at its entrance. The cathedral looks . . . normal. Nothing outwardly demonic. If anything, it looks clean and proper, like something from a movie set. Small and quaint.

It's just after eight p.m., and just beyond the dark wooden doors, the parish is silent.

The door creaks open as I push it. But it's just that—a creak. There is still no sign of a demon. No smell of sulfur.

"Hello?" I call out. It echoes around the church, bouncing on the dark wooden pews, up to the domed ceiling, through the sanctuary where Jesus is spread on the crucifix, and up into the small balcony above the Holy Father, where an ornate organ sits. The gold of the pipes catch my eye, the ivory keys, the espresso-colored wood. It's beautiful. Just like the crucifix, and just like the window.

I make a mental note to ask about the budget for this place and how it was funded. Surely, the diocese wouldn't pay from their pockets for a church in as small a town as Belmouth. Not with Boston and New York City and all the rest of New England available right there.

Maybe it was the fire at the convent. They built this place with the insurance money. And if so, was that the plan all along?

Exorcists are trained to see every possibility *other* than demonic possession. Rule everything out and *then* we can continue. I have seen too many "possessions" stem from the sins of man. Mothers believing their children are possessed when really they are just traumatized. Men claiming possession to get away with touching someone in their parish.

It's disgusting.

A door opens beside the sanctuary and out walks a tall man, dark blond hair slicked back, and a soft smile. "Father Marcelo, I presume?" The man hurries to me down the aisle of the pews, his pale hand already outstretched.

I nod, firmly shaking his hand. "Father Callum, yes? You have a beautiful church here."

He grins widely, and it lights up his whole face. Callum is the picture of a perfect priest—reserved, joyous, kind. I'd say he's probably in his mid- to late-fifties. He definitely takes care of himself, but isn't cut like he goes hard at the gym every day. His black slacks are modest, a little gray from wear, and his shoes are scuffed all around the toes, which tells me he isn't a big spender. His clean-shaven face tells me he cares about his appearance, but the grays combed through his blond hair indicates he doesn't care about his appearance for his own sake—no, there is no pride here—he cares about how he represents himself to his parish.

A spiritual leader through and through.

But I know first-hand, no picture is as it seems. There is always more. Depth, secrets, truths. So, what are Callum's truths?

"I am so grateful to have you here to help us with our little . . . problem." He huffs a breath. "Shall I—"

I drop my bags to the floor and slump into the nearest pew, lifting my ankle onto my opposite knee. "Tell me why you think your parish is being possessed by demons, Father."

My eyes don't leave Callum's. Not as they falter for a moment, waiting, watching.

It is my common tactic, be friendly when I first greet them, and then drop the bomb of my true personality.

It's a tactic that reveals something about my fellow priests every time. The look on their faces when they realize they've been duped. When they realize they've entered a war of dominance. When they realize they have to walk on eggshells around me, if they're hiding anything.

It's my first test. Will they succumb and fight me for power? Will they become stumbling messes with something to hide? Or will they be grateful someone is finally here to help?

Callum's eyes, and the falter within, tell me everything I need to know about him. The man is pussy-whipped. And the pussy in question? The Church, maybe. God. His parish. Maybe his damn self. But the flinch of fear is so much better than the flinch of pride and greed I usually see.

It tells me that maybe the man before me isn't lying. Maybe there are demons here.

Maybe.

Callum clears his throat and his shoulders slump. "It's bad, Father. I've been receiving complaints of odd visions, strange dreams. In just the last month, I have had triple the amount of people come to me for private prayers than I ever have."

"What is the parish claiming are in their dreams?"

"A mix. All the carnal sins." Callum sits in the pew in front of me and turns toward me. "And some have even been seeing things, here, in the church."

"Like what?"

He shrugs, letting the joyous mask slip a little more. In truth, the man just looks tired. Behind his smile lines are dark bags under his eyes, a pimple on his chin.

This man is stressed.

Callum runs a hand down his face. "Shadows, things I can't even give a name to. Blood running down the walls. Their faces distorted in the bathroom mirrors. All sorts of profanity."

I nod, listening, digesting. "And you, Father? Have you seen things?"

His dark eyes hover on me as he presses his lips together and slowly, almost painfully, nods. Callum sighs again, stretching his hands over his knees. "I—I live here. On the property. At night, when it's empty, when I do my final round, I sometimes see things."

I don't speak. I wait for him to continue.

"Shadows, mostly. Probably a trick of the eye. But sometimes—*sometimes*, I see more. It's my dreams I am worried about most. They are so vivid, so real."

I fold my arms over my chest. "What are you doing in these dreams?"

"Sinning. All kinds." He pauses and looks to the floor. "Please don't make me elaborate, Father. Not at night."

I nod.

"I want more information. But . . ." I stand and shove my hands into my pockets. "I have been on the road for two days. I think everything can wait till morning."

"Excellent. I'll show you where you'll be staying, and

after Mass, I'll give you a proper tour and tell you everything you need to know in order to begin."

As he stands, I lift my bag over my shoulder and do
another once over of the church.

But there is nothing to see.

4

JUNE

The notes echo all around me, consuming every thought—every doubt—twirling in my mind. Every shred of regret in my stomach eases the moment my fingers touch the keys. Every self-deprecating thought and every reserved restriction melts off of me.

Mother says it's the worshiping, that God is embracing me with his love, and that's why I feel *so good* when I play. But I know it's not that. I know, because I feel it even when I don't play for Him. It's the only time I don't feel so different, so broken, so ugly and damaged and foul. It's the only time I don't care what my mother thinks or who's looking at me or if my breasts still look too large in the frumpy sweaters I wear.

The music *I* create is all that matters, the notes that come from *my* fingertips.

I play and play, hitting pistons and keys in time for the

music, until the hymn comes to an end, and once the final note vibrates around the room, only then does my spirit reenter my body.

Only then does everything flood back into me, like a weight pressed firmly against my chest in the middle of the ocean, drowning me under the waves.

I pull my hands back from the keys, stretching and cracking them. I'm in the cathedral, on my normal balcony above the sanctuary, hidden behind the railing. I can hear Father Callum continue morning Mass, but I can't see him from my bench, as he stands directly under me. So unless I stand at the railing and peer over, I don't see anyone. It is such a nice reprieve. I'm sure Mother will scold me. She always does if she doesn't see me watching Mass, but after last night, I can't stomach standing just to please her.

Not when her words are still ringing through my mind, clawing at the walls till they're ingrained into me.

I skipped breakfast, taking Mother's advice. I guess I'll skip lunch, too.

After I snuck into my room, Mother went to her women's meetings held at the church three times a week, and the entire time, I heard Daren prowling the house, back and forth.

Once, he even came up to my door, but after a few minutes, his heavy presence returned to the living room.

It wasn't always this way. Well, it was with *Daren*. But some of my mom's past fiancés were fine. Normal. Kind, even. But Daren just makes me uncomfortable. Like waiting for a jump scare when you know it's about to happen.

The memory of his eyes on me last night and his "discomforts" make me cringe.

I sigh, and slump my shoulders, my lower back grazing the cold keys on the organ. My posture hasn't been good since the fifth grade, when these boobs grew into my short body. I still remember the pain of wearing the binding bras the first few years, when Mother started saying it was improper to show them off. Something she hasn't *stopped* saying, even though I only wear sweaters three times too large, and two sports bras at all times.

Which, of course, pushes down on my tummy. Maybe Mother was right about me gaining weight. Skirts have been tighter. Bras dig into my skin more. And . . . I guess my stomach is a little squishier.

Maybe, maybe, maybe . . . that's all I seem to say these days.

Below, I hear Father Callum starting the final prayer of Mass—which is my cue to start winding through the cathedral to meet everyone downstairs to take Communion.

I stand in my little mezzanine and stretch out my fingers one more time. Mornings in which *I* get to be the organist fills my utterly dull life with purpose. At twenty-five, I thought I'd be out of the house already. I thought I'd have graduated college, with friends, have an apartment somewhere far from here, and spending time creating something for myself. But then Mother threw the college acceptance letter into the trash.

"You don't play for fame, Junia. You play for God, and that's it."

There went my full ride to Tisch School of the Arts, my one ticket out of here. Mother likes to say we're broke, but she also insists I don't get myself a job. I've offered countless times, to help pay rent, with bills, to buy us gas, but . . . she always refuses. She says I have to be devoted to my time at the church. So, I don't have even a penny to my name.

Not like I can do anything without her. I don't even truly know if I could wash a load of laundry without her guidance.

So instead, I'm here. Stuck. In St. Mary's of Belmouth.

Playing the organ four times a week for a God I'm not even totally sure I believe in.

If he were real, why would life be this hard? I know the Bible is all about suffering, but . . . haven't we had enough?

Father Callum likes to say we are paying for the sins of our brothers. Jesus's sacrifice was good. For a time. But the sins of man have raged rampant once more. He likes to comment on the younger generation—*my generation*—being too obsessed with self image and having physical attachments to phones and the internet.

The first time he said that years ago, Mother took the hand-me-down phone she'd given me. The one with so few minutes, I couldn't access the internet even if I wanted to.

We've been coming to St. Mary's for as long as I can remember, and Father Callum has always been the lead priest. Others have come and gone; sometimes there's up to three secondary priests besides Callum to lead the daily Masses and take confessions. But Callum has been the only constant, and takes pride that we are *his* parish.

He's a tall, attractive, older man, and for as long as I've known him, all twenty-something years, he has seemed perpetually in his mid-fifties. Mother is just a little bit ob-sessed with him—as obsessed as any woman could be with a priest. But his holy virtues and her devotion to the Lord—nor her devotion to whomever she's dating at the time—doesn't stop her from curling her finger in her hair or biting her lip whenever they speak to each other.

To Father Callum's credit, he seems blissfully unaware of every advance. And Mother seems fine with it. As if she just enjoys fighting for his attention.

After another organ player for the church switches off with me, I wind down the dark wooden staircase that leads from my tiny mezzanine to the room just behind the sanctuary. The room holds the vestments for Mass and I wait here a moment until Father Callum calls for Communion and finally walk through the small door leading into the sanctuary.

Mass is sparse today, a weekday morning, but families are getting up, shuffling out from between the pews to join the line of Communion as Father Callum stands at the front, the host in hand. The second organ player begins a new hymn and the parish make their way to the front, one at a time. We do Communion three times a week, Wednesdays, Fridays, and Sundays.

I see Mother and Daren in line and quicken my step to join them.

"Junia, there you are," Mother says. "I didn't see you watching homily." She pops her hip out and leans on it. "Where were you?"

There are only a few people in front of us. Daren hasn't even turned around to look at me.

"I—I listened," I stutter. Heck, she hates when I stutter.

On cue, Mother raises a blond brow. "Listening isn't the same as watching. It isn't the same as *worshiping*." She huffs a breath, and another two people leave the line. "We'll talk about this when we get home, young lady."

She turns, and I immediately pick at the flesh around my thumbs, digging at them with the nails of my index fingers.

It hurts, but I don't think about it. All I *can* think about is, *"We'll talk about this when we get home."*

Daren looks over his shoulder at me, a small smirk on his lips. I want to believe it is meant to be comforting, but my brain tells me it isn't. It's . . . enjoyment.

Mother drops down on her knees before Father Callum, opening her mouth wide. I watch her, noting the stare down she has with the priest, noting the . . . *something* in her eyes. Just as the host is placed on her tongue, she makes an *O*-shape with her lips, closing them around the Father's thumb.

Once again, Father Callum doesn't react, and Daren's eyes are still locked on me. When I meet them again, they dart up into mine before he raises a singular brow and turns to take his own Communion.

"June," Father Callum says with a smile as Daren steps away, and I drop to my knees. The dark red carpet fuzz presses into the skin, and I can already feel them embed marks on me. "Excellent playing today. I really felt your love for the Lord in each note."

I smile, then open my mouth.

As he places the host on my tongue, I use it to stop from admitting the truth. It's not my love for the Lord that fuels my music. It's my desire to escape from here.

The host feels thick, like cardboard, in my throat as I swallow it down, and not even the small sip of wine helps. I rise to my feet and join my mother on the side. She's conversing with some of the other women of the church, boasting about the dress she's wearing, but it all drowns out through one ear. Daren is standing next to her, smiling and nodding. The women ogle at him as though he's anything to look at. Others are busy ogling at Father Callum.

No one ogles their own husbands.

St. Mary's didn't always seem so foreign. I don't know when or what changed, but suddenly the men grew nicer and the women grew crueler. Maybe it has always been this way, and I'm just finally old enough to see it.

After Father Callum says the closing prayer, many families are exiting the church—not ours, we're almost always the last to leave—and the room quiets, save for the chatter of my mother and her friends.

But suddenly, even the undecipherable noise of the women evades my senses. My head swims, and my cheeks heat. *Not now*, I think to myself. I squeeze my thighs together, begging for the sensation to go away. I can already feel a slick dampness building in my panties, and my core clenches tight.

These . . . spells of . . . whatever this is, happens more and more often. Sudden attacks. It doesn't stop until I submit to them.

Breathe. It's okay, I remind myself. A shaky exhale escapes me, and I quickly excuse myself, not expecting anyone to actually hear me.

When Mother stays locked in her conversation, I turn and nearly bump right into Father Callum. The closeness and warmth of another human makes my entire body feel wound tight. I'm almost ready to hump his leg like a feral dog, when I look up to see him smiling.

"June, I was thinking tomorrow we can change up the order of the hymns. I'll leave the sheets up on the stand for you in the new order."

My cheeks are flushed, and I *know* if Callum looks down right now, he'll see my nipples poking through my sweater's material. Curse the eternally pointy nips.

"S—Sounds good," I nearly moan.

I feel slickness drip onto my inner thighs, dampening the hot area under my skirt, as I clear my throat—trying desperately to compose myself.

Hell.

Father Callum smiles warmly. "I'm going to go say hi to your parents. I'll see you in a bit!"

I nod, cringing slightly at the word *parents*, and sidestep him before he can say another word.

Normally, in times of crisis, I run to the organ. It's safe

and private, and the height of the console is perfect to rub against.

But it isn't close enough. Not when I feel this building at the level it currently is.

As I hurry across the pews, I can feel Jesus's eyes on me from the crucifix, judging me for the sinner I am. But until I touch myself, this won't stop. I've tried. I've waited. I've fallen asleep with it and woke up the next morning with a pool of wetness on my sheets. I've ignored it and moaned in the middle of Mass. Thankfully, I was also in the middle of playing, so no one heard.

It always hits so, so suddenly, as if someone snapped their fingers.

I ignore everything around me and hurry into the small confession booth on the left side of the church. I know no one is on the other side, because Father Callum—the only priest here today—is speaking to my mother.

As soon as the dark wooden door is shut, the church on the other side disappears, silencing the noise all around me.

Now, it's just my breath, shaky and hot.

I hate this. I hate this. I hate this. I hate this.

It may feel fantastic. It may set every nerve in my body on fire. It may even make me feel more alive than I ever do.

But masturbation—carnal pleasure—is a sin. And I know if Mother *ever* found out, I would be strung up and crucified. She would say I'm touched by the Devil. She'd say I'm a slut, a whore.

And, I guess, I am. Because as I fall onto the wooden bench in the small confessional, I feel the pressure so blissfully pressed against that wonderful spot between my thighs. The warmth coating my blood, making my toes curl, and stomach flip—it is as though I *live* for this right now.

"You're going to Hell, slut." I hear my mother's voice. But

my body and brain aren't lining up. My body doesn't care about the absolute disgust I feel for myself right now, the turmoil making me want to vomit as my hand drifts up my milky thigh, pulling my calf-length skirt up, up, *up*.

I throw my head back as my fingers graze the already-wet spot on my panties. *There.* That's where it feels best.

"Slut, slut, fat slut."

My middle finger presses firmly against *there*, and my entire body shudders. It feels *so* good, and not for the first time, I wonder how it'd feel if it were someone else's hand pressing on me, grabbing my panties, tasting me.

Squeezing my thighs together, I suck my lips into my mouth to hold back a moan, but a small whimper escapes me as the pressure builds.

"Oh *God*." I breathe, unable to help myself, and I have *never* heard my voice like this before. I have no idea what's prompting me to do this, what's guiding my hand. Surely not the Devil, right? Not something that feels *this damned good*?

Immediately, I know I'm lying to myself. Mother would say it's the Devil's hand that's touching me, and I'm letting him.

My free hand lets go of the edge of my skirt and I lift it, toying with my pebbled nipple, slamming my head back again.

It feels *too* good, and being in the house of God, sinning, touching myself *here*—it makes me coil even tighter. My legs spread as much as they can in the tiny room, and I feel myself building, building, building, as I press the flat of my fingers against myself, moving it back and forth. My movements jerk and get more aggressive as I feel a wave rushing through me.

"Oh, God!" I moan again, rubbing myself faster and faster. I buck my hips against my hand, making love to myself.

"Fat, stupid slut. You're going to Hell."

"Oh Father," I say through gasps, "forgive me for my sins." I'm so close, I can feel myself just on the precipice of complete and total pleasure.

And through the heat and absolute bliss in my body, I feel a hot tear drip onto my cheek. I am so utterly disgusted with myself. So disturbed and . . . and . . .

Broken. Damaged. *Tainted.*

But I can't stop. Not if I want to walk out of here. If I stop now, my body will stay this high. Will stay this wet, this needy, this demanding. I'll be a moaning, flustered, horny mess—in front of the parish, in front of creepy Daren. *In front of Mother.*

And it'll stay, torturing me, dragging me to Hell.

The only way out is through damnation.

I grind against the wood of the bench, my hand digging against me, and with another whimper through bitten lips, I give myself over to sin.

5
MARCELO

uck, fuck, fuck. This is bad. I've trapped myself, with no damned way to escape now.

I told Callum I didn't want to catch the eye of the parish. Not for the first Mass. I wanted to watch, to take in, to see everyone in their natural state, without knowing a stranger was in their midst. I wasn't here for the congregation. I was here for the demon, and getting to know the parish always managed to complicate things.

And, damned me, the confessional booth seemed like the best place to simply observe.

I began my prayers, asking God to guide my hand in this town, this church, this exorcism. Thanking him for my safe journey and apologizing for the sins I keep fucking making—swearing being my number one offense. I'm working on it.

But I wasn't expecting a damned test of faith today.

The little organist caught my attention the moment I saw her. She was . . . different from the other women of the parish. Reserved, quiet.

Scared.

She didn't ogle at Father Callum like her mother had. She didn't pay much attention to the gruff man beside her mother and his lingering stare. I clocked the man as the mother's boyfriend—no, fiancé. The mother wore a ring. He did not.

The little organist just left, sauntering behind the sanctuary, and next I saw her, she sat high in her mezzanine, her fingers playing the organ like she was *born* for it. Sculpted of clay and given life by our Father to play that instrument.

It was a shame this would be the farthest her talents would reach.

As she played something . . . quieted within the church. Nothing tangible, but an energy. A feeling.

Then, next thing I knew, I saw her Mother roughly grabbing her wrist, the fiancé staring at his soon-to-be-stepdaughter's tits, and then she was on her knees before Father Callum, opening her pretty plump lips for him.

A streak of violent jealousy shot through me when I saw his thumb near her tongue. I wanted to jump from my hiding place and pull her away, take her far. But then she was standing, and a moment later, hurrying toward me.

No, not me.

The confessional booth.

No one but Father Callum knew I was in here, and no one but Father Callum should've been available to *be* in here. She wasn't here to confess her sins, so . . . why?

I turn, peeking through the small window, but the patterned metal over the opening obscures my view. I hear her take a deep breath. All I see is an orange sweater, the wisp of light, mousy brown hair, and her head pressed against the inside of the door as her pale white, delicate hands fist next to her.

She makes another small sound, almost like a whimper, and—for some reason—I'm left entranced. Entranced and stuck, afraid to give away my position.

She sits roughly on the wooden bench, and I hear the shuffling of clothes, then silence for a long beat.

"Oh, *God*," she moans.

My cock reacts before it even fully processes what I'm listening to. And before I can stop myself, I lean closer to the window. I see one of those delicate hands pressed tightly between her milky thighs. God, they're so thick. *I want to press my face between them*, I fleetingly think. Fuck.

Chastity, Marcelo, purity.

I can't help but watch. She rubs herself as tiny, heated breaths and whimpers continue to escape her full lips. It may just be my new favorite sound. The little songbird can sing too.

My cock throbs in my pants, pressing against the fabric hard enough to cause pain. But I *can't* touch myself. I *can't* give in to temptation. No matter how much I might want to simply *hearing* her.

I'm so fucking hard right now, though, it hurts.

"Oh, God!" she moans again, a little louder this time. And part of me likes how daring she's become in solitude.

I can't just leave. If I do, she'll know. She'll be terrified. At least, that's what I tell myself.

God, why did you put me in this position? Is this your will? Or a test of faith?

"Oh Father," she breathes. "Forgive me for my sins." She moans again, and the sound nearly ruptures my being.

I want to take my hand and pump myself. I want to barge through this wall, take my cock, and thrust in into her wet pussy, fucking her till we're both condemned to Hell as the fucked-up parish watches at my back.

I lift my hand to the wall, temptation pulling at every fiber of my being. I can practically *feel* her soft skin under my palm.

Her whimpers decrescendo, muted, and some sick part of me hates her for silencing herself. Her shaky breaths are all that's left as I hear the shuffle of fabric, and the pale panties I briefly spotted are gone and she fixes her long brown skirt back into place.

My songbird sighs heavily, her voice shaky, and for a moment, it almost sounds as though it's caught on a sob.

I can just barely make out her shape slumped back against the wall as she regains her breath.

She seems . . . dejected.

I haven't had sex since I was nineteen years old, when I first became a priest after a short stint in college. I haven't touched myself since, and—until now—I haven't felt this overwhelming need to. Yeah, I still get horny. What man wouldn't? But it's hard to think of something tempting enough when your day-to-day is killing fucked-up psychopaths and exorcising demons trying to eat babies.

Just jerking it in bed has never seemed worth risking my vows.

Not until I heard this woman's sounds of pleasure.

Guilt fills me at the thought, but if I pulled my cock out right now, with her sounds still echoing in my ears, I don't think I'd be able to stop myself from bursting.

I rub my hand over my face, trying to suppress the thoughts of this woman. Trying to suppress my sins, my desires. I'm here on a mission, to find a demon—if there is one—and exorcise it.

But those sweet little whimpers . . .

They're enough to drive me wild. So much so, I can't help myself. I graze my hand over my cock, feeling so compelled to just touch myself as she had done. Compelled to touch myself for her.

But I want more. So much more.

I pull my cock out from my pants and languidly stroke myself to the thought of her wet, dripping cunt. Her pussy would already be prepped for me to slide inside of her, to fuck her hard. I wanted more of those sweet moans to crescendo within the confessional booth, to trap each and every whimper and keep them all for myself.

My fist tightens around my dick, and I groan out, "Songbird."

My songbird stands and I'm snapped to reality. *My hands are in my lap, my cock is in my pants, and the girl on the other side of the confessional still has no idea I'm here.* My songbird, without a second of hesitation, leaves the confessional booth, shutting the door behind her.

What the fuck just happened, I think to myself. *Maybe there is a demon here after all.* Something that forced her to touch herself just after Mass. Something driving me to want to touch her, too. Something that just forced that vision on me. It was . . . surreal. I know it wasn't real, but as it happened, it felt like a video playing in my head. A video where I could feel *everything*.

Fuck. With that in mind, maybe the demon is at play here. And if so, I have work to do. *And* I have my first lead. *My songbird.*

I wait a moment, readjusting to hide the still-hard dick in my pants, and then exit the confessional, walking through the now-empty nave. I was too focused to realize her parents and Callum disappeared, presumably into his office. I cross the room, adjust my collar, and lightly knock on Father Callum's office door, before pushing it open and entering.

And when I do, all I see is *her*.

The milky skin, the mousy-brown hair, that orange sweater doing her tits all kinds of favors. I want to run across the room and rip it off, see them for myself. She is fucking gorgeous, and my cock is already straining against my black jeans again.

Her eyes widen when they land on me, and it sends a thrill through me, my lips lifting in a smirk.

"Ah, Father Marcelo, these are the Foresters," Father Callum explains, but I don't take my eyes off my little songbird in front of me. Her bangs hang low over her fore-head, curled at the ends, dipping into her eyes, which are the deepest shade of blue, like the ocean in the middle of a storm. Her rounded cheeks are rosy red from her little display, and her full lips are parted as she watches me with equal fascination.

She looks even more gorgeous close-up.

A shrill, incredibly thin woman with sagging skin and too-thin lips steps between me and my songbird. "Father Marcelo," she repeats, mimicking a thick accent I can't even place; it's so bad. "How exotic. Are you from Vatican City?"

I tilt my head at her, feeling my eyebrows come together. "Excuse me?"

"You're Italian, no?"

I press my lips together, and it takes everything in me to smile politely. This is the exact kind of Catholic woman I despise. I can read so much about her, just from the red lipstick she wears, the perfectly curled hair, the outfit so prim and proper, not a wrinkle could be seen—but covered in the tiniest moth holes. I think back to how she grabbed my songbird's wrist, the dark expression now hidden behind a picture-perfect smile.

This woman is evil.

With a huff of fake laughter, I say, "No, Miss . . . Forester, was it? Latin. Born in Puerto Rico, raised in Miami." I look at my little songbird, her eyes still locked on mine. "I'm Father Marcelo Serrano. I will be joining your parish for the next few weeks to assist Father Callum in development plans."

And then, against my own will, I stick out my hand to my songbird. I know she'll take it, and when she does, it'll be with the hand she used to fuck herself with. A part of me wonders if they'd still be slick with her come. If they'd taste like her. Smell like her.

She startles a bit, her eyes dropping to my hand. And I know she is wondering the same thing, unaware that I am counting on it.

Her mother elbows her, a flicker of the darkness drifting past the fake smile. Pressing her lips together, my songbird slowly takes my hand, and the heat in her fingers makes my cock throb.

"H-Hello. I'm Junia. Uh—You can call me June."

June.

"Though she prefers Junia. After one of the apostles of Christ." Her mother forces a smile, and my distaste for the woman only grows. "And I'm Jill. This is my fiancé, Daren," she says, pointing at the vile man next to her. "We're so happy to have you here," the mother continues, though Daren seems to be sizing me up, staring between me and June.

But I haven't let go of her hand. And her eyes haven't broken from mine. "It's good to meet you, June," I say, only to—only *for*—her. Her rosy cheeks turn an even more violent shade of red, bringing a smile to my lips.

"Yo—You too," she mumbles, pulling her hand back.

All of a sudden, I come to my senses. Remembering the priest I am. I take a step back, closer to Father Callum, and shove my hands into my pockets.

"Thank you for inviting me into your parish. St. Mary's is beautiful, and I am honored to call it home for the next few days."

"Days?" Father Callum asks, his eyebrow raised. We haven't spoken about my process really. I haven't told him how quickly things could move.

I bob my head back and forth. "More or less. Depends how long the . . . development takes."

"Surely, you'll be here until Sunday though, right, Father? For Sunday Mass?" the mother—Joan? Jill?—questions.

I turn to her and weakly nod. Truth is, I don't know how long I'll be here. If things go well, I'll be skipping town tomorrow. If they don't . . .

I find myself once again turning to June.

Maybe I can stay for just one Mass. It's been a long time since I've seen a full service. And I would love to hear her play again.

But I tell myself, *she also is my first lead.*

Of course, she could just be a horny little church girl, fucking herself like that in private. But it feels like more. And that vision and the raging hard on in my pants seems like a good sign I'm right.

I mean, June is gorgeous. Her ass is fucking phenomenal, and I want to drown in her tits, and squeeze every part of her to hear those little soft noises she'd make . . .

I—fuck. My thoughts spiraling out of control is *exactly* what I mean. I'm not a horny man. I'm not so easily seduced, I don't fall to lust. It's just not one of my sins, and it hasn't been in a *very* long time.

But the sight of June? The *sound* of June?

It is driving me off the fucking wall, begging me to sin. I *could* be just making excuses, but I feel a heaviness shroud the walls. A primal need settling into my blood.

If there's a demon here—and I'm starting to truly believe there might be—I think it may just be attached to my songbird.

6

JUNE

My cheeks are still warm as I blindly follow after Mother and Daren to the car. That priest . . . Father Marcelo . . . I was unable to take my eyes off him. He was so *handsome*, and his deep voice with his strong accent was so melodic, it felt as though each syllable uttered wrapped around me, snugly fitting around each and every curve.

Capturing me.

Priest, I remind myself. *He's a priest.* Not that it matters. Even if he weren't, there is no way on earth a man as hot as *that* would ever look at me.

"June." The sound of my name from his mouth alone is enough to send my stomach into somersaults. Maybe it's the recent plague of horny bouts, but I haven't . . . *ogled* at someone like this before. Not even Father Callum, who was arguably the most attractive man in my life.

Most attractive till now.

I shake my head, trying to get the thoughts of Father Marcelo and his chiseled jaw, scruffy facial hair, and curly, mussed dark brown hair, out of my mind. His tan skin was near golden, and his dark eyes were absolutely intoxicating as he looked down at me.

And he was tall. Very tall.

"I haven't heard such a thick accent since the last time I was in Jersey. Could barely understand a fucking thing that guy said," Daren spits, forcing my attention back to them as he moves to the driver's side of my mother's old, beat up, white Toyota Corolla.

Mother shrugs. "I don't know. I thought he was *exotic.*" A small smile curves her lips, and pink rises on her cheeks before she catches me watching her. Her face quickly switches to a scowl. "What? Don't look at me like that. I haven't forgotten that you skipped Mass."

I slide into the car and startle. Not thinking, I utter, "What? I didn't—"

The sharp noise reverberating in my ears shocks me faster than the sting on my cheek.

Mother's body is spun in the front seat, facing me, and only then do I realize she just slapped me.

"You were such an embarrassment. What's everyone gonna think when they realize you weren't praying with the rest of us?" she hisses.

Daren huffs a breath, almost a laugh, and drives out of the church's lot as Mother's voice only grows louder.

"It's like you think you're better than us. Sitting up there, above the rest of the parish. What, do you think you're closer to God 'cause you're up there, Junia?" Her white face is now stark red, and I shrivel farther into the back seat.

I know this look.

A shaky breath releases from my nose and I can feel a familiar quivering in my chest, almost as if my lungs are shriveling up, with no room for air.

"She must," Daren says, provokingly, "and the whole dang parish knows it. You saw how Tonia looked at her when she came into the sanctuary for Communion?"

Mother spins to him. "No. What'd she do?"

"Looked at the girl's tits poking through that tight sweater."

I stifle a gasp, trying desperately to stay as still as possible.

That wasn't Tonia, jerk, it was you.

Mother's eyes snap back to mine before they dip down to look at my chest. I instinctively cross my arms over them, but she yanks my wrist away.

"That is *it*. What the Hell is wrong with you?"

"I-I'm sorry," I stutter, not even sure what I'm sorry for. Perky nipples? A sweater that is *obviously* not too tight? My existence? "I-I'll get rid of this one. I th-thought it was okay."

Slap.

My face stings from the impact, and before I can recover, I feel wetness on my lashes, pooling in my eyes.

"My daughter, acting like the town fucking slut." Mother rolls her eyes and spins in her seat, facing the front again.

"Girl deserves a whoopin' if ya ask me."

Mother nods, and I can feel the life drain from me as she says, "Oh, I intend to."

My throat is so dry, no matter how much I swallow, it just feels like cotton. The ride goes on forever, and I can already feel the burn on my back, my legs, the familiar sting of the belt, the stabbing pain of the metal buckle that always manages to catch me.

Every breath is forcing its way out of me, but no matter how much I breathe in, it's never enough.

Daren's voice sounds far away as fear captures me, but I manage to hear him say, "Who do you think she's doin' it for?"

Mother looks at him. "Doin' what for?"

Daren shrugs as his eyes find mine in the rearview mirror, but his gaze doesn't linger there—it drops. "Lookin' sexy, showing off her tits." He turns to Mother abruptly. "You think it's Callum?"

Ass. Hole.

Mother's silence is louder than any curse she could've mustered, her rage simmering in the unbreathable air in the small cabin of the car. I see her jaw lock, her eyes stay forward.

And I know, Daren just added so much more fire to her rage. So much more force to each whip. I can't move, I can't make a noise. If I do, I don't know what will happen.

If I do, I don't know if I'll make it home.

I cry out again, my hands holding the back of the worn suede couch as my knees are propped on the sunken-in cushions. But no matter how hard I plunge my fingers into the soft material, it doesn't ebb the pain.

Whip. Whip. Two slashes, back to back, as the leather snaps against my bare back. Mother had me strip to my underwear, my sweater already thrown into the trash. The teddy bear panties I've had since middle school, with tears all along the seams and a faded period stain, are all that protect my butt from the ravage whips. My bras, circa teddy bear panties, are old, worn, and way too small. The once-white color of the top one has turned a gross yellow from years of washing. The underwire has long since poked into my skin, and the band has stretched so wide, it's holding on by a thread. The one I wear under is a sports bra as tight as can be, from before I even wore regular bras, and that strip is all that protects my back. But my mother purposefully doesn't aim where her blows would be cushioned, and I can already feel the burning slashes rising, red and angry. Like her.

Mother stands behind me, her rage taking up all the space and air in the small living room. But I can feel Daren's eyes on me from the hallway. Watching. Enjoying.

"Are you trying to seduce Father Callum?" she yells, whipping my upper thighs right under my ass.

The leather snaps on my skin and I cry out, "No!"

"Then *who*?" she hisses.

"No one, I-I'm not doing anything!"

"Liar!" Another whip. I've lost count already.

"Pl-Please, Mother," I whimper pathetically. The pain on my back is radiating, spreading all over my skin. Sweat dots my forehead and I can't help but squeeze my eyes shut to the pain, even as tears drip down.

Suddenly, I stiffen.

The sound of metal on metal.

I jolt up, trying to turn around. I know that sound. I *hate* that sound. But Mother knees my lower back, pushing me back toward the couch.

"You don't wanna tell me, Junia. So, you get the buckle. Three lashes for your heresy in church today. Three lashes for the father, the son, and the holy spirit."

My spine straightens as I hear the metal prong hit the

buckle, jingling again, and before I can brace myself, I can feel the sharp cold snap into the flesh at my back. The juxtaposition of cold creating a raging heat singes my back, as fresh waves of violent stings explode. I don't even know if I'm bleeding yet, but I can *feel* my skin torn open, exposed to this rotten room.

She snaps it against me again, and this time, the prong catches on my skin, tearing the flesh down and away.

I scream and lie flat on the couch, trying to escape her, escape the belt.

But then she hits me again, so fast I'm not ready. This time, the metal tears into my butt cheek, just beside my underwear, ripping skin once more. Stupid teddy bears. They couldn't even protect me.

Over my silent sobs, I hear Mother huff a breath and step back. The metal jingling once more as she drops the belt.

Slowly, so slowly it feels like I'm not even moving, I ease up, leaning on the back of the couch as I turn to sit.

Daren steps back into the room, and I do everything I can to avoid him.

"Want me to take over?" he asks Mother, pointing at the belt.

I catch her reaction. She scrunches her eyebrows and shakes her head in confusion. "No. I said three for the trinity, and she took three. She's done." Then she turned back to me. "Go to your room. I think you could afford to skip dinner." She looks at me with such disgust in her eyes, dropping her gaze to my stomach, my thighs, and it takes everything in me to hold back the bile in my throat.

Somehow, I manage to stand up, even with the pain of the fresh wounds screaming at me. I lift the skirt from the floor, hold it to my chest, and run. Past Mother. Past

Daren. Our house is so small, yet the run feels so long. So far. And as soon as I'm in my room, I lock the door behind me, and slump to the old, smelly carpeted floor. All I can do is cry.

7
MARCELO

Junia Forester. June. My songbird. Shortly after she was taken from the cathedral by her overbearing mother and *Daren*, I excused myself from Father Callum, telling him I needed to scout out Belmouth, get supplies, see what I could find.

In reality, I just followed them home.

After a quick trip to my room, I removed the collar and changed into a fitted black tee and hoodie, shoving the metal rosary into my pocket just in case I needed to exorcise whatever I assumed was following June. And, just so she wouldn't recognize me if she *did* see me, I tucked my mask into my hoodie.

Now, I'm parked down the road from her shitty little house, mask on and hood up, standing about ten paces from her bedroom window.

It's still daytime, but she doesn't even notice the figure in all black staring at her as she bursts into her room.

In . . . just her underwear.

What the fuck?

June slumps to the floor, her knees buckling under her, and just a moment later, her entire body shakes with what look like sobs. All I see are her pale shoulders shaking, and her thick brown hair covering her face.

This was . . . not what I was expecting.

Why is she just in her underwear?

After watching her for what has to be over an hour, her shoulders finally relax, but she doesn't move. The sun is nearing the horizon, creating a lilac sky with orange and pink clouds.

I have *never* been good with crying women. If my mother or sister cried in front of me, it was over. I would do anything they said. Same for Willow years later. If she cried over a stupid boy, I'd go beat him up for her. She cried 'cause someone said something awful about Rowan? I made sure they never said *anything* about him again.

Seeing June cry strikes that same *need* inside of me. The need to protect, to help, to *make it right*.

Before I even know what I'm doing, I step forward. Actually realizing what I'm about to do, I still take another step.

Something, or someone, made this little songbird cry herself to sleep before nightfall.

The dry grass crunches under my black boots with each step and, with the mask on, it feels like every shred of hesitation or second guessing falls away. If she wakes up, she'll be terrified, and I don't quite hate the idea of that. I reach her window, and though my shoulders are nearly the width of it, I'm determined to climb in. I test it, making sure it's not locked, and when it slides up with only a little hesitation, I ready myself to enter.

The masked me is supposed to be saved for killing those too evil to be alive. Those summoning demons and devils into our world, sacrificing innocents for their hellish goals. It's meant to fight the root of the problem, as the priest fights the results of the problem.

But right now, the masked me wants nothing more than to sneak into this girl's bedroom and ease all her sorrows.

I push the window up, and carefully—quietly—climb in.

The room is small, and it smells of wildflowers and laundry detergent. Her small bed is centered, with nightstands on either side, one holding a Bible and the other a notebook. Across her bed is a small, old dresser and beside it is a full-length mirror.

And that's it.

Nothing on her walls, nothing on her floors. There's a small closet door on the other side of the dresser, but when I peek inside, all I see are blankets.

I can tell they're not well off, but this girl has . . . nothing. There is absolutely no character to her room, not a single book, I don't even see a phone.

What twenty-something-year-old doesn't have a phone?

As expected, June is asleep, her breaths like a small animal.

And as I come closer, I see them—the raging lashes. Blood is dripping from two wounds on her back, and another on her round, plump ass. Beside them are angry swells coating the backs of her thighs, red lines marring that porcelain skin.

My gloved hands fist tightly, and my jaw hurts from how tightly I clench it. It takes *everything* in me not to

throw open that door she's slumped in front of and murder those two dumbfucks who did this to her.

But then I'd be leaving my broken little songbird alone.
And I *can't.*

I quietly ease down and move her, just a bit, to make
sure she's fully asleep, then I pull her toward me and lift
her up.

Fuck. She's gorgeous. These porcelain thick thighs, her
little belly. It makes me want to bite her. Kiss her. Lick her.

And her fucking tits? They're so much larger than I
thought they were in that frumpy sweater she wore earlier. I knew she was hiding *something,* but Father in
Heaven, I didn't know she looked like *this.*

A gorgeous, thick goddess. I could drown in her and it
still wouldn't be enough.

I don't realize how tightly I'm gripping her thigh as I
cradle her to me until she jostles in my arms, whimpering,
before settling back down again.

Fuck. What the Hell is happening to me?

I walk June to her bed and gently place her on it, turning her onto her side, away from me. Absently, I notice
she's wearing two bras that are digging into her skin.

I can't leave her room, so instead of properly cleaning
her wounds, I dab at the drying blood. *Saliva has healing
properties. I could lick them,* I think to myself for the briefest
moment before coming to my senses. Again.

After making sure none of the wounds are still bleeding, I cover June in the heaps of blankets she has on her
bed and stand above her. Watching her.

My hard cock is begging to be set free, begging to be
shoved inside of her, and take her—even as she sleeps. It's
pressed so tightly against my pants, it's almost painful. I
take a shaky breath, trying to calm myself down. I've

never felt desire as strongly as I have today. I feel . . . unlike myself. Like an animal. A demon.

And it is the one reason why I don't leave.

Because I am convinced a demon is influencing my poor songbird, and now me along with her.

I sit on her bed beside her—probably a mistake, but one only me and God will ever know about—and I pray. I pray for June, for her troubles and her soul.

"Hail Mary, full of grace, the Lord is with thee. Blessed art thou amongst women, and blessed is—"

June shudders beside me, and a small, faint moan escapes her breath.

I go absolutely, wildly feral.

I throw the blankets off her and watch as her thighs squeeze together, those little teddy bears getting lost between them. Perky nipples are pressing through the fabric of her bras, and it takes everything in me not to rip the final threads of these things apart and take those glorious breasts into my mouth.

Lowering myself beside her, I breathe her in. She smells nothing like laundry detergent and everything like wildflowers and tears. It sends jolts to my cock, and the only thing I can do is press it into her round ass as I lie next to her sleeping body.

Fuck, fuck, fuck, fuck, fuck.

I am committing a carnal sin. But, as long as I don't break my vows—as long as I remain abstinent—it's okay.

Right?

June backs her ass into my cock, and I curl my arm around her waist, hugging her to me. I can hear her deep, sleeping breaths.

But it's not enough.

I need to *feel* them.

I trail my arm up her abdomen, refusing every urge to grab her stomach and squeeze her. My hand drifts between her breasts, resting on her chest.

Up, down. Up, down.

I tune my breathing to hers, feeling each inhale of life, and as I drive my cock against her ass cheek again, I *feel* another moan escape her chest.

Before I can stop myself, I pinch one of her perky nipples between my finger and thumb—and I *twist*.

June moans again, jerking into me. It takes everything in me not to touch her. Not to rip those little teddy bear panties away from her cunt and shove my gloved fingers into her desperate pussy.

This is all, I tell myself. *I will not indulge more.*

But I keep toying with her breast, cupping it in my hand and squeezing, pinching her nipple and rolling it between my fingers.

She turns onto her back, giving me better access to fondle her. Fuck, she really is gorgeous. Her bangs fall into her eyes, and her perfect, plump lips are open.

Wait.

Her lips are pressed together.

It's her eyes that are open.

She freezes, like a little deer caught in the headlights, and I can tell that she's trying to figure out if I'm even human. After all, all she can see is a black mask with a thin white cross coming down on her.

Her wide doe eyes study me as her plump lips quiver. She's terrified. Justifiably so, but it still stings to know *I* do this to her. And some sick part of me also finds it a little hot.

June's breathing has completely stopped, and I can tell before even she can that she's about to scream. The change in her eyes, the sudden stiffness of her body, the recognition of something not being *right* painted all over her face. As she takes a sharp inhale, I pin my body over hers and press a gloved hand tightly over her mouth, grabbing her scream and *taking it.*

Tears prickle her eyes and I can't help but find her absolutely stunning like this. She tries to fight, jerking under me as if to get away, but a sharp hiss leaves her lips and escapes between my fingers. She spasms, and I can tell it's from the pain raking down her back with each welt her wicked family left on her.

I don't want my songbird in pain.

Still holding her tightly, I straddle her wide hips and pin her to the bed with my knees, easing my weight from her chest and hovering over her.

She exhales, her eyes closing in a form of relief.

Something compels me to speak. God, the Devil— maybe my cock. But I *need* her to know she won't be hurt, not by me. "I'm not going to hurt you." I deepen my voice, trying to suppress my accent as much as possible. Fuck, how do British people pretend to be American all the damn time?

June blinks her eyes up at me.

"Are you going to scream?"

She hesitates, then shakes her head.

"Good girl," I mutter, and slowly lift my hand from her mouth, testing—waiting—to see if she truly is a *good girl.*

When she doesn't scream, I brush the tears from her cheek. She whimpers, swallows, and then whispers, "Wh- Who are you?"

Instead of answering, I ask, "Why did they hurt you?"

8
JUNE

The black face with a white cross hovers above me like an angel come to punish me for my sins. Only, the angel is currently touching me in ways I've never been touched, making me feel so, so good.

So maybe he's not an angel at all. Maybe he's a demon.

Arousal has woken me before, and though I am no stranger to wet dreams, my new . . . *illness* has forced me to consciousness before in dire need of a reprieve.

I thought this was just another bout.

But I am *very* wrong.

The masked man hovers over me, his weight pressing on me as he straddles my hips. There are no eye holes in his mask, and something about that makes him feel even more unreal, even more of a monster than simply a man sneaking into my room.

And for some very, *very* deranged reason—I'm not

really afraid. Maybe I'm naive, but . . . when he said he wouldn't hurt me, I believed him.

I open my mouth to answer, but a shuddering breath escapes instead. The masked man watches, patient, and I take a deep breath in to try again.

"I was bad," I say—though I'm not even sure that's true. "I was bad and sinful in church."

He tilts his head. The mask absorbing the small amount of light and making it look like a void spot in my bedroom. It isn't leather, at least not in the way I know leather to be. It's thick and stiff, and with his hood pulled up, the white cross jaggedly painted across it almost glows.

"And what sins are those?" he asks, gently wiping my other cheek of tears.

What's wrong with me? Why am I not fighting this man off at all? Why am I not screaming for help or trying to get away?

I see the impressive bulge in his pants, feel its hard length pressed against my lower belly.

And, disgustingly, I'm so wet. I am so turned on by the smell of tobacco and not-quite-leather engulfing me, or the way I just *know* he's studying my near-nude body. Some twisted part of me wants him to shred these teddy bear panties the rest of the way and touch me like no one has ever touched me before.

I can't believe myself. My mother is right, I am a slut. I desperately want the man who's breaking into my room to have sex with me. The *masked* man. It makes me sick, and I just know I'm broken. Damaged.

"M-My body." I don't know why I admit any of this. I don't know why I'm entertaining him. My hands aren't even bound. I have no excuse. "What are you going to do to me?"

The man straightens and I can *feel* his eyes devouring every inch of me. I stiffen under him, needing to avoid his gaze, trying to squirm away from it, but with him on top of me, I'm not going anywhere. And suddenly, I am so, *so* embarrassed by the shitty two bras I'm wearing. My cheeks heat and I feel the need to squeeze my eyes shut—to just get *away*, even if it's visually.

He places a leather gloved hand on my ribs, and the touch feels absolutely forbidden as it sends a shiver down my spine. I can feel the goosebumps all over my arms and legs, and as the leather begins to trail up, I have to bite my lip from crying out.

"Your body is *no* sin, doll. It is a fucking miracle from God. Don't let anyone else's jealousy ruin that." I gasp at his words, as his hand cups the bottom of my breast, massaging just where the underwire digs into me. His finger finds where it pokes out, jabbing into my skin.

In a blink, the masked man pulls a knife from his pocket, flicks it open, and slashes my bra just where the two cups meet in the center.

The cold bites my skin, but the relief of my breasts being released—and of finally being able to breathe—floods me.

"The wire . . ." He breathes, his fingers still grazing under my breasts, his knuckles brushing just under my nipple "It was stabbing into you."

A shaky breath leaves me and heat pools between my thighs like never before. I clench my core, praying this mysterious man doesn't realize what he's doing to me.

I work to swallow around the lump in my throat. "Yo—You didn't answer . . . what are you going to do to me?"

With his thumbs, he follows the curve under my breasts once more, squeezing both ever so gently. And then he lifts himself off of me.

"Nothing."

The masked man caresses one gloved finger over my cheek, then walks back to the window. He turns, keeps his eyes—well, cross—on me, and then slips through my window. His form slowly backs away, disappearing into the bushes at the edge of our yard. But even once he's gone, I still feel his eyes on me. All throughout the night.

Somehow, it makes me feel safe.

Maybe he is an angel after all.

I fall asleep after what feels like hours of staring at those bushes, trying to catch another glimpse of my Peeping Tom. But the hours of making men out of shadows quickly turn into tired, droopy eyes, and the next thing I know, it's morning.

I'm still in my underwear and sports bra, the sliced bra now split in half around me, and the bushes outside my window are just regular, common junipers. No masked man in sight.

If it weren't for the torn bra, every rational part of me would think what happened last night was a trauma-response dream. A masked man—a superhero—who came to help me after a slew of pain.

Only I would make my superhero a terrifying, jacked man in black who definitely should've made me fear for my life but instead made me incredibly horny.

But . . . the bra does prove it. He was real and here and . . . he didn't hurt me.

Banging on my door snaps me out of my thoughts, and just as I jerk up from bed, I wince. My back is still raging, and every welt feels just as swollen as when the belt first touched my skin yesterday. The tears in my skin feel fresh and raw—and possibly infected.

"Junia! Wake up! We're going to be late!"

Church. Again. Every day, and twice on Sundays. It's never ending. Mother acts like she can't stand that I'm still at home but . . . she doesn't let me do anything that would let me get out of here.

"Coming!" I yell back, and try to ease myself out of bed. At least the slash on my butt won't be too hard to clean, but I have to figure out if I should brave asking Mother for help on the two on my back.

I hobble toward the small dresser of clothes I have and try to pick the least offensive outfit I can. Nothing too tight—I don't want to look like a slut—and nothing too frumpy—I don't want Mother to point out how fat I am again.

It leaves me with another sweater and skirt combo, but the skirt reaches my ankles, and I add another cardigan over the sweater to cover my boobs even more. And as an added extra, I lay a sock flat on each of my nipples, just in case they feel like ruining my life by being pointy again. I trade out the teddy bears for *Thursday* panties I seldom wear on Thursdays, and then I hurry to the bathroom.

Just as I reach for the door, Daren throws it open and his body collides into mine.

"Well, good morning to you too." He smirks, his gold mustache catching the light.

"Good morning," I mumble.

He takes a step forward, his chest staying against mine, forcing me to take a step back in turn. "About yesterday . . . I want to apologize for goading your Mother. It's awful what she did to you."

I look up at him, a line forming between my brows. "From what I remember, you asked to take over."

Daren runs his tongue over his teeth and raises an eyebrow, nodding slowly. "That I did. See, June, you ain't got a daddy figure in your life. I want to be that. I wanna be your daddy. And if that means punishing you for the wrong you do, then that's just tough love." He places a hand on my upper arm, slowly trailing it down. "But it's still love. I ain't gonna let you be anybody's little whore."

"I wasn't—"

His eyes meet mine, his entire face darkening as he says, "Now. Go get ready for church." He yanks my body against his once more and moves his hand to my back. As he steps beside me, he pushes me into the bathroom, his hand digging right into where Mother whipped me the night before.

I whimper at the pain, nearly falling forward, but Daren doesn't stop. His hand only pushes deeper, and once I'm fully in the bathroom, he closes the door.

I don't hear his footsteps leave the doorway for several moments. All the while my back radiates to new levels of pain and tears dot my eyes.

A shaky breath escapes my lips as the buzz of the fluorescent light above the mirror eats it up.

Finally, Daren leaves, and when I look up in the mirror, my eyes are bloodshot and the tears pricking my lashes become full sobs.

Spending the night watching June left me no closer to any answers on the demons plaguing this town.

June made me feel like an animal last night. I had the primal need to protect her, to take care of her, to fuck her. It was early morning when I was finally able to tear my eyes from her, to leave the shadows of the trees outside of her window. My chest twisted with each step—a gut feeling I haven't felt in years. I'm not sure what this sick obsession I have with her is but there's more than lust. I have a bad feeling leaving her alone. A guilt, a fear—that something might happen to her.

But I very well couldn't stand at her window in the light of day, not when the mask has to be tucked away, and Marcelo the priest must take the mantle.

Now, I'm on my knees, rosary tangled between my

fingers, and I'm praying. The frankincense drifts around me as I beg for forgiveness for everything I did last night.

It's odd. I *should* feel so much more guilt for the sins I've committed. For touching her, lusting after her, stalking her. Not only are they against my vows and the church, they're against the law. I broke into her home last night.

But I don't feel guilty for any of it.

I don't feel guilty for anything related to June and something about that should be . . . troubling. But, instead, it just leaves me to wonder—maybe this is a part of God's plan for me. Maybe *she* is a part of God's plan.

I have never been a perfect priest. It's part of the reason Father Rodrigo asked me to become an exorcist so early on. I can't even remember the time of priesthood before I exorcised demons. It was always part of the lure to the church.

To fight for those who cannot fight for themselves.

To get a chance at revenge.

I've probably broken every vow I took, yet I am still embedded with the power of the holy fire to execute foulness from the world.

Maybe I'm special, sure. But in reality, I know it's not that. I know it's the false rules man set to follow a God they couldn't see. Rules set to favor *themselves*, not the Father. The one and only thing I believe in is Him. The Bible be damned. The Church be damned.

So I won't fight these lustful thoughts for June. I will taper them. I will restrain them. But I will not fight them, I will not stop them.

Because something about that woman *sings* to me. My little songbird.

And I am desperate to match her tune.

The first service is set to begin in just a few minutes, and I stand with Father Callum at the doors, greeting all the parish as they enter. My *official* introduction into St. Mary's. I can tell the "devout " from the casual attendees. The "every morning, three times a day" visitors, from the "on holidays and when I need something more from the Lord."

I always seem to favor the latter.

The "everydayers" look at me with confusion, fear, and something akin to distaste. They don't like *new*, they don't like *change*, and they definitely don't like a grumpy priest with tattoos on his hands.

But who fucking cares?

The faces go by, bland and boring, telling me their names as if I'll remember any of them. But I can feel my entire demeanor change when I spot *her*. My shoulders roll back, my spine straightens—I even puff out my chest a little.

June hobbles behind her family, and I can tell she is trying her best to hide the pain beneath the old, moth-eaten sweater. The equally drab cardigan she wears over it weighs her down.

She shyly peeks up at me through her honey brown bangs, and the smallest smirk tilts her lips. I go to greet her, but the moment I open my mouth, her mother's in my face, pushing herself at me.

"Ah, Father Marcelo, Father Callum, good morning!"

Her makeup is caked on, and her dress is cut low at the cleavage. Unfortunately for whatshername, June's figure must've come from her father's side. Where June is filled out wonderfully, curves and soft spots in all the best places, her mother is as thin and flat as plywood. And where I don't regularly find myself commenting on women's bodies, I do find the bodacious nature of her outfit is only making her thinness *more* apparent.

She looks almost sickly. And the smell of cigarettes on her breath doesn't help.

"Good morning," I mutter, and let Father Callum take the reins of the conversation.

The mother's fiancé—Daren? Darien? Whatever—stands between the two women, his arms crossed over his chest almost as if he's acting as a personal bodyguard to the two.

"Ah, Daren, I meant to tell you—the men's group is rescheduled from this Friday to Saturday," Callum says.

And as I watch, June takes the smallest step from him, just enough so his elbow doesn't touch her arm.

I hear Callum continue speaking, but the words don't register—not as I *watch* the man notice the lack of contact with his almost-stepdaughter. *Watch* as annoyance and rage . . . and something more disgusting—something like *challenge*—enters his eyes.

It's a second of time. A moment. But it tells me so much more of this dynamic. It tells me that all the fear I had leaving June this morning . . . is possibly valid. Yes, she's being abused at home. Her mother is vile, June is sheltered, and this man is disgusting. But that singular *look*—the look of a man who thinks he is *owed* what is not offered—is cause for concern. That tells me this isn't just an overly zealous mother.

This is danger.

Before I think any better, I place my hand on June's upper arm.

"June." Her name on my tongue feels like honey. Her

stormy blue eyes meet mine—they look like the ocean in a storm, full of gray clouds and massive waves. But on her cheeks, there's a warm sunrise welcoming a new dawn. "Father Callum has told me you are here nearly as often as he is. I still have not properly toured the cathedral. Do you think you could show me?"

The sunrise turns into a full on blush, and—thankfully—she steps closer to me. Away from her stepfather.

"I would be happy to, Father Marcelo." *My* name on her lips nearly brings me to my knees. My sweet songbird.

Marcelo, I imagine my name on her lips in the dark. Her voice whimpering as I touch her, love her, show her just how perfect she is. *Marcelo,* she'd moan, and I would be completely undone.

"—prefer after the service?"

Fuck. She was speaking. I mentally curse myself and the growing hard-on in my pants. "*Perdón.* Can you say that again?"

She presses her lips together. I wonder if my Spanish turns her on.

"Would you like a tour now? Or would you prefer one after the service?" Her full lips raise on one side.

Mere moments have passed since she walked up to me. Her mother and stepfather still stand beside her, but for all I care, they could not exist. Even Father Callum has blended into the background.

It is only the ringing of the church bells above that forces me to realize this moment is more than just between June and I.

"Well." I chuckle lightly. "I think the bells just answered for us. I believe after will be wonderful. But, if you don't mind, I'd like to join you in the mezzanine. I want to see you play."

Her cheeks turn a bright red, and I give her a moment by turning to Father Callum. "If that is all right with you, of course, Father. I think I'd rather watch the parish than join them for my first service."

Callum's eyes widen for a moment before he nods, clearly thinking of what I am actually here for. "Of course."

I turn back to June. "Well then, Miss Forester, please lead the way."

Without another glance at her parents, I follow June into the church. The pews are still filling, but most of the parish is seated, facing forward. We walk between them. The sunlight shines in through the stained glass windows, creating a kaleidoscope of colors all around the dark wood and cream marble flooring. Before we get to the carved crucifix, June turns right, exiting through the same espresso-colored wooden door I'd take to get to my quarters. The moment the door shuts behind us, the chatter and rustling of the morning crowd muffles, and all I can hear are the taps of our footsteps.

"How long have you been coming to St. Mary's, June?"

She looks back at me over her shoulder as she turns into a small alcove leading directly into a spiral stairway. "Pretty much as long as I can remember. I wasn't born in Belmouth, but I've spent most of my life here."

I nod, following behind her as we ascend the stairs. "Where are you from originally?"

She shrugs. "Boston, I think? My mother doesn't talk about it much, but I know I was born in a hospital there. I think we moved here before I was even five." She pushes a plain door open at the top of the stairs, leading to the mezzanine balcony looking out over the parish. "Right around the time Father Callum became priest here, actually. It was just a year or two later, I think," she adds.

The half-circle shape and tall railing make it difficult to

see the people below, especially from the backside of the balcony. I imagine I'd have to stand right against the railing to see everyone. All that can be seen is the gorgeous brass pipes of the organ.

As June walks up to it, I marvel at its beauty. For a church so small, the organ looks priceless. It's massive and warm, with numerous sets of keys, and several buttons on panels to both sides—she tells me they're called pistons and stops. The small bench sits over pedals with even more of those buttons and a number of other nobs. Truthfully, I can't even fathom what I'm looking at, nor how one person is supposed to use *all this*. It looks like a contraption, like a time machine from a sci-fi movie, or a box that could take you to another realm.

June pulls one of the random chairs strewn about over to the balcony—facing away from her. "Would you like to sit here?"

I smirk and tilt my head before walking over to the chair and lifting it with one hand, placing it directly next to the organ. "I've seen a million services. I wanted to watch *you*."

She takes in a sharp breath. "Ah—oh. Of course, I just thought—no one has wanted to watch me play before. I didn't—"

"Really? I heard you yesterday. You were amazing."

The blush on her cheeks deepen, and something about it makes me absolutely feral.

"I—Thank you. I think most people come here to hear Father Callum. Not me."

I plop into the chair and cross my ankles.

"Well, I am honored, then, to be your first audience."

June presses her lips together again to hide her smile, and I think it might just be my new favorite sight. Still clearly frazzled, she sits on her bench and scoots across it. When I see her ass struggle to slide, I have never been more jealous of a piece of wood in my life.

I take her in once more as she begins to organize her sheet music, fumbling the papers. There is so much movement in so little an action, it seems as though her entire body is reacting to . . . well, me.

Her breasts are nearly falling out of her bra. I see the plump line where the seam is cutting into them, nearly overflowing.

Another bra for me to cut apart tonight, when I sneak into her room again as her Salvation.

But I can't think of that right now. Not while the collar is on. I dart my eyes away, trying to find anything else to focus on.

The little songbird riffles through her sheet music, placing them in front of her. "Ho—How was your first night here?" she breathes, and my chest feels like it's running a marathon.

"Good. It was a quiet night." I grin—lying. If only she knew *I* was the one laying atop her. "I hope you don't mind me sitting up here? It just seemed like the best seat in the house, and I did want to see you play. If it's too uncomfortable—"

She finally turns to me, a smile lifting her lips. But it falters, like it slipped of its own accord without her permission.

"I don't mind at all. Just a fair warning, it's really loud up here during the music, but during the sermon you can hardly hear a thing. Father Callum isn't too great at projecting." She shrugs a shoulder, and I can't help but smile.

"To be honest, neither am I. That's ninety percent why they don't have me leading my own parish," I say jokingly.

Her eyes meet mine. "What's the other ten percent?"

That I am the farthest thing from a good priest there is. That I want to take you over this organ and fuck you till you're singing for me. That I want to make you mine in every sense of the word.

"I-I'm sorry." She waves both of her hands in front of her. And *fuck*, she must've seen *something* on my face. "That was way too personal."

I shouldn't have come up here . . . not alone with her. I feel the familiar sliver of what I felt in the church yesterday. What I felt listening to her finger fuck herself in the confessional. Lust, yes. But deeper than that.

Desperation. Need.

"Not at all, don't apologize." I clear my throat, deciding to give her some truth. "The other ten percent is that my bishop is also the man who raised me, so he knows just how much of a lousy priest I make."

At that moment, the opening procession begins, and it's June's cue to start playing, but instead, her eyes find mine once more.

"Father . . ." Her blue eyes search mine, and I can feel the seam between my eyebrows deepen as I search her face in return.

She knows something. And she's incredibly afraid of what she knows.

I put my hand on her shoulder. "June, what—"

And then Father Callum walks out, and June scurries to the keys, her long delicate fingers on the white bars, and begins to play the most beautiful song I've ever heard.

I stand, taking a step back in amazement, taking in *all* her glory—watching her and only her. Her fingers fly over the keys, her hands pulling on stops, then pushing on the little piston buttons. Her feet are everywhere, pressing pedals and pushing against more below. She truly is a masterpiece, working the giant contraption all by herself, and creating such beautiful sound with each of her movements. It should be a chaotic mess, but instead, it's like watching a waterfall, stunning and gorgeous as it flows, but loud and destructive all the same.

Fuck the parish downstairs, fuck the procession, fuck everything.

All that matters right now is June's playing, and the image of her beautiful fucking ass hanging off the bench.

Something takes over my mind again, as I find myself staring. God, what I would give to just squeeze her ass.

Fuck it, I think, and go to unbuckle my belt. I want her ass, right here, right now. I step toward her and push her over the keys of the organ, creating a jarring blast of notes that echo throughout the entire sanctuary. But no one notices. At least, I don't notice if they do.

"Father Marcelo, what are you doing?" she squeaks. But she knows exactly what I'm doing, exactly what I want. Because it's what she wants too. With her bent over the organ, I pull her big ass back toward my hard cock and shove her skirt up to her waist. God, I nearly come just at the sight of her exposed for me, exposed above the entire congregation and no one has the slightest idea what I'm going to do to her.

"Shhh," I hum behind her.

"B-But you're a priest! Your vows?!"

I glide my fingers under the seam of her pink cotton panties, and pull them over her hips and down her thighs, till they reveal her to me completely.

Fuck, she's perfect.

"My vows . . . they're not worth denying this." I slip my index finger between her already-damp folds, and a small whimper escapes her lips. "I want you to moan for me, songbird."

I run my finger over her throbbing clit.

"Ah, God," she moans, looking at me over her shoulder.

"Not for him," I say, not even recognizing my own voice. "For me." I slide my middle finger into her wet, hot cunt, and she breaks.

"Father Marcelo," she whimpers, pushing herself back, taking my fingers deeper, "I want you—"

"I know what you want. I watched you touch yourself, and I know exactly what you need."

I slip my finger out of her, eliciting another moan to fall from those plump lips. God, I want to fuck every part of her. But I return to what I really want.

I rub my hand over the soft, smooth skin of her ass, before I slap it hard, leaving a red handprint, and then I do it again.

She shudders with each smack, and my cock is so fucking hard, I feel like it's going to explode in my black slacks. I pull it out and fist myself as I touch her.

"You're so fucking naughty," I breathe through gritted teeth. "Making me want to break my oath to God. Making me want to sully myself with sin. God, June, I want to fill you up with my come and have you beg me to be sinful. I want to do so many things to you."

I spank her again, my pinky hitting the plump lips between her thighs, and she jolts, her back arching from pleasure.

"You like when I spank you there, songbird? Let me hear it."

I do it again, and she moans my name. Fuck, it's so hot. I continue fisting myself, and it's been so long since I've given into pleasure, I can already feel the tightening heat in my core, begging to burst out. I'm not even inside of her and I already want to come for her.

I pull her hips back again and slide my cock between her ass cheeks, pressing myself against her hole as I continue thrusting into my hand.

"June, you've done this to me. This is your fault. Fucking thank you." *I feel my balls slapping her pussy with each rock between her cheeks.*

I want her to come. I want her to scream my name. I want to fill her up and have her leaking my fucking come.

I reach around, shoving my fingers between her folds and find that sweet little bundle of nerves. "Ah, Marcelo! Father Marcelo!"

"That's right, June. Sing for me, songbird."

"Marcelo!"

"Father Marcelo?"

My eyes flash to June as she sits on the bench, looking at me over her shoulder. Her skirt is still in place, and I stand a few steps behind her, hands gripping onto the balcony's copper bar like it is the one thing between me and death.

Which, in this case, it might be.

What the fuck just happened? Was all of that an illusion?

June watches me in concern, but all I can think about is my hand on her ass, on her clit. All I can think about is how fucking hard I just was—fuck, *am.*

"Father Marcelo, are you okay?"

I let out a shaky breath. "Of course. Why?"

June shakes her head, saying, "I'm not sure. I heard you say 'Sing for me,' and when I asked you what you meant, you didn't respond."

Fuck, fuck, fuck.

"Sorry, June. I think my mind was elsewhere." *My mind was apparently too busy thinking about trying to fuck you than actually listening to you.* "Are you done with your set already?"

She eyes me strangely—I don't blame her, I just fantasized about bending her over the organ and trying to get her to come above the entire congregation—and then nods.

But her gorgeous ass is still hanging over that seat.

I bite my lip and grip the railing harder. I need to adjust my dick *now*, before she notices . . . if she hasn't already.

I turn my back to her, pretending to look over Mass, while I discreetly adjust myself. June stands behind me, taking a tentative step closer.

"C-Can I ask you something?"

Fuck.

"Of course, June."

Is this about last night?

"Before I had to play . . . I asked if you were actually here for church developments."

I turn to her. "Yes. What else would I be here for?"

Or maybe she'll tell me of the demon.

She fidgets with her hands, rubbing them together, and looks from me, to the floor, and then to me again.

"You can ask me anything, June," I reassure. If it's the latter, I need to know. So far, all I have is a feeling—and that is not enough to perform an exorcism.

She nods softly and then takes a breath. "You—" She pauses, looks me over, then shakes her head. "Did you like my set?"

I don't know why I couldn't bring myself to ask him. Maybe because it is ridiculous to even *think* someone as gorgeous—as *holy*—as him would ever degrade himself to want me.

There's no way he was the masked man.

But there was a moment. An ... *essence*. When he spoke about his past, when he sounded ... real, and not like the persona of the traveling priest—where he sounded *like* my masked man. His voice. His cadence.

It's not lost on me he arrived in my life on the *same day*.

But to delude myself into thinking *this* man would ever ... touch me? It's insane. Absolutely delusional.

No, the man who touched me has to be grossly disfigured. Maybe with three eyes and no teeth. He has to be clinically insane or an absolute figment of my imagination.

Some real *Phantom of the Opera* type.

Though, I always was Team Phantom.

Father Marcelo smiles before me, nodding his head. "It was the most gorgeous thing I've ever heard."

After the service concludes, I walk Father Marcelo down to the main floor and instead of meeting up with Mother and Daren first, I show Father Marcelo around the cathedral.

He seems to already know most of it—it's not a very large building. There's the priest's office to the left of the sanctuary, the sacristy to the right, and then more empty rooms beyond my little staircase—two plain offices, one room for gatherings, and, finally at the end of the hall, the guest living quarters. I know behind that cherry oak door is a small bathroom, a tightly packed kitchen connected to a living area, and a small bedroom with one window. And all of Father Marcelo's things.

I can't help but wonder what they smell like. Would they have the lingering scent of cigarettes and frankincense? Like the deeper, intoxicating scent that makes my knees weak?

"It's very quiet in my quarters. Almost unnervingly so." Father Marcelo chuckles. The rectory sits behind the church, so Father Marcelo's apartment is the only one in the actual cathedral.

"It's a little like a horror movie, right? Sometimes I'm here alone, Father Callum in his cottage, and I can't help but feel eyes on the back of my neck."

He smirks, but his eyes linger on me for a moment too long.

"Yeah." I shrug. "Like a horror movie."

Once we turn back and walk down the passage, it's only a matter of moments before we're back at the doors to the sanctuary. Every fiber of my being wants to *stay*. *Stay* here, stay with Father Marcelo.

But reality is ready to steal it all away.

I press into the door just as a hand gently wraps around my arm.

"June . . ." His voice is just as soft as his touch.

A lump forms in my throat.

Masked man, masked man, masked man. My eyes fall to his hands, those hands that were possibly soothing my pains, rubbing where the bra wire had repeatedly stabbed into me. Then I meet his eyes—eyes I couldn't see in the dark, but eyes that potentially saw a *lot* of me.

Suddenly, it feels too warm in this small, dim hallway.

His eyes are such a dark brown—not quite black, they're too warm for that. No, they're almost like a cherry-coated chocolate, a burnt umber, or the darkest shade of maroon imaginable. They're rich and terrifying, yet utterly captivating.

Father Marcelo takes a small step back, scratches the back of his head, and says, "You played beautifully today. I look forward to hearing you tomorrow as well."

A blush creeps over my cheeks. "T—thank you." I turn back to the door just as Father Marcelo pushes it open for me.

The congregation sits on the other side. Father Callum is speaking to my mother and Daren, again. The rest of the parish either lingers about or makes their way back to their regular lives.

But something isn't right—

I flinch back into Father Marcelo, my back bumping his chest as my heart stops dead in its tracks.

It's gone between blinks—where now all I see is a stained glass window, reflecting shimmering blues and reds—before I saw a black mass, shadowy and moving like smoke. It stood at the back of the church, watching . . . me? Father Marcelo?

"What is it, June?" Father Marcelo's hands are wrapped around my arms as he holds me to him, almost as if he's ready to toss me behind him at the first sight of danger.

When I look back to the spot with the shadow, there isn't a single trace of it left. Just the window, light shining through.

"N-nothing." I blink a few times, willing my heart to slow down. Lord, getting scared of a shadow? I need to stop sneaking horror movies.

"Junia?" my mother calls. When I find her, her eyes are locked on Father Marcelo's hands. As are Daren's.

"Coming," I call, and step out of Father Marcelo's grasp, leaving a cold wake in its place.

The day has been long, and I have begged for night to come like no other. Mother didn't take kindly to my . . . closeness with Father Marcelo today, so it was another whipping, this time, with Daren holding me down. I can still feel his dirt-covered fingernails digging into my hair at the base of my skull, pressing my face into the back of the couch as he watched Mother whip his belt across my back.

It was less than yesterday, but it hurt so much more.

Skipping dinner, I slunk into my room as fast as possible. I couldn't deal with them anymore. I just wanted . . .

Salvation.

And Salvation is here again, waiting, as if he knows I need him. He's standing outside my window, watching. Just like last time. His black hoodie is pulled over that terrifying mask, but . . . I don't feel afraid. I should. I most *definitely* should. Scary huge man outside my window watching me? What's *not* to be afraid of?

Especially with that thin white cross jaggedly painted over the thick black material. Is he mocking my faith? If that was his goal, it's not working. If anything . . . it's just making *him* my new faith.

He isn't scary. Or, at least, I'm not scared. Maybe it's because I've already dealt with enough horror for the night. My threshold is maxed out and nothing new can affect me. Maybe it's because my masked watcher has already done this before and everything was fine.

Maybe it's because, compared to the shit that is my life, the masked man feels more like a protector than a stalker. Like a comfort than actual danger.

He sees me watching him through the window as I curl in bed, his head tilts to the side. I think some part of me hoped he'd come tonight, and I can only assume he's seeing that on my face. If he *can* see through that thing. It looks so alien and . . . unhuman. No eye holes, no mouth — nothing but black and the thin cross drawn across it to face me. I don't even know if he *is* human.

I wipe one of the tears from under my eyes and lean up in bed. The masked man tenses, but doesn't move, staying just in the bushes a few feet from the window. But I see the stiffness in his shoulders. It's like he didn't expect me to acknowledge him.

Tossing the blanket off, I stand, completely unsure of what I'm doing. I walk over to the window and stand just in front of the glass.

I don't know if it's the anonymity of it all, but . . . I *like* the masked man watching me. I feel oddly safe under his sightless stare, knowing that if he hurts me, it's my own damn fault and not some made up, gaslit version of the truth.

I unlock my window, push it open, and step back, meeting the face of my watcher.

He once again tilts his head, then steps forward. Within three long strides, he stands at my window, and my chest hurts from the lack of breaths I've taken since standing.

A gloved hand hovers over the windowsill, and the thought of *those* gloved hands tangled in my hair, holding my face down, sends shivers all throughout my body. I suddenly realize what my body has known all along.

I want him to touch me.

I want him to taint me—before someone else does. With each day, I realize how *afraid* of Daren I am becoming. Each day, I realize he isn't here for my mom—there's no love, no security, and no money. No, Daren is here to play a game. A game in which he decided *I* was the prize for winning.

But he can't have his prize—it's not his to claim.

The masked man easily swoops into the opening, and as he stands at his full height, I feel my thighs clench with wrathful need.

I can pretend.

I can pretend whoever I wanted was under that mask.

My first thoughts are of Marcelo, my raging desire for him, knowing I'll never have him. I'll never feel him touch me beyond his gentle hands wrapped around my arms, his chest pressed against my back.

But this? This I can have. And what consequences will there be when a masked man wants to stay hidden, and a virgin slut wants to just *feel anything*?

I blow out a shaky breath and step closer to the man, slowly lifting my hand to touch him. He grabs it in the air, clutching it so tight, it almost hurts.

I wince, but I know what I want. I want his touch. I *crave* it.

With his hand wrapped around my wrist, I guide it toward my breast, grazing his knuckles just along the underside once more.

Within a breath, the man is on me, pushing me back into the wall next to my bed. Alarm bells ring, but I still don't think this was a mistake. Not as I feel a hard length press into my hip, not as his hand pins my wrist to the wall, not as his masked face hovers just above mine.

"Is this what you want?"

The shock of a robotic, altered voice jolts me to reality — to the decisions I've just made, the very *real*, very *stupid* decisions.

Unlike last night, he has a voice changer in his mask. This isn't just some creep lurking outside girls' windows. This is someone with a purpose that brought him here.

The man leans back to look at me, releasing my wrist but raising both arms to either side of me, locking me within.

"What? You scared now?" He presses his forehead against mine, forcing me to see nothing but the cross on his face. "You want me to leave?" The man digs his hips into me further, the length between his legs pressing into my damp core.

Fuck, it feels good. Better than I imagined. A shuddery breath escapes my quivering lips.

"Needy little church girl letting a stranger into her

room when Mother's back is turned." Another thrust, and I throw my head back.

"M-m-mistake," I stutter.

He nuzzles my cheek, the thick material dragging on my skin. It feels like . . . rubber. Or silicone. Not leather at all.

"Was it?"

His hands drop to my thighs, and by some act of God, he grabs them and lifts me against the wall, pressing directly against that sensitive spot I've only ever touched myself.

How he is able to carry me is beyond me, and a rushed gasp turns into a vicious moan when he presses into me.

The man chuckles under the mask, sliding a free hand up my stomach, between my breasts, and around my neck before finally settling over my mouth.

"Shh. You don't want to wake Mommy, do you? Not with those sweet little moans."

Maybe this was a mistake. I can admit that. But as his firm body is pressed to mine, it feels like anything but.

I shake my head and buck my hips forward, grinding his length.

He chuckles, and I swear he kisses me through the mask. "There's a good girl."

The masked man grinds against me, and for a moment, I lose myself in it. I think of Marcelo again, his sweet voice calling me a good girl. His hands on my body. His erection pressed against me.

I shudder—just *thinking* it feels so wrong. But I find my toes curling all the same.

The man takes a step back, letting my legs fall back to the floor before he completely unpins me from the wall. It's . . . odd. The gesture is . . . thoughtful. Almost kind. He doesn't let me fall. And though he's been slamming me around, the fresh wounds haven't stung once.

"Take off your clothes," he orders. I blink, unmoving. But the masked man doesn't let me think. He tries to lift my sweater over my head, saying, "Show me the wounds she gave you."

I don't know if it's the way he said it, but even through the robotic voice, I can feel an inkling of warmth.

I take a half step back, closer to the wall. "N—no," I whimper half-heartedly. I don't want him to see more of me. He's already seen too much.

"Now, songbird. Or I'll do it for you."

I bite my lips. I know he will. He already tried to take off my sweater and has proved he has no fear of cutting my clothes off of me.

But . . . if I do, then he'll see me.

The masked man pulls something from his pocket—his knife. He waits a moment, letting me see it, before flicking it open.

Quickly, I unbutton my skirt and let it fall to the floor around my ankles.

"Fuck," he groans. His hand holding the blade travels to my outer thigh, and he slowly caresses his gloved hand along my goosebumps. "I want these wrapped around my body, my face—" The masked man squeezes. "I want to feel these between my teeth." His other hand travels to the hem of my sweater again. "Continue."

I feel my cheeks heat, but I pull it over my head and let it fall with my skirt. It only took mere moments, and I'm yet again, standing in nothing but my underwear and socks in front of this man.

"So fucking beautiful," he breathes, and I can feel his eyes taking me in. I go to fold my arms over my stomach, feeling my heart pound in my chest, but the masked man quickly grabs them, tossing my wrists to my sides. "Don't you dare fucking cover yourself. You are stunning, and I want to admire every inch of you."

He steps forward, reaching for my breasts. I shut my eyes, anticipating his touch again, but instead, I just feel a tug.

As I open my eyes, I want nothing more than to super glue them shut forever as mortification swallows me whole. The masked man tugs on the two socks I laid flat against my nipples this morning, pulling them out from behind my bra.

"I've heard of women stuffing their bras, but . . . I don't really think you need it, songbird." The masked man chuckles, tossing the socks over his shoulder. "Your tits are already perfect as is."

I take a step back from him, trying to hide my shame, but his fist curls around my hair, the leather gloves tugging harshly at my scalp—just like I want—as he pulls me forward and tosses me onto my bed.

I fall, sprawling over the mattress and propping on my elbows to meet his gaze. He stands over me, so large it makes it seem like the room is too small for him, and I feel those sightless eyes careen down my body.

"You're so fucking wet already," he hisses, almost to himself. I look down at myself, and a small wet spot has formed just between my legs, just under the word *Thursday*. My lips fall open, but he doesn't give me a chance to respond. "Do you want me to make you feel good?"

Silence beats loud through the space between us. His chest rises and falls, waiting for me to answer.

I should say no.

I'd only be proving my mom right—I am a slut.

But . . .

"I want to admire every inch of you."

The words rattle in my mind, repeating over and over. He makes me feel . . . seen. He makes me feel warm.

So instead, I nod. The man tilts his head, and I add, "Please," just for good measure.

He looks down at himself, unzipping his hoodie to reveal his fitted T-shirt snug around his thick biceps.

I swallow, imagining this man *must* have a hideous face. Something that would make him stoop low enough to want to touch *me*.

Maybe I've been the only victim willing.

The masked man stands tall, tossing his jacket on the foot of the bed, his arms covered in stunning dark ink, and as I study the art over his muscles, he steps forward, nudging my thighs apart to make room for him.

"I'm not gonna hurt you, songbird."

And for some reason, I believe him.

Delicately, carefully, he lowers his hand to my hips, gently sliding against my skin. I feel the pores of the leather, the softness, rub against the goosebumps I now have.

With a violent, unexpected tug, he flips me onto my stomach and pushes my hair off my upper back. The lashes down my back, old and new, sting from the cold bite of the AC.

There's a beat of silence, heavy, as I feel his eyes roam the length of the cuts, the scars underneath, as his gaze wanders down my spine, over my hips, my . . . ass.

"What was your *sin* this time?" His voice drips with disdain, even with the robotic filter over it, like the mere thought of my punishment is the sin—that nothing I could've done would warrant this.

I've never had someone on my side before, about

anything. His words, his tone, it fills me with a sense of . . . self preservation, of hope.

Of not feeling alone.

As this all dawns on me, my masked man slowly comes around the other side of the bed, and crouches down to my eye level. He doesn't say anything more, waits for me to respond, and carefully works a small towel and water bottle from his bag. He dabs my back with the towel, cleaning the fresh ones.

Being with him, it makes me realize how . . . empty I've been. He may be the one wearing the mask, but he has shown me more of his personality in these two nights than I think I've been capable of showing anyone—even myself—for years. I . . . I don't know who I am. I don't know what I want. I don't know what I like—other than playing the organ— what I don't like, what I care about, what my interests are— nothing.

Except, now I know one thing. I like *him*.

"I was punished for being seen."

His hand pauses just over another slash. "Explain."

I rest my cheek on the mattress below me, my head turned to the side, facing the mask dead on. "She wants me to be a shadow. Always following behind her, but never outshining her. He wants me to be *his*. Today, they saw . . . someone . . . notice me. And they didn't like it."

The masked man is absolutely still, but I can see the muscles strain in his neck, the bulge in his forearm under his fitted black long sleeve.

"Listen," he says through gritted teeth. In a quick motion, he cups my chin between his thumb and finger, pinching my cheeks to meet his eyes. "You will *never* be his, because you are already *mine*, songbird."

My heart stops, the claim doing more for me than I

thought possible. Heat coils between my thighs, my core tightening.

His thumb on my cheek rubs small circles before moving to tuck a loose strand behind my ear. I haven't breathed since he called me his, but the masked man stands, and sits beside me on the bed. He reaches in his bag once more, pulling out an ointment, and dabs it on the welts down my spine. "You are so much more than a shadow, songbird. You're a ray of sunlight in this shithole," he whispers. His voice is gruff behind the mask, and somehow I still hear the cadence, the tone.

The care.

Once he finishes, he helps me sit up, my thighs touching his, my shoulders against his biceps.

"I got something for you."

I flinch back and look up at him. "You did?"

He reaches into his bag again and pulls out a small pink shopping bag. "To replace what I ruined." The masked man stands and steps in front of me. My eyes are level to his belt, and I—suddenly—want so badly to see it undone.

His gloved hand comes under my cheek again, forcing my eyes on his. The leather feels so soft on my skin, but his grip squeezes, and I couldn't look away if I wanted to.

The pink bag is placed on my lap, cool to the touch, but I can't look into it as the masked man bends at the waist. I can smell the thick leather—it's intoxicating. His breath is heavy as he hovers just a few centimeters away from me.

"Open your mouth for me and stick out your tongue."

I don't even think about it—I do as he says.

He closes the gap, my tongue on the thick leather, licking the small pores just over where his lips should be—the tip of the white cross.

And I feel his mouth through the mask.

My breath catches in my throat, but before I can regain it, before I can throw my arms around his neck, before I can go farther, he's taking a step back.

"I want you to think of me when you wear those," he says, pointing at the bag. He then grabs his bag and leaves through the window.

It's only after my eyes follow him for as long as they can see him, only after his silhouette completely disappears, do I look in the bag.

Inside is the softest baby-pink lace bundle I have ever felt—a bra and panty set.

I did not plan on calling her mine, but better she knows it now. It took every fiber of my being to leave through June's window, to not storm out into the hallway, find that fucker of a stepfather, and force him on his knees, begging her forgiveness, before I ripped his fucking eyes out of his skull.

I wanted to take her away, to steal her from that place and keep her with me. But I'll settle for that kiss, for her tongue on mine, even with the material between us.

It's all I can think of the whole way back to the church, as I try to fall asleep, as I don my collar the next morning—all the way to the bells chiming for Friday's Mass.

The hall is empty, but I hear chatter come from the sanctuary—the parish slithering in. Just as I'm about to join the masses, my phone buzzes in my pocket. It's a text from Rodrigo.

Rodrigo: Anything?

Me: Nothing confirmed but I feel something here.

I'm ashamed to say my mind has been . . . elsewhere—apparently too busy following my dick than my holy duty. I'm usually in and out of these jobs, a few days max. But the way this has been going, the way my mind is very *un-invested*, I can't begin to say how long it might take. Which will just make Rodrigo ask more questions, more often.

Me: Hoping to find something tonight.

Rodrigo: Vaya con dios.

I shove my phone in my pocket, already upset I won't be able to sneak into my little songbird's room and see her in the underwear I bought her tonight. My cock is rock hard simply imagining the lace covering her tits, her hard nipples teasing me underneath, the straps of the thong melting into the soft curves of her skin.

God, she'd look like a fucking saint. And now I have to stand her up while she waits for me.

Fuck work. Fuck demons. And fuck cultists.

I adjust my dick, the image of her still tickling my mind, and push my way into the sanctuary. It's packed, more so than the last two mornings I've watched over, but my eyes glaze over every single sinner here, searching for the one *good* thing in this place.

And they find her. June is side stepping into a pew, her

perfect tits bouncing with each step under another frumpy gray sweater, her mother and Daren filing in just behind her.

So, she's not playing today.

Her mother side eyes her as she sits, and shoves a Bible into June's lap, before practically turning her back to her daughter. I watch as June's eyes fall to her lap, her shoulders slumping—the shell slowly closing in around her.

The welts last night were bad. I'm no stranger to whippings. In my years before taking my vows, I tried many things. I *know* the intensity needed to break skin with such a thing. I recognize the cuts of a buckle instead of leather. June's mother does more than she needs to. Especially considering she's beating her adult daughter.

It's vile and evil. I'd almost think the supposed demon in St. Mary's was her—but she is an evil only sick humanity can breed.

The bells chime again, signaling Mass is about to start, but my eyes still don't break from June, not as she finally looks up and meets my eyes.

She's stunning, those dark blue doe eyes, the light brown hair and pale skin, perfect lips. God, how'd they feel around my dick. I want to shove myself to the back of her throat, feel those cheeks hollow around me. I want to hear her gag and moan and cry, her eyes tearing up from how much of me she'll take.

I just know she'd be perfect at it.

"Father Marcelo," Father Callum says, placing a hand on my shoulder and pulling me back into reality. June's eyes are still on mine. A small, shy smile saying hello appears on her lips, before she lets her head fall back down.

I can't help but grind my teeth, mentally cursing Callum for ruining that moment I had.

"One of the altar boys is sick today. Will you help with Mass?"

I put on the mask—the fake me, the obeying priest, the good, smiling man, knowing full well the real me is the one that wears the leather, the one that kills in the name of God, the one that sneaks into June's room at night and touches her aching body.

"Of course. What can I do?"

My eyes haven't left June. Not as I stand off to the side for the two-hour long Mass, assisting where I am needed. Her eyes have met mine a handful of times, but each time she blushes and quickly looks away. And each time, I catch either her mother or Daren spotting the eye contact. I tell myself to be careful, to keep in mind *I* won't be the one punished for these stolen glances—but I can't help it. June has my full, undivided attention. Something about her calls to me, draws me in. She's so fucking gorgeous, and she doesn't know it. I want to tell her—to *show* her just how stunning she is.

But more than that, her soul is a fucking wonder. The glimpses I've seen of it are enough to bring the strongest to their knees. It's hidden, caged behind iron bars, but I'm going to break them. I'm going to break *her*—in order to set her free.

It may have been years since I've been with a woman, years since I've pleasured myself—Hell, it's been years since I've felt the need to. But before my vows, I was . . . active. Rebellious youth with a taste for pain and violence.

I lost my virginity six months after *it* happened, when I was fourteen, and I didn't stop having sex till my vows. I fucked some one-night stand the night before my ceremony—thirteen years ago—and while I can't remember her face or name, I do remember the hand prints I left on her ass.

And in the last few days, that lingering memory has shifted. It's now June's ass I see my hand on.

Sex is a beautiful fucking thing. It brings pleasure and joy to both parties, how the human bodies can even entwine like so is a work of art. The idea that God would consider it a sin has always been lost on me. But still, I upheld the vow of celibacy, and now—I'm starting to understand why.

Do not worship false idols. Don't worship anything or anyone *but* God.

I am ready to drop to my knees and sing praise for this woman to simply give me a taste of the forbidden nectar between her legs. I want my tongue on her, my fingers in her, my cock filling her.

I'd give anything.

June looks up at me again, blinking those long, dark lashes, and I have never been more thankful for the ridiculous, oversized robes—chasubles—we wear for Mass. The green flowing fabric, hopefully, covers my straining cock. I smile at her, and the pink returns to her cheeks before her eyes turn to the center of the sanctuary.

I had forgotten what blue balls felt like, but fuck. Every night since seeing her in that confessional, I'm plagued with a pain strong enough to keel me over. It feels like the hand of Satan is squeezing them till they pop, and every shift or rub against my pants feels like being stabbed by a billion angry hornets.

Fuck, I *really* need to get off.

But June had somehow slipped into my very being. She was more than just a rogue fantasy, more than just someone to get my dick wet with. I may not believe in them much, but I committed to my vows. And I dignified myself in being a man of my word.

I've seen beautiful women in the thirteen years I've been a priest. I've had women throw themselves at me—but never *once* have I even been tempted.

Which is why June has stricken me so hard.

I need her like I need air, and it is absolutely terrifying. But more than that, I want to protect her from myself. She has all but given herself to the masked man—a man she doesn't know, a man that could be a monster in the dark. And she has offered herself so . . . willingly. It takes everything in my power not to fuck her senseless in her bedroom every night, a gag stuffed in her sweet mouth so her parents won't hear and interrupt us.

But I can't do that to her. I *won't* do that to her.

"Through Christ our Lord, Amen," Father Callum says, bowing his head and signing the cross. I mimic him, as does the entire parish. "Now, we will take Communion and end for the day."

As one, the parish rises, and lines up in the center of the aisle between the pews. Callum ushers me over and hands me the golden chalice filled with the bread, as he carries a similar chalice of the wine and stands next to me before the parish.

I've held Communion enough times to autopilot through the ritual. I wait for the bow, they drop to their knees, and either hold their hands up or open their mouths.

"The body of Christ," I whisper.

"Amen," they reply.

The bread is stiff between my fingers and so damn

breakable. It always surprises me that the body of our Christ can feel like little more than sandpaper and taste just as similar.

It isn't long before June's mother is the one next to stand before me. She smiles, her lipstick smearing along her teeth, and drops to her knees, keeping her eyes locked on mine. Slowly, she sticks her tongue out, a smirk still curving her lips and her eyes still trying to lock on mine.

She makes me feel sick.

"The body of Christ," I mumble, and practically toss the host into her awaiting mouth, my fingers going nowhere near her.

She coughs as the host hits the back of her throat and then stands. "Amen."

I hold the next host up for the next person—Daren. He bows but that is as close to the ritual as he gets. As he steps closer, I smell the stale beer on his breath, see the crusts from sleep and dried drool still on his face. He's . . . crusty. Disgusting. If grime could be a person, it'd be him. His hazy blue eyes are locked on mine, eyebrows furled.

I match his expression, resisting every twitch in my body screaming at me to rip this guy's head off.

He wants me to be his. June's voice filters through my ears from last night, with the quiet, terrified expression on her face.

The host cracks between my fingers, but Daren snatches the two halves from me, shoving them in his mouth and stomping toward Callum.

A sharp exhale escapes my nose and my teeth grind together. How I'd *love* for the masked man to pay *him* a fucking visit.

"Father Marcelo?" a small voice whispers before me.

June shuffles on both feet before me, and drops to her

knees as my gaze settles on her, her tits bouncing all along the way.

Fuck, she looks so God damn gorgeous on her knees. Her breathing is quick, sharp, and I can see her chest rise and fall in quick bursts.

It's only a moment, but it feels like an eternity as I watch her—just *her*—in this room. Her eyes dilate, and under the long droopy skirt, she clenches her thighs together—just as she did last night in her bedroom.

I don't know what compels me, but I hold up the host, and demand, "Open your mouth, June."

Her full lips part on a small gasp, but then she does as I say, sticking that sweet tongue out for me like the good girl she is.

She's panting now, waiting, and seeing her like this—on her knees before me, obeying me, her tongue out and ready for *me*—I just can't stop myself, I can't protect her, I can't *stop*.

I drop the host at my feet, tossing the rest of the chalice behind me. Gasps rise from the parish and Father Callum turns to me, but nothing matters now that my songbird is kneeling, begging, waiting to please me. I rip the green chasuble over my head and throw it at the person standing in shock behind June.

"Will you take this offering?" I ask, unbuckling my belt and stepping closer to her. She nods feverishly, begging.

I pull myself out, and—of course—I'm already hard from the simple sight of her. The parish gasps again, but they might as well not exist. No one moves to stop us. They just watch, transfixed, as if what we were doing was the vilest show they couldn't take their eyes off.

June's beautiful doe eyes grow wider at the sight of me, and somewhere in the back of my mind, I reason that this must be the first cock she's actually seen.

She sticks her tongue out farther, trying desperately to close the space between us. I stroke myself, groaning at the sensation I haven't felt in too fucking long, but I can't tear my eyes off hers, seeing how hungry she is for me.

"Please," she begs.

And I obey. I shove my free hand in her hair, gripping it at the base of her neck.

"Taste me, little songbird."

She pokes the tip of my cock with her tongue, testing, shuddering everywhere. Then she takes more, she sucks my head into her mouth, and fuck, *is she hot and slippery and* desperate. *She sucks me down a little farther, startling when her lips meet metal. She pulls back and sees the Jacob's ladder piercings I got on my eighteenth birthday. Two piercings, four small silver balls just along the frenum of my dick. Her eyes go wide, starving, as a small, insidious smile curves her lips.*

June doesn't hesitate. She wraps her hot tongue around me, toying with the piercings, and I guide her head forward. I want to feel the back of her throat. I want to feel my piercings on the flat of her tongue. I want her to take all of me.

I fuck her mouth in front of everyone. Her hands dig into my ass, as small gags come from her.

"Fuck, yes," I breathe, and I love the slurping, wet sounds her tongue makes as she drinks me in. "You're doing so fucking good." I slam my hips forward, shoving my cock farther, farther.

It's only been two fucking minutes and I feel the tension build in my back, my legs—I'm going to fucking come all over my little songbird, and I want her to swallow every single drop of me.

Her hot mouth closes around me and . . .

"Amen," she says before her plump lips wrap around

my thumb, the host separating her sweet tongue from my skin.

Her blue eyes aren't on me, they're dazed, unfocused, and staring at the cross tattooed on my index finger. But her lips—*fuck*—her *perfect* lips are wrapped around my thumb.

Not my cock.

I blink. And blink again.

I'm still wearing the green chasuble, white knuckling the chalice, the parish going about their own business.

None of that was real.

My cock was never in her mouth.

But . . . my thumb *is*.

I give myself a moment to feel how her lips *really* feel around me. Soft, pliable, fuckable. Just like in my fantasy, they're hot and wet, and desperate.

She releases me with a *pop*, and as she pulls away, her gaze slowly, painfully, refocuses on me.

And I can see the moment sheer terror corrupts that blissful expression.

June abruptly stands, her cheeks on fire. "Ah—I am—I'm so sorry." Her doe eyes don't meet mine. I can practically hear the iron cage door that had just been open for me slam shut in my face. She hurriedly steps away from me, not saying a word more, taking the fastest sip of the wine, and running from the room, past her parents, and out of sight.

I jolt—ready to run after her—but beside the door she just ran through stands a dark, tall, oppressing figure.

A figure with horns.

A figure that fades through the door June just ran through.

12
JUNE

What the Hell? *What the Hell did I just do?* One minute I was dropping to my knees for Father Marcelo, feeling that all-too-familiar, all-too-consuming warmth between my legs, the slick wetness dripping past my panties, down my thighs, and the next, my lips were wrapped around his thumb as if it was . . . something else.

My chest squeezes, and my face feels like it's on fire. I have never wanted to stop existing more.

Another voice in my mind says, *but . . . he didn't pull away.*

I—I haven't heard . . . *felt* that voice for a long time. It's my voice. My *voice.* The one I muted when I turned eleven. The one I muted after my mother's view of me changed from child to woman. The one I smashed deep, deep down, and never let speak.

She's back—err, I'm back.

I don't know why now. Maybe it's my attraction to Marcelo—my first real attraction to a man on more than just a surface "he's nice to look at" level. Maybe it's the masked man making me feel like I deserve a life more than *this*.

Maybe it's the raging spouts of desire I suffer through every few days.

Whatever it is, it scares me. *I* scare me.

I can't have this voice, this voice that wants and thinks and feels. This voice *with* a voice.

The brown walls of the church hallway crowd in around me. It was the same hallway Father Marcelo and I stood in yesterday—alone. Where his bedroom waits at the end.

I need to breathe. I need air. I can feel the smoke from the frankincense wrap around my throat, strangling me, filling my lungs and smothering me. I need—

"June!"

I turn to see Father Marcelo slamming through the door from the sanctuary, sprinting toward me. His body moves like an actual god, muscles shifting, chest pumping.

But before I can start drooling over him, a small, clawed hand grabs my ankle.

A scream escapes my lips before my mind finishes processing what it's actually looking at. With tiny, sharp-pointed teeth, the face of a baby smiles up at me. It's cherub-like, with a curl of blond hair, pink cheeks, and giant blue eyes . . . only, with pupils like that of a goat—actually, his entire lower body is goat-like, with hooved feet and matted, curly brown fur. Like that satyr from *Narnia*. But unlike Mr. Tumnus, an obscenely long and pointed *erect* . . . member . . . protrudes from the tufts of fur. The monster's smile widens as I see him—*it*—and the clawed hand reaches higher, shoving my skirt up my calf.

I feel its claws on my skin, and take a few steps back—away—but, suddenly, I'm surrounded. It's not like they just appeared, but more like . . . like they just slipped into my periphery. As if they've always been here, and I can just see them now.

I scream again as another hand digs its claws into my skirt, but Father Marcelo is on it before it can get any closer. He kicks the beast away, a silver rosary wrapped around his hand. He's speaking in another language and in the chaos of everything, I can't tell if it's Spanish or Latin.

But whatever he's doing, it's working—the cherub-faces are disappearing into plumes of black smoke that smell like rotten eggs.

Father Marcelo doesn't give me another moment to process. He grabs my hand and pulls me with him, jumping over and weaving between more of the demons. All the while, he continues with the prayer.

I glance behind me, feeling the ghost of more claws grabbing my skirt, claws on my calves. But instead, I completely forget how to breathe.

Behind us is a large, shadowy mass. The same shadowy mass I glimpsed yesterday. I thought it was my mind playing tricks on me, the masked man weaving into my brain and confusing me.

But this is . . . *real*.

I can barely make it out, but I see broad shoulders, nails like talons, dark hair, and large, curving horns. The figure is easily seven, maybe eight feet tall, and it sucks the air and light right out of the room.

Thank God it's not looking at us. It's busy attacking the

cherub-faces, grabbing them and squeezing them into more of those black puffs.

"My room," Father Marcelo grunts, "has an exit to get outside." Just like the door into this hallway, Marcelo slams himself against the door to his quarters, pulling me through and slamming it behind him. I stumble to the hardwood floor, breathing heavily. Or, trying to.

It's more of a rapid wheezing.

My vision is tinged with darkness, but all I can do is try to suck down air. It tears my throat, a sharp, twisting pain forming in my side. I keep breathing in, but there is nothing coming out.

Father Marcelo drops to his knee in front of me and cups my face. "Breathe, songbird. You need to breathe." He takes a deep inhale through his nose, and releases through the mouth. "Now you." Together, we breathe in, hold, and breathe out. Then we do it again.

I'm shaking uncontrollably. His hands are the only thing keeping my brain from rattling, but slowly my lungs don't feel like they're shriveling to raisins, and the black around my vision ebbs. The room is bright and warm, with a small living room and kitchenette. It all looks like it belongs in a cottage, not a catholic church. The couch looks worn; there's a single table in the kitchen with two chairs, and two doors—one leading to the bathroom, and the other into a bedroom. *His* bedroom.

I shift my eyes back to him, and he gently squeezes my cheeks.

"Good?"

I nod, taking another deep breath.

"What was—"

He presses his thumb against my lips. "Not here.

Outside—I'll tell you everything outside." Father Marcelo quickly stands and holds both hands out for me.

It's now I see—they're calloused and scarred. His knuckles bulge in odd angles, scar tissue built upon scar tissue.

This man . . . he's more than a priest.

And . . . I know it wasn't another trick of the mind.

I know . . . he called me songbird.

Father Marcelo called me songbird, just like the masked man.

13

MARCELO

June's hands feel soft and warm in mine as she takes them. I easily pull her to her feet and guide her to the back door behind the kitchen. We need to get out of here. I need to tell her.

Fuck. As exorcists, we're meant to keep the existence of demons as a belief, not a fact. Meaning, I am supposed to act covertly. June should've never found out about why I'm really here. She never should've been in that situation. But the fucking imps revealed themselves to her, lusting after her. It's been a long time since I've encountered a demon strong enough to have imps around. The tiny demons are nothing more than a nuisance, grunts to the big guy in charge, and based on the shadowy figure I saw, I'd guess *that's* their big guy.

He's finally made himself known.

And June was there to see it all.

As I pull her outside and around the back of the church, I realize they were going after her. Maybe she's the target.

I can't think straight, not as I see the tiny hands of the imps on her skin, not as I watch the claws tear at her skirt. I pull June toward me and press her into the wall in the alley beside the church. The smell of trash breaks the clogged scent of sulfur filling my nose, my shoes seeping in the mud underneath us.

"Keep breathing."

"What was that?" she demands. It's the firmest I've heard her since we met. "What were those things?"

I debate not telling her, sending her home, and just leaving her to wonder. I debate calling Rodrigo and Rowan and letting them handle this.

But instead, I tell her everything.

"I lied. I'm not here for church developments or whatever bullshit I said a few days ago." My shift of tone startles her. But I want to drop this facade I've worn every time I've faced her as Marcelo. She's liked the masked man enough—the real me. I think she can handle where the two meet.

I take a step closer, surrounding her as she presses herself into the wall.

"A-are you even a priest?"

I huff a laugh. "Unfortunately. I'm an exorcist."

She doesn't laugh, just scrunches her eyebrows, and I can hear her words before she says them.

"Yes, like the movies. June, those were demons. *Real* demons—hellfire, pitchforks, all that. And I think they were after you."

I can see her mind digesting my words, her eyes flitting back and forth between mine.

"And you're here . . . to exorcise them?"

I nod. "Father Callum called me here. He said the parish was under oppression."

Her throat bobs, lips quivering no matter how hard she presses them together.

"And you think . . . you think they're after me?" She pauses. "Why?"

Well, fuck. I can't very well tell her I know about her time in the confessional booth. Nor that I know the demon makes her incredibly horny. Nor that the demon, in turn, makes *me* incredibly horny *for her*.

So, instead, I say, "The imps were chasing you, grabbing you. And . . . I know you feel things. I can see it on your face sometimes."

Great, Marcelo, leave it vague and weird.

June blushes, and I quickly add, "Do you feel eyes on the back of your neck sometimes? Or like something is standing in the room behind you, but when you turn, nothing is there?"

She thinks for a moment, and slowly nods before biting her lip. "There's more."

I realize how close she is, how warm. Her chest rises and falls, her tits so close to my chest. Fuck, what I'd give to feel them pressed against me, to see her hardened nipples and take them between my teeth.

Her sweet lips quiver again, and I try to tell myself it's the demonic influence doing this to us.

But I know it's not.

Her bouts of arousal may be from the demon—even the intensely real fantasies I've had may be from it—but my desire for her is *all* me.

"I—I don't think I can tell you like this. Not face to face." She tilts her chin up, her eyes dropping to my lips, then back to my eyes. Fuck, that look. Those eyes.

How badly I want to take her on the side of this church.

It'd be easy.

No one is around.

She's wearing a skirt. I could tear the panties right off her ass and shove my cock deep inside her.

At the least, I could lean down mere centimeters and take her lips.

"It'd be easier if—"

A black mass slams down next to us, on top of the giant green trash can. June jumps into me. I throw my arms around her and pull her behind me, ready to fight whatever may come for us.

"Fuckin' Hell," I curse as a familiar pair of golden eyes stare at me, the little demon licking its long, sharp teeth.

June fidgets against me, her chest pressing against mine, and it makes me want to collapse on the spot from bliss. Still gripping my shoulder, she looks behind me at the cat now licking its paw. She gasps, her eyes lighting, and she quickly pushes away from me.

"Oh my goodness, and who are you?" she squeals, the cat immediately rubbing its head against her palm.

"*El diablo*," I mutter.

She turns to me and pouts her lip. "That's what you named this cutie?"

"It's a devil."

"*He's* the cutest kitty." Her wide eyes fall on the cat again, and she gingerly picks him up. The bastard actually snuggles into her arms calmly, rubbing against her as he starts to purr.

"As I said, Diablo."

June huffs a laugh and looks at the creature in her arms, then back up at me. "He actually kind of looks like you, Father Marcelo."

I lower my brows.

"Look." She points at the white tuft of fur on his chest. "He has a white collar, just like you."

I groan. "Maybe he's an exorcist too."

June presses her lips together. "Mmm, I think he's more of an exterminator. Someone's gotta get rid of the church mice."

I chuckle, and June's smile in response is igniting my insides like fireworks. It makes me melt.

"You can drop the 'Father,' by the way. Call me Marcelo, please."

I want my name on her lips, with or without her calling me Father, but maybe it'll put her more at ease with this version of me. Maybe, soon, she'll be as open with this me as she is with the masked man.

Her cheeks warm once again. "Okay, Marcelo," she tests, her lips lifting as the *o* leaves her lips.

"Much better." I smirk. There's so much more I want to talk to her about, so much more I want to tell her. But I know her parents must be growing impatient and I could only imagine the welts they'd give her if they catch her in this alley with me, alone. "I should get you back to the parish," I say. "I don't think I even have to ask this of you, but please don't tell anyone about the demon, nor about what I'm really here for."

She nods. "Oh, of course!" June places Diablo on the ground, scratching between his ears a final time, and stands up straight. "And if you need any help—I don't really know what I could do—but . . . I'm here if you need me."

Her offer chips even more of the "lone wolf" barrier around my heart away. There's no way I'd ever put her in harm's way, but I've been at this game alone for a long time now. At no fault of my loved ones; Hell, Rodrigo,

Rowan, and even Willow — with no stake in the church at all — have been begging to help. I've just never let them.

It's specifically something about *June* that makes me want to nudge that door open enough only for her.

"I'll keep that in mind. Thank you."

Her perfect, pure smile beams up at me and I have never, so desperately, wanted to taint someone so corruptly with my love.

It's him. Fath—Marcelo *is* the masked man. *My* masked man.

It took the entire conversation with him outside, the intensity in his eyes as he had me practically pinned to the church wall, and the entire drive home to come to terms with it. Someone as beautiful and kind as *that* has been stalking me, stealing away into my room at night, touching me.

I think of his fingers grazing the underside of my breast as he cut my bra off me, of his hands on my back as he aided my wounds, of his tongue on mine with only leather between us.

My core is hot and I feel like I haven't taken a full breath since the service, since before Communion, when I wanted nothing more than to rip his pants open and suck on him there, in front of everyone. In front of my mother, in front of Daren.

The arousal from then hasn't quieted — not one bit. Not as I sit in the backseat of Daren's car, not as I walk into our small house, and not now, as I touch myself under the stream of a cold shower.

I think, if his skin would've touched mine, even once more, I would've leaped on him, begging him to break his vows of chastity.

But somewhere between the first and second orgasm in the cold shower, just before Mother slammed on the door and told me to hurry up, I came up with an idea.

Tonight, I'll wait for him in nothing more than what he gave me.

Shit. I already regret promising Rodrigo intel tonight. I imagine June at home, waiting for me. Hopefully, there are no new lashes, but who will be there to help her if there are? Is she wearing the lingerie I got her? I hope they fit right. I'd hate to have gotten her anything more restricting than what she had before. I know women typically feel much more confident when they feel sexy, and while June doesn't need anything extra, I'm hoping it'll make her feel just as fucking hot as she truly is.

Picturing her solves none of my problems, but damn, do I love it.

Instead of being outside her window, watching her as she slips on that lacy thong, I'm here—in the church after dark, scoping the grounds.

Being an exorcist is all about finding the right place at the right time—something the movies don't really show you. We cannot summon demons to us, not without actual summoning rituals or taboo items such as spirit boards—both of which are banned in the Order of the Exorcists, as they give more power to the demon in question.

No, instead, we must hunt. We investigate. We . . . *find*.

Demons don't always show themselves. Sometimes they hide within the bodies of others, and sometimes, they're more like ghosts, here one moment and gone the next.

I highly doubt the black shadow or its imps will reveal themselves to me tonight, but it's worth looking.

Creeping from my room, I push into the large hallway June was attacked in this morning. Compared to then, it's now silent, the only sounds being the air conditioner and my footsteps.

The imps made themselves known to us today *after* I saw the shadow, and it was the first time June has seen them at all. And there's no question that they were after her.

The hallway is pristine, the floor practically spotless, as if someone had cleaned it mere minutes ago—which, I guess, they would have. Afternoon Mass concluded about an hour and a half ago. After that, people were all through-out the church doing their nightly cleaning.

So, there goes that plan.

I hadn't spoken to Father Callum much about why he called us in the first place—nothing more than that first night here.

If he knew about the demon, does he know about its connection to June?

Before I think of another option, I'm leaving the church and walking to his small cottage. The Belmouth air is crisp, almost sharp, as I walk through the autumn night. It's wet; red and gold leaves cling to the black ground, and each step is silenced by the layer of dew just below my feet.

I pull out a cigarette—I haven't smoked all day, and the itch is only growing and growing the more unclear this case is becoming.

The moment I ignite the lighter, my foot bumps into something . . . pliable. Small white fangs and golden eyes shine from below me, as Diablo hisses at me once more and jumps back.

"Yeah, fuck you too," I grumble, finally lighting the cigarette. That first pull fills my lungs so deliciously, I can practically feel the tar building on them. I know it's not good for me, but fuck. Right now, it's one of my holier vices. It's this, or abandon my vows, kidnap June, kill her parents, and fuck her over their still-warm corpses.

Choose your sins wisely, Marcelo.

Surprisingly, Diablo follows me. He keeps his distance, but the cat trots at a pace matching my own. His eyes stay straight ahead, on Father Callum's little cottage. I wait a moment, Diablo stopping next to me, to finish the rest of my cigarette, the smoke clouding with my breath in the air.

Once I snub it out, Diablo doesn't follow me the rest of the way to the cottage. Instead, he sits, watching as though he were waiting to see what I would do next.

I walk up to Callum's door and rap my knuckles against the wood. A few beats of silence, and I knock again.

Then again.

The cottage is utterly silent on the other side. Either he's a heavy sleeper or Father Callum isn't home.

But where would a priest—one without a masked alter ego—be on a Friday night?

Maybe Father Callum isn't as devoted as I pegged him for. Or maybe he's running a local food drive. Who fucking knows.

I turn to the devil cat behind me, his gold eyes watching me, and all I can think is, *this cat knows something.*

16

JUNE

I have never felt sexy, or hot, or . . . pretty. Mother snuffed that out of me very early on. My eyes were too big for my face, my cheeks too round, my belly too squishy. No boy would ever deem me pretty, so I should take what I could get.

Of course, I should take what I could get only after marriage—anything earlier would make me a slut.

I was eleven years old when she first used that word on me. I had just gotten my period, and the only man she'd ever been married to—after my real father—made a comment about finally having another woman in the house. I didn't even know what a period was—I thought I had broken something inside of me during school. I stuffed the panties in the trash can, hoping whatever was broken would unbreak, and that everything would go back to normal the next day.

But Daddy found them.

My blood-soaked panties dangled from his finger as he sat at *the square dining table, a brown bottle dripping condensation at his elbow. He smelled like earth and smoke and skunk, and his eyes were as red as my panties.*

My mother's eyes shifted to me the moment I entered the room. I still remember her upturned eyebrows, the small frown, the sympathy in her eyes. Guilt, I think.

"Whaddya say, Jill? Should I test out the newer, younger model?"

And just like that, those soft eyes became daggers. Her small frown turned into a hard line, her pale skin turned red.

But—it was directed at me.

"I mean, she is a woman now."

"Get out." Mother's voice was like freezer burn. So cold, it clung and burned and rotted.

My stepfather slowly spun around. "Jill, I was just kid—"

"Not you, idiot. Junia, get out."

My stepfather and I were both stunned into silence. I still didn't know what I had done wrong, but I was convinced I did something. That's why something inside of me was broken. That's why I bled. Because I must've done something wrong— even if I didn't know what.

Mother squinted her eyes at me, the daggers pinning me to the spot despite her words telling me to leave. "How come Malcolm found your underwear? Did you just leave them out for him to find?" She placed her hand on her hip, her words never slowing. "You wanted him to see them, didn't you? What were you hoping he did with 'em? Lord, Junia, you are acting like such a little slut. I raised you better than that. Get out. Now!"

Three months later, Malcolm began crawling into my bed after mother was asleep. His hands never touched me, he'd just lay there, pressed against me.

Eight months after that, Mother kicked him out of the house.

Their divorce was finalized two months later, and he moved from Belmouth. We never saw him again, and Mother started dating her next boyfriend, Ian.

It took me months to finally learn what a period was —when I bled in school and a teacher had to explain it to me. I remember the daggers in my mother's eyes when she was called down to the school to pick me up. She almost refused letting me out for the day, saying something along the lines of, "The embarrassment she faces today with blood all over the back of her skirt will make her remember to never do it again."

But my teacher and principal were women of St. Mary's, and after one dirty look, Mother agreed to take me home. I remember the beating I got after that —it was one of the first.

Most important of all, though, that night in the kitchen, with my panties dangling from Malcolm's fingers, was the last time I ever saw any remorse or compassion or love in my mother's eyes.

Since then, it's been nothing but daggers.

17

JUNE

I felt sexy right now. For the first time, possibly *ever*, I felt sexy. Hot. Pretty—maybe even beautiful.

I knew men wanted my body. Malcolm's comments and his hard body cuddled against me all those months eventually clicked into place in my aging brain. He wasn't being affectionate with his supposed daughter, he was being a filthy old man who wanted something he shouldn't.

Daren is the same. He has the same predatory look in his eyes, the way they devour me every time I walk in the room, the way they linger where they shouldn't.

But *never* have I taken their looks as anything more than a fetish for them to get off on. I know I have big boobs, a big ass—but it comes with a tummy roll and thick thighs. I was too big for all the boys in high school. Every single boy I've ever had a crush on ended up dating a girl much, much skinnier than me.

And I couldn't blame them, the dumb boys or the pretty girls. No, I could only blame myself and God for giving me this body.

But when I look in this mirror, wearing the light pink lingerie set Marcelo bought me—I can see what's to like. The straps of the thong hug the curves of my hips *just* right, as if they were made to cradle the pouch of my belly. When I turn in front of the mirror, the thong gets lost between my plump cheeks, making me feel like a cute peach.

The bra is somehow even more flattering. For starters, it actually fits. The soft lace feels wonderful against my skin, and the underwire is simultaneously lifting and supporting, while being covered by enough material so as to not feel like it's digging into me. I didn't realize they made bras this comfortable. I thought they were all medieval torture devices meant to suppress the true strength and power of women.

A comfortable bra feels more like witchcraft and sorcery than the demonic imps I saw earlier.

My boobs have honestly never looked better. I can see the faintest peek of my nipples through them, but the pink lace masks the pink peaks perfectly—like a hidden secret only I know about.

Seeing myself like this—no, *feeling* myself like this . . . it's liberating. Intoxicating. Arousing. I have never liked myself more.

I pose in front of the mirror, grabbing my breasts, sitting on my knees, my butt resting on the back of my feet. My thighs are so big like this but, Lord, do I look good. Heat pools between my thighs, as a breeze from my open window wafts into the room. I can't wait for Marcelo to see me like this, for the masked man to creep into my room, and find his little *songbird* waiting for him.

I wonder what he'll do to me. Part of me feels bad for

trying to make a priest break his vows, but the rest of me—the rest of me *craves* it. To have a man go to such lengths for me, to want *me* more than anything, more than God and Jesus and eternal glory.

To be *wanted*—it's something I always only thought to be a fallacy, but now it could be real.

I stand, turning toward the window. It's late enough but still no sight of that Salvation I seek hiding in the shadows beyond my room.

Maybe he's toying with me, waiting for me to see him, like the night before.

I walk to the window, sticking my head out of it. It's just started to drizzle, the droplets fall on my bangs, on my cheeks, and the autumn air is cold on my skin, the wind blowing my brown hair all around. I can almost hear a whisper in the wind, "Junia."

But no masked man. No Marcelo.

"Junia!"

The whisper in the wind turns into a bellow. My hair is yanked back, pulling me from the window. I don't even fully land on my butt before I feel her hand slap across my face. Each hit stings new, and I can't see a thing behind the mess of hair covering my eyes.

"What the *fuck* are you wearing?" she yells. "Where did you get that? What were you looking for out the window? Were you waiting for someone?" *Smack, smack, smack.*

I fight out of her grip and scramble to a standing position.

My mother's pale skin is as red as the devil, and her heavy breaths match my own. But it's her eyes that freeze me to the spot, that terrify me to my core. Her pupils are so dilated, they're practically hidden within the raging blue storm aimed directly at me.

I can't even question what she's doing in here. Dammit. I knew she had a key to my door, but I never thought she'd use it when it was actually locked. Or at least she could've knocked.

But . . . she's caught me. Like this. It's my fault. I should've never worn something like this, something so . . . so . . .

"You fucking slut. I knew it. I knew you were up to something."

"No—no, it's not—"

She stalks toward me, and all I can do is back up until my thighs hit my bed. The moment I lose my balance, my mother rushes on me, her fist connecting with my jaw, my eye, my nose—over and over.

I try to fight her off, but she screams through her fury. I can taste blood, I can *see* blood, but she doesn't stop, not even after I stop feeling my face entirely.

"Please, please, please," I beg, and still she hits me.

"I knew you were trying to steal him from me. You wanted Daren to see you like this? Well, let's go fucking show him."

Her hand wraps around my upper arm, and she yanks me up, dragging me from my room. Her fingers bruise my skin as I'm pulled from the only safe space I've ever known.

Such a small woman, but she is the source of all my fears, all my nightmares, and all my scars.

I try to fight her, try to pry her fingers from me, but her grip is ironclad. I stumble behind her and she doesn't slow a bit as she yells, "Daren!"

We make it to the old, worn couch far too quickly—the TV is on some old movie I don't recognize, the volume loud like always. Mother shoves me toward the couch and I fall into it. These cushions have become my jail, my dungeon. I can't sit on them without feeling tense, without waiting for the next impact on my skin. It's where she *always* uses the belt on me.

I spin around, and just as I do, Daren walks in. His sunken eyes find me immediately and devour me whole.

"What's going—" he starts, but Mother quickly cuts him off.

"Gimme your belt. The fat slut wanted to dress up for you."

I sit up, trying to cover myself as much as possible as I feel Daren's eyes locked on my breasts, my stomach, my thighs. "Mother, no, I wasn't dressed up for him—"

"Shut up!" She leaps on me again, pounding her fist into the side of my head over and over again. "I see the way you look at him—you want him for yourself!" Mother hisses. She knocks my eye and I feel it immediately pulse under my skin; my lip splits in the corner, and my ear is brutalized. Each hit stings and hurts, but it all comes too fast to stop.

Daren pulls Mother off me, and when I finally look into her eyes, they're—so far away. They look absolutely mad, wild. Her skin has gone nearly purple, and it hadn't dawned on me till that moment that with each wail against me, the smell of vodka leaked from her breath.

I slump back on the couch, still covering myself as much as possible. Blood drips from a gash above my eyebrow into my eye, and my ear is ringing.

Movement calls my attention, and when I look, Daren's eyes are still traveling up and down my body as he pulls his belt from his jeans. There's a noticeable bulge just where his hands are, and he quickly gives my mother the belt.

He's not even trying to hide how turned on he is right now.

And Mother's too angry, too drunk—too hellbent on punishing me—to notice.

She grabs the belt from his hand and I squirm farther into the cushions, hoping they would just swallow me whole.

"Didn't you want him to see you? Why are you coverin' yourself now?"

Crack.

She whips the belt against my arms covering my breasts. The buckle slams into me and I can already feel the welt growing on the back of my hand where it hit.

"Let him see, like you wanted!" Another hit, this one on my stomach.

The thin table behind the couch rattles with the force of another impact. Nothing is on that table save for a small statue icon we have of the Virgin Mary—to watch over the home.

The irony is not lost on me.

Where is she, as another impact whips across my thighs? Where is she, as Daren's eyes are fucking me from the corner? Where is God, as my own mother snags my chest with the metal of the belt, tearing a layer of skin away?

Fucking no where.

At some point, I turned, trying to save my front and revealing my ass to my mother. She strikes me again and again, not relenting. The welts from a few days ago tear as they're impacted again and again with fresh hits. Nothing on me is allowed to heal. *I'm* not allowed to heal.

Mother slows, and while I don't face her, I hear her labored breaths as she tries to catch them. The pain all around me buzzes, like they're all connected by live wire, and the moment one goes off, my entire body will feel everything all over again.

And I wish . . . I wish I'd die. I don't have the strength or courage to kill myself. I've thought about it. A lot. I can't imagine plunging a blade into my wrists. I can't imagine tying a rope around my neck or pulling the trigger to the gun at my head. I can't even get the fortitude to swallow a bunch of pills and never wake up.

But . . . if someone could kill me? If I could just cease to exist? Then my will to live won't be a problem.

I wonder, in those moments I hear her chest deeply rising and falling, how much more of this it would take for her to kill me.

"I think that's enough, Jill."

I turn as much as I'm able to and see Daren taking the belt from Mother's hands. She's still catching her breath as she lets him take it.

"But—we need to cleanse her of her sins. She's not repentant yet. And she sure as Hell ain't forgiven."

"I'm not sayin' that's enough punishment, babe. I just think you've done enough. You need a break. I can handle the rest."

There's a beat of silence. Mother has *never* let Daren punish me before. Ever. Somewhere deep in her soul, she has to know what he thinks of me. She has to see how he stares—has to know it's not *me*, but *him*.

Mother watches him now, completely still. Will she deny him? Will she . . . protect me?

"Here." Daren fishes in his pocket and draws out a wadded up bill. It looks like a fifty. "How 'bout you run down to the store, get yourself a lil' treat, get us a six-pack, and by the time you come back, I'll have this taken care of."

No. Fucking *no.* She wouldn't. She wouldn't leave me here with him. She . . .

Mother stares at the money then glances at me. Her

eyes are still filled with those painfully familiar *daggers*. She snatches the money and walks toward the front door.

"Mother, no," I whimper as she's putting on her shoes. "Please, don't—Mom, he'll—"

"That's what you wanted, isn't it?! You fucking whore!" She shoves her jacket on and turns her back to me.

I cry out, sobs raking through my broken chest, "Mommy, please, don't—!" She ignores me, slamming the front door shut. Leaving me alone with Daren.

She left me.

She left me alone.

She knows and she left me.

ow why the fuck are you actually wearing this?" Daren saunters forward, falling back onto the couch next to me. "Don't get me wrong, it's fuckin' hot. I've dreamt of you lookin' like this for me. But I know you ain't like this *for me*. So you see where my problem is?"

He runs his knuckle along my thigh, and I scramble back, balling up as tight as possible. I know what's about to happen. I know, and I don't think I'm strong enough right now to stop it. To stop him. My body aches, every movement hurts, and seeing mother's back as she left me—

Daren laughs. "I'd say I'm not gonna hurt you, but I've heard it always hurts the first time and I like to be a little rough." He grabs my ankle and pulls me down the couch closer to him. The fresh welts on my back drag against the rough material of the cushion, and I yelp. "Plus, your momma hasn't put out since we started dating. Says she's waiting for marriage. I think I fuckin' hate that religious bitch." He pulls me closer, forcing me to be face to face with him. "He said if I wait till the time is right, I can have you. Well, what better time is there than you looking like this?"

He?

Daren didn't give me time to think. He threw the belt over my head and looped it around my throat like a collar and leash, each pull tightening around my neck, choking me.

I claw at the leather, trying to pull free—but each pull only leeches the air from me more. The thread in the leather digs into my skin, pricking my neck, but it's Daren's free hand that scares me more than anything.

Calluses and grime touch my thigh, gripping and groping at the soft flesh. His thumb rubs over the lace of my panties, and I buck to get him off of me.

"Such a feisty little thing, never woulda pegged that of you." He pulls the belt closer, and a choked gag escapes my lips. "God, I wanna see those lips around my dick. Sometimes, when I hear you in the shower, I fantasize about walking in on you, forcing you to suck me off till I finish all over these pretty titties." He cups my breast, squeezing hard. "Fuck, these are nicer than I thought. Lemme get a good feel."

I smash my palm into Daren's face, but he grips my wrist tight and pulls, using the hand wrapped around the belt to pull it tight. Somehow, he positions me on his lap, my back pressed against his chest. His hard length grinds against my ass.

"Let go of me!" I hiss.

"Why? Your mom left us, practically giving me permission to do whatever I'd like to my little whore." He gropes and fondles my chest, yanking the pink lace aside to reveal my breast to him, and pinching my nipple between two dirty fingers. I whimper, trying to push his hand away, but Daren pulls the belt again.

"Lemme hear you moan again, I liked the sound of that." He roughly squeezes me, his nail digging into the small peak, and I yell out. "That's a good whore. Do as daddy tells ya."

He lets go of my breast and it takes everything in me not to let myself slump back against him in relief.

"P—please, stop," I whisper.

Daren's hand trails down my stomach, past my belly button, and his fingers glide just under the seam of my panties.

Nuzzling my ear, he breathes against my neck. "Call me daddy, and then maybe I will." His lips move along my neck, his tongue flicking my skin.

I swallow, disgusted with myself for being in this position. Disgusted at Mother for leaving me here. Disgusted at Daren for making me beg, for making me say things I don't mean, for touching me, for hurting me.

"Pl—please, Daddy. Stop."

He bites my neck, licking just after.

"No."

His hand cups my pussy roughly, his fingers blindly trying to find my slit, trying to find anything, but I don't stop moving, don't stop fighting. The belt tightens around my neck, but I push my body back against Daren as hard as I can. I reach back for something—anything. When my hand finds something hard, I grab it. In the same breath, Daren rips my panties from my crotch, his hand grabbing me again, but the moment his fingers slither up my slit, I swing the hard thing in my hands down across his head.

The Virgin Mary statue shatters into a million porcelain pieces as it meets his forehead. Dazed, Daren's grip loosens on me and the belt. I don't take a second to think about anything. I jump off his lap, the belt still around my throat, and I bolt to the door.

"You fuckin—" he slurs, but he hasn't gotten up yet. He's still clutching his head, a small stream of blood spilling between his fingers. I don't wait to see if he's okay. I don't wait to hear what else he has to say. I'm fucking *done* being here, being his play thing, being Mother's punching bag. I'm done being a shell of myself, I'm done hiding behind frumpy clothes and Bibles, pretending nothing matters and nothing hurts.

I'm fucking *done*.

I throw on the oversized gray hoodie from the coat rack at the door, and with no shoes or any of my belongings, I run from this Hell house and into the rainy, dark autumn night.

It's been a long fucking night of nothing. It started pouring while I snooped around the church grounds, and I got drenched on the short run back into the cathedral. I should've known better when that damned devil disappeared from sight just before the rain began.

Thankfully, I had forgotten to lock the back door of the church leading to my room. I push into the room, slamming my shoulder against the damp wood. The heat inside is relieving, instantly warming the cold bite on my skin. Hair and beard dripping, I hurry to the small bathroom and attempt to towel dry the locks curling on my neck, but my thick hair will need much more than a towel to dry it fully.

I remove my belt and let it fall to the floor, pulling the collar loose from my clergy shirt. The soaked black linen sticks to my skin, and I itch to take it off, but just as I undo the top few buttons, I hear something deep within the cathedral.

My hands pause on the second button.

It's well past midnight, and though Father Callum wasn't home, I highly doubt he's the one wandering the church in the middle of night.

Wandering like a ghost.

I silently exit my bathroom, leaving the belt and collar on the tile floor. Just like my shirt, the black slacks I wear cling to my thighs and legs, making it difficult to pull the silver rosary from my pocket. The sound of metal hitting metal is far too loud, giving me away, but the moment the long strands are free, I twist it, wrapping it around my knuckles with the cross hanging from my palm.

The hall is silent on the other side of my door as I crack it open, peeking into the darkness.

No scent of sulfur, no feelings of rage or arousal or . . . general otherness. I'm alone, there are no eyes on the back of my neck. At least, not in this hallway. The only sound is that of my footsteps. But the noise I heard was deep in the heart of the cathedral; deep in the sanctuary.

I take another step and hear the sound once again, finally deciphering what it is.

A note.

A single note on an ornate, gorgeous organ.

I don't waste another second. I run through the hallway, my arms pumping despite the stiff hold my clothes have on me. I know whose fingers are on the organ. I know there is no demon tempting me into the belly of the church.

I may have not gone to my songbird tonight, but she came to me.

I nearly fall over as I lumber through the door to the sanctuary just as another singular note permeates through the room.

"June!" I call, not slowing as I hurry up the steps and crash through the small door to the mezzanine, not as I trip over myself on the wooden stairs, not as I crash through the final door keeping me from her.

Not *till* I see a bloody, wet, nearly nude goddess sobbing on the organ bench, one finger hovering just over a single key. Her shoulders shake, her naked legs are scratched and bruised, and blood seeps through all over her back her heather gray hoodie. The hood is pulled tight over her head, blocking her face completely.

Her finger falls, playing the note again, snapping me to movement. The rosary falls from my hand, thunking to the floor.

"June? June!" I run to her, dropping to my knees and sliding the rest of the way. "June, what are you doing here? Are you okay?"

Small whimpers come from her, and I see more than just her shoulders are shaking. She's absolutely freezing, the hoodie soaked through, and her skin is wet to the touch. Gently, I move closer, placing a hand on her arm. The moment I touch her, she winces and balls up even more. The hem of her hoodie rises, and I see she isn't wearing anything—no shorts, no underwear—and while I desperately want to ogle at her bare ass, I can't help but stare at the new and broken welts marring her skin.

There are so many. Her entire ass is as red as hellfire, and that's not even accounting for the actual broken flesh dripping crimson blood along her porcelain skin.

And I'm *sure* this is just what I can see. I *know* there's more hidden.

My jaw is clenched so hard it's difficult to pry open to speak.

"June. I need you to tell me what happened." I know

what happened. "I need you to tell me who did this to you." I *fucking know who did this to her*. And it takes *everything* in my goddamn power to not stand up, shove the mask on my face, and go butcher her parents till there's nothing left of them.

This isn't fucking punishment. This is abuse. This is torture.

June whimpers again, and I can see the barest shake of her head.

I swallow the knot of anger in my throat threatening to consume me. I will fucking *end them*, but not right now, not tonight. My little injured bird needs me, and I will *not* leave her alone.

"June, *mi amor*, let me see." I try to gently pull her toward me, but she shrugs out of my grasp. I sigh and stand. If she's not going to *let* me help her, I'll have to do it my own way. Careful to avoid the marks I can see, I tuck an arm under her thighs and my other around her shoulders. When I lift, she squeaks and is forced to fall into me.

I see a glimpse of purple and red, but she quickly throws her hands in front of her face.

"I'm going to take care of you. Is that okay?"

Slowly, June nods.

Adjusting her in my arms, she curls into my neck and grips my shoulder like a vice. As I wind down the spiral stairwell and enter the sanctuary, I feel warm droplets mix with the cold drops from my wet hair. Her hot breath warms my neck, lingering just where the white of my collar is meant to be.

Shouldering the next door open into the long, dark hallway, I can't help but wonder what went down tonight—and more importantly that I *could've* stopped it had I been there like I was supposed to be. My fucking timing sucks.

How did she end up here? Why is she naked? I get running away from home after a bad beating. I've wanted nothing more than to take her from that shithole. But why now? Why like this?

June doesn't say a word on the long walk back to my room, but her shivering has turned violent. I lightly squeeze her to me, trying to give her all the warmth I have mustered within me.

Once we get to my door, I knee it open, and walk inside. "We're safe," I whisper, "*you're* safe." I bypass the room, walking straight into the bathroom, and I carefully seat her on the closed toilet seat, knowing how much it might hurt the wounds on her rear. I take a small step back, then kneel to be eye level with her, finally taking in the damage done.

She keeps her face hidden behind delicate fingers, but there is so much more to see, so much more, my eyes can't focus on any one thing. There are welts *everywhere*. Her legs are covered, and her thighs are especially bad. The gray hoodie pulled over her head is forcing her hair into her face, concealing her even more, but it's only zipped a little past her belly button.

Below the hoodie June is wearing the bra I got her and nothing more. It's rumpled, and one of her breasts is barely inside the cup—but worse, there's a black leather belt tightly looped around her neck, the buckle pressing into her skin. Her stomach has more welts, her chest is cut up, and her neck is already bruising from the belt.

I swallow again, feeling the anger rise once more and forcing it down.

"Show me your face," I grit out, trying my best to sound calm.

She timidly shakes her head.

I huff out a breath and place my arms on her lap, fiddling with the zipper on the hoodie.

"Can I take this off? To help with the rest of the wounds?"

She hesitates, and the smallest voice I've ever heard from my little songbird comes out between sobs. "I—I don't want . . . I don't want you to see me."

I scrunch my brows together. "Why?" I ask, expecting to find worse.

"I—I'm fat. I don't want you to see me."

My heart cracks a little bit. Ay coño, *that fucking mother of hers is to blame.*

"June—Junia—you are *fucking gorgeous.* I am grateful God gave me more of you to love." I swallow, hoping that despite the collar I wear, despite her thinking I am nothing more than a priest, she knows I fucking mean it.

She blows out a shuddering breath, and I can hear her ready to sob again. "I'll blindfold myself," I rush out. "Then I'll help you in the shower, and I won't see a thing. Would that be okay?"

"Yes," she says quietly.

A sigh of relief escapes my lips. "Great. But you have to do something for me, okay, June? You have to let me see your face. I need to know what I need to help you with," I say gently, praying she'll finally lower her hands.

June's shoulders tense, but slowly, she lowers them. I follow her lead, gently pushing the hood off her head, and tuck her hair behind her ears, cupping her face.

Fucking Hell. I don't know how many more reveals I can take. The crack in my chest threatens to burst open, and I feel every punch, every smack, every whip she took tonight against me. I want to scream and break things. I want to get in my car and drive over there. I want to show them just how much pain this beautiful creature has been in due to them.

But I also *need* to be here.

Keeping my face stoic even as a monsoon is crashing through me, I analyze her face—a black eye, a split lip, her nose seems okay, but a small trail of now-dried blood drips from her ear. Her black eye is swollen, but thankfully the eye itself seems okay, even though blood seeps into it from a gash on her forehead.

I clear my throat, trying to stay sturdy for her. "Let's stop the blood on this one, then we'll get you a nice hot shower, okay?"

June swallows, then nods.

I stand and take all of two steps to grab a small face towel when June flinches so hard she nearly falls from the porcelain seat. I hurry back in front of her, cupping her face again. "What? What is it?"

Tears pool in her eyes and quickly fall as she shakingly lifts a finger toward my forgotten belt on the floor. Fuck.

I kick it out of the room and slam the door shut behind it, promising myself to trash the thing the moment I'm done here.

"I'm sorry, it's okay. It won't hurt you—I won't hurt you," I try to soothe.

June breaks, finally giving into the tears. She throws her arms over my shoulders and sobs into my neck. She shakes so much, my chest feels like it's being squeezed like one of those chickens with the popping eyeballs.

I pull June into my lap, her thighs warming me despite her shivering. I let her sob into me, gently rubbing her back—something my mother used to do for me whenever I cried.

Kicking my shoes off, I lift June again and step into the

shower. It's a relatively small space, but large enough for the two of us, with the glass door and white subway tiles. I put the shower on hot, letting the water stream down as I move us to the floor. June still sobs against me, but the shivers *finally* begin to slow.

"It might sting at first," I breathe into her soft hair, "But it'll calm all the angry wounds, I promise."

With the glass door open, I reach up behind me and pull one of the towels loose. As promised, I tie it around my eyes, blindfolding myself. "I can't see a thing, June. So let me take this off you." I pull at the zipper on her hoodie again.

June nods against my shoulder. "Okay."

I make quick work of the hoodie, unzipping it and gently pushing it from her shoulders, before I toss it out of the shower. I skip asking her if I can remove her bra, and go to unhook it anyway. She gasps as my fingers quickly pull the straps and fling it outside as well.

Knowing this will be the hardest part for her, I give her a moment to just breathe. "I'm going to free your neck now too," I warn. Pulling her hair back behind her shoulders, I slide my finger underneath the buckled belt on her neck, careful to not tighten it anymore than it needs to be. Slowly, I pull the buckle through, loosening it, and the moment she's free of it, I toss it too. A sob escapes her lips, and she slumps back into me.

"You can cry," I say softly. "Shower cries are a different kind of healing." As a man, I'm not afraid to say I fucking cry—and crying in the shower is like free therapy. As the water pelts us, I feel her tension slowly ease away.

Blindfolded, I'm extra careful not to . . . touch anything. But with every movement, my fingers graze her round, soft tits—wondering how far my fingers are from her nipples—

or her soft curves, cursing myself for not getting even a glimpse of it under this towel. I want to squeeze her hips, her thighs. I so desperately want to touch every single part of her—

I let my head thump against the shower wall. *Get a fucking grip, Marcelo.* She doesn't need some horny priest trying to touch her right now. She needs a friend.

She *needs* her masked man.

20

MARCELO

After June finally calms enough for me to leave, I ease from beneath her and let her relax in the shower.

"Don't come out till the water gets cold," I tell her, taking the belt used to torture her with me. "I'll get you something to wear for after."

I leave the bathroom door cracked just a bit, and immediately remove the rest of my dripping clothes, throwing it all into the kitchen sink before I hurry back to the bedroom. I throw on a white T-shirt and some gray sweats before pulling out another T-shirt, boxers, and socks. Hopefully, it'll make due for the night, and tomorrow I will figure out how to get her clothes.

"I'm putting the clothes here," I call as I nudge the door open just a bit more, and place the folded bundle on the sink.

"Th-thank you," she says, and I'm happy to finally hear her put more than a singular syllable together. Even if it's just two.

Turning back to the small living room, I put the TV on just for the background noise—funny enough, it's a ghost hunting show claiming they're being scratched and oppressed by demons. Fucking fakers. The host would shit his pants if he ever came face to face with the bullshit I've seen.

I search the floor, quickly finding my belt I tossed from the bathroom earlier. No more belts. Shrugging on a hoodie, I take the two belts and run through my back door, back into the rain.

It's still pouring, but thankfully the large trash cans are relatively close to my apartment. Without a second thought, I throw both belts into the garbage—wishing I could burn the one that'd been wrapped around June. Hell, I wish I could use it to do the same to the two fucks that did that to her.

As the dumpster door slams shut, a small *meow* comes from under it.

Fucker.

He'd make June happy right now. She needs happy.

Fucker.

I drop to my knees and look under the trash to find two gold eyes staring at me.

"You wanna come inside or what?"

Diablo hisses at me, but after another beat, he inches his tiny paws forward and crawls from under the trash. I pick up the beast quickly, not giving him a chance to second guess, and shove him under my hoodie.

"Fucker!" I yell, as he hisses under the fabric and claws at my skin, scratching my chest and biting my arm.

Instead of letting go—like I definitely should do—I run back to the apartment, back into warmth, and close the door behind me. As soon as I'm through, I let the hellbeast fall from my hoodie, but the bastard predictably lands on all fours, turning back and hissing at me.

I hiss right back, baring my teeth to the fucker—

"Marcelo?"

Looking up, June steps from the bathroom, steam following her. My black T-shirt looks oversized on her, as it reaches down to her hips, the shorts fitting her wide thighs snuggly, but not uncomfortably, my socks too big on her, the heels well past her actual heels, scrunched just above her ankles. Diablo hurries up to her and rubs against her legs, knocking his head on her shin, before squeezing between her calves, and making a figure eight.

"A—Are you comfortable?" I ask. "I can get you a different shirt, or a jacket, or—"

"I'm okay. Your clothes are so soft."

I choke down how desperately I want to run over to her and take her *out* of my clothes right now. Being Marcelo the priest is too fucking hard when it comes to this woman. Marcelo the masked stalker? Now he's easy. I so desperately wish to be myself in this moment, so desperately wish to take her and show her exactly how beautiful she is, how safe she is, how *nothing* will *ever* hurt her again.

"I put the TV on," I say instead.

June bites back a small smirk. "I see."

I scrunch my eyebrows, wondering when exactly I became such an idiot. "Are you hungry? I can make you something."

"Ah—not right now. Thanks."

I stand there, not quite sure what to do with myself— should my hands be in my pockets? Do I move to the couch? Am I just *assuming* she'll be staying here? Maybe she has somewhere else—somewhere better. Fuck, I thought I was suave, but I am totally fumbling this right now. I try for anything, picking the first thing that pops into my head.

"How are you fee—"

"I need to make a confession," she blurts, her fingers gripping the hem of my T-shirt like it's a lifeline.

"Okay? I'm listening."

"A . . . a holy confession . . ."

It takes me an extra moment to realize what she's actually asking for.

"O—Okay. I'm all ears."

June is staring at the floor, refusing to meet my eyes. "I don't think I can say it to your face, I don't—I don't know."

"Would you like to go to the booth or—"

"I think I need the other you."

I pause. All my senses are on full alert, as if a fight were about to break loose, as if I needed to run. My hair stands on end, even as the damp hoodie drips raindrops onto the hardwood floor underneath me.

"Other me?" I breathe out.

She continues fidgeting with my shirt, and I fight to stay here, across the room from her. Fight to not take those few strides toward her and pull *my* fucking shirt over her head, revealing her perfect fucking body to me, to force her to confess to me, to force her to tell me what the fuck happened.

"I know you're the man that's been sneaking into my room." She exhales. "I know you're the masked man."

A flurry of emotions punch into me. How the fuck was I so obvious? Did I say something? Did she read it in my eyes when I pinned her to that wall outside? Did she see the cross tattoo on my ring finger one of the nights I snuck in?

Fuck, how could I be so stupid? Of course she's uncomfortable. I'm her *priest*—she should feel completely safe with me, not lusted after and stalked and—

"And I *really*, really need *him* right now."

The thoughts racing through me shut the fuck up.

She needs *him* right now. The masked man.

Him. *Me.*

Thank fucking God.

Marcelo seems like a deer caught in the headlights when I first tell him. But the moment I tell him I need him, his entire face darkens. It takes a single breath, and he's moving, his stride is fast—determined, and he's standing before me before I can catch my next breath. Diablo runs, disappearing into some dark corner, but I can't track him as Marcelo grabs my hands, making me finally look up at him, finally meet his eyes. They're so dark, but . . . so warm. The brown is a shade so dark, they nearly look red. They're so different than they were moments ago. It's like . . . he's a whole different person. What was once soft and careful, is now hard and demanding.

It's what I need.

He's what I need.

The kind Marcelo from the shower was what I needed at that moment. But I felt how much he was holding back.

And I just *know* the real Marcelo will take care of me. He won't hurt me.

I swallow the fear in my throat, but don't break the stare down. He needs to know I am not afraid of this version of him.

Marcelo clenches his jaw, his fingers tightening on mine.

"You want the masked man. You sure?"

Holding his gaze, I nod.

"Will you do as I say?"

I nod again.

In a swift movement, he pulls the shirt over my head and lets it fall to the floor. The air is cool on my nipples, but I can feel his warmth against them from how close he is to me.

And his eyes don't dare flinch downward. No, they're locked on mine as if they are the only things he can see in a tunnel of black.

"Shorts too, songbird," he grunts. "You'll get them back *after* you fucking show me what they did."

My core tightens at the command. *This* is what I want. But not entirely.

"Put the mask on," I demand back.

A vicious smirk spreads over Marcelo's lips.

"My little songbird has teeth. Okay—a deal's a deal." Marcelo saunters back to his bedroom, disappearing for only a moment. In the time he's gone, I shimmy out of his shorts and let them fall to the floor.

Marcelo comes back into the living room, mask already secured to his face, and his hoodie is gone, revealing the skin I've only seen in the dark. The stunning tattoos start at the simple black cross on his index finger, but from his wrist up are stunning pieces of black and white work.

Angels and demons, a sacred heart, lions, doves, faces of three people who look eerily similar to him. They disappear under the sleeves of his shirt, and I so desperately wish to see what's under the thin cotton. To see his chest, the rest of the artwork that came together to make this beautiful man.

And here I am, naked, in front of this god of a man, naked in front of a man for the *first time*, and I'm a bloody, bruised, and beat up mess.

But I know he *wants* me to be the one on display right now.

"So fucking beautiful," he says under his breath. Then, louder as he walks up to me. "Couch. Now."

I feel his eyes on me as I walk past him. My cheeks are on fire, and it takes everything in me not to cover myself—to try to hide—but I agreed to this. There was no other way I was going to show him everything. There was no other way I was going to tell him what Daren did to me.

I sit on the couch, crossing my arms over my stomach, but leave the rest on display.

My nipples are hard and perky as usual, but I swallow the embarrassment as Marcelo walks in front of me. He kicks the coffee table away, giving himself room to stand, as the stupid ghost hunting show still goes on in the background.

"Fucking perfect," he breathes. "Except . . ." Leaning down, he grabs one of my wrists, and tosses it to my side, and doing the same to the other. I don't move from where he's placed me, letting him take in all of me. "There she is. A fucking work of art. A masterpiece of God's creation. Don't you ever dare cover yourself. Especially your tummy. I fucking love it."

And . . . I *see* he loves it. Holy shit, people weren't kidding about gray sweatpants on men. The bulge in his pants is at my eye level, and it's . . . difficult to look away from.

"Tell me what happened," he demands, either not noticing me drooling about what's in his pants, or not caring.

He walks back to his bathroom, searching under the sink for something.

I take a deep breath and close my eyes. "I was waiting for you. In the underwear you bought me. My mother walked in, saw me like that, and I guess . . . I guess she thought the worst."

He comes back with a store-brand ointment and cleanser, then he kneeled before me.

"I'm sorry," he grits out. "It's my fucking fault this happened to you."

I sit up, cupping his face. "No! No, it is not. I—I don't blame you. I don't blame the underwear. That—that was the nicest thing anyone has ever done for me."

He covers my hand with his. "And that is sad. You deserve the fucking *world*, Junia Forester. Not some lingerie from a creep outside your window."

I huff a laugh. "Maybe. My mom didn't think so."

"So she beat you?"

I nod. "She thought . . ." It makes me sick to even say. Marcelo starts cleaning the wounds, applying the ointment, then moving to the next. I get lost in his rhythmic touch, his fingers delicately dancing over my skin. "She thought I was trying to seduce Daren."

His hand flinches, but he doesn't stop, letting me continue.

"He had to stop her at some point."

"I'm surprised she actually did," he grunts.

"She did 'cause he gave her money to leave."

Now his hands come to a complete stop. But I don't.

"He gave her money to leave the house for a bit. And she took it. She left me. She *left me with him.*" Fresh tears fall from my eyes, and I'm shaking all over again—but I know it's not from the cold, not in this toasty room. Not in Marcelo's warm touch.

"He . . . he's the one who put the belt around my neck. He touched me."

Marcelo's head jerked forward. "What. Did. He. Do."

I swallowed, following the cross painted across the mask despite my blurry vision. "He groped me, grabbed . . . down there. Ripped the panties you gave me. But that was it."

"*Puta mierda!*" He slams his fist against the floor and grabs my hand. "Tell me to stay." His fingers interlock with mine, his palm squeezed to mine. "Tell me to stay, and not to go there right now, and chop his fucking hand off. Tell me to stay so I don't go fucking kill him right now."

I grab his other hand, the ointment falling from his grip. "Stay." I beg. "Stay with me. You said the other night you could make me feel good. I need you to make me feel good right now."

Shaking in my grasp, Marcelo shoots up, standing abruptly and letting go of my hands.

"Lay back," he demands, guiding my shoulders into the couch cushions. I flinch, feeling the material on my welts just as I did earlier tonight, just before my mom left me.

Somehow, that's the traumatizing part. I think part of me had been mentally preparing for Daren's unwelcome touch for a long time, and while it was still awful and disgusting, it is *nothing* compared to that final look in my mother's eyes, *nothing* compared to the image of her back to me as I *begged* her to stay.

"Please," I whisper. "Please stay."

Marcelo runs his hand through my damp hair, brushing it surprisingly gently. "I will, songbird. I'm never fucking leaving you again, you hear me? Wherever I go, you go."

I release a shuddering breath. I hadn't realized how desperately I needed to hear that.

He sighs and crouches again in front of me. "Once I finish putting this ointment on you, I'm going to make you food, and you're going to eat. Got it?"

I nod.

"And . . . And then will you make me feel good?"

I squeeze my thighs together, hoping he understands what I mean. I want his touch. I want his touch to replace the feel of those grimy hands on me. I want *Marcelo's* hands on me, and no one else's.

As I stare into the mask, I regret making him wear it. I wish I could see his expression underneath. Is he . . . interested in touching me? Or . . . disgusted?

He squeezes my thigh roughly—in a spot with no welts.

"You have no idea how good I want to make you feel. I want to fucking worship you, to praise you with my fingers, my tongue, my cock. I want to hear you moan for me, to scream for me—I want you to *sing* for me." The heat coils between my thighs, and God do I want his fingers to trail just a bit higher. His thumb is already so close to me, all it would take is a little shift—"But I don't think I should do that tonight. I want you to *feel* everything I do to you, to relish in just how good I make you feel, not use it as a retreat. When I touch you, June—and please, be aware I *will* touch you, vows be damned—I want you to know without a doubt it is because *I* want to, and not because you asked."

He tucks a strand of hair behind my ear, and though

everything he said makes sense, I can't help but feel a little disappointed.

"But I will do something for you."

Marcelo pulls the mask from his face and tosses it onto the coffee table.

"I won't touch you. But you can use me."

I tilt my head, scrunching my eyebrows together. Marcelo stands, lifting me along with him.

"What do you mean?"

"You don't want the ghost of his hands on you. Use mine. I won't move, and you can use my hands as you want."

He pulls me with him across the room, and pushes me against the wall between the bathroom door and the kitchenette, crowding in front of me.

My breasts press into his chest, and I see the small vein in his neck in response. "Know this will be *very* difficult for me."

Holy shit.

He's really giving me full rein to use his hands. I . . .

"Put it between my legs. Please."

Marcelo braces a hand on the wall beside me and leans into me, his warm hand drifting between my legs.

His fingers against my thighs are like lightning. It sends chills all along my body, heating my center.

"Fuck," he breathes out.

I reach between us, guiding his hand *exactly* where I want it—cupping my pussy.

"*Fuck*," he curses again, stepping into me just a bit.

"Are you going to stay still?" I ask, teasing him. I don't know when I started *teasing* but . . . it feels hot.

"Y-Yes," he says breathlessly.

I inch my hips up, sliding his stiff fingers against me. Marcelo bites his lower lip, and the expression is enough to make my knees weak. As I slide against him again, his fingers slide between my wet slit. He curses again and moves his knee between my legs, supporting his hand with his thigh.

"Rub your clit on me, make yourself come," he demands—no, *begs*.

I guide his fingers to that bundle of nerves and it is like fireworks going off in my brain the moment I feel the friction. I suck in a sharp breath at how *damn good* it feels. I'm basically using his hand to masturbate and somehow it feels *so much better* than my own hands or anything I've rubbed up against.

"God," I moan.

"*Coño*. Moan again, songbird."

I grind my hips again, sliding myself against his hand as I moan.

"So wet—God, I'm regretting every decision I've ever made right now."

I snicker, but keep my hips moving, slowly grinding against his calloused, strong hand. His fingers are long and perfect and, God, I'm really going to come all over his hand.

"Have you always shaved?" he asks through gritted teeth.

"N-no. I shaved earlier . . . just in case you came and . . ."

Marcelo keeps me pinned to the wall, pushing back as he raises his thigh, pressing his hand harder against me. Obediently, he doesn't move his fingers even a centimeter.

"You did it for me? *Fuck*. Grind that pretty pussy on me," he begs again, his hard cock pressing into my hip. God, I want to be grinding myself on *that*. "Make yourself come, *mi amor*."

My legs have gone out from how damned good this

feels, but he keeps me up. I grind my hips quicker, feeling his rough skin on my clit with each movement, pressing him into me.

"Ah—Marcelo!" I moan, throwing my head into his shoulder, slumping into him.

Marcelo props his elbow on the wall, and reaches his hand behind my head, yanking my hair back so I'm forced to look at him.

"Don't hide from me, June. I want to see that gorgeous face as you come for me."

He's so close, I can't look away, not as he watches me intently. The eye contact heightens *everything*.

"Ah," I moan again, as the crescendo takes over. I drive my hips back and forth, sawing myself against his hand, the friction growing so, *so* deliciously. My toes curl and I feel the familiar warmth pooling in my belly as my clit becomes sensitive to every touch. I can feel the end of the song coming to an end. It's just there—I just need to play the final note.

I throw my arms around his neck and grind my hips against him, and the moment my clit slides over him, I scream.

But it never reaches the room.

Because Marcelo's lips are on mine, swallowing my moans as I come all over his hand.

22

MARCELO

I can't help it. The moment I see her eyes start rolling back, I *need* her. I kept my promise. I didn't move my hand. But I didn't say *anything* about kissing her.

Her lips are just as soft as I thought they'd be, and I want to fall into them every moment of every day. I try to remind myself to be gentle. Her lip was split earlier that night, but the moment I lick the wound, I'm fucking feral, devouring her. Her tongue is like honey, and I want to swallow it down and make it mine.

June's wet, hot come coats my hand, and I make the painful decision to not have a little taste I so desperately want. Why have a sample, when I can have the entire feast later? And anyway, right now, I can't pull away from her lips.

I kiss her and kiss her, and kiss her. I kiss her as easily as breathing. I kiss her like kissing her *is* breathing, and I cannot survive without it.

I hoist her up, cupping her ass, and she wraps her legs around me, grinding into my hard cock with that shaved, tight pussy.

God, I want to fuck her.

But I said I wouldn't.

Like a fucking idiot.

I take June back to the couch and sit her down, slowing the kiss. She tastes fucking delicious, she feels incredible, and I would give anything not to stop.

But I also know she's covered in fresh wounds, should eat, and has had a long fucking night.

Unwrapping my tongue from hers, I give her a final, long kiss before pulling away from her. Her eyes are still closed, her cheeks an adorable pink, her lips red.

My songbird bats those long lashes open and looks up at me. Out of breath, I smile at her. "I just found out what my paradise in Heaven would feel like."

June's beautiful doe eyes are wide, and her pink cheeks only become a deep crimson. I chuckle and stand, moving to pick up her clothes and the ointment long forgotten.

"Ointment. Food. And then we can talk more, okay?"

June's chest rises and falls quickly still, her beautiful fucking tits bouncing with each inhale. It took everything in my power not to bury myself between them earlier when I first took her shirt off, everything not to stare at her naked body and ogle at everything God created.

"Okay," she breathes, still catching her breath. I chuckle and kneel in front of her again, working first on her thighs.

"Want me to change the channel?" I ask, dabbing the cream on her thighs.

She shakes her head. "Nah. I like these dumb ghost shows."

After the ointment, I help her back into my clothes, and then make her one of my childhood favorites—scrambled eggs, chopped up hot dogs, white rice, and ketchup. June eyes it skeptically at first, but her eyes light up the moment she takes a bite. We eat together in silence, save for the little moans and happy dances she does after each bite.

At some point, Diablo snuck out of his hiding place, and now sits at her feet as June sneaks him pieces of hot dog.

"You can take my room," I say between bites. "I'll sleep out here."

June blinks at me, then nods.

I considered sleeping with her, but just because I let her fuck my hand doesn't mean the girl needs some space. She's had a traumatic night, and the last thing I should be doing is presuming anything.

After we eat, I quickly wash our dishes and clean up as June carries Diablo to the couch and flops back on it.

"Can we watch a movie?" she asks as I pull the bag of frozen veggies from my freezer and walk over to her on the couch.

"Yeah, what do you wanna watch?"

She taps her chin, puckering her lips. "Mmm. Can we watch something scary?"

I arch an eyebrow at her. "You like horror movies?"

June's cheeks redden as she shrugs. "Yeah. I can't watch them whenever my mom is home. She thinks they transfer the spirits or whatever to the house through the TV."

Bullshit.

"Wait, you'd know!" she says quickly. "They don't, do they? I never believed her, but if she was—"

I chuckle. "No, it doesn't really work that way. Just like watching these shows," I point at the ghost hunting show still somehow playing in the background, "can't summon the Devil to your house."

"Knew it." She scratches Diablo between the ears, who has now become more of a liquid croissant than a cat. "Anyway, I've always loved movies. But . . . movies were weird at my house. We always watched them as a family, and usually whatever my mother chose and approved."

"Which meant no horror movies."

June shakes her head. "But, in the third grade, I stayed home sick from school and Mother couldn't skip work, so she left me alone for just a few hours. It was eleven a.m. and some channel I wasn't supposed to be on was playing *Creature from the Black Lagoon*."

"Good choice," I say, leaning back.

"I remember thinking how dumb the girl was in it—to not love the creature back."

My girl's a damn monster fucker. Hot.

"Right after that, the original *House on Haunted Hill* came on. And I don't know . . . I was so young, but it made the house a little less lonely that day, and it distracted me from my cold. Since then, horror has been sort of a comfort for me. It's been impossible since Daren has moved in to watch anything, but before him, it would often be my go-to whenever the . . . whenever *this* became too much." She taps her forehead.

Horror as a coping mechanism. That's not so hard to believe. I mean, the adrenaline from the movies might overwrite adrenaline from anxiety, watching someone else's life be fantastically awful—it creates the illusion of your life being pretty okay compared to the teen boy getting axed by a masked killer or the family being haunted by demons infesting their house.

"I usually just smoke a pack of cigarettes and go for a drive. Both of which are very bad."

June squints at me. "How is driving bad?"

"Because," I shrug, "if I want it to be a coping mechanism, I usually go forty over the speed limit."

She huffs a laugh and leans back, too. I can feel her warmth, but our bodies don't touch, and I can't help but feel like she's too far.

"When did you start smoking?"

Grabbing the remote, I click to a streaming app and start scrolling the movies absently as I tell her, "Since I was fourteen."

June whistles. "Wow. And they didn't ask you to quit when you took your vows?"

I chuckle. "Oh, they did. They still do. But, and this may shock you, songbird, I'm not a very good priest."

"Ya know," she laughs, "I'm starting to see why. Maybe it has something to do with the stalking?"

"The mask is . . . a whole other thing." I sigh. A whole other can of decrepit gross worms that I *really* don't want to get into right now. "The stalking? They probably wouldn't think too highly of that either."

From the corner of my eye, I see June picking at her thumb.

"And . . ." Her eyes stay locked on Diablo's sleeping black mass. "What about what you did a little while ago? Or . . . when you said you'd touch me, vows be damned. What do they think of that?"

Leaning over, I place a hand on her cheek and force her to turn to me. "If you're asking if I've done that with any other woman, or anything of that nature, no. I have not even *thought* of touching another woman since I met you." Her cheeks heat under my palm, but I continue. "I'm a priest for the sole intention of being an exorcist, June. I have a relationship with God, but it isn't how the Catholic church wants it to be. It isn't how the Bible wants it to be. And it sure as Hell isn't how your mother would want it to be. My faith in Him is my own, and my ideas of what he wants for me are by what I feel as a priest. I have *always* believed the vows to be ridiculous, and I have always believed the church to be a bunch of power mongering idiots who believe they are the voice of authority because they are closer to God. But that is not me. I don't think he would want me to stop feeling love. I don't think he would create our bodies to feel such pleasure and then devoid it of such. I do not believe he would want us to hate each other for the sins we have or haven't committed. If it comes down to it, I'm fine revoking my vows—the politics of it all are too much, and it's never been why I've invested myself into an organization I don't truly believe in. But I do believe in protecting the world from evil, and I will always be an exorcist.

"So, no," I breathe, looking at June's plump lips again as she sucks them between her teeth. "They don't know I want to worship your body with my tongue and praise your mind as I learn more and more about its intricacies. They don't know I want to fuck you, day and night, till you scream my name instead of God's. They don't know I want to kill anyone who even touches you or that I want to steal you away and never let go."

I stare into June's eyes as a sharp inhale rakes her body again. Her cheeks are a crimson so deep, it almost looks like a crime scene.

"Now, do you believe me when I say I'm a fucking awful priest?"

I can't even remember when I fell asleep. One minute I was leaning on the arm of the sofa, Diablo warming my thighs, watching some newer zombie movie I hadn't heard of, and the next it was morning. I'm covered with a blanket, the sun shining through the windows, my body in a completely different position and—and Marcelo nowhere in sight.

Diablo is still cuddling against me as my brain focuses on the room around me. I hadn't really noticed last night— not with everything that happened that I am actively try- ing to avoid, and not with everything that happened with everything I am hyper fixating on—but it's pretty odd. I've been in here once or twice long ago, and I don't remember it being so . . . eighties. The walls are all either a chestnut brown wooden overlay, or a bright yet somehow dark hunter green; the rug is a kaleidoscope of browns and tans while the couch is bright yellow; even the small kitchen-ette is covered in lime green subway tile with what looks like a mint-colored vintage formica dining table pressed against the wall.

Hell, the only things *new* in here are the TV, the bath-room, and the hot Latin man currently in the shower. The sound of the water running pulls me further from sleep, and I can't help but try to imagine what he must look like in there—the water cascading down his tan skin, drench-ing those soft curls.

The water shuts off and my thoughts race back to real-ity as I hear Marcelo open the shower door. Oh god. He's going to think I'm such a sloth if he comes out, ready for the day already, and I'm still tangled in sleep, hair a mess, breath gross, eyes crusty, and overall just a literal hobgob-lin.

Disturbing Diablo, I throw the blanket off me and scramble up from the couch. My head immediately feels woozy, but I ignore it as I—

"Oh, you're up."

As I forget every thought I've ever had, every word I've ever said, my own name, and what woozy even means.

I forget because there is a god in front of me. An actual god. And his name probably has something to do with abs and pecks and just general hot manly *umph*ness.

This is better than what I just made up in my head about him in the shower. *So* much better.

Marcelo exits the bathroom, shirt off and sweats slung low. His hair is still dripping, forcing the curls to elongate, making it drape just past his neck. The tattoos I only as-sumed were spread across his chest are absolutely breath-taking, and so much more detailed than I ever could've imagined. He has three large pieces spread across his chest, making an entire mural so stunning, and then they transition into his shoulders, and down his arms.

Marcelo isn't shredded, but the definition of muscle—the *man*ness of him—makes me froth at the mouth, and the trail of dark hair disappearing into those low slung sweats might actually cause a heart aneurysm. Or brain aneurysm. Whatever.

The god before me clears his throat, and as I finally unglue my eyes to his gorgeous body and meet his eyes, his smile is wide and wicked and . . . also stunning.

"You good there, *princesa*?"

Fuck. Caught. Whatever, I'm allowed. After he stared at my body under the mask all those nights in a row, let me use his hand the other night—and dared be the first man I ever wanted *like that* appear *like this* in front of me, I am damn allowed!

"Yes!" I say, a little too excitedly. "I am. Good shower?" *What the fuck did I just ask?*

He snorts. "Yes. Good shower. Does June want good shower too?"

Oh no. Even his caveman is hot.

"I can wait."

Smirking, Marcelo nods. "Good. Now get back on the couch. We have plans, you and I."

I squint at him.

"After you fell asleep, I ended up finding a horror streaming service. I've already picked out the best horror movies from the last few years I want to show you. I'll order pizza, get snacks—but there's one rule."

My heart pumps from everything he just said and swells from the idea of it. A movie day. With him. Watching *my* favorite genre. That *he's* planned. But . . . one rule?

"Which is what?"

"We are not allowed to leave the couch."

And we don't break that rule (I mean, obviously we get up to get the pizza and go to the bathroom and stretch). After Marcelo replaces his shirt, I am thrown into horror movie after horror movie, blissfully ignoring the haunting image of my mother's eyes, blissfully ignoring the feeling of grime dripping down my body.

I am engulfed in a horror that is not my own and I could not be more at peace.

T he TV glow lights up the small room as a monster chases after the screaming final girl, but I haven't bothered glancing at the movie even once. Not when my little songbird is fast asleep next to me, looking like the most gorgeous angel that could ever walk this earth.

The day was mostly quiet, but I could sense her peace with each passing fright, like the trauma that happened to her last night was being pulled away, tucked into her chest for another time.

I can't stop thinking of her stepfather's hands on her. His fingers even grazing the spots I long to worship. He grabbed her pussy, and he tried to steal from her what wasn't his.

June holds Diablo to her, and for some reason, the cat lets her. He's cuddled in her arms, acting as the perfect little spoon. I lean over and pat his butt. The cat jerks up with a guttural meow and looks over at me.

"Keep her safe," I whisper. "I'll be back soon."

Diablo only flops his head back onto her arm, snuggling his fur against her skin.

Standing, I creep back into my room. I haven't wanted to leave June's side—even last night when the rage was threatening to boil over. Even when she fell asleep and all I could think of were the welts marring her skin, the black eye we'd been icing all day. Even when I thought about her in nothing but that drenched gray hoodie.

I didn't leave her then. But tonight, she's fast asleep. Tonight, she has a little more peace.

I'll make it quick.

I pull up to the small little familiar house, its white exterior dirty and in desperate need of a power wash. I can't help but think of June and her fucking stepdad as I see the grime slither up the white wood, mold and dirt, and who knows what else slowly infecting the house.

Shutting the car off, I step outside into the cold night and zip my hoodie all the way up, tightening the leather gloves covering my hands. My mask is already pulled snuggly over my face, but unlike when I was here for June, there will be *no* Salvation in the home tonight.

Taking an empty bag with me, and a kitchen knife from the church's apartment, I walk around back—back to June's room, back to the window I *know* is still open for me. I'll grab some clothes for her, anything that might look important to her, and then she'll never have to come back here.

And what I'll do to her parents? I haven't decided yet. My hands are aching to be wrapped around Daren's throat or plunging the blade into his gut, but I only brought the kitchen knife just in case. I have only ever killed cultists, those who attempt to bring *true* evil into our world, who try to sow chaos and hurt and fear, who sacrifice, rape, and butcher innocents in the name of their gods. I have never killed anyone for anything else.

Yet for the first time, I want to. I want to kill the man who touched June. I want to slice his fingers off, one by one, and feed them back to him. I want to burn his palms for grabbing her tits, and I want to stab his eyes out for even *daring* to look at her. But just because I *want* to, doesn't mean I will. I have a code I try to live by, no matter how fucked it is. It is the only thing that can tell me I'm better than them. I'm not delusional enough to believe God will grant me mercy since I'm killing his enemies. I know I'm not getting into Heaven. He said murder is a sin, and I am in no way absolved from that. But I don't want to become another evil on earth either.

I slide the window up, and it smoothly opens as I expected it to, and when I swing myself into June's room—it's a total mess.

There are clothes and things everywhere, most torn up, but some . . .

My jaw clenches and for a second, all I see is red.

Her underwear drawer is pulled open, the panties all thrown about and . . . riffled through. It isn't till I take a step closer that I also see they're covered in dried cum, with her pink panties that *I* bought her sitting right at the top, covered completely.

"Fucking creep," I hiss, trying to breathe through the leather. Taking a few steps back before I kick something, I look for *anything* June might want, a journal, a dress, a coat, a stuffed animal—anything. But everything in here feels as though it doesn't actually belong to her. The clothes are more of the frumpy worn pieces I've seen her wear. The books are all ancient and shoved in a bookcase with a layer of dust covering them—and they're all weird religious books that *I* wouldn't even touch.

The only thing I find that *might* be anything worthy to her is a small songbook I find in the drawer next to her bed. It's full of notes and worn sheet music for the organ. I stash it in the bag, and after another sweep, I realize I've taken what I can.

Fuck. I can't even take her a fucking pair of underwear because of the bastard. Does her mother know what he's done in here? What he's done to her?

A door opens from somewhere else in the house, followed by footsteps wandering into the hall. It's not that late, June fell asleep by nine and I had to be in my car by ten, so it's gotta be before eleven. But as I continue to hear the ruffling of clothes and the jingle of keys, I realize this is more than just a nighttime bathroom trip.

Someone is going somewhere.

As the front door opens and closes, I also hop from the window. The house's lights are off, but the neighbors and streetlights are all illuminated, making the sky seem more black and devoid of stars.

I creep around toward the front of the house, staying close to the wall, and spot Daren falling into the seat of his car with what looks like a Bible in his hands.

As soon as I see his taillights, I dash to my car and get

in. I keep my headlights off and follow from a decent distance behind, making sure not to be too obvious.

Though it doesn't help being two of the only cars on the road.

Daren drives through Belmouth, passing St. Mary's where June is sound asleep, and doesn't come to a stop until he is just outside of town. He swings the car just behind the *Welcome to Belmouth* sign, where I notice a handful of cars have already parked. At least five others line up, including a patrol car, and vehicles I recognize from the church.

What the fuck is this?

Still keeping my distance, I see Daren get out of the car with the Bible still in hand. He's sporting a large bandage on his forehead where I can only assume June hit him with the idol.

That's my girl, I think.

I count to ten, waiting for Daren to just barely be visible before I get out of the car and follow after him. He walks into an alley between two buildings before disappearing into the woods.

The moment I pass through the line of trees, every sense in my body is telling me to *run*. I feel the cross tattooed on my finger begin to itch and burn as the smell of . . . charcoal and rotten eggs clouds my nose.

Demons.

Fuck. What the fuck is Daren doing here?

I follow him farther, stepping carefully and keeping to the shadows. But I feel something watching me from behind — something that has been following me since I entered these woods.

And it isn't human.

I veer away from Daren's path. I can come back tomorrow and try to retrace his steps, but I can't do that if he finds out I'd been following him. So, I lure the thing following me away. If it's going to attack, let it do so where Daren can't see, can't hear.

The woods are dark, the moon hidden behind the clouds of the tops of the trees, and each shadow puts me on edge. Is it just another tree? Or a demon waiting to rip my throat open?

After I feel we're far enough away, I pull the rosary from my pocket and come to an abrupt stop. The moment the cross emerges from my pocket, the leaves around me rustle, and a tiny hoard of imps peer out from between the trees, in the bushes, and out from the shadows.

There has to be at least fifteen ugly baby faces grinning with those disgusting tiny, sharp teeth and gleaming those golden goat eyes.

"Blessed Michael, archangel," I begin, and the beasts lunge toward me, wicked claws displayed and aimed right for my gut. "Defend us in the hour of conflict."

I slump back to the car, my fists bloodied and bruised, but content that I was able to send all the fuckers back to Hell. Imps are like mosquitoes, more annoying than anything else—but like mosquitoes often hovering near water, imps hover near demons.

If Daren is a cultist, that just made my life a whole lot fucking easier.

Sliding into the car, I drape the metal rosary on the rearview mirror. It's hot to the touch from use, and the three scratched up beads call my attention. If all goes how I want it to, there will soon be a fourth scratched bead to match the other.

I turn to see the small bundle of what I rescued from June's, and can't help but wince. It's nothing—less than nothing.

Sighing as soon as I turn the car on, I send off a quick text.

> *Me: Hey, call me when you wake up. I need to borrow your ear.*

Before I can even put my phone back in my pocket, it vibrates with a notification.

> *Willow: Still up—call now?*

Of course she fucking is.

I click the call button, and at the end of the first ring, I hear a loud and long, "Well hello, hello, stranger."

Willow has been my best friend for nearly twenty-five years—maybe more honestly. Her and Rowan are twins, and though he was who I became friends with first, that has never stopped her from being *all* up in my business.

"My ear is yours to borrow."

"What the Hell are you doing up?" I grunt into the phone.

"Oh, you know." The phone ruffles in the background, and I can tell she put me on speaker and then threw her phone across the room. "When creativity calls."

Willow is a video editor. She works freelance for a handful of clients on rotation, and because of the flexible schedule, she is always up way late into the night. Which suits her just fine, as she's always been a "stay up till morning and sleep till the afternoon" kind of person.

"Anyway, I know you didn't call to ask about my latest ad run, so what do you need?" She huffs a breath. "And why has it taken you so damn long to call me?"

I huff a laugh as I pull onto the road back to St. Mary's. "I've been busy."

"Ah, of course, exorcising and shit."

"Hey, you're talking to a priest."

"*Hey, you're talking to a priest*, my ass."

I shrug. Fair enough.

"I need your opinion—or your help, I guess. But Will, you *cannot* say anything to Rowan or Rodrigo."

She laughs. "Ooo, is it as juicy as all the tattoos you've been hiding from *Padre* all this time?"

I don't answer, letting the silence wean her into agreeing. Eventually, she does. "Urgh, fine, I won't tell RoRo." A name she's given the two since her brother became a priest. *They're basically the same person now*, she said to explain the God-awful name. "Anyway, tell me *everything*."

"I, uh, met someone."

I don't even know how to explain June, how to convey all the feelings and emotions I've developed for this girl in just the last few days. So, I tell Willow everything. All the nights of stalking, the beatings I've found on her, and now—the pinnacle of it all from last night.

Willow is silent on the other side, and *this* is why she's the person I trust with anything and everything. She never judges, she only lets me explain and then offers her help. Even in my dark days, even in my *darker* days, she was always there, always my soundboard.

"Whoa, she's had it rough," Willow whispers, shock coating her voice. "Is she . . . is she okay? I mean, of course she's not, but—"

"She's managing," I say. "But, Will, she's got nothing. Like, less than nothing. Not even a pair of socks to her name."

"Does she have any friends she can talk to?"

I sigh. "Not that I know of. She's twenty-five and doesn't own a cellphone. I think her mother didn't *let* her have a life of her own at all."

Willow sighs also. "Fuck. Do you want me to go up? Maybe a little girl time'll help her. And lord knows I need a break from this place."

"I think it'd help."

"All right, give me a few days. In the meantime, maybe take her shopping. If it was as bad as you said it was, June's probably never been allowed to pick out her own clothes. It might help her, I don't know, find some part of herself she had locked away."

Which is exactly what I want. I've seen glimpses of the real June. I *know* she's in there.

June has seen the real me, the savage, crazed, obsessed version of myself—and has preferred it to the fake version of myself I convey at church.

Now, I want the real her. Even if I have to pull it out of her myself.

The power of the car thrums underneath me as the array of fall-colored leaves zoom past my vision. Marcelo wasn't kidding, he likes to drive fast—and right now, I couldn't be more thankful for it.

I woke up this morning thinking today was going to be awful. No, *preparing* is the better word. I *prepared* for today to be awful.

It's Sunday, the one day a week church is more of a duty and less of an offering. The one day everyone always expected us to show up on time, prim and proper, and on our best behaviors. The one day other families might *notice* if we weren't there, so we'd have to go even if we weren't feeling well. The one day they used to stone townspeople as punishment for not attending back in Puritan Massachusetts.

From the moment I woke up when the first church bell rang, I knew Mother and Daren were *somewhere* under the very same roof I was, ready for Mass. I didn't have a phone, so it's not like Mother could've called me to ask where I was, but . . . I get the feeling she didn't even try. Or care.

Luckily for me, Marcelo is making sure I don't have to find out.

I have no idea where we're going, but wherever it is, it's *away*. Which is exactly where I want to be. Not in the church, not at the organ, and definitely not with my mother.

From the corner of my eye, I see Marcelo shift gears. His knuckles are bruised and there's a small gash just under the cross tattoo on his index finger as he palms the shifter. He's not wearing his regular priest attire, but looks more like my masked man—in all black, with a fitted T-shirt and a hoodie to hide all those tattoos. All that's missing is the mask itself.

After that first bell, he put a small pile of clothes on the couch next to me and gave me a tiny steaming cup of coffee.

"Get dressed. We're going out."

I sat up, taking the coffee. "Where are we going?"

A corner of his mouth lifted. "You'll see."

The coffee was absolutely delicious, and nothing like I've ever had. It was rich and *so* fucking strong with the perfect amount of sweetness, I felt wired after the first sip.

"*Cafecito* straight from Miami. That shit's like cocaine." Marcelo laughed, watching my expression.

After downing the rest of the drink—and feeling like my heart was going to explode out of my chest—I threw on the sweats he gave me, swimming in the too-long pants and hoodie.

Now, in the car, my butt is way too big in them though, and I feel the fabric pull every time I adjust in the seat. I even had to wear some of his shoes since I showed up at his door with *nothing*. And while it has been such a nice break not wearing a constricting, painful bra for the last two days, the girls are in desperate need and my back has never been angrier at me.

"I think I got a lead last night," he says, breaking me from the hypnotizing view of passing trees. "Are you okay checking it out with me?"

"Is that where we're going now?"

He shakes his head. "Later, if you're okay with it."

The idea that I'll be . . . part of something absolutely thrills me. That I can help with something, that he *wants* my help in the first place. "Of course," I say. Hunting demons—hopefully it'll go better than how it does in the movies.

"Great, then I want you to wear this. Don't take it off unless *I* tell you to." He hands me his metal rosary. "It should keep you safe in case of anything."

I slip it over my head and tuck it under the hoodie. The metal is cold against my skin as the beads and cross land between my breasts, sending a small shiver over my body.

"Speaking of the demon . . ." I start, not sure where the confidence to say this to him comes from. "There's something I never told you. I wanted to, but I . . . I got scared."

Marcelo stays quiet, listening.

"I don't know when it started, but . . . I get these bouts of—of arousal. It always starts when I'm in the church, and it doesn't go away until . . ." I can't say the words, not without combusting into a small sun. But I hope he knows what I mean. "Anyway, it always felt like something happening *to* me, rather than my body reacting to something outside."

He scrunches his eyebrows. "What do you mean?"

"Like—like—"

"June, you came all over my fingers two nights ago, and I am dying for you to do it all over again. Now, use your big girl words and tell me what you mean."

The memory makes my toes curl and an instant heat spreads from my core.

"Wh—When you did that to me, I was . . . aroused because of you, because of the moment. When it happens at church, when I can't stop it, it feels like something is forcing it on me. Like my body just warms up and *needs* to be touched. It doesn't stop until I orgasm—and sometimes one isn't enough."

"Do you feel touched when it happens?" he asks, and his voice sounds more clerical, as if he were a doctor asking about my condition.

I think back on the feelings, my face hot from even *saying* these things in front of him. "Not really. More like I *need* to be touched, I *need* to orgasm—"

"Well," Marcelo says, "next time that happens, let me help." He looks at me from the corner of his eyes, and my God, he looks stunning with one hand gripped on the wheel, and the other holding the gear shift. The veins on his hands pop as he squeezes the leather just a little. "Okay?"

I nod, squeezing my thighs together. He let me use his hand the other night, but I have a feeling that doesn't even scratch the surface of what *he can do to me*, how he'd use those hands on my body, how he'd use them to make me come. "Yes," I breathe, and I'm not sure it doesn't sound more like a moan. Clearing my throat, I say, "I'll go to you."

Marcelo smirks. "Good girl."

And before I can fully melt at his words and ask him to touch me right now, we're pulling into a massive parking lot to a huge mall in the next town over. I used to come here in my teens, but it's been years.

"The mall?" I question.

He parks the car and fully shifts in the bench seat to look at me. "I went to your house last night to try to get you some clothes, but I realized . . . most of it wasn't actually yours, was it?" Marcelo eyes me up and down. Last night? Is that what the bruises on his hands are from? "Or, if it was, it wasn't something you actually wanted, and definitely wasn't something that fit you."

My stomach sinks. I don't want to go home, but it's not like I have money to shop. "It's fine, I can still wear—"

"No. You can't. For starters, you're not going back there." He takes my hand and pulls it to him. "And you're not wearing underwear from ten years ago that digs into your skin."

"Marcelo." I wince. "I don't have any money. None. My mother didn't let me have a job and any money I got from the church went right back to her."

His grip on my hand tightened. "I didn't bring you here for *you* to spend money, June. *I'm* buying you whatever you want." He cupped my face, and brought my eyes to meet his. "*Whatever* you want, June. Not whatever you need. I want you to pick clothes *you* like, stuff *you* want."

"But what about—"

"Don't worry about money. I get paid to be an exorcist but all my expenses are also covered by the job. So, I have a lot that I never use." He rubs his thumbs along my cheeks. "Let me do this for you," he whispered. "Let me take care of you."

All I hear is my mother's voice screaming in my head, "*No, no—don't accept handouts.*"

"Okay."

Marcelo takes my hand the moment we're out of the car, guiding me into the mall. It's a little surreal being back here, and much more quiet than I remember it being in my youth. There are a few families walking around, but it's early on a Sunday morning. I only assume people are sleeping in or in church.

But I'm thankful for it. With my eye still not totally right, no bra, Marcelo's clothes and shoes, and the general anxiety of being seen next to this gorgeous human, I would like to be perceived as least as possible.

My hand feels so small in his as his fingers intertwine with mine. I find myself rubbing the little cross with my thumb, and something about it is just so soothing, it immediately quiets my racing heart.

"What first?" he asks.

Like ripping off a bandaid, I'd rather get the worst over with first. "Underwear."

He nods. "Remember, anything you *want*, June."

Marcelo guides me into a store filled with neon purple and a brilliant lights. Bras, underwear, and other lingerie sets line the walls and counters.

I hesitantly pick up a very normal beige bra. The underwire looks a little intense, but it also seems . . . reliable? Useful? Able to get the job done?

Marcelo pulls his lips in and huffs a breath. He takes the bra from my hands and places it back where it was before rubbing my back. "Pick whatever you'd like, whatever calls to you," he says, letting go of my hand and gently pushing me to the table. "Whatever you want to wear, or be in, or try—" He leans into me from behind, whispering in my ear, "or whatever you think looks sexy."

I blush at his words again, imagining how different the night would've gone if he had come to my room when I was wearing the pink set he'd bought me. How his eyes would've devoured me, and how turned on that would've made me.

I look around, immediately spotting a few things I think I like. Thankfully, it seems the store is pretty size in-clusive, so most of the styles that catch my eye are easy to find in my size. Something that was *very* rare where my mother and I shopped. I also had to size down at least by two cups in order to find anything that would fit, and up in band size to compensate. And *nothing* that ever actually came in my size was this cute.

I grab a few things, including some normal bras and panties, others strappy or more like a corset with matching thongs, a lacy bodysuit, and a black chemise sleep teddy. Marcelo carries the store's black shopping bag, holding it open for me whenever I grab something new. I don't miss the small smirk and eyebrow raise he gives the teddy and matching thong the moment I throw it in the bag.

A gorgeous woman in fitted black clothes and a name tag walks up to us. She has a gleaming smile shining at us as she asks, "Are you finding everything okay?"

She's so gorgeous, and the way her eyes are lit up on Marcelo has my gut twisting in such an ugly, uncomfortable way.

"She's skinny, so she's prettier than you. Marcelo is going to think she's prettier than you, too. Why can't you be skinny? No man is ever going to choose you over someone like her."

It's my mother's voice again, saying words in my head that she's never said aloud.

Marcelo's warm and heavy arm wrapped around my shoulder, pulling me into his hard body. "Yeah, she was actually just getting ready to try this stuff on. Can you show us to the dressing room?"

The woman guides us to a small hallway of dressing rooms tucked deep into the store. It's incredibly private and with so few people in here, even more so.

"Let me know if you need anything else or if you want me to grab different sizes." The woman smiles and then walks away.

Marcelo hands me the bag and sits on the small couch just outside the door, also smiling at me a final time before I shut it behind me.

The moment I take off his clothes, nothing feels right and I don't feel I look . . . good.

Fat, fat, fat, I hear my mother say again and again.

But, I don't feel *ugly*. Not necessarily. Sure, I have a tummy. Sure, my thighs are big. Sure, I'm wider than most. But . . . doesn't *this* still look good? Why did Mother always say fat as if it meant ugly?

I put on one of the lingerie tops, fitting my breasts into the cups, as a small knock sounds on the door.

I know it's Marcelo before I even open it, but the moment I do, he's squeezing through the door and stumbling into the small changing room.

"I couldn't stand being on the other side of this door, waiting, wondering what you look like in all these. I wanted to see." He turns to me, and just as I imagined, his eyes absolutely devour me. His chin dips as his eyes darken, roaming over every curve of my body.

"Fuck," he grunts. "Look at you."

The plum-colored corset hugs my breasts so nicely, and ends at my waist, accentuating whatever hourglass figure I have.

As his eyes drink me in, I see the exact moment Marcelo notices—I haven't put the matching panties on yet.

His eyes go wide, and his nostrils flare as he stares so intently at me.

"You are absolutely breathtaking, and you don't even realize, do you?"

I feel stunned into silence, biting my lip and waving my arms back and forth like an idiot.

"Come here," he demands, beckoning me toward him with one finger. The moment I take a step in his direction, he grabs my hips and turns us both, pulling my back flush to his chest as he forces me to face the mirror. "I want you to look at yourself, songbird. Look how fucking sexy you are." His hands begin to roam my body, cupping my breasts, and gripping my hips. "See how much you turn me on?" He grinds his hardening length against my ass, and I have to stop myself from moaning.

"Does this make you feel sexy?" he whispers against my ear, and the tickle of his beard against my neck sends shivers all along my spine.

"I—it does," I breathe.

"Okay, then we'll get it." He kisses my neck, his lips so terribly soft. "I want you to never question whether or not you're beautiful, because you are the most devastating thing I have ever laid eyes on. You ruin me, June Forester." His tongue claims my skin and I can't help but lean into his kiss, his touch. What he just said should be so . . . heartbreaking. But it only makes me believe him. He said he'd break his vows for me, and his tongue on my neck is showing me just how much he means that.

Marcelo's hands slip behind me as he starts undoing the corset.

"Let me show you how beautiful you are."

26

JUNE

Marcelo pulls the straps of the corset down my shoulders, revealing me to the mirror. Of course, my nipples are already perky, but without the support, my breasts fall heavy and I immediately raise my arms to cover myself.

But my wrists are snagged the moment they do. "Why," Marcelo hisses, "would you hide from me? Why would you hide at all?"

Instead of answering, I give a lame shrug, unsure how to respond. Because I'm repulsive? Because my boobs sag and I don't want you to see? Because my stomach looks like I could be pregnant with ten cheeseburgers and an ostrich egg? Or maybe because I don't want you to see all these stretch marks marring my skin?

I bite my lip, deciding I'd rather choose my answer by Russian roulette. After all, whatever I end up saying will

187

definitely be the end of me—of this . . . thing between us, whatever it is.

"Be—"

"Look how fucking gorgeous these are."

When I find Marcelo's eyes in the mirror, they're not on mine. They're not hard and disgusted, they're not terrified or nervous. His dark eyes are full of lust, full of want, full of *need*.

He cups my breasts, hard, staring at the way his fingers massage into them, his lips part as if he's imagining them between his teeth. A small moan escapes me as his finger brushes against my nipple, as *I see* the way he holds me. He wants me—bad. But more than that, I see how attracted he is to my body, how much he admires and wants it, and how much he cares for it in every single touch.

The metal rosary dangles low, the cross resting between my breasts. I see the moment Marcelo's eyes land on it through the mirror, feeling his erection grow hard as he grinds into me.

"Fuck. My little angel," he groans, grabbing the cross. "Don't you see how beautiful you are?"

I look at myself in the mirror, and with his hands wrapped around me, I *do* feel beautiful. I feel wanted and lusted after and cared for, all at once. For once, my curves are . . . nice.

There's also something about being totally naked before him while he is fully clothed that sends fire between my thighs.

Marcelo kisses my neck, roaming his hands down my body. He squeezes my waist before splaying them over my hips. "So fucking sexy," he breathes as his fingers dig into my skin, pulling my hips back against him. "I want to touch your pretty cunt so fucking bad."

I tilt my head, giving him more access to my neck. "Please, I want you to."

He grins, his facial hair rough against my skin. "Do you want my cock, songbird? My fingers? Or would you like my tongue?"

A shuddering breath escapes me as his fingers dance along my thighs, slowly and delicately drifting up.

"Everything," I moan. "All of you. You can do anything to me, Marcelo—just . . . no belts."

He huffs a laugh, his hot breath tickling me. "No belts. Anything else?"

I think for a moment. The idea of the masked man taking me, whenever he'd please—it makes my toes curl at the mere idea of what he might do. I remember how desperately I wanted the stranger to have his way with me, how hot I thought it would be. And Marcelo seems to be equally down for the experiment.

But one thing does cross my mind. "I don't want to be choked." I meet his eyes in the mirror, and he's already watching me intently. "I can still feel the belt around my throat if I think about it too much," I admit, my hand resting where it was a few nights ago. "Maybe eventually but—"

"No choking," he repeats, kissing my neck gently. "I won't force that on you."

Taking a deep breath, I grab his hand and place it between my legs. He groans at the contact, his fingers immediately sliding between my folds to find wet heat. "But," I say on a shuddering sigh, "everything else."

"Can I chase you?" His finger slides along my core, grazing the bundle of nerves that sends a moan slipping from my lips.

"Yes."

"Can I bite you?" He nibbles my throat.

I nod, giving him more access.

"Can I fuck you, whenever I want, however I want?" His fingers dip into me just the smallest amount, and it is like explosions behind my eyelids.

"God, yes, please—anything."

"If you ever don't want me to do something, just tell me. Otherwise…" His free hand comes up and grips my cheeks, forcing my eyes on his through the mirror. "You are mine to do with as I please. Got it?"

"Yes," I whimper as his fingers slip out of me again.

"How'd you get so fucking wet? Was it from looking at yourself in the mirror? From my hands on you?" He easily finds my clit again and pinches it between his fingers.

"Marcelo," I moan, grabbing his wrist.

The hand holding my cheeks lets go and completely covers my mouth, pressing tightly. "Or, is it that we can be caught right now? Does my little songbird like to be touched in public?"

I hesitate, wondering if that's what it is—if knowing that the beautiful woman could come back at any second, knock on this door, and might hear me moaning on the other side.

"I wasn't going to tell you this," he says against me, pulling my chin down once more to meet his eyes, "but the first time we met, I knew your hands had just been used to get you off."

I freeze.

"I was on the other side of the confessional, songbird. I heard you sing as you touched yourself, as you made yourself come. I nearly busted the wall down just to get a better view."

His fingers on my clit don't relent as he roughly rubs in small circles. I squeeze my thighs together, but it only makes the pressure more intense. But the embarrassment of having been caught, of that settling into his mind all this time, makes my knees weak, but the hand at my pussy keeps me upright.

"Tell me, has anything ever been inside of you?" Marcelo moves his hand to play with my nipple again, squeezing and pulling.

"N—No. Nothing."

"Not even those delicate musician fingers?"

I shake my head. I'd always been too afraid to . . . *break* anything, I'd never done it.

"Then I cannot wait to stuff and claim every gorgeous hole—this beautiful mouth, your tight ass, and your perfect fucking pussy."

I moan again, his words making my body shake as his fingers work me up and up and up.

But then he completely stops.

"Not right now, though, not here. I want you so hot and bothered during our shopping trip. I want you to be dripping wet by the time we get back to the car, barely able to stand, so that when I claim some part of you, you'll be begging me for it."

"Wait, I want it now—"

"I can't wait to have this"—Marcelo takes a step back, his hand moving from between my thighs to gently rub my ass—"riding my cock, bouncing up and down for me."

I'm just about ready to faint from everything he's done and said, when he lifts his fingers and sucks on each one that'd been between my legs.

His eyes practically roll to the back of his head as he moans around each one. "So fucking delicious." Marcelo grabs his cock, rubbing his palm roughly against it before he adjusts himself. "Take a bra to put on now and give me the tag. But—" he snatches up all the underwear I'd brought into the dressing room. "Keep the panties *off*."

I do as I'm told, and getting dressed again as Marcelo goes to pay. Sliding *his* pants back on, I can't help but notice how much of a mess I already am. He's going to have so much of *me* on the crotch of his sweats, and knowing that makes me even more desperate for him. As we shop at the next few stores, I find myself still mad at him for stopping so suddenly—but, damn, he was right. It's making me *want* so much more.

As we shop, I find that I am *really*, continuously, drawn to black—black dresses, black skirts, black shorts. I've seen the way the "goth girls" dress in horror movies, and that style has always been so cool to me and now that I can *choose* how I want to look, it's what I'm finding the most appealing. Not to mention how short all the dresses and skirts I'm choosing are. Guess Mom was right, I am a slut.

Once I pick a few outfits, Marcelo makes me choose a few more, then grabs socks and pjs for me as well. At one point, while in one of the dressing rooms, Marcelo slips into the room behind the curtain. I'm trying on a pair of jeans—with underwear on—I decidedly hate, as he slips something into the butt pocket. His hand squeezes my ass around the object as he whispers in my ear, "So you can *always* reach me."

I pull it out to see he'd gotten me a phone.

"My number is already saved."

I stare at it blankly. "Why did you get this?"

"Every twenty-five year old needs a phone. But also, how am I supposed to call you if I'm, for some reason, not with you?"

I blink at him. How — how is this man . . .

"Why are you being so nice to me?" I mumble.

He shrugs. "I'm a priest. It's in the job description."

I squint my eyes at him. "But you're a bad priest?"

His gorgeous lips lift, a sly smile making him look dangerously handsome. He rubs his thumb along my bottom lip. "The absolute worst."

27
MARCELO

After getting everything June wanted, we grab a couple mall pretzels and head back to the car. June wears some of her new clothes, shoes that actually fit her, and a pair of sheer tights that make me desperately want to tear them apart. Fuck. Shoulda bought those in bulk. She looks too damn sexy in them.

Sliding into the bench seat, I turn the car on, blasting the heater, and tell her about my night.

"Daren? A cultist?" She raises an eyebrow. "I mean—the guy is evil, but I've never noticed anything like that. He goes to church every day with my mom since he's moved in," she explains.

I shrug. "I don't know for sure either, but it feels a little convenient. I think I have to check it out, if you're okay with that?"

June fidgets with her fingers. "Will I . . . have to see him?"

I grab her hands, holding them tight. "Not if I can help it."

She stares at our hands for a moment. "Okay." She nods. "Let's go."

The car thrums under us as I drive through the back roads of western Massachusetts. June is slouched in the seat, staring out the window as my music plays from the stereo. From the corner of my eye, I see June tapping her thigh to the beat.

"It's a love song," I tell her, raising the volume a little, the reggaeton beat vibrating through me just a little more. "He's talking about her body, and how she'll be the end of him."

She scoffed. "Sounds romantic."

I smirk. I love this sassy side of her. "*There would be no better way to die, with the beat of your heart in tune with your moans, as the last thing I hear,*" I translate. "In Miami's standards, this is probably the most romantic thing a guy could say." I laugh.

June laughs, and it sounds . . . so genuine, so different from anything I've heard coming from her. It sounds so free.

"What is Miami like? I've rarely left Belmouth, let alone Massachusetts."

"Hot. Sweaty. Palm trees everywhere." I settle further into the seat. "But it's also home. The salty, humid air, the loud shitty cars, the echoing base of reggaeton down every street—there's something different about it. Something I haven't seen in any other city or town I've been to. The nights are late, and the people are always so . . . *alive.* Parts of it are like the movies, yeah. But everyone also somehow knows everyone, and the little grandparents in the corner bakery will give you free coffee if they simply recognize your face."

I never miss home. Not really. At least, not cognitively.

But when I really think about it, Miami *is* home. It sings to my blood and calls to me when I'm gone for too long. I yearn for the gorgeous sunsets and horrible drivers, for the buttered *tostadas* and five a.m. dinner trips after a night of clubbing. For early mornings sunbathing in front of the ocean and naps on the beach.

"That sounds amazing. I'd love to see it someday."

"You should come with me next time I go."

June's eyes widen before another smile pulls at her lips. "I'd like that."

When we finally get back to Belmouth, I follow the path Daren took last night, trailing right back outside of the quiet town, and pulling over next to the *Welcome to Belmouth* sign. No cars linger around it now with it being the early afternoon—another good indicator that whatever happened last night was something secret, something nefarious.

As I shift the car into park, I turn to June. "Do you want to stay here?"

Her eyes are hard as she looks at me. "No way. I'm going with you."

I smirk, pinching her cheeks between my thumb and fingers. "Good girl. Remember, you're never leaving my sight."

Her plump lips capture my eyes, and with them pouted like this, they just look so . . . delicious. I pull her toward me, sliding across the bench to get closer to her.

June's breath shudders as I near her, but she doesn't pull away—instead, she opens her mouth just enough for me to pull her bottom lip between my teeth. A soft whimper rumbles in her throat as I suck on her lip, scraping it with my teeth. She tastes like cherries and coffee and salty pretzels.

Her lip falls from my mouth with a pop, but

immediately, she's on me. June pushes herself into me, crashing her lips to mine once again. Long fingers drag through my hair as she pulls me down to her. Her hot tongue finds mine as easily as breathing and it is everything I can do to not completely dissolve into her, become one with her. My hand falls to her waist and I pull her onto my lap, her ass warming my thighs.

The kiss the other night hasn't left my mind. It's been almost fifteen years since I've done such a thing, but kissing June feels like kissing for the very first time again. I told her I'd have no problem breaking my vows for her, and I was telling the truth, but a shred of guilt has followed me since. Yet, when I kiss her, every shred of guilt melts away and I can't help but fully give myself to her.

She kisses me as if she's starved. It's clumsy and her tongue doesn't quite know what to do once it collides with mine, and it drives me to absolute ferocity. I cup her face and slide my tongue across her lips, sucking her tongue into my mouth. I show her how to kiss me, how to take my lips, nibbling her to remind her to breathe.

I groan June's name into her mouth, moving my lips across her face, along her jaw, down her neck, pulling her closer, closer, closer—till I feel her soft warmth all over me.

"So fucking delicious," I huff, licking her neck. I want to leave marks all over her, kiss her till her lips turn blue, bruise her skin with hickeys, and show her how real affection feels.

June pulls away, her lips plump and red from my kiss, and her cheeks rubbed raw from my facial hair. She looks stunning, her eyes sparkling as she catches her breath.

"I could've been doing this my entire life?"

I chuckle, tucking the loose hair behind her ear. "You could've. But I'm happy you waited for me."

June instantly throws herself on me again, her lips warm as she kisses me with just as much ferocity as before.

My hand is entwined in June's as we traverse the woods, following the same path I took the other night. It's odd—the atmosphere is completely different today. The eerie shadows have been replaced with a pleasant breeze, the shadows of possible demons for colorful leaves. It is almost as though the woods changed overnight, became something else.

June and I cut through the trees, stepping over branches and dying foliage, as I follow the path Daren took last night.

"This is near where I lost him," I tell her.

"Where the imps swarmed you?"

I nod, pointing west. "It was a little farther down that way, but I felt them from here. Hell, I felt them the moment I entered the woods."

June studies the ground, her eyes moving from where we stand to a few feet ahead. "And they didn't follow him at all? Just you?"

Good point.

"So . . ." she says, and I can see the gears in her brain turning, putting pieces together. Pieces I may have not seen yet. "You were called here because of a demon infesting the church."

"A supposed demon, yes."

"And now there might be a cult involved."

"Correct."

"Is that normal?"

"Lately, yes. Cultist activity has been ridiculously high in the last few years. Most demonic sightings have been caused by summonings."

"So it's not out of the question that this . . . *cult*," she says it like a dirty word, "is what brought the demon to the church in the first place?"

I nod.

"And the imps you fought last night, they were protecting the cult." She meets my eyes. "Which means we're in the right place, going the right way."

"They wouldn't protect somewhere unimportant," I agree.

June bites her lip, her eyes falling. "Which means Daren *is* probably involved."

I squeeze her hand, letting her make the next connection herself.

"And which is possibly why I've been affected?"

I nod again. "I believe so."

She cringes, her eyes squeezing shut, but I quickly pull her into me. June thumps her head on my chest, leaving it there.

"I remember something from *that* night. It didn't really make sense then, but it's starting to."

I swallow hard, afraid to hear whatever she's about to tell me. "What is it?"

"He said something right after my mom left. '*He* said if I wait till the time is right, I can have you.' It was such a weird thing to say, it stuck out to me. But, obviously, I didn't really get any time to ask questions."

I squeeze her tighter, my jaw clenching. June is not something to be offered, not something to be given, and definitely not something to be taken—by anyone but me. I've stolen my little songbird. She is mine, and mine alone.

And she knows it.

June pulls back just a bit, but stays within the circle of my arms. She meets my eyes once more. The ghost of memories sweeping across her features is being shoved away, back into the box she keeps within herself.

The box I plan on destroying.

"Should we continue? We're in the right place," she asks, stepping back more.

But I grab her arm.

I want her to know who she belongs to. That she is mine, and mine alone. That being mine means she will forever be safe, that being mine means she doesn't have to fear the demons from her past, or the demons trying to find her now. That being *mine* means she is free.

"He can't have you, Junia." My voice dips as I squeeze her arm, reminding her she is here with *me*—not Daren. "Ever."

Reaching into my back pocket, I pull out her Salvation. June's eyes widen a bit, but as she pulls her lips between her teeth, I can see just how much she wants this—to be dominated, to be cared for, to be *mine*.

I feel the shift within myself, the shift from priest to . . . other. The depravity has been present since I touched her in the dressing room back in the mall, and again with her tongue down my throat in the car. And now, I want her tongue around my cock.

With the mask on, I meet June's eyes again. They're wide, and a sliver of fear traces the gray ocean of her irises. But there's also arousal and lust and *want*.

She wants to be dominated. It's all she's ever known. But to be dominated by someone who actually *cares*, who knows how to take care of her? It's the missing part of herself she's never had.

June takes another step back. She swallows, and a small smirk appears across her lips. Her back straightens, and a new-found confidence I've only seen a handful of times overtakes her.

"Why? Because I already belong to you?" she goads.

I take a step forward. "That's right."

"I'm not yours," she says. "Not until you *make* me yours." And without so much as another breath, June turns from me and runs deep into the woods.

28

MARCELO

It only takes me a moment to start chasing after her. But I know what she's doing. My little songbird *wants* to be chased after, to be caught. She wants me to claim her and force her to be mine.

I will give her just that.

Like a wolf chasing a small rabbit, I follow close behind her as she weaves between the trees. Her tits and ass bounce with each step, and it only drives me more wild to see her run from me. But I also let her run. I let her feel like she is just a step ahead of me.

A branch snags her foot, and as she crashes down, I'm on her. Straddling her thighs, I push her dress over her ass to see the glorious view of it in tights. She's still not wearing any underwear, as I had instructed, and it makes me want to weep from how fucking hot she is.

June struggles underneath me, and I give her ass a light smack. "Gotcha, songbird. Will you sing for me?"

"No," she spits back.

I flip her over and straddle her hips, letting her feel how hard my cock already is.

"What will it take?" I tease, roughly squeezing her tits in my palms. So fucking soft, and I can feel her hard nipples under the bra. I want to *see* them. I start slipping the coat she wears off her shoulder, the strap of her dress and bra with it.

"Marcelo," she barks. "If you want me to be yours, *make me* sing for you."

She wants me to fuck her in these woods.

And, God, do I want to. But I won't. Not here, not with Daren on her mind, not with her body as a consolation prize.

So no, I won't fuck her. But there are other ways to claim her.

I drag my thumb along her lips.

"Show me your tits," I demand. I back up a bit, bringing her into a seated position with me. She scowls at me, but I know it's an act—I can feel her body practically vibrating from adrenaline and excitement under me. June shrugs out of her coat, then I help her pull the dainty straps past her elbows and she removes them the rest of the way.

Still scowling at me, pouting those plump lips, she holds the dress to her chest.

"Show me, songbird." Yanking at the hemline, she lets me pull it down, along with the bra, to reveal her swollen, perfect tits. Her pink nipples are hard in the cold, and my hands instantly find them like a magnet, twisting the hardened pebbles. Her tits are heavy and full, and I can't help pressing my groin against them, feeling them against my cock.

I grab her chin and force her to look up at me, to look at the cross on my mask. "I want you to praise me, songbird. Worship me. Show me your devotion."

Her act falters as her eyes fall to my strained zipper. "I—I don't know how—" She looks up at me again through those thick dark lashes. "Will you guide me?"

I grunt, gripping her chin harder. "Yes."

She takes a deep breath, and the determination returns to her eyes, her lips set, and her eyes focused. Her fingers shake, just a bit, as they reach for my pants, unbuttoning and unzipping me.

"Good, now reach into my briefs and pull me free."

She does as I tell her, and a jolt of electricity sparks down my body the moment she touches my cock. Her hands are cold, but fuck, they feel better than the fantasies I've had of this. Her long fingers grip my shaft, her thumb dancing along a vein, as she pulls my cock out.

Immediately, June gasps. Her cheeks are so red, it's hard to say how much is from seeing me and how much is from the cold, but her lips pop open in shock as she studies me.

"This is supposed to fit inside of me?"

I chuckle. "Ideally. Take your time looking, *mi amor*."

Her fingers glide over me, her doe eyes widening further as she finds my piercings. She presses one of the metal balls, and it makes my cock twitch. June startles as I groan through another chuckle.

"Are priests allowed—" she starts, but I cut her off.

"Got them before. When I was nineteen. I heard they'd make sex great for both parties."

She blinks. "And . . . and do they?"

"Unfortunately, the healing process takes a long-ass time. Only got to try once before I took my vows."

"And?"

"And they did."

June licked her lips, her thumb still pressing gently into them.

"They'll feel good against your clit too," I tell her, working her up. "I can grind my cock against you, and these little balls will feel as though they were made to pleasure you."

Her breath grows shaky, and I know she's thinking about it—imagining it.

"All right, songbird, squeeze your tits around me," I demand.

She startles again, but does as I say.

"Fuck," I groan, and thrust into her, feeling the softness envelop me. "You feel so good." I thrust between her a few more times, but stop myself. It's amazing—too amazing—but it's not what I want from her right now.

I want her mouth on me.

Still on my knees, I shuffle back. Her tights are torn at the knee, the sight sending my cock twitching yet again.

"On your hands and knees, songbird. Come suck my cock."

June hesitates a moment, biting her lip before she swings her legs behind her and crawls to me. The sight of her tits hanging heavy nearly has me coming as she nears me, her ass in the air.

"Do I just . . . ?" she asks, her bottom lip quivering. I know she's nervous, but she literally cannot do anything to make this bad for me. She could sink her teeth into my cock and I'd still erupt just because she's touching me.

"I'll help you. Open your mouth nice and wide, *mi amor*." I pull her lip down. "Stick your tongue out, and remember to breathe through your nose."

As she does what I tell her, I guide my cock to her

mouth. The moment the tip of my head touches her sweet tongue, I nearly burst. June gasps around me, and it pulls another groan from my throat as my Jacob's ladder presses against her tongue.

"That's it, songbird," I praise. "You're doing so well already." I thrust my hips, letting her mouth get used to the size of my head, the girth of me, before I force more of myself on her. "Ready for more?"

She nods, crawling closer as she sucks more of me down. My hand tangles in her hair, and it takes everything in me not to force her to take all of me, to feel my cock in the back of her throat, to hear her sweet gags around me.

With my free hand, I pull her dress over her ass again and reach over, squeezing her in my palm.

She moans around me, and it sends my hips bucking farther into her mouth. "Fuck, June. You're so fucking good at this."

With one hand gripping the hair at the base of her neck and the other squeezing her ass, June takes initiative. She closes her lips around me, creating a suction that makes me see stars before my eyes, as she also starts using her tongue around me. It's hot and wet, and I can't help thrusting farther into her.

"Fuck yes, good girl," I push her head down my cock, hearing her gag. "Breathe, songbird."

June bobs her head—the ambitious little she-devil—sucking more and more of me down, her tongue wrapping around me.

Suddenly, I want to feel how wet she is, feel how much she's enjoying being used like this in the woods. My girl's got a kink for being in public, and at any moment, cultists or demons can walk up on us. I know she must be dripping, and her pretty little cunt is right there, for any stranger to walk up and see as she's on her hands and knees for me.

I move my hand, grabbing her ass and cup her pussy, finding exactly what I expected. She's soaked. June stiffens under me, her tongue pausing.

"Don't be embarrassed, songbird. I like how wet you get for me." I grind my fingers against her, letting the wetness seep from her tights. June squeezes her thighs together, and I desperately want to plunge inside of her, force her thighs open. Force that tight cunt to swallow me whole.

But her mouth is doing wonders for now and I can feel the heat coil in my gut, ready to blow all over her.

She pauses again, letting my cock fall from her mouth, as she moans from my fingers pressing against her again.

"Does your jaw hurt, *mi amor*?"

She nods, breathless.

"Let me help." With the hand tangled in her hair, I grip her jaw, massaging under her ear. "Just open wide for me. I'll do the rest. I'm already so close."

June does as she's told, sticking her tongue out.

I thrust my hips into her hot, wet mouth, massaging her jaw with each stroke.

I thrust my hips all the way to her lips, forcing my cock to hit the back of her throat. "I'm going to baptize you, Junia. You will be mine in body and soul, and I will cleanse your past, so you never have to be afraid, never have to fear being unwanted or uncared for. You are *mine*, Junia Forester, and I will make sure you know it."

June closes her lips around me again, sucking me as I thrust into her.

"Good fucking girl," I tell her. "Show me your mine. Use your tongue, baby." Curling her tongue around my head, and laying it flat against me, pressing into the piercings, I feel myself ready to come.

I thrust a few more times before—

"Ah, June," I moan, pulling out of her mouth just as I come hard, spilling myself all over her gorgeous fucking tits. Fifteen years—fifteen fucking years since I've allowed myself to come—and it was worth waiting every second so I could come for her.

She pants, sitting back on her calves, her tights stretching over her thick thighs. "I am yours, Marcelo." Her cheeks are still so red, even as she dips one hand between her thighs and rubs herself, letting her fingers gather her wetness. She pulls me closer and rubs her delicate fingers against the mask, pressing against my lips. "But you are just as much mine."

I chuckle under the mask before leaning back like she is. I take my thumb and, using my come, I draw a cross between her tits right where her heart pumps rapidly in her chest.

"And so I shall cleanse you in pleasure. Amen."

29
JUNE

My knees burn with each step. Dead leaves are tangled in my hair, my clothes are damp from being pinned to the ground, and as I shiver traversing deeper into the woods, it is the best I've felt in — ever. My body is electric. I feel like I could scale the tallest tree, climb the tallest mountain, and scream at my mother for all she's ever done to me.

Marcelo may have pinned me to the ground, fucked my mouth ruthlessly, and made an absolute mess of me, but by doing so, he has also shown me what it is like to be *seen*, to be cared for despite his intensity. Right after he came on me, he immediately pushed me back to the ground to examine my knees.

"These need to be cleaned," he said, but I didn't want them healed — not yet. I *want* to feel them. I want the physical reminder that he chased me, he caught me, and he claimed me. And if I get a few scars from it, oh well. Add them to the mess all over my back from belts over the years, the stretch marks along my upper thighs.

I did let him clean me up, using his jacket sleeve to wipe off the excess. He chuckled as he did so. "God, I haven't come in fifteen years. Sorry, it was a lot."

Resting my palm over his veiny hand, I smiled at him. "I wouldn't have known the difference between a lot and a little, anyway." Marcelo laughed again, and it took all my willpower—and my already aching knees—not to throw myself at him again. I'd happily suck his cock all night if he wanted me to, even if my jaw hurt, even if my knees bled, even if my pussy dripped down my thighs.

But once he pulled me to my feet, put my coat over my shoulders, and took my hand, I could tell by the shift in his body language that he was eager to keep searching for the cult. He left his mask on as he tread the woods with me, and I can't help but feel . . . safe. As if he's my super-hero, he'll fight all the demons that try to come for me. But more than that, I'm *his* now, and the cross on his mask isn't letting me forget.

I want him to drop everything and *really* claim me, fucking me till I bleed, till I scream his name through these woods, till I come all over his cock—my pussy is begging for it as I feel how wet I am with each step.

But if my demonic oppression has taught me anything, it's that I can wait to get off. Waiting sometimes is half the fun.

"How do we know we're following his path?" I ask, trying to keep up as my knees burn.

"We don't. Not really. But wherever he went has to be in these woods."

The woods aren't big. I can already see the light of

another road at the far end beyond the treeline, and we haven't been walking for all that long.

"Wouldn't we have seen—"

Thunk. I yelp as my foot slightly gives way and grab onto Marcelo immediately, wrapping myself around his arm.

We both look down to see a metal hatch, large enough to look like basement doors. Leaves are brushed over it, almost *too* conveniently, as if they were placed there on purpose.

"Well, looks like you found it." He pulls me off the trapdoor and sits on his haunches, examining it.

"Are you going to open it?"

Reaching in his pocket, he pulls out a small vial and dabs it onto the metal. Immediately, the metal sizzles.

"Acid?" I ask, crouching down too.

"Holy water."

My mouth falls open, watching the liquid simmer into bubbles before completely dissolving as if being burned away. "So . . . demons."

He nods. "And a cult. Fuck." Marcelo stands, kicking the leaves around him as he scratches the back of his head, breathing deeply. With his back turned to me, he pulls out his phone, dials a number, and puts it to his ear.

"*Hola? Padre? Si—puta madre, es un cult.* It's a long story, but I just found—yeah. Okay. Tell Rowan I'll call him in a bit."

He hangs up the phone and turns back to me. His fist tightens on the phone, gripping it like it's a stress ball. "We have to get out of here. Now."

My eyebrows pinch. "We don't have to go down there? What if we're wrong?"

"We're not wrong. But I told you I'd keep you safe, and

that is exactly what I'm doing. I'm *not* taking you down there."

I stand and step forward. "Keep me safe but also do your job. I don't want to stop you." I grab his hand. "You said you would stop me from having to see Daren. I highly doubt he's down there—not when he's probably still at the church with my mom."

Marcelo clenches his jaw, his eyes lingering on our entwined fingers before moving to the metal hatch.

"The *first* sign of danger and I'm carrying you out. Got it?"

I nod, excitement pumping through me. I feel like . . . like Indiana Jones or something, traveling through caves in search of treasure—or in this case, demons.

Marcelo throws the hatch open, the leaves cascading around us as the smell of wet dirt and—

"Frankincense!" I blurt.

He turns to me, and I hear him smelling the air through the thick mask. "Does the church have a basement?"

I think for only a moment. "Not that I know of."

Grabbing my face, he forces me to look at him, at the cross. "June, stay right next to me."

Nodding, I say, "I will."

Marcelo's hand trails along the back of my neck, his thumb sliding between the rosary and my skin. Carefully, he pulls the cross out from my dress and lets it fall over my coat as he takes another deep breath, shrugs out his shoulder, and finally swings himself over to descend the ladder into darkness.

I follow right behind him, trying hard not to think about how easy it'd be for him to see my ass again, how all he'd have to do was look up. God, I *want* him to see my ass again.

Once he reaches the ground, his hands quickly find my waist, and he eases me the rest of the way. The underground path is lit by lanterns lining the wall, similar to that of old mines or caves. It's narrow as can be, packed with dark dirt, and I can't make out the end of the path—it just looks like it goes on forever.

Marcelo takes my hand again and guides me forward. I keep my free hand wrapped around his upper arm, just in case. It's colder down here than it was in the woods, goosebumps lining my skin. All I hear are our footsteps on the packed ground and my beating heart.

It feels like one of the horror movies we watched last night, like something will run at us from the end of the dark hallway, sharp teeth ready to rip our faces off, eyes unblinking. I can't shake the image, even as Marcelo rubs his thumb over the back of my hand, even though I know I'm safe with him.

At least, I *hope* I'm safe with him. I don't know anything about demons—Hell, I barely know anything about Marcelo. How long has he been an exorcist? This isn't his first case, is it?

Suddenly, my masked man is a total stranger again. In my soul I know he'll do what he can, but . . . what can he do compared to a literal *demon*?

"June," he whispers, and I nearly jump out of my skin at the hushed sound. "I can feel your mind spiraling." He jerks his arm, making me realize just how tightly I'm holding on to him. "We can still go back if you're scared."

He pauses to look over his shoulder at me, the jagged white cross illuminated as if it were backlit in this dark space. I can't see his eyes, but I know they're on me, waiting for me to say something—to answer him. I also know he'd do anything I ask him to do right now. But . . . with the cross on me like this, somehow I feel calmer. This isn't just a stranger in a mask. It's *Marcelo*, my masked man, my Salvation. He's already proven to me he can protect me from demons when he pulled me from that hallway all those days ago.

"I'm fine," I tell him. "Just a little scared."

"We'll just see where this goes, and get out of here." Marcelo pats my hand and continues down the long hall. We walk for several long minutes before a door finally comes into view at the end of the hall. It's large and wooden, with old, black iron decorating the door with a large symbol in the center.

Marcelo stops, tilting his head as he studies the symbol as well.

Slowly, we progress forward. The door is old—very old. Mold has grown within the cracks, making it weak, as the iron has rusted in some parts. Tentatively, Marcelo lifts his hand, but before he can even touch the wood, the door creaks open.

Almost as if it's *inviting* us within.

"This is the part of the horror movie where someone usually dies," I whisper, swearing I see the ghost of a smile tilt the mouth of his mask up.

"Shh, songbird," he chides, his voice light.

We creep through the door, and on the other side is a room completely made of gray stone. Or, rather, *remade*.

This is definitely a basement, but not under the church.

Marcelo huffs, "Where the Hell are we?"

"We're—we're in the old convent." I realize as the words spill from my tongue. "The one that burned down in the eighties. They've never built anything on top of it, and . . . maybe this is why."

The room is vast and freezing cold; the stone clutching

onto the frigid air like a vice. But it's also completely bare. There's no sign a cult would meet here—it looks like nothing has touched these walls in the forty-something years since the fire.

"Look," Marcelo says, pointing out a set of stairs at the other end of the room. "A building that's been abandoned for years wouldn't smell as though someone was recently burning incense. Someone has been here. And I bet, whatever they were doing, it was up those steps." He squeezed my hand. "Are you ready?"

I take a deep breath and nod. Then I follow him up the stairs and into the next room. As I climb the final step, a gasp lodges in my throat, my entire body being doused in imaginary ice water.

The room looks like a small chapel, filled with pews and a small sanctuary in the front of the room. But what surprises me isn't the presence of a worship hall in the convent. But what's *inside.* More symbols are painted on the walls, the floor, every piece of furniture—in what looks like blood. Half-melted candles line the space, an altar standing at the front of a room just before a bed of stone. Above the altar sits a painting—a silhouette of something . . . inhuman. Tall, red, with a hunched back and hoof-like feet, a crown of wire rests on the creature's head, broken up by two large horns not unlike the black shadow figure I saw in the hallway the other day. Though, these horns aren't curved—they twist into spirals, pointing straight up.

This *isn't* the demon from the church.

"What—" I take a step and, suddenly, the air is tight in my throat—almost heavy and thick, as if it's more like water than oxygen. My legs don't budge, a weight thrown over my shoulders, rooting me in place.

I try to move, but my body doesn't listen to me—my

fingers won't even twitch. All I can do is rapidly blink and look all around me, look for what is watching me, look for what is haunting me.

"I feel it too," Marcelo grunts. "It's the—"

A few feet away, as if my thoughts themselves summoned him, the shadowy figure emerges from the darkness—*with* the darkness—in the corner of the room. Like before, it's tall with broad shoulders, and I once again see the essence of curled horns atop its head—*very* different from the one in the painting. But due to the shadows all around him, I can't make out a single other feature. No eyes, no mouth, nothing—save for the fact this demon isn't red. He's made of shadow and darkness—charcoal grays and midnight blacks.

Marcelo's hand tightens in mine, the rosary at my chest beginning to rattle. His body tenses, his shoulder slowly moving in front of me.

The black shadow shifts and flows, raising what looks like an arm, a long finger pointing directly at us.

A noise like nails on a chalkboard, like a metal fork on a porcelain plate, like metal rubbing against metal, screeched through the empty room.

"GET OUT."

We haul ass back to Belmouth, the Mustang speeding down winding roads as the sun has begun to stretch to the horizon, painting the sky in golds and oranges—yet through the kaleidoscope of color, I cannot get the black figure out of my mind.

A true demon. Not an imp. And this is the third time I've seen him. Based on his horns alone, I'd say he's of the upper echelon. Maybe even a—

No. I don't let myself think about it. The *idea* of it is enough to end entire nations.

The convent, I tell myself. *Focus on the convent.* It's the first real lead I've had since my songbird.

June hasn't stopped shaking since we got back in the car, her knees once again red and raw from the mad dash we made back through the tunnel, the woods. Her fingers are clutched around my mask, taken off and discarded the moment we got to the car. But now she uses it as a crux, holding it for dear life. I place my hand on her thigh, squeezing to bring her back to me. She jolts and turns to me.

"You okay?"

She swallows, once again locking her eyes on the road before us. "Just . . . processing."

After I park the car in the St. Mary's parking lot, I send a text to Rowan.

> *Me: Find everything you can on that burned down convent and call me as soon as you find anything.*

Immediately, he responds.

> *Rowan: On it. Call you tomorrow. Don't do anything stupid.*

I roll my eyes. My definition of stupid is *very* different from Rowan's, and I fully believe every decision I've ever made would be deemed stupid in his eyes.

"Can . . ." June mumbles as I shove my phone back in my pocket. I turn to her, resting my arm on the back of the bench seat and the other on the wheel. "Can we sit in the sanctuary for a bit?"

I smile. "Of course."

June heads inside the main door as I take all the shopping bags back to the cathedral's apartment. As soon as I open the back door to enter, the small black fuzz ball dashes past my leg, escaping into the night. I know he'll be back in a few hours, scratching at the wood and meowing. It's what he's done for three days now.

Putting the bags in the bedroom, I sigh, scratching out

my hair. Another long fucking day here, and somehow even more confused.

I zip my hoodie up, and leave the apartment, walking through the hall to meet up with June, when Father Callum exits one of the doors in the hall. He turns to me, a smile lighting his lips.

"Ah, Father Marcelo. We missed you this morning." The man stops, steepling his hands in front of him as the door to another small office is ajar behind him, revealing books and tomes typical in a cathedral.

"I had a few errands to run."

He raises a hand. "All good."

"Actually, Father, I wanted to speak with you."

Callum raises his brows, then motions for me to follow him into the office he was just in. Instead of sitting at the desk, he sits at a small side table, pulling out a chair for himself and indicating for me to sit across from him.

"I've actually wanted to speak to you as well, Father Marcelo. I wanted an update on the search, if you've seen anything. I feel so sorry I haven't had much time to help you or give you the full rundown."

Sitting, I say, "It's actually what I wanted to discuss as well." I'm skeptical of Callum. A cult in his town—a cult he either didn't tell me about by choice, or doesn't know about. And considering this priest has been living here for at least twenty years, according to June, then only one of these options seems plausible.

"In honesty, Father, I don't know what's going on. Members of the parish are . . . different. This was a peaceful town with kind people. Now, I look at their faces and everyone is . . . warped."

"How so?" I lean back in the chair. Men love to speak. They love to *tell*. So, I'll let Callum speak, I'll let him tell me what he knows—what he *thinks* he knows.

"Take the Foresters. I know you've become close with Junia—" he pauses, his eyebrows kneading together in the center as his eyes reach mine. "She hasn't come in a few days. Do you know if she's all right?"

I nod. "She is."

He sighs, "Good. Her mother is a prime example of what I mean. She's an . . . interesting woman. An interesting Catholic, if I'm being honest. She's been coming to the church for years, and her choice of partners has always been questionable. She's been through divorce, which the church does acknowledge, but Daren, her fiancé—I don't like the way he looks at her. I don't like the way he looks at June."

Callum watches my face. "You've noticed, no?" he asks.

"I have."

"Well—" he sighs again. "I have refrained from telling you. Maybe I'm not a great Catholic either. I am letting my pride get to me. I do not want the church to revoke my priesthood, and possibly more threatening, I do not want the church to think less of me." He places his hands on the table, fiddling them back and forth. "But I have noticed the brewings of something strange in this town. And in that time, the demons have come."

Feigning ignorance, I tilt my chin and raise an eyebrow. "What have you noticed, Father?"

"I believe there might be . . . rituals or *something*. A group— a group that came together to summon that demon."

"A cult?"

He licks his lips and shrugs. "I don't know what to call it, but perhaps. Last night, I was . . . out late." He groans and blesses the lord before biting his lip. "I have more vices than just pride, Father. I also seem to worship false idols . . ."

Once again, I wait to let him explain.

"I like the bottle a little too much. At first it began with a . . .

need to be close to God. I felt closer once I drank the blood of Christ. But wine is not my only poison now. Anyway, last night, I went to the store to buy more, and as I was walking back I saw a number of cars—Daren's included. I think Daren is a part of it." I find myself believing him. Not only is he telling me things that *could* get his priesthood revoked, but he also smells of stale alcohol, and his flesh has a strange sag to it that only comes with excessive alcohol use. Father Callum is just a sad man, married to the church, but trying his damned best in this fucked up world. He licks his lips again, and I can't help but wonder if Callum is wishing he currently had another bottle with him. "And, worse," he coughs, "I believe he is trying to use June for it."

Now I am surprised. "How?"

Callum leans forward. "The demon has been apparent since Daren began living with the Foresters. In that time, Junia has become even more subdued. She comes to Mass limping more often than not. I've caught glimpses of scars on her legs. She retreats to her organ more and more often, and she is more timid—more jumpy—than ever before. As a child, Junia was so bright, so joyous, singing louder than all the other children in the choir."

I imagine my little songbird, and I know that child is still within her—just hidden away, forced to retreat and hide behind an iron gate.

"Well," I say. "She's safe now."

Callum looks up at me. "She's with you?"

"Yes."

Callum clenches his jaw, and I immediately feel my body tense, as he clears his throat and raises a brow. "Well, Father Marcelo, last night, I also saw your car."

I can't help but burst with a laugh. "You did indeed. I followed Daren." I cross my arms over my chest. "Like you, Father, I am not a perfect Catholic. That man *hurt* June. I had half a mind to *hurt* him. That's when I saw all the cars from *your* church. That's when I followed them and saw them congregate. That's when I saw the demons protecting their hideout in the woods."

I keep the convent a secret. Whether he's involved or not, he doesn't need to know I'm aware of it yet.

Callum sighs in relief, his shoulders slumping. "I guess I should've known better."

"What else can you tell me about that . . . congregation."

"That's all I know, really. I can give you the names of the men I saw yesterday."

"That'll be a good start."

After Callum scurries around the room to grab paper and jot down the names, he sits and again goes over everything he knows. Which isn't much. He's seen shadows, and he thinks there is a group of men at the church that are meeting up.

I stand, thinking of June waiting all alone in the sanctuary, desperate to be by her side again, to sooth her worries.

As I start to walk to the door, excusing myself, Callum calls behind me. "Also, do you think you will be able to assist me in confessionals tomorrow before Mass? I had a few special requests for it today, but with the after-Mass festivities, I just couldn't get to it." He smiles. "Maybe it'll even give you some insight into the parish. Maybe someone knows something I don't."

I'm still not totally convinced he's innocent, but I can't pin what Callum's goal of being part of a cult would even be. He's already a man in a high place, he confessed to sins he could've kept to the grave, and he seems to be genuinely concerned for his parish.

"Of course, Father."

31

MARCELO

s I enter the sanctuary, my eyes immediately find
June. Her big doe eyes are trained up at the crucifix, and I see her lips moving, her hands clasped
together as she kneels at a pew. I wince thinking about her
already-hurt knees and how they must feel now.

"Sorry that took long," I say, announcing my presence.
"I spoke to Father Callum for a bit."

Her eyes light up when she looks at me, and I realize
what I would do to have her always look at me that way.

"It's okay," she says. "I think I needed a minute anyway."

I slump in the pew next to her as she eases back into the
seat. My thigh touches hers, her arm against mine. She's
still so cold, but at least she's not shaking anymore.

"This might sound odd—" she begins.

I huff a laugh. "June, we just faced down a demon
together. I don't think anything could be odd between us."

She smirks at me. "Well, while we were in the tunnel, I realized I don't really know anything about you."

"Shit." Chuckling, I sit back. "I've been mostly on the road for fifteen years. I think I must've forgotten how to make friends."

She smiles, but it doesn't reach her eyes. "I stopped having friends after high school. Once we graduated, they all went on to college—left this small, shitty town. While I was stuck here." She sighs. "So, I think I forgot too."

"Then," I start, "maybe we can work on it together."

She turns to me, placing her hand on my thigh. "I think . . . I think that'd be nice."

I swallow. It's been so long since I've told anyone about . . . about my parents. But I've seen June on what I could only hope was the worst day of her life. I've seen her naked, I've let her use me just as she's let me use her. I've brushed away her tears, and cleaned her wounds, and shown her the real side of me no one has seen besides my little family of misfits in Miami.

I want to tell her about them. I want to tell her about *me*, and how they are the reason I am all that I am today.

But . . . I don't think I can relive that night.

Turning my palm up on my knee, I wait till she entwines her perfect, dainty fingers in mine. It fuels me like a car on empty, like a battery completely depleted.

"My parents and older sister died when I was fourteen. I've lived so long blocking out the memory of that night, I can't conjure the details."

She gasps and her fingers squeeze mine in an instant. Rubbing the back of her palm with my thumb, a corner of my mouth twitches up.

"It's okay. It was a long time ago." I meet June's eyes again, the dark blue already misty with unshed tears. "I didn't believe in demons growing up. Ghosts, sure. What kid doesn't? But demons? They were the obsession for the wholly devout. While we went to church every week, it wasn't really ingrained in our life like it was yours." I rub my thumb along the back of her palm again, her soft skin grounding me. "But . . . that changed. A demon . . . a demon killed . . . " The words lodge in my throat, unwilling to come out as flashes of memory cloud my mind. Blood, my father's dark brown eyes turned a hideous orange, my mother crying and begging with blood on her hands, my sister's body bent in ways I struggle to recreate even in my mind.

My jaw is locked, teeth grinding, as if they, too, know the words that threaten to spill will ruin me.

June's warm palm cups my chin, pulling my face toward her once more, her other hand still squeezing in mine.

"You don't have to continue. Not if it hurts this much." She smiles, and something about it breaks my heart. I *want* her to know, so why can't I tell her? "Sometimes," she says, her eyes shifting back and forth between mine. "Sometimes, it's harder to remember, harder to focus on *what* happened instead of just knowing *something* happened." A knowing, sad smile curves her lips as she releases a shuddery breath. "I'm grateful you told me something happened, and if that's all you can tell me, that already is more than enough."

June—June, June, June.

I don't even know when it happened, but I have undoubtedly, wholly, fallen for this woman. I've been obsessed with her from the moment I saw her—and I knew it was lust, but I also knew it was so much more too. I knew love could spark from that obsession, and the more she sees *me*, the more that love wraps its glorious, delicate claws around my throat and keeps me in a chokehold.

I lean toward her, slowly, my lips desperate to feel her as they're drawn to her own. The kiss is soft and tender, her plump lips open with mine pressed against them, warming my soul as the breath is pulled from my lungs.

"Thank you," I hum against her lips, and I feel the smile in her kiss.

Her smile lights my soul brighter than any hellfire.

I'll tell her, I promise myself, *but not tonight.*

Tonight, my wicked mind is conjuring other plans as I slowly kiss her. I told her this morning to keep her panties off, and the image of her wet pussy in those sexy little tights as she sucked me down her throat still clings in my mind. I want it. I want *her*.

"You've been *such* a good girl today, June," my voice rumbles against her, as she quivers against me. "You deserve a reward."

She releases a shuddering breath into my mouth, and her body goes taut in my arms.

"A—a reward?"

"Mhm," I hum, smirking at the goosebumps my voice gives her.

As I trail my lips along her jaw, I feel her lips fall open. But she doesn't speak right away, she hesitates. "Here?"

My perfect little songbird. Instantly, I know she is asking in fear—and hope. She wants to be taken advantage of in public, and I can sense the thrill of being caught in a *church* of all places running through her racing mind.

God, I can't even imagine how wet she must be from the idea alone, my little exhibitionist.

"Yes, here." I pull away from her, far enough to see her perfect, terrified face. "I want to bend you over these pews and eat your pussy while you scream for our Lord."

The moment the words register in her mind, the instant

her cheeks turn that adorable shade of pink, I'm pulling June over my lap and shoving her forward, bending her over just as I said I would. Her legs are just long enough to bend against the back of the bench in front of us, her glorious big ass in my face.

Nearly falling forward, she slams her hands on the seat of the bench in front of us, holding herself up as she faces the sanctuary of the church.

"My perfect little church girl. Ready to pray for me?"

"Marcelo," she nearly moans. "A—Are you sure this is okay?" June looks over her shoulder at me, her eyes pleading, *begging* it to be okay.

Sliding my hand up the back of her thigh, the material of the sheer tights under my palm stirring my cock to life, I round her ass and push the hem of the dress over it, baring her to me.

I pause. "Do you want this?"

June sucks her bottom lip between her teeth. "S—so much has happened today. The demon—and you were just—" she pauses. "And Father Callum is still here."

I press my nose into her ass cheek, feeling its roundness against my lips. It's so fucking soft and squishy, so grabbable. I open my mouth and press my teeth into it, biting her ass. A whimper escapes her, but she presses her ass into my face rather than pulls away.

Releasing my teeth, I meet her starry eyes once more. "Do. You. Want. This?" I repeat.

June presses her lips together and nods. "Yes."

32

JUNE

I feel so . . . dirty. Not just for what we're doing—but physically filthy. We've been out *all* day, no underwear, I've been wetter than I ever have, I ran through a forest, and now I'm here. With his face pressed against my ass, ready to do things to me I've only ever fantasized about.

The bite still stings, but I want him to bite me more. I want him to leave marks all over my thighs, my ass—the idea of my rear bruised and marked by *him* has my knees already wobbling.

As if he could read my mind, Marcelo bites me again, sinking his teeth into the curve where my thigh meets my butt. I yelp, feeling his sharp canines poke and his blunt molars press into me. But I also feel his tongue swirl on the flesh in the middle, and the moment his teeth loosen, his tongue and lips are on the bite marks, soothing them with languid licks and kisses.

"You're so fucking hot, June." His hand slides up the back of my thigh again, making my entire spine straighten as goosebumps follow his warm palm. "So fucking sexy. And all for me."

His hot breath engulfs my already over-heating pussy as he draws near, and it takes everything in me not to buck away from him—or worse, buck my hips right into him.

"You have plagued every thought in my mind since I've met you, Junia Forester. Every waking moment, every stirring dream. You have made me realize who I am more in the few days we've been together than all my years wearing that mask or this collar."

Marcelo presses his lips directly on the wide seam of my tights, right over my waiting clit.

"In just a few days, you have become my Devil and my God, and I want nothing more than to worship the ground you walk on. To sing your praise whenever you're in my sight. I want nothing more than to baptize myself in the pleasure of you and be reborn as a man made for worshiping you."

Hot and wet. Those are the first feelings to cross my mind. Then utter bliss. His tongue presses into the tights, starting at my clit as he flicks the seam back and forth, teasing me just before he languidly drags his tongue up my slit and licks me completely.

I moan immediately, my arms giving up, and I bend over the pew even deeper, giving him more access. His fingers dig into my hips as he licks me again, nibbling the back of my thigh, nibbling my swollen lips.

"God, it feels good," I moan.

"Don't tell God, tell me."

He bites me hard.

"*Marcelo!*" I hiss and moan all at once.

Immediately, he licks where he bit, soothing the plumped, swollen skin. "Fuck, I want more. You taste so fucking good, so sweet." His hands fumble around my ass, squeezing and groping along the way, as he reaches for the waistline of my tights. Digging his fingers under the waist, he yanks them down, pulling my hips back into his face. Marcelo licks me feverishly, yanking the tights farther and farther over and down my ass, revealing my wet pussy to him, till they're all the way down to my knees.

The cold church air is like an ice bath against my hot center, and as I feel Marcelo's hungry eyes on me, I clench my thighs together.

"No," he demands, smacking at my swollen lips. I shriek another moan, jolting forward. The smack vibrated right to my clit, setting me on fire. "Don't hide away from me. Let me see you. Let me see *everything*."

His thumb pokes and prods my upper thighs, pulling them apart and squeezing. He jiggles his hands so my ass shakes in his face, and from over my shoulder, I see just how enamoured he is with me, as his eyes are glued to everything being presented to him right now.

"I know you shaved for me—for that night—but do you often shave?" he asks, startling me. His finger grazes the mound between my thighs, running over small cuts and razor bumps.

"N—no. This was my first time shaving. I—I thought you might like it more."

"I do like it. But only if you do too. I'd like you anyway." He hums again as drives his fore and middle finger between my slit and splits me open. "Fuck. I love the sight of you. You big pussy lips, your swollen clit. It's so fucking sexy."

Marcelo doesn't give me a second to respond as he

immediately presses his lips between his fingers, sucking my clit into his mouth.

"Ah," I yelp, back stiffening once more. He sucks my clit harder and harder, his tongue licking it up and down. His coarse facial hair rubs against my mound, pressing into my skin in all the right ways. I'm about to see stars when he finally pulls away from me with a loud, resounding *pop*.

"Like honey," he breathes.

His fingers slide from their spot, and instead anchor onto my lower ass cheeks, his thumbs prying apart my lips as wide as they'd go.

"I worship thee," he groans, and he completely devours me. His tongue is everywhere, his teeth scrape places that have never been touched by another person—never been *seen* by another person—his lips suck and kiss, and I just know those marks I so desperately wanted are being left on me with each touch. A coiling heat swirls in my lower tummy as my toes curl in their boots and I have never felt so exposed, so mortified, and so horribly, wickedly, turned on.

"So fucking wet for me, my sweet honey," Marcelo grunts between licks. "Such a delicious feast you make."

The wood of the pew digs into my stomach, almost hurting now, but it doesn't matter—nothing matters. Not when his tongue feels this good.

"Are you going to sing for me, songbird?" His tongue laps my pussy again, and I know he's drinking in every single drop of me.

"Ah—yes!"

He licks and licks, occasionally breaking his rhythm by sucking my clit into his mouth, and each time it nearly sends me to my knees. But it feels too good to give up.

Worship me, I beg in my mind, *worship me, worship me, worship me!*

And he does. His hands pull me to him, his tongue taking everything I give him, and as I edge the precipice of ecstasy, he holds me tight, sucking me through each shuddering moan and rapid breath.

His teeth graze my clit, and it lurches me over the cliff as I come all over his face.

33

MARCELO

My perfect, sweet, delicious songbird. Fuck. I can't get enough of her. I lap every delicious drop of her as she comes on my tongue, drinking her sweet honey as she shudders in my grasp. Hearing her sing my name makes my cock ache with pleasure. I think about just how easy it'd be to simply stand and shove myself inside of her tight pussy, to break her hymen and have her virgin blood on my cock, to hear her scream for me louder than ever before.

But this was a reward *for her*. A show of worship as I fucked her with my tongue in the church, her eyes on the crucifix. And to show for that worship, I'll sacrifice my own pleasure, my own need.

I ease June back onto my lap, and she immediately slumps back against me. Her breath is ragged and her bottom lip is swollen from how much she bit it.

"Let's get you cleaned up," I whisper in her ear, so tempted to touch her pretty cunt again and feel my spit on her.

Instead, I cup her jaw and pull her lips toward mine, sliding my tongue against hers. She sucks it into her mouth, tasting herself on me.

As I pull away, I smirk. "See? Just like honey."

June is knocked out in my bed, Diablo once again curled against her. The bastard was scratching at the back door the moment June stepped out of the bathroom, fresh and clean in her new pajamas. She looked so damn sexy in the black teddy, it took everything in me not to rip it right back off of her. But the moment she heard the cat, it seemed like all sexual thought left her brain, and all she wanted to do was cuddle the damned fuzzball.

Diablo even sat between us on the couch as we watched our nightly ghost hunting show and ate leftover pizza.

"I'm a little sleepy." June yawned, and I knew she was definitely more than *a little* sleepy. We had a long fucking day, and even I was exhausted.

"Let's go to bed," I said, turning to look at her. It was the first time we'd sleep in there—we'd both fallen asleep on the couch every night since she's been here. I also knew *this* was the reason she wore that adorable little teddy. June *wanted* to share my bed.

The cuddling was fucking fantastic. Her soft skin pressed against me, warming every inch of my body, it was enough to make a man weep. And more than enough to fuel my energy through the next week. With my cock pressed against her ass, my hand so close to her perfect tits, I'm finding it difficult to properly sleep. But laying here, with her, is enough. More than enough.

Her soft breaths are like a symphony, and combined with Diablo's purrs, it truly feels like I've died and gone to Heaven. I still can't believe how much my little songbird has come out of her shell. There is so much more to her than initially meets the eye: she's smart and thoughtful—incredibly sweet and funny. Her love of horror and for that damned cat, her lust, her kinks, that spicy little attitude she gets when she's teasing me, even her fears—it all has come together to define this woman. I don't even think she has realized how much of herself she's revealed to me, how much she has blossomed in just these few days away from her mother.

She was always more than her mother's little shadow, but now she's finally embracing that.

I haven't told her about being needed in church tomorrow. I don't know how she'd feel about returning, even if she hides away with me in the confessional. I can't imagine she wants to even see her mother or Daren, but I also don't want to sneak away in the morning and leave her to wake up alone.

June shifts in my arms, wiggling her ass just a little, and the simple motion reignites the hard-on I've had for what feels like hours. All day. Since I met her.

I kiss her shoulder, sucking her skin between my teeth to leave yet another mark on her, but she doesn't stir. Her soft breaths are heavy with sleep, and I know my little songbird is totally out.

A wicked thought crosses my mind yet again.

I could do anything to her right now. Everything. And

she wouldn't even know. My hips twitch, rubbing my cock along her ass cheek, just next to the seam of her new underwear. Black, lacy, cheeky—that's how the store described them—and *fuck*, are they cheeky. Her thick, smooth thighs are so fucking warm, I can't even imagine how'd they feel on my bare skin. The idea makes me want to combust, want to . . .

Makes me want to pull my cock out and fuck her right here as she sleeps. How hard can I thrust inside of her till she wakes up? How wet can I make her before she bats those pretty eyes at me? Will she scream when she sees my cock covered in her come, her blood? I know she'd like it. I know how desperately she wants it.

But I want to see her eyes when I push myself inside her for the first time, I want to see her face as I force myself into her tight cunt, to see her eyes roll back as the pain and pleasure take over and she gives herself to me.

And yet, despite that desire, I still want something. *No—I* need *something.*

I pull my cock out and kick off my pants—I don't know why I even bothered sleeping with clothes on when I knew it would always come to this. Her soft skin is drawing me in, driving me mad, and I want so much more of it.

I position my cock between her thighs, the drop of precum marring her perfectly smooth skin as my head throbs against her. June's soft thighs make me groan, and I can't help myself as I squeeze my dick between them, grinding against her pussy. She squirms, just a little bit, but grinds her ass against me, her body welcoming my touch. Fucking her thighs is almost as hot as her lips wrapped around me, its soft and plush but so fucking sexy, and the more I press into her clit, the more wet my songbird becomes.

June releases a breathy moan, and I pray she's dreaming of me touching her, tainting her, loving her. I've been dying to let her feel my piercings she seems so interested in, to rub the ladder against her clit, to let her grind on me till she's dripping down the length of my cock, only to plunge it into her—but this angle isn't letting me do that. So, instead, I saw myself between her plump pussy lips and grind myself on her clit. Fuck, it feels good as her panties get damp, her come seeping through and making lube for my cock.

My hands roam her soft skin, fingers slipping under her nightgown as I grope her, squeezing her nipples between my fingers as hard as I can. I cup her tits, wanting desperately to fuck them too, to drive my dick between them and watch as I come all over them.

"Wake up," I beg. "Wake up and let me fuck you."

But her deep breaths tell me she's still fast asleep.

I don't know if I can keep holding myself back. My cock needs to know what she feels like, how tight she is. Sliding her panties to the side, I continue sawing myself between her. I shudder a moan into her ear as I feel just how wet she is, my cock smoothly sliding through her folds—and as my head pushes against her clit, grinding into it, June moans and rocks into me, her sleeping body begging for more, more, more.

Fuck it. I know she wants it just as bad as I do.

I pull her hips toward me, angling my cock at her entrance. She's so wet, so ready for me. I can't wait to hear more of her beautiful moans, those soft little whimpers.

I can't wait to hear her sing.

I throw myself back, falling from the bed, the blanket tangled around my waist coming with me. I crash against the wall, my ass already hurting from hitting the floor. *Fuck.*

June jolts upright, her eyes wide as they search for me in the dark room, as Diablo skitters away.

"Oh my God, are you okay?" She crawls toward me, and I have to lift a hand to tell her to stop as I desperately try to catch my breath.

It was another vision. Another *fucked up* vision.

"Fuck," I groan and push myself to standing. The blanket slumps to the floor, and I'm surprised to see I still have my sweats on. June is watching me, her eyebrows knit together as she bites her lip.

"What happ—"

"The demon," I grunt out, cutting her off.

Finally, she sits back on her feet. My eyes linger on those milky thighs, even thicker now that they're in this position. If my twisted imagination hadn't just happened, I'd be in complete awe of her like this, so beautiful even half asleep.

But my lingering desire to ravage her and take that sweet purity she has kept for so long kind of sours the mood.

I scratch the back of my head and gaze around the room before I toss the blanket back onto the bed.

"Go back to sleep, songbird." I crawl onto the bed and gently push her shoulders back so she lies down once more. "I'm going to go for a walk to clear my mind."

June grabs my arm. "I can go with you."

I smile and kiss her forehead. "No, *mi amor*. I woke you up. Try to get some more sleep and I'll be right back."

She pouts, but after I rub her arm for just a moment more, she nods and lets me tuck her back under the covers.

Once I hear her breath return to that deep rhythm, I ease off the bed and throw a hoodie on and grab the silver rosary off June's night table.

The demon has to be near if he forced his influence on me. And I'm going to find him.

34

JUNE

I'm dreaming. I know I am as I still feel Marcelo's lingering touch on my arm, still feel the ghost of his presence next to me. But I'm not in bed, I'm not in his apartment in the church—I don't even think I'm in Belmouth.

I am . . . elsewhere. Other. Nowhere, maybe.

No, no—I am somewhere. *As the fog begins to clear in the dream, I slowly recognize things I've seen before. Stone, gray and brown, broken, crumbled. Pillars. Symbols.*

I'm in the burned convent.

It looks different than it did earlier, the burn marks almost seem fresh against the stone. Pieces of blackened wood are scattered around me, and the candles from earlier look brand new, barely used, if used at all.

This is a different time, I realize, before the sigils were drawn everywhere, before the painting was added. This room I now stood in was just the beginning of . . . of whatever it was that happened here.

I pad across the room, not sure exactly what I'll find. It's strange—I'm not afraid like I was earlier. I don't feel like a trespasser, but rather a fly on the wall, another stone amongst the many, an unlit candle with all the others. Where the altar had been in reality now sat a box filled with papers and books, things so very human. Peaking through, I found a notebook with some of the sigils drawn scattered amongst the pages. Notes in a language I didn't know were written all around, and I couldn't tell if it was actually another language or just effects of the dream. But four words stood out to me throughout the notes, four words that weren't written in letters exactly, at least not the English letters I recognized. But the words still engraved themselves into my brain, decoding, deciphering, becoming *words I did recognize.*

Asmodeus.

Leviathan.

Bael.

Devil.

The last one cut through me like a knife.

Of course I've heard of the other names; TV shows, books, movies—they were all familiar. But something about them feels like *more. Like . . . like they're what connects* everything.

A piece of wood skitters across the floor behind me, as though it were kicked. The book falls from my hand as I jump and swiftly turn around. All the air—fictional or not—leaves my lungs, my eyes are wide, unblinking, and I can't move an inch, no matter how much I will my body to. I'm stuck, frozen, paralyzed.

Before me stands the black shadow I've seen so much, only now . . . now the shadows are leaving him, melding into the darkness of our surroundings—revealing him.

He's tall. Really tall. Towering, even. Maybe eight feet tall. The demon wears a billowing cloak, hiding his body, but I can tell even with it that he's massive, broad, and terrifying. His skin is a deep, deep red and his long curled hair is like an ink spill.

But as I'm frozen, paralyzed in his shadow, the main thing I can't take my eyes off of are those huge, looping horns. They jut out from the sides of his head, curving far up before sloping down into a small spiral around his ears—like horns somewhere between that of an antelope's and a ram's.

The demon's face was mostly covered in the shadow of the robe, but those looming horns moved, as if he were slowly looking up to face me.

"Your priest is not who he seems." His voice is a fiery mix of sultry and menacing, gravely in all the right places, but the timber so low and deep, it vibrates through the floor and up my spine. But more than that, it's his words that shake me. Marcelo, not what he seems? I strongly believe I've learned exactly *who he is, mask and all. If there's more to him he's hiding, then . . .*

The demon takes another step closer, his clawed feet peeking under the long hem of the robe. That step is just what I need to finally kick myself out of this paralyzing fear. I scrabble back, fully aware that while this is definitely a dream, who fucking knows how Freddy Krueger this horned man is about to get. "Your fear is misplaced, Junia Forester. Here and in your church." The demon stops shortly, still halfway across the room. His glowing eyes squint at me before he sighs and shakes his head. The act is so very . . . human. It looks more unnatural on him than his red skin, his horns. The demon scratches the back of his head before looking back up at me. "Protect him. Promise me you'll protect him. That is all I ask of you."

Him? *I think.* Who's him?

35

MARCELO

Puta mierda.

Those fuckers. What or whoever the fuck is trying to oppress and influence me into fantasizing of fucking June, I'm going to butcher them. I want to do the things I've imagined to her anyway—I don't need some twisted pendejo forcing that want onto me.

It's between *us*, not us and all of Hell.

I stomp through the cathedral, searching for any sign of the demon—that tall fucker with the horns. It's about damned time I exorcise the bastard and send him back to where he belongs. Fuck the cult—I'll figure them out later if I have to. All that matters right now is finding this demon and stopping him from coming between June and I.

I stalk through the halls of the church, searching in rooms I hadn't been in before: the room I was in with Callum earlier today, the sanctuary, the garden outside,

June's balcony—but I don't pick up even the faintest hint of demonic activity. No imps, no demon—nothing.

Slumping onto June's organ bench, I lean forward, my elbows on my knees and my face in my hands. I haven't felt this useless since . . .

Since my parents.

I groan and slam my fist down on my knee, ignoring the sting of pain and grunt through it. Fucking Hell. It's been *days* now, and I don't feel any closer to exorcising this thing. I've been distracted, prioritizing what *I want* for the first time in thirteen years instead of what God wants, instead of what the church wants. Yet while it has felt *so damn good*, I know I'm failing my duties. And, worse, by failing those duties, I'm failing June.

This demon is just as much after her as it is now after me. It wants something from her, I just don't know what. It could only be Daren. But I doubt he'd get all those men I saw outside the forest to commit blasphemy and turn from their God to a demon. Not when his motives were as revolting as forcing his step-daughter to be with him. No, it had to be more than that. The *cult* was more than that.

My mind feels fried, like putting a fork in an electrical socket. I've never been this frazzled on the job, not even the first time I wore the mask, the first time I killed a cultist. And I can't help feeling that it all has to do with June. The stakes are higher now. I *have* to protect her—keep her safe from the Hell that's *here*, in this world, rather than the next. I can't handle having her suffer, even in the slightest. Not anymore. She's suffered enough. And my God let that happen, let her mother abuse her.

I sigh again, scrubbing my hand through my hair. The curls tangle around my fingers, still damp from my shower before bed.

It's a thought I hadn't even allowed myself to voice yet, even in my mind. *My God let that happen to her*. I know the implications. I'm doubting Him. I'm doubting everything. And therefore, I am weak. My faith isn't strong enough to cast away demons . . . it's not even strong enough to cast away these thoughts.

Somewhere, I know He didn't guide Daren's eyes to June, He didn't guide the belt in her mother's hand. But . . . He didn't stop them either. He didn't give June *anything* to protect herself with.

All He gave her was me.

And I'm a damn awful consolation prize.

I tilt my head to either side, cracking the column of my neck in numerous places. I need a plan. A plan that'll get me back on track, get me closer to finding these sons of bitches, and a plan to exorcise the demon plaguing June and I.

But first, I need to atone. First, I need my strength returned to me, my power over the demons.

First, I need to confess my sins and reunite with God.

I make my way back downstairs and head into the confessional booth, closing the door behind me. I don't have my rosary to pray the Hail Marys, but I do them anyway, my hands clasped together, my head bowed before God.

"Father, forgive me for my sins . . . they are plenty."

And then I pray. I pray for forgiveness, for strength, for union. I don't pretend to hear God's voice speak directly to me. That's for saints and Mormons. No, I just follow my feelings. I believe God feels *through* me, and what my heart wants is what God wants for me. And what my heart wants is June.

I don't ask for forgiveness for touching her, for wanting her. I can still feel the ghost of her tongue wrapped around my cock, her lips on me, and I *know* her Heavenly mouth is no sin. Just like her hands that come together in prayer are no sin, her breasts that protect her heart are no sin, and her perfect, tight cunt that will one day bear my child is no sin.

My feelings and want and desire for her are not a sin. Not a sin God planned for man. How can God have created Adam to not desire Eve, but still expect man and women to love each other, to lie together, to make love and bear children together? No. God created desire. God created love. And my God *is* a god of love.

Man created the sin of desire, for desiring that which he could not have, that which he wanted to take without permission, without want. *That* is sin.

"God, forgive me for my distance," I say, sorry for it. Sorry for my anger at Daren and Jill. Sorry for my lack of attention to my faith. Sorry for my distance from my real family, from Rodrigo and Rowan and Willow. And sorry for not meeting June sooner, for not saving her the moment I first laid eyes on her, for not stealing her that first night I crept in through her window.

I feel God in my heart then, guiding me through my confessions, strengthening me with each moment. And not once does he guide me to confess any sins of my body, of my wants, of my passions. Not once does he guide me to confess of June. Because I am not sorry for my affection toward her. I am not sorry for my desire for her, my want to break my vows and make endless love to her. I am not sorry for my love—because loving Junia Forest is not a sin.

Marcelo never came back last night. Which doesn't surprise me. He was more than a little on edge when he fell out of bed. I know the demon is getting to him more and more with each passing day, and we're no closer to finding him.

Even if he was in my dream last night—even if he warned me of . . . of something.

I turn over in bed, Diablo nestled like a little croissant between my thighs, and click on my new phone. There's no notifications, of course—I've only downloaded a reading app and a few books I've barely started, and the only phone number I have saved is Marcelo's. But it's not why I check it. It's already 7:10. Mass will start in twenty minutes and it's only a matter of time before people—my mother—start showing up. And Marcelo left last night in a simple T-shirt.

I crawl out of bed, knocking Diablo from his place. The cat chirps but stands and stretches, waking up with me. He yawns wide, those razor-sharp teeth revealing themselves to me—teeth he hasn't used against me even once. He scampers across the bed, and bonks his cute little head against my hand, demanding attention as I scratch between his ears.

"Marcelo needs his collar if he's going to serve confessionals today," I tell him. "So I have to go, but I'll be right back."

I quickly get dressed as Diablo goes to eat his kibble. I throw on a black, nondescript dress, a cropped cardigan, and combat boots I easily zip up. My plan is to find Marcelo, give him his shirt and collar, and get the Hell out of there and back here before anyone shows up and asks where I've been—or worse, meeting my mother.

I grab what I need, let Diablo out the back door, and leave the safety of the apartment. The halls are silent but for the shuffle of feet of the altar boys and attendants preparing for Mass.

Hurrying through the hall, I push my way into the sanctuary. A few early birds are already standing amongst the pews, chatting or finding their places, but I don't look at anyone for more than a breath. I don't want eye contact, I don't want looks of concern or confusion or disgust. I just want Marcelo.

The first bell sounds throughout the cathedral. Flinching, I hurry my step once more, crossing in front of the sanctuary and the pulpit. *Hopefully, he's already in the confessional,* I think, as the idea of wandering St. Mary's looking for him sounds more terrifying with each passing moment my mother might walk in and see me. I reach the confessional booth and lightly knock on the wood. The booth sits on the far side of the pews, but pressed into its own little alcove, slightly hidden and private for anyone looking to confess.

"Yes?" Marcelo's voice is raw, raspy—and incredibly sexy—coming from the other side of the door. He sounds exhausted and just about done with everything. Not really like a welcoming priest ready to listen to the parishes' woes and tribulations.

"It's me," I whisper. "I brought—"

A small yelp escapes me in place of words. I don't even get time to finish my sentence as Marcelo pushes the door open, wraps his arm around my waist, and pulls me into the small booth with him.

"Hello, songbird." He grins, placing me on his lap. The booth is small, tight, and incredibly closed in. I feel each of his breaths against my cheek, my neck, as his smile widens. "Sorry I didn't come to bed."

I pat his knee. "It's okay. I brought your shirt and collar. Didn't think you would be allowed to hold confessions with just a T-shirt on." I smirk and pluck the shirt from his chest as I hand him his priestly attire. He throws it around his shoulders, working his hands around me so he doesn't move me even an inch further from him. But his eyes feel distant. "Are you okay?"

He pursed his lips a little, looking past me. "I think so. I spent the majority of the night in here."

"Confessing your sins?"

He smirked again, but the smile didn't reach his eyes. "Yes."

I stare at him a moment, the dark circles under his eyes making his brown eyes even deeper, like the color of freshly brewed espresso or forest dirt with a damp layer of morning dew—there's still a warmth in them I'm not even sure he realizes he has.

Those gorgeous eyes meet mine.

"But *you* are not one of my sins, Junia. The things I want to do to you—though vile and wicked and downright perverse—are not a sin. I am not ashamed for wanting you as badly as I do. For pleasing you, for wanting your moans and your screams. I may have broken a vow, but it was a vow made by man, not my God. My God would not bring you into my life and then force us to deprive each other of what we truly want—what we need." His hand slides around my waist again, pulling me closer.

"June," he continues, "I—I don't think I've ever said this to a woman. I don't think I've said this ever, to anyone other than my parents, but . . . I love you. I'm *in* love with you. And loving you . . . it isn't a sin."

The air catches in my throat, and for a solid moment, I forget how it works to breathe—how to inhale from my nose, letting air move through me to fill my lungs, how it is to release the air, exhaling. I simply forget. All I can do is process his words, over and over again, and be consumed by the deep, warm eyes I've simply become obsessed with.

I cannot remember the last time someone told me they loved me—never a boy . . . a man. Since her eyes became daggers, I haven't even heard my mother utter the word.

Marcelo cups my chin, his soft touch reminding me to inhale. I breathe in a little too sharply, hiccuping from the effort.

"Don't answer now, songbird," he whispers, his eyes searching mine before falling to my lips. He knows how I feel about him, he has to. "I want to show you first. Prove it to you."

The next chime of the church bell vibrates through the tiny booth, and the cacophony of voices finally reaches my ears. There are so many people, people I know, people I've seen every day of my life, right beyond this piece of wood, right beyond this tiny box.

My mother is even with them.

I close my eyes, closing them to all of it—shutting them out. They can't take this from me. My *mother* cannot take this from me. It's mine. *He's mine.*

Marcelo guides my chin toward him, and I feel the second his soft lips meet mine. Those lips that spill words of love and adoration, of praise and desire and everything that is good in this wretched world. He kisses me with those lips, showing me just how much truth is in his words, how much he meant them. And I can feel it—all of it—every thing in this one kiss.

His hand pulls at my waist, pressing me into him, and he groans as my breast pushes against his chest. I didn't wear a bra, thinking I'd be running right back to the apartment after giving him his things, and I can tell by the way he slides his tongue between my teeth that he is so incredibly grateful for it.

"I love you," he says again, against my lips. "I love you, June." His hand on my chin glides past my jaw and burrows deep into my hair at the base of my neck. He pulls lightly and I can't help but moan into his mouth. Our tongues dance together, and it takes all but a moment to feel his hard cock pressed against my thigh. "Let me show you. Please," he begs, "let me show you how much I love you."

I pull away, waiting for him to open his eyes, to look at me. I want him to see that I agree to it, that I want it— him—just as much as he does. Marcelo bats his eyes, his gorgeous lashes slowly opening, and then, he finds my eyes instantly, his deep, almost-maroon eyes piercing me. I nod, slow and sure. I don't care if the entire parish is just on the other side of this door. I don't care if they walk in on us, or hear us. It's time for confessionals, and Marcelo is ready to confess that he loves me.

He spins me around on his lap, facing the dark brown wood of the door, my ass sliding over his cock as he does. Marcelo moans in my ear, sending shudders all down my spine. With quick fingers, he unbuttons the cardigan and slides it from my shoulders, leaving me in just my dress.

Digging his fingers into the hem of the dress sitting at my thighs, he pauses. It's so dark in the confessional booth, just enough sunlight making its way in to see, but the shadows are everywhere, his dark clothes one with the room.

"May I?" he asks, and it sends a funny tingle between my thighs, him asking for so much permission when he knows full well he could take what he wanted and I'd like it. But I like this too.

"Please," I breathe, leaning my head back. I've only had a taste of what his fingers felt like till now. When he let me use his hand, and when he toyed with me in the dressing room. And only once did he slip a finger inside of me, just to the knuckle. But nothing has even been *there*, and I want him, now, to be the one to break that barrier.

Marcelo slides my dress up my thighs, over my hips, and around my ass. A small gasp escapes him when he sees I'm also not wearing any underwear, the sound making me wet.

"You naughty little thing," he jokes, biting at my earlobe. "Were you hoping I'd fuck you in the confessional when you brought me my collar?" He keeps sliding my dress up, leaving it scrunched high at my waist.

"No," I admit. "But . . . I do now."

My words send him wild. He falls to my neck, kissing and sucking my skin between his teeth as he thrusts his hips up, letting me feel just how big and hard he is.

"Don't regret those words, *mi amor*." Marcelo slipped his hand to the sleeve of my dress, yanking it down. "You know I love to play with these," he says, revealing my breasts and pulling my arms out of the sleeves so I'm fully exposed. "Your tits are so full and heavy, and these hard little nipples just beg me to pull on them." He cups my breast, pulling at my nipple then rolling it between his fingers to soothe it. "Fucking perfect," he utters.

Outside, I hear Mass begin, the singing of hymns, the first prayer led by Father Callum—all while Marcelo touches me in ways that make every part of my being feel alive.

His hand slides down my stomach, pausing between my thighs. "I want to touch you here. To push my fingers inside of you, and feel how tight you are." He kisses my neck between words. "I want to feel you squeeze around me as I stretch you for my cock."

I don't wait for him to ask for permission again, I don't wait for him to make his move. I buck my hips up, forcing his hand to touch me exactly where I want him. He startles, but his fingers quickly find my clit, putting pressure exactly where I like it. "How about you show me exactly what you did in here, right before I first met you? I can't get the ideas out of my head. Your hand between your sweet thighs. Your beautiful musician hands circling your swollen clit to completion." I feel his smile against my neck and it makes me desperate, so desperate, I grab his wrist and push his hand farther down. Marcelo hisses as his fingers graze over my wetness, and he bites my neck—the smile still there. "Maybe I'll have you show me another time."

He is loving every second of this.

"Look at me, June," he orders. I turn my head, leaning back against his shoulder. His lips are only a breath away from mine, as he looks down on me and demands, "You can't make a noise, not if I'm to fuck you like you want me to. We can't let anyone know you're in here with me. Not yet. No one is ruining this for us. So, no singing, my little songbird. Got it?"

I nod feverishly. I just want him to touch me.

He presses against my core with his index finger, moving so slow, it drives me wild. I feel the immediate pressure as his finger pokes into me, it's such a small amount, but it's a pressure I've never expected, never experienced.

"Easy, *mi amor*, easy," he coos against my neck. "Be a good girl and relax for me." With his other hand, he grabs my hip, digging his thumb into my lower back and massaging me. His hand cups my curves, pressing into my skin, and for once, I'm not embarrassed by the extra skin there, the stretch marks that line it. For once, I feel like they're being loved and cherished and . . . goddamn *treasured*.

I lean back on his shoulder, his beard tickling the curve of my neck as he keeps whispering into my ear.

"You are so beautiful. Every single inch of you is absolutely perfect." He squeezes me as he kisses my neck, and I feel all the affection.

Marcelo presses his finger deeper inside me, the pressure once again there, but as he kisses me and whispers, I relax immediately.

"You're doing so well," he whispers. "So, so well." He pulls his finger out, before going back in, and I feel how slick it is as it smoothly moves inside again. He repeats this, going deeper and deeper each time, and I grab onto his knee for support, closing my eyes to just *feel*. I feel it— him—inside of me, pressing against those inner walls, and it makes my toes curl. I fight hard not to moan, biting my lip, and winding my body tight to hold in all the pleasure.

"How does it feel?" he breathes.

"So," I stop myself, holding back a moan. "So good." Before I realize, I find myself rocking my hips in tune with his movements, greedily taking his fingers deeper and deeper, faster and faster. "More," I beg, reaching for the cloth as his chest and clutching it between my grip. "Please, please."

Marcelo smiles. "My needy little songbird," he coos. "Beg me some more."

"Marcelo, please," I moan, unable to help myself as he cups his finger inside of me. My God, does it feel amazing.

"I like when you beg." He pecks my cheek and then adds a second finger, sliding it into me with the other, spreading me even wider. I bite my lip on another moan, trying to stay as quiet as possible. On the other side, Father Callum is preaching the Bible and in the confessional, I'm pleading to God to make this last forever. Now, with both fingers, I feel Marcelo move even deeper, rubbing my walls and adding all the blissful pressure.

"Does anything hurt?" he asks.

I shake my head against his shoulder. "No, no—it feels good."

Marcelo keeps going, his hand still massaging my lower back as his other hand fucks my pussy. And just like with his tongue, it feels like total bliss.

He licks my neck, kissing me again. "I want to play with you, June. I want to *keep* playing with you till you can't take it anymore. And then, I'll finally fuck you. I want you dripping by the time I shove my cock in you. And then I want you to come all over me as I tell you I love you, over and over again." His fingers find that spot I like so much, and he cups them against it, harder and faster. "You may not be able to scream for me in here, songbird, but you'll definitely be coming for me. Again and again."

37

MARCELO

I t doesn't take long to get June to come for the first time in her confession. I clap my palm around her lips and let her breath into it, moaning around my fingers as she grinds against my hand. Her wet pussy is making me see stars, and it's all I can do to not bend her over this bench and shove my cock into her.

But all in due time, I tell myself. All in due time.

I slide my fingers out of her as she huffs, trying to reclaim her breath. My fingers are covered in her, coated in her come. Her eyes watch them, her lips slightly parted.

"Do you want to taste yourself again, songbird?"

"Is—is that weird?" She looks up at me, her large doe eyes searching for confirmation, concerned of her own desires.

"Not at all. Lots of people are curious." I slip my fingers between her lips and press down on her tongue. "You never have to feel like *anything* you want is weird with me. I will do anything you ask, anything you desire."

She wraps her tongue around me, sucking harder, and I have to knock the back of my head against the wall behind me to stop from groaning. Fuck. I wish it were my dick in her mouth.

And she fucking knows it.

"Ahh, so my songbird wants to play too, huh?"

I quickly spin her around and grind my cock against her wet pussy, not caring if my pants get her come all over them. Her head falls back, and she sucks her lips into her mouth to keep from crying out.

With my cock still pressed against her, I cup her tits in my hands and squeeze as hard as I can just before I suck one of her nipples into my mouth.

I keep playing with June throughout the next hour, hearing the service go on just beyond the wall, and over and over again, I make June come. Her cheeks are stained red with heat and lust, her lips swollen from kissing, her stunning doe eyes dilated with want, and she's finally pulled my cock from my pants, desperate and begging for me.

"Please," she says after finishing again. "I want you."

Now, she's a gorgeous sopping mess. And I think I've held both of us back for long enough.

I pull her even closer to me, her thighs straddling me. Thrusting my hips up, I grind my cock between the seam of her pussy, pressing first against her dripping hole, and then against her needy, desperate clit. She shudders as she feels my piercings press along her skin, and I focus on it a little longer, grinding these four metal balls against her till a small breathy moan escapes her lips.

"Are you sure you're ready?" I ask again. I'm desperate to take her, virgin or not. But that's not what I want *for her*.

I want her to claim me just as much as I claim her. To be as ready for this as I am—

June slaps her hand over my mouth. "I have been begging you to fuck me since the first night you found me, Marcelo. If you don't fuck me right now, I'll take your cock and do it myself."

Her heady gaze was trying so hard to look dominating—but she just looked fucking adorable.

So much so, I couldn't deny her.

I grab June's waist tightly, my fingers digging into her delicious curves, and lift her. She sits up on her knees with me, her perfect tits in my face as she does. I can't help but lick and suck another nipple into my mouth, even if her tits are already covered in my hickies. Slowly, so slowly it hurts, I guide her to my cock, positioning myself at her entrance. Her thighs shake around me, and I know despite her words, her bravado in wanting me, she's terrified right now.

June has been told for so long how her desire was sin, sex was evil, and her body was a curse. Yet in the short time I've known her, I have broken every single one of these ideas, and I plan to show her just how holy her desire is, just how pure sex can be, and just how miraculous her body is.

Her nails dig into my shoulders, bracing herself, so I ease her down. I let the tip of my cock dip into the warmth between her thighs, pressing into her sweet, wet cunt. She stiffens, immediately biting her lip.

"Easy, *mi amor*, easy," I huff, holding myself back. I want to ram my hips into her, filling her with me completely, hear her singing my name as loud as she can. But I also want to keep fucking her—and if I want to do that, no one can hear us in here.

I ease her down, just a bit, and feel her squirm and

flinch between my palms as my cock slowly starts to spread her apart. Her cheeks are on fire, her nails digging into me as if she's holding on for dear life.

But, fuck, it feels *so good*. So fucking tight.

Holding onto me, she lowers herself, taking more and more of me. I feel her shaking, but she doesn't let it stop her.

"You're doing so good, mi amor, you're taking me so, so well." I nearly groan as I slide into her more, pausing every so often to let her acclimate to me. "Does it hurt?"

She bites her lips and nods. "A little. But it feels really good too."

"Keep going at your own pace," I coo.

I throw my head back as my piercings squeeze into her, rubbing against her wet inner walls.

A tiny, breathy moan escapes June's lips as I finally fill her tight cunt. If I didn't know better, I'd think her pussy was Heaven—actual Heaven. A Heaven I would *happily* die to be in for the rest of eternity.

Clamping my hand over her mouth, I slowly thrust my hips back and then forward. Her doe eyes are pleading with me to do more, more, more, her hot breath warming my palm pressed to her lips. June's cunt is perfectly stretched around me, ready for me to do as I please without hurting her.

Too much.

I thrust back again and slam into her perfect pussy. She bucks forward, crying into my palm, biting the fleshy meat of my fingers to silence herself.

My songbird is singing just a little too loud. I can't let this be interrupted. I reach around the booth, picking up the small leather-bound Bible from the small wall pocket rack and lift it to her lips. Her eyes widen as she sees it, flicking to me.

"Bite," I mouth.

She hesitates, but the moment she opens those plump lips, I push the leather spine between her teeth, pushing it as far back as it'll go, gagging her.

The Bible hanging from her mouth, I thrust again, and again, feeling how far I can go as she rides on top of me, her entire body shaking with each thrust.

It's fucking bliss, utter perfection—I've never wanted to lose myself more, falling into her body over and over again. I don't remember sex being *this* good, this . . . otherworldly *good*. My cock is begging for more, more, more, never satiated with each thrust, never satisfied with how much of her I have.

I *need* more.

"In the name of the Father, and of the Son, and of the Holy Spirit."

June freezes on top of me, her entire body going incredibly stiff, rigid. Her pussy clenches around me, as do her thighs, her jaw, her arms—everything.

"Forgive me, Father, for I have sinned."

I stop moving as well, freezing like a deer caught in the headlights, my cock half inside of June as her thighs start shaking from holding herself up, my hands clamped around her hip.

We didn't hear Mass come to an end, we were too busy in our own lustful world. We didn't hear anyone approaching the confessional booth. And we definitely didn't hear anyone enter.

I quickly turn toward the other person in the booth, checking the tiny grated window, and thanking God the window is closed shut.

She can't see us.

June's breath grows ragged, her heart beating so loud,

I can feel her vibrating through every place our bodies are touching, hear it as if it were my own heart beating.

Her doe eyes must match my own, because they look as afraid, as shocked as if a semi were driving straight for her, high beams blasting—nowhere to run.

Because on the other side of this wall, June's mother just walked in to confess her sins.

MARCELO

I haven't seen June's eyes this terrified since the night I found her nearly naked, wet, and beaten lying by her organ. They weren't like this as we encountered the demons, not when we were in the burned convent, not even as I crept into her room the first time as the masked man. I've only seen her *afraid* twice—and both times were because of her mother, Jill, who now sits waiting to confess.

"It has been two weeks since my last confession. These are my sins."

I don't say a word, make a single sound, June frozen in my arms.

"I—" Jill shuffles in the other booth. "The screen is closed, Father. Will you open it?"

June stiffens further. Fuck. I steel myself, looking deep into June's eyes. I want to tell her it's okay, it'll *be* okay. I will handle it. I will comfort her. I will make Jill go away.

I clear my throat. "Sorry, Miss Forester, I'm not feeling my best today. I offered to hold confessionals for Father Callum, but I do not wish to get anyone sick."

She giggles and I can hear just how fake, how rehearsed it is. "Oh, I don't mind. You can open it."

This woman grates my nerves. "I do. So I'll be leaving it closed." Before she can speak again, I say, "Your sins, please."

Jill slowly begins to drone on about artificial sins. Being jealous of the other ladies in the church for their nice clothes and rich husbands, for looking at Father Callum and other men in the church when she should be purely devoted to Daren, for cursing here or there—but she *never* takes the Lord's name in vain, thank you—for gossiping to others, for not honoring her parents because she hasn't called them in months.

It all is artificial. Fake. And it fills me with rage that she doesn't confess for the *actual* sins she's committed. For hurting her daughter, body and soul. For leaving her to get raped by the sicko she's planning on marrying.

My hand grips on June's hip, digging into her beautiful curves. Her warmth fills my palms, easing my mind and—

And June starts to move. My cock is still buried inside of her, and slowly June takes more of me, filling herself with me. I turn to her, her eyes sparkling, a little mischievous. She's ignoring her mom. She's taking what she wants—pleasure—and she's not letting her mother take it from her. June's eyes flick to me, looking up at me through her long lashes, asking for permission to keep going, to keep pleasing herself.

I swallow, placing both hands on her hips as June bites into the Bible to stop herself from moaning, nodding. June leans back, placing her hands on my knees, opening her chest and giving me full visibility of her huge tits.

As Jill drones on, June picks up speed, using her thighs and balance on my knees to ride my cock, her tits bouncing with each move. I watch where our bodies connect, entwine, and the sight of me sliding out of her, covered in her wetness, will forever be ingrained in my mind like a world-class painting. My cock feels like it's being milked as she sucks me in with each movement, her back arching more and more as her tits bounce in my face.

I throw my head back, ignoring Jill's voice completely and only focusing on my sweet songbird, riding my cock as I've always dreamed—taking what she wants. My horny little she-devil. June is so tight and warm, my breath catches as my head hits the wall again. I'm covered in her wetness as she drips down my cock. I want to fill her with my come so bad, watch as it slowly drips out of her pussy, know that as she walks through the church with her little dress on, she's not wearing any panties to stop it from leaking down her thighs. Another little secret for just the two of us.

My little songbird is a fucking sight to behold, and seeing her bounce for me is far superior to every single dirty thought I've had in the last fifteen years. Her pussy pulses around my cock, and I cannot wait to see my dick covered in her come as my fingers had been. I cannot wait to keep fucking her through it, to—

"And then there's the matter of my daughter," Jill's voice somehow makes it past my ragged breath, June's accelerated heart rate, even as June's pussy clenches around me. "I feel the need to confess for her sins, because they are mine as well."

I stiffen again, clutching June in my grasp, holding her still.

A knot in my throat grows, and I struggle swallowing around it. "And what sins are those?"

"You haven't known her for long, Father Marcelo, but Junia is troubled. She *loves* attention. Needs it like a whore. She uses her body to manipulate men into wanting her, tempting them."

June flinches, the Bible finally falling from her lips and between us on my stomach, her fear making my blood boil. She doesn't need to be hearing this bullshit, this—

"I mean, she's a bigger girl. Fat, even. Which is no fault of mine. I've *told* her to eat less, but the girl just *loves food*. But I guess it tempts men."

The lump in my throat is back, my jaw feels locked as I grind my teeth together. This woman—

"Daren has fallen for her temptation recently, and June ran away for attention. I *know* she was just trying to have him chase after her. She hates me and wants everything I have. She doesn't want me to be happy, she just wants what I have—"

How could a parent be so vile, so awful, so—

I think back, remembering June covering herself in the mirror. Of her arms wrapped around her stomach to hide herself. Of her small flinches whenever someone moved too quickly around her. Of how much my girl fucking hated herself when we first met.

The answer is *no* parent. This woman isn't her mother. She's the evil fucking woman who birthed her and nothing more.

I pull June off me, shove my dick back in my pants, and storm out of the booth. The church looks black in my vision, the darkness tunneling around my eyes as I throw the other door open, the wood slamming into wood and leaving a deafening silence in its wake.

Jill yelps, sitting in the tiny booth, but I don't give her

the opportunity to open her disgusting mouth again as I storm into the confessional, grab her wrist, and *pull.*

"You're not confessing for God's forgiveness, you hypocrite. You're only saying things you *want* to believe." My grip on the frail woman's wrist tightens. "You're saying things to make yourself feel better for being an awful mother and an abysmal Catholic."

"What are—let go of me!" she demands—and I do. Immediately. But it doesn't stop my wicked tongue from forcing this woman to face her truth.

"You have drained the youth of your daughter. You have chewed her up and spit her back out. You've *damaged* her, more than your stupid little brain can even comprehend because you are constantly too busy focusing on your fucking self, you condescending, self-absorbed—"

"Hey!"

Loud footsteps resonate on the marble floor, approaching me with a ferocious speed I recognize. It's one I take up every time I don the mask.

"What the *fuck* do you think you're doing?" Daren yells, his finger pointing at me.

I don't grace the fucker with an answer—in fact, it is already taking everything in my power not to rip his fucking throat out.

From the corner of my eye, I see Jill's eyes roam around the room—but . . . she's not looking at Daren. Rather, past him, to the parish at large. Onlookers are watching us, not a ton, but enough. I meet Father Callum's eyes as he presses his lips together. He's not going to stop me. Not unless he needs to. He *knows* these two fucking hypocrites deserve punishment. I don't care what the parish thinks of me—in a few weeks, maybe even days, I'll be long gone from here with June by my side. No, I want the parish to see this—to hear every wicked thing these two demons on earth have done.

"Hun," Jill hisses. "No cursing in church."

"I don't give a damn, Jill. Who the fuck does this fucker think he is, touching my woman?"

"Nice," I snarl. "Real fucking nice."

Just then, Jill's head snaps to right past my shoulder, and her eyes shift. It's almost like watching an actual demonic possession as her eyes sharpen, darken, becoming more like weapons than anything else.

And then a small hand gently wraps around my arm, a soft body presses against my back—shaking.

"Junia?" her mother hisses. "You—you've been *here*? With *him*?"

Daren's face darkens as well, his eyes locked on my songbird. "More importantly, what the fuck was she doing with you *in there*?"

"You tempted the *priest*? My God, you're worse than I thought!" June flinches, but neither of us says a thing. "You *slut*," she hisses and I jerk toward her, resisting every muscle in my body, every voice in my head *begging* to shut her up. Permanently.

Daren straightens, looking between June and I, and as his gaze lingers on June—taking in her legs on display, the dress she wears hugging her hips, the red tint to her cheeks from moments ago—he noticeably softens. "June, sweety. You can come with us. Come home with daddy." Jill balks at her fiancé, but Daren doesn't flinch. He raises his hand up, expecting June to actually take it.

But her hand just tightens on my arm.

"She is not going *anywhere* with you."

His bloodshot eyes finally meet mine. "And why the fuck not, *priest*?" The way he said it was like a slur, vitriol spewing from his mouth. "You mad she only callin' *me* 'daddy'?" His smirk was full of yellow teeth, chapped, torn lips, and overgrown facial hair.

I step forward, moving out of June's grip and into Daren's face. "I don't need June to call me daddy. Not when she already calls me *Father*."

Daren takes the bait, rearing back and attempting to punch me in the face, but the moment his fist extends, he's wobbly. I sidestep him easily, and throw an uppercut into his jaw, stunning him back a few steps.

"Daren!" Jill gasps, and I hear others in the church do the same as Father Callum finally makes his move to diffuse the situation.

"Now for your penance, both of you—your sins will go unforgiven. No amount of Hail Marys or Our Fathers can absolve you of these sins. But be warned . . ." Jill grabs Daren's arm, helping him straighten just as Callum reaches us. "Salvation *will* be hunting you. Will you finally be fucking smart enough to see it?"

39

JUNE

I play a song, my fingers hitting the invisible keys along the notes. I can't remember the name of the song right now, only that I haven't played it in years. Yet, somehow, I still remember the notes. I still remember where my fingers go, when to hit the pedal, the crescendo and the finale. I play it over and over again on the leather seat under me. It's not nearly as beautiful sounding as my organ, but it gets the job done. It tosses the daggers away from my mind. It rinses the grimy touch from my skin. It forces the voices to silence, because all I can hear is my imaginary song.

Well, my imaginary song and the revving of the car engine as Marcelo races across Belmouth.

The windows are rolled down, blowing the crisp air into my face as we speed along the dark road. It's gray and dreary outside, the rain making it even colder, like a splash of ice water against my skin. Marcelo takes another puff of his cigarette, the smoke swirling between us as he exhales another drag. The smell of cigarettes used to bother me so much—my mother and so many of her boyfriends smoked, our couches and carpets getting tainted by the gross scent. But since I met Marcelo, the smoke lingering around those gorgeous lips, his chiseled jaw, the scuff I loved feeling against my skin—it is nothing but utterly intoxicating.

I can tell he's still obviously raging from earlier by the way his teeth bite into the white paper. The moment he'd essentially told my mother and Daren to screw off, he grabbed my hand and whisked me out of there. I remember their eyes lingering on me, my mother's on where his hand held mine, and Daren's on the short hemline of my dress. Thankfully, Father Callum immediately reached them just as we were enough space away, stalling either of them from coming after us.

Marcelo opened his car door for me, slammed it a little harder than he meant to, immediately apologized under his breath as he slid into the driver's seat, and then sped away. I still have no idea where we're going but . . . I don't care. I wanted to get the Hell away from there just as bad as he did, and if that means he's taking me far, far away to never return, then that'll be fine.

Except, I'd demand we grab Diablo and *then* leave.

Since he peeled out of the church parking lot, Marcelo has still not said a word. I can *feel* his mind working, raging, and the loud heavy rock music blasting from the speakers adds to his visage. He'd pulled his collar and button-up off at some point, only leaving on the black T-shirt he'd worn last night to bed. The short sleeves cling to his biceps, the artwork lining his skin on full, delicious, display.

Marcelo's hand tightens on the steering wheel, his veins popping from beneath his skin, and I can't help but imagine those same hands gripped around my ass just a few minutes ago.

Of course it'd be my life that my *mother* — of all people — was the one to interrupt us. But . . . I didn't want to let her win again. I didn't want to let her take that moment from me — from *us*. Plus, it was really hot.

I squeeze my thighs together, remembering just how it felt to have him plunge inside of me, those piercings truly working wonders. I knew I had been about to come when she started talking about me, when Marcelo and I both froze, when he got up to defend me. It was like bungee jumping. I thought I was about to leap off a cliff into pure, utter, bliss, only to be aggressively yanked back toward the rocks.

And though I knew he was angry — and I should've been too — all I could focus on was finishing what we started in that confessional booth; that I hadn't told him I love him too. That I have, since the first night he snuck into my room in that mask. Since he stood up against my mother, wanting my attention alone. Since he carried me into that shower and let me cry all over him.

I bite my lip and turn to face him as he takes another drag of his cigarette. "Marcelo, I—"

Just then, he pulls off the main road, the car bouncing as he offroads between dying sequoias and a number of other trees shedding their brightly colored leaves. The car swerves and bounces as it battles the terrain, climbing over small muddy slopes and descending leafy hills. Finally, we reach a small clearing, just slightly bigger than the car itself, and Marcelo puts the Mustang in park and turns the engine off. The forest is loud with insects and bugs, the engine rumbling to cool off the only man made noise out here.

Marcelo calmly puts the cigarette out in the small ashtray he has just under the center console, and then he finally looks at me. I gasp, unable to control the sharp inhale flooding my lungs, as he looks at me with eyes full of sorrow and remorse and worry—not anger.

"Are you okay?" he asks, placing his arm on the back of the bench and resting his hand on my shoulder.

I can't help but stare at him. "You're . . . not mad?"

He raises an eyebrow. "Oh, I'm mad. But I'm also worried about you. I'm so sorry you had to hear or see any of that. That you had to see *them*. I just—I want to make sure you're okay."

I nod slowly.

"Do you need anything?" The hand on my shoulder squeezes, and as it does, my eyes blur, my cheeks become wet. It's only after another breath do I realize I'm . . . crying?

My chest flutters as the tears well, dripping in big, ugly drops. I have no idea why I'm crying, why I feel this . . . this hole inside of my chest, why—

Marcelo pulls me to him, cradling me in his arms. "It's okay, *mi amor*, I won't let them touch you. Ever."

Another sob racks through me.

The hole. The hole in my chest is where the flutters are coming from. I—I'm not sad because of my mother's words or Daren's glances. I'm used to that.

I'm not alone anymore.

Someone . . . actually cares.

The realization sends my body folding into his. It's not tears of fear, or sorrow, or anything of the sort—it's . . . relief. Not quite joy, but something so akin to it, my body doesn't know how to process it other than crying. Marcelo pats my hair, lightly rocking me back and forth.

"I'm here," he whispers, "I'm here."

I've only ever been met with anger. My mother's dagger eyes, her abuse, her sour words. Any emotion I've ever conveyed, any tough situation, any time the weight of the words felt heavy on my shoulders—it was always met with rage. And so, for as long as I could remember, I've suppressed any reaction. Suppressed doubt and fear and loathing and sorrow. I've suppressed all emotion, hiding behind a wall of my own creation. So much so, I've trained myself to just accept her words, her disdained looks, absorbing them into my wall. Into me.

But Marcelo has been cracking that wall, chip by chip. He's *here* with *me*. He *cares*—no, he *loves me.*

And that's more than I can ever say about anyone else in my life.

"Shh, *mi amor*," he says, his fingers tangling in my hair. "Tell me what you need."

I sniff, knowing exactly what I need. It's what he's been working toward all along. Except now, I'm finally ready for it.

"I need you to break me."

Marcelo pauses. "Are you sure?"

I nod against him. "Anything you want. No restrictions. Choke me, spank me, use a belt. Just—cleanse me. Break me. And then make me yours. Make me whole again."

I look up at him, his lips are parted and his hand finds my cheek, rubbing it softly.

"I'm tired of being a songbird in a cage, Marcelo. Break me free."

He clenches his jaw, his thumb still gentle on my cheek. After a moment, he nods. "Okay."

"I want to say no. I want to fight you off."

He swallows. I know he wants that too. Has wanted it from the first night he touched me.

"But what if—"

I cut him off, placing the tips of my fingers to his lips. "I know you would *never* hurt me. Not in any way I didn't like or want. I want this."

Marcelo's dark eyes search mine before he grabs my wrist and places a delicate kiss on my fingertips before moving them away.

"Then you deserve to be fucked by the real me."

Now I swallow, knowing exactly what he means—and it's exactly what I want too.

He reaches past my thighs, opens the glove box, and pulls out his black mask, the white cross catching the morning light through the windshield as he pulls it toward him.

"You'll be screaming your love for me by the time I'm done with you." Marcelo pulls the mask over his head, his eyes disappearing behind the blackness. "You can be as loud as you want out here, songbird. No one will hear your screams." He pulls the strings tight in the back of his head, his brown hair curling around his neck with each tug. Once it's secured, the white cross faces me and I feel a jolt in my chest, fight or flight kicking in. "You look so pretty when you cry," his hand wipes at my cheek, smudging the fallen tears across it, "but you look even prettier when you cry with my dick in your mouth."

Immediately, it's like my body is set on fire. I'm fully tense, ready to run, ready to throw myself at him, ready for anything. But my pussy is already craving his rough touch, his blissful torture.

"Now, *princesa*, get out of the fucking car."

40

JUNE

I fall as I jump out of the car, tripping already on the wet leaves covering the ground. I don't know if his plan is to chase me, or if he'll grab me the moment I even try to run away, but it doesn't matter—the idea makes me wet all the same.

I push myself up, running into the trees, just as I hear heavy footfalls behind me. Marcelo is coming toward me, but he's not running. No, his steps are fast and hard, but determined, purposeful. I can hide, or I can keep running, knowing he'll eventually catch up to me. Or I can turn around right now and try to fight him, trick him, and run past him to get back to the car.

I think of the only other time I've ever fought back, the shattered pieces of the Virgin Mary statue clattering by my feet. Of the blood that marred Daren's forehead. And then I think of the only time I've run, when I ran from that house—my bare feet pounding on muddy dirt and rocks as I ran to the church in nothing more than a hoodie in the cold rain.

But hiding? I've hidden my whole life. I *know* how to hide.

I round a tree, springing myself out of sight from my pursuer and serpentine around another few trees before finally stopping, and crouching under a fallen log. Wet leaves cling to my cardigan, my hair, and I see spiders and other small bugs crawl around just in front of me. But I stay absolutely still, my pussy pounding in tune with my heart as I try to quiet my breaths.

Marcelo's loud foot falls slow as he nears me, and I see his black boots stop a few steps away from my hiding place. I stop breathing altogether, afraid he'll hear me. Thankfully, his shoes are pointed away from me, turning in a semicircle till he pauses, and picks up his pace in a different direction.

But I've seen a lot of horror movies. I know this is the moment I let my guard down and he appears behind me, ready to attack.

I know, but I do it anyway.

I exhale, wanting him to find me, wanting him to punish me and give me exactly what I want.

But nothing happens. Marcelo doesn't come for me. He doesn't pull me out from under the log by my ankles, forcing his cock inside of me as he lifts my dress, my clit pressed roughly against the cold, wet ground as he fucks me hard. No, instead I stay there, waiting, breathing. And aching. My core is begging to be touched, begging for friction. I feel like I can't breathe, not until I feel *something*.

I throw every single reservation I have away.

I'm a filthy slut, and I don't fucking care anymore. I want to be touched. *Need* to be touched.

I thank God once more I didn't wear underwear today as I slide my hand along my body, toward my thighs. If he can't hear my breath, maybe he'll hear my moans. Maybe he'll find me as I come all over myself, upset to have missed his opportunity to do it himself.

The moment my hand passes the hemline of my dress, big hands roughly wrap around the ankles of my boots and pull—just as I imagined he would. My front scratches against the branches, rocks, and leaves lining the floor, and I kick hard, trying to break his grasp.

"I've been watching you squirm, songbird. My little *princesa* is so fucking needy, isn't she?" He easily flips me around and I see he isn't wearing his shirt, his tattoos on full display. The artwork mesmerizes me, and I find it hard to take my eyes off all the different pieces. *Later*, I tell myself, *later I will study each and everyone of these, learn them as if they were my own.*

It's at that same moment I feel what he's actually done with his shirt. Or rather, what he plans to do with it. He straddles my hips and yanks my hands above my head, tying the shirt snugly around my wrists. I try to knee him in the back, wiggle out from under him, but it does nothing.

"Let me go!" I demand. Marcelo chuckles, leaning forward as his hand slams right next to my head. The mask is clouding my vision, the white cross the only thing I see in the sky of black.

"You think I'd let you touch yourself? And let you get off that easy?" He chuckles again. "No chance in Hell. I told you, June, you're going to be screaming your love for me by the time I'm done with you, and for that you'll have to be nice and patient." His other hand slowly drifts up my thighs, his touch feather light, sending goosebumps all over my skin.

Fuck, just a little closer.

His index finger toys with the hemline, before slipping under, and I can feel the juxtaposition of his cold fingers on my molten core. God, how nice it'd feel if he just—

"You dirty little slut," he whispers into my ear, before he chuckles again.

The air is stolen from me as my mother's words leave his tongue. But, not because they hurt. No, when he says it, it sends that familiar pulse to my clit, begging for attention. For *his* attention. And no one else's.

I am a slut. *His* slut.

"Mine," he groans as he dips his hips, grinding against me just once. "*My* little slut."

"Fucking tease," I breath, and it pulls another chuckle from behind the mask.

"Oh, love. You have no idea."

He sits back up, straddling me once more as he yanks open my cardigan. The buttons tear from the fabric, flying off all together as he pulls it up my arms and wraps it around his T-shirt where my hands are tied. Then, he stands and pulls me up with him. I fight, but my feet barely reach the floor as I'm halfway thrown over his shoulder. I kick at his thighs, not finding any purchase, until he throws me back. I slam against a tree, the air leaving my lungs, as he pulls my arms over my head again, lifting me off the ground. I dangle, too dazed to realize how at first, only noting how much this position hurts my shoulders.

"There—now, I'll only let you off if you're a good girl. Are you going to be good for me, songbird?"

I don't reply, fighting to pull my arms back down in front of me, trying to reach the ground as the toes of my boots barely graze the dirt. It's no use, I'm stuck. I look up, trying to see what's holding me. Like a jacket on a hook, the bundle of fabric tying my wrists are hung over a branch, thick enough to hold my weight. Marcelo grabs the branch, shaking it lightly, reminding me he just asked me something.

"I'll be good." I nod.

Reaching in his back pocket, Marcelo pulls free a knife. As he switches it open, another small gasp leaves me.

"First, you need to be punished for trying to cheat." He doesn't give me a moment to react, instead he slashes forward, and I flinch, covering my face in the crook of my arm. I wait for pain, for the sting of the knife, for the warmth of blood.

But I feel nothing.

I feel a breeze.

And then I feel a rough hand cup my breast.

"I haven't had enough of these today. Seeing them bounce up and down for me is all I ever want to see again. I want to be drowned in that image and live in it forever. Your beautiful fucking body moving like that—for me? Fuck, I don't know what I did to deserve you."

Marcelo had cut the straps of my dress, the front falling to my waist to reveal me to him and the rest of the forest as I dangled from the tree.

"Do you know how badly I wanted to suck on them in that confessional booth? How badly I wanted to slap them back and forth? I feared we'd be too loud if I did that, though. But here—"

He lightly squeezes, his thumb pressing into my nipple, before he pulls back and slaps the side of my breast.

"*Fuuuck,*" he groans. "That jiggle is everything." He does it again, harder, and a small yelp escapes me at the sting left behind as my pussy clenches, desperate to feel that same sting.

He rubs the red mark he left, before moving to toy with my nipple.

"W—" I try, biting back a moan as he pulls on the sensitive, peaked bud. "What's my penance, Father?" My heady eyes meet the white cross again, and I can feel him staring at me, watching me, worshiping my body as he touches and slaps and pulls.

"Hmm," he hums, and the vibration in his throat makes me desperate to feel it between my thighs, his tongue on me again. He takes the knife into his dominant hand once more, and softly glides it across my breast, letting the blade come dangerously close to breaking the skin.

"Should I carve my name into what's mine?"

I shudder at the idea, wincing at the thought of the pain, but . . . the idea also makes me incredibly wet. I squeeze my thighs together again. He slaps my breasts again, and immediately plucks my nipples between his thumb and forefinger, pulling roughly before massaging them back. I moan as his fingers toy with me, leaning my head back on the tree, my shoulders already numb. "For your penance, you must become mine. Completely."

I already am, I think. But I don't tell him that. Not when there is so much more I want him to do to me.

Putting his knife away, he plucks me from the tree, lifting me by my hips and slowly placing me on the ground. It takes me a moment to gather my footing, to feel stable, as the blood rushes back through my arms, my fingers buzzing like a staticky TV.

Marcelo yanks my wrists toward him, untying me, letting my cardigan and his T-shirt fall to the floor. I don't know what he's planning next. Half of me expected him to fuck me against that tree, and the other half knew there was more he had up his sleeve.

He lifts my chin up to meet the white cross again, holding it in place. "You're going to be my good little girl?"

I lean up, licking the spot on the mask where I know his mouth to be, and as I pull away, a smile lifts my lips. "I'm going to be your good little slut."

I push him back, as hard as I can, and I run back toward the car. I know he let me push him, let himself stumble back and give me a slight head start, and while I have no plan for what I'll do when I get to the car, the thrill is intoxicating, absolutely invigorating.

I run through the trees, jumping over roots and under branches, skidding around the damp leaves, and—finally, the cream of the Mustang meets my eyes. I've made it, I've—

A hard body slams into me, but instead of tumbling to the floor, he pulls me into him, his hand like stone shackles around my upper arms. I feel Marcelo's hard cock on my ass, his sweaty chest pressed against my upper back. His heavy breaths are steady, different from my rapid and ragged breathing.

"Inhale," he whispers softly into my ear, breaking character for just a moment, reminding me how much he cares about me, reminding me this is all a game, reminding me I am his everything.

I do as I'm told, despite the "brat" persona I'm playing at, despite the fact I'm trying to run away *from him*. I inhale deeply and exhale through parted lips. Marcelo gives me a moment to do it again, and as I exhale the second time, one hand drifts up my body. He's slow, methodical, as his fingers graze against the skin between my breasts, along my chest and collar bone, until his large hand wraps around my neck and squeezes.

"No!" I choke on my next inhale, my hands clawing at his arm as the air lodges in my throat. I can breathe, but barely. My vision doubles and for a moment, his calloused hand becomes a leathery belt. It tightens like a snake, pulling the life from me, the very air I need to breathe. Darkness starts to creep in, turning the world into a vignette photograph, it—

"Inhale," he whispers again, in the same way. I try, and, surprisingly, the breath reaches my lungs, slithering past his tightened grip. Marcelo's hand tightens a little bit more, and I am still able to just barely breathe. The realization of his utter control, and the overall feeling of being at his mercy—knowing he would never hurt me, not really—it sends a wave of heat through my body. I feel myself dripping down my thighs, desperate for more, more, more.

Marcelo half lifts me, half drags me, his hand still clamped around my throat, over to the Mustang. I don't fight him, ready to take whatever he is willing to give to me. If he forces me on my knees to suck his cock, and nothing more, I'll take it. If he teases me to madness, never letting me get off, I'll happily oblige. If he slides me back into the car, never to fuck me again, I'll accept the time I've had with him.

But Marcelo doesn't do any of those things. He walks to the hood of his car, and bends me over it, slamming me down. I scream as the cold metal presses into my sore breasts, my hot body instantly cooling.

"Don't fucking move," Marcelo demands, stepping back. I hear him prowling in a semicircle around me, looking at me from every angle. After seeing what he wants, he steps up to me again, flicking my dress over my ass with an easy movement, revealing my ass and pussy to him.

He chuckles then, seeing how wet I am. "My needy little love. Look how fucking wet you are." He slides a finger along my inner thigh, coating himself in me. "So desperate to be touched by me. Tell me, songbird, is it my attention you want?"

With his hand between my thighs, he easily finds my clit, giving me just the right amount of friction I need.

"Do you need it?"

"Yes," I moan.

He slips his hand away from me.

I lift myself, trying to look back, needing more. "No—"

He smacks my ass hard, the sound echoing through the silence of the woods.

"Do you need it like a whore?"

My mother's words once again spill from his mouth, but it's nothing like what I felt earlier when she said them.

"Ye—yes," I moan again as he spanks me. "I'm your little whore," I repeat. "Don't stop giving me attention. Ever."

He spanks me, again and again, and I cry out each time, my body rocking against the hood of the car. He kicks my legs open, spreading my pussy open as I'm forced to stand with them far apart.

"God, this pussy." He pulls his mask off and drops to his knees behind me, and the next moment, I feel his teeth biting the back of my thigh, claiming me.

"Taste me," I beg. "Taste me, please. I want your tongue on me." I buck my hips, trying to grind against the car, his face, anything I could find. I *need* the friction, need his touch.

"Are you manipulating me, June? Tempting me with your perfect fucking body? With your gorgeous, tight cunt, and your big hips? With this ass I can't help but grab and spank?"

"Yes, yes, yes," I breathe as he bites me again, closer to my pussy.

"What about with your eyes? And your shy, breath-taking smile? Do you tempt me with those too?"

My breath shudders, those same tears from earlier threatening to spill.

"Have you tempted me into loving you, Junia Forester? Because I can't stop. I won't ever stop. You are all that matters, you are the only thing I desire, the only one I seek, the only temptation I'll ever need." His hot tongue languidly slides over me, just once, the tip of his tongue flicking against my clit.

"I love you, Marcelo," I moan, the tears finally overflowing. "I love you."

I feel him pause behind me. Then he rises and, after what sounds like him putting his mask back on, leans over me, his hot body pressed against my back, his cock pressing into my red, stinging ass. His masked face appears just next to mine, so close I feel his breath through the leather.

"Then let me love you," he whispers, once again in that soft voice so out of character, out of the hungry, violent demeanor of my stalker. It's where my masked man and Marcelo the priest meet. It's where my Salvation is. The true version of himself, where his ferocious heart joins. And I love all of it, every version of him.

He doesn't wait for my permission. Marcelo pulls his cock out, and pushes all the way inside of me in one long, hard thrust. I'm so wet, there's no resistance, just pure fucking bliss.

"God, fuck. You feel even better than before."

He pulls all the way out of me, and slams into me again, my ass jiggling against him from the impact. He spanks me again, uttering, "My little whore," as he does it again. "My perfect slut," again. With each thrust, my clit grinds into the cold metal of the car, creating a whirlwind of friction and pleasure and ecstasy.

"Sing for me," he demands, and I do. I moan so loud, it's enough to rattle the birds. I scream his name as he fucks into me again, his body slamming into mine, violently, messy, and so fucking good. "So fucking tight," he breaths. "My little slut is so fucking tight, and she's taking me so fucking well."

"Marcelo," I moan, already feeling that familiar cliff as his cock hits deep into me, his piercings rubbing against my inner walls. I feel my cunt clenching around him, pulling him into this bliss with me. He slams into me more, harder, faster, finding the exact rhythm my body needs, the exact spot his cock hits inside of me, over and over again. I curl my toes, my entire body stiffening, as I push my ass back, desperate to have him inside of me each time he pulls out.

A breathy laugh escapes his lips. "My needy little songbird," he says again, his hand on my ass, shaking it to take even more of him. "Do you want to come?"

I nod, unable to speak and I feel my grip on reality loosening.

He groans and spanks my ass. "Tell me, June. Beg for it."

"Please," I breathe, my eyes rolling back as he keeps hitting that perfect spot. "Please, please, Marcelo, please let me come. I'll be your good little slut if you let me come."

"Ah, June," he moans, still thrusting into me. I feel his balls slap my thighs, and it has my spine straightening even more. "Such a good fucking girl. All right, baby, come for me."

He pulls himself out to the tip, and slams into me. My back arches immediately, and as he keeps the motion, I feel myself burst. The tension all over my body explodes as I come all over his cock, screaming his name as he continues pounding into me with each wave of ecstasy.

This time, I jump from the cliff. There's no cord to snap me back. Just him. Just Marcelo and his perfect arms, his gorgeous smile, his loving gaze. I jump off the cliff, and the moment he feels me come all around him, he comes, filling me completely.

We are both panting messes by the time I come back to earth. He's still inside of me, his forehead dipped and leaning on my back as he inhales and exhales, trying to catch his breath.

"Ah fuck," he huffs. "That was . . . " But he doesn't say more. Instead, he plants soft kisses all over my back as I fight to catch my breath again. I feel his scratchy facial hair against my spine, as he kisses again, he mutters along my skin, "I love you, June."

I had to carry June back into the car, her legs too wobbly to stand straight. I ease her into the back seat, sliding in with her. I position her on top of me, resting against my chest as we both continue to fight to catch our breaths and acclimate to this new . . . existence. This existence where I could do *that* whenever I wanted. To feel *her* whenever I pleased. Fuck. I didn't ever think I deserved such a life, but here I was.

"I—" she says, before huffing on another breath, "I didn't bleed."

I pat her hair before trailing my hand down her back and shrug. "A lot of women don't."

She scrunches her eyebrows. "I thought—"

"It's not as black and white as that. Sometimes it breaks and bleeds from everyday activities. Sometimes it breaks with sex, but just doesn't bleed. And sometimes it does."

She bites her lip and nods.

"Does that bother you?"

"N—no. I just thought I would."

I cup her cheek. "Well, do you feel okay? I've heard sometimes women feel—"

She leans up, folding her arms over my chest. "I feel better than okay. Maybe a little sore, but . . . I think that's hot."

I bark a laugh. "Well, then good."

We stay in blissful silence for a while, her fingers tracing my tattoos and my hands rubbing her back. It's so utterly peaceful, I'm half asleep when she asks, "Who are they?"

June traces the three faces lining my upper arm. I knew she'd ask about them one day, and . . . I think after what we just did, I finally feel ready to tell her.

I clear my throat and grab her hand, entwining my fingers with hers. I'm going to need them if I have to get through this.

"My parents and my sister."

Her big doe eyes meet mine, her chin resting on my chest. "What happened to them?"

Tucking a strand of hair behind her ear, I cup her cheek. "They died when I was young. It's . . . not a good story. But I'd like to tell you about it if you'd let me?"

She nods, already moving to sit up, but I hold her to me. I need her warmth, her soft skin against mine, the feeling of her body engulfing me. June settles back, curling on top of me as her fingers start to dance over my hand, tracing the lines and grooves, delicately outlining the scars on my knuckles, the calluses on my palms. Her touch grounds me, reminds me I'm *here*. In the car with *her*.

Not in my own personal Hell—the memories of that night—as I begin to finally tell her.

Friday nights were movie night in the Serrano household. It didn't matter if we went out or stayed in, we'd gather every Friday and spend time together. Ana and I were never allowed to make plans with friends—though there had been multiple Fridays in which our friends joined *movie night—but at its core, it was* familia *time. My mom always ordered us pizza from our favorite spot in town—the box always dripping grease by the time the acne-spotted teenager would deliver it to us; and my dad always made the popcorn—adding real butter and M&M's to the microwave mix for the Serrano special.*

Movie night started when I was in fourth grade. I remember because I had been a week away from my tenth birthday party at the roller skating rink, and a baby tooth, one of my canines, fell out, right into the bowl of popcorn. It's weird how similar a tooth could look to a kernel of popcorn. Needless to say, no one touched the popcorn after that, and those birthday pictures all came out awesome.

Ana was in the sixth grade by then, and the teenage angst came early for her. My mom wanted us to do movie night as a way to "bring us together" or something like that, but what had started as more of a punishment, quickly became a fundamental tradition. So much so, that we never *skipped movie night. Not once in the five years we did it.*

I remember Ana's eighth grade graduation landed on a Friday night. Instead of hanging out with her friends after, she decided to come home with us. That night, we watched The Thing *for the first time, and it became her favorite horror movie.*

"Carpenter can do no wrong," she said after the credits began to roll.

"Yeah? What about the Halloween *movie where Michael Myers was just a possessed cult puppet?" I laughed.*

Ana then shrugged and rolled her eyes. "That one wasn't Carpenter, dumbass."

"Language," Mom scolded.

And then Dad snickered, "I can't even begin to fathom how much Carpenter hates that movie."

For 272 Fridays, the Serranos came together and watched a movie. Sometimes my mom would choose her romantic comedies, Dad would pick horror, I'd always choose whatever was popular at the time, and Ana would pick some arthouse flick or a "cinematic masterpiece" that probably won Oscars or some shit.

For 272 Fridays, the Serranos were unbroken—even if Mom and Ana fought, even if I was grounded, even if Dad had to work a little overtime and come home late. We always did movie night.

So when Dad was too sick to join us one night, it felt like the earth had suddenly ended. Like all humanity had been zapped away, taken in the rapture, and only Ana and I were left, unaware and completely confused as Mom took care of Dad.

It was August, the hottest month in Miami. The sun had been blazing down on the black street all day, steaming the recent puddles from a midafternoon rainfall into more humidity that carried on deep into the night. Sweat in places you couldn't even fathom accrued along our skin as the hair curling at our necks grew frizzier and frizzier with each passing moment. Drops of rain clung to the windows after the evening shower, and while the palm trees still dripped, the weather had all but cleared.

But it was always like this, every summer. Hollywood made it seem like Miami was the place to be during the summer, but for us natives, it was rather ungodly. We stayed inside, AC blasting as much as possible, readying ourselves for the approaching school year and end of another round of freedom.

Ana was about to be a junior in high school and was probably one of the smartest girls in her grade—and one of the most popular. Everyone loved Ana, and she adored me. I was her little baby she'd parade around, even when I started wearing all black and thinking I was too cool to hang out with her.

We were already sitting in our respective seats, Ana on one end of the long couch, me on the other as my feet kicked into her leg to get her to move. Mom sat on the love seat, where she usually snuggled up under a blanket with Dad. The bowl for popcorn was already set out in the kitchen, the wrappers shed, the box of M&M's opened.

But there was no Dad. Ana and I hadn't seen him in four days.

We'd been under the same roof, breathing the same air, but he'd been locked away in his bedroom since Tuesday, before either of us got home from school. It was unlike Dad to be so . . . distant. He was always *involved, always there. And his absence left a gaping hole every night he didn't join us for dinner.*

"Lemme go talk to him," Mom sighed, sitting up and tossing the blanket off her. It was supposed to be Dad's turn to pick a movie, but he hadn't been feeling well for almost a week. None of us knew what was wrong with him, and he refused to go to the doctor's.

As Mom went into the room, the door closing behind her, George Lopez *droned on in the background. I remember Ana was painting her nails—the smell was so strong, I kept kicking her just to annoy her as much as that smell was annoying me.*

"Pendejo," she hissed, the red smudging onto her fingers. She smacked my leg, then immediately went back to what she was doing.

BANG!

The obnoxious laugh track from the TV was cut off by a heavy thud in the room behind us. The vibration moved through the house like a ghost, rocking the couch under us, rattling through my entire body with the force of it. The windows buzzed, the TV shook. Ana and I shifted to stare at the dark wooden door, closed, maybe even locked, with no way to know what happened on the other side. Something must have fallen, I thought—it couldn't be more than that. But the more Ana and I stared at the closed door, the more the thud rang in my ears, the more it echoed over the TV, through the silence of the house, passing the frogs and crickets outside, muffling the last of the raindrops from the trees.

It was only a thud, but I knew—somewhere in my wretched soul—it was so much more.

"Mami?" Ana called out. "Are you okay?"

There was no answer.

The door became alive, breathing as my heartbeat rang in my ears. George Lopez became nothing more than a haunting thrum, the outside noises joining the void of sound.

I wanted to call out to my mom, my dad, but the words lodged in my throat, my voice caught like I swallowed a bite too big, took a gulp too large. I swallowed again, feeling my throat tighten.

"Ma—" Ana started again, but as quickly as she began, her words were cut off as everything in the house surged. The volume on the TV blared, followed by the iPod plugged into a speaker in the garage and Ana's CD player upstairs—blasting a cacophony of music we couldn't pick out from each other. The lights blinded us, the TV satirized George Lopez to look more like a sleep-paralysis demon than an iconic late-night sitcom star. Clocks went off, electronic toys, the Furby my sister still kept in the den, the Tamagotchis resting between us, begging to be fed—all of it.

I covered my ears as Ana hopped to her feet, nail polish completely forgotten as it shattered to the ground, paint going everywhere. She was always the braver one, always the fighter.

"Mami!" she yelled again, taking a step toward my parents' door.

And then everything went black. Silent. The surge ended, taking all the power and electricity with it. No more music blasting through the house, no more buzz from the lights ready to explode, no more George Lopez.

Nothing but a silent void, and then—

"Ah, fuck!" Ana hissed. Glass crunched under her foot as she shuffled another step forward, stepping directly on the fallen nail polish.

My eyes were still adjusting to the dark, I could just barely make out Ana's silhouette, could just barely make out her heavy, ragged breathing.

"M—Marcelo?" she whispered, her voice small. "Is that you?"

Finally, her silhouette was visible. But . . . she wasn't looking at me. And her voice—her voice wasn't coming from where I heard the breathing.

I quickly turned my head, following her gaze, and my entire body froze. Another silhouette stood at the now-open doorway to my parents' bedroom, a shape I'd recognize anywhere.

My dad was breathing hard, a piercing whistle following each time he exhaled.

Seeing him finally gave me strength. "Dad, what's going on?" I said, sitting up on my knees and bracing myself on the back of the couch. His gaze jerked to me, but he didn't move a step. All I saw were his shoulders, shifting up and down as his labored breathing continued. And all at once, the smell of nail polish was completely overpowered by a stench so potent, I gagged. A rotten mango sitting out in the sun, a trash bag leak- ing brown, muddy liquid, eggs overcooking in a hot kitchen— all these things assaulted my nose as our Dad stared at us.

"Papi?" Ana squeaked as his labored breathing became a growl. "Where's Mami?" Her voice was quivering, and I re- member thinking, Is it the pain in her foot? Or is she just as scared as I am right now?

Suddenly, another silhouette appeared behind Dad, moving so fast, it broke the spell of stillness the last few moments forced on us. Dad didn't have time to move before Mom lugged the electric-blue portable stereo at his head.

Ana and I screamed as bits and pieces of plastic broke around his skull, scattering to the floor. Mom rushed past Dad, running to Ana and tightly squeezing her into a bear hug.

"I'm right here, mi niña, right here," she soothed.

But my eyes couldn't break away from Dad. He'd slumped down, immediately, blood already dripping onto his shoulders, and—

Mom grabbed my arm, pulling me into the hug.

"That"—her voice was shaky, even more so than Ana's—"is not your father."

42

MARCELO

I stared at the man prone on the tile floor. It looked like my father, but . . . that was about where the similarities ended. It didn't sound like my father, didn't smell like him, breathe like him, stand like him, move like him—it didn't feel like my dad.

"Wha—Who is it?" Ana asked, pulling back.

Mom was bleeding too, a large gash marring her forehead as the blood dripped into her right eye.

"I need you both to do everything I tell you," she demanded, not answering us. "Okay?"

We nodded.

"Kitchen. Now." Mom threw her arm around Ana's waist, half-lifting her to the kitchen as I followed closely behind. Ana's bloody foot stained the white square tiles, the red nail polish just a few shades lighter than the blood seeping from her skin. Mom helped her into one of the wooden dining table chairs, and turned to pull out hydrogen peroxide and tweezers out from the medicine cabinet. "Start taking out the glass," Mom ordered as she turned back around, grabbing the landline off the charger.

Mom dialed too many numbers for it to be 911, but she quickly put the phone to her ear.

It rang. And rang. Until finally, "Hello? Father Rodrigo? It's Rosa Serrano. It's happening, Father—what we talked about." She paused, for only a moment, turning to us. Tears sparkled in her brown eyes. "Yes. The kids are here. Can you come?"

I had never heard my mother sound so . . . desperate. For all the years she'd been my mother, she had been the strong one. While my dad sobbed at sad Superbowl commercials, Mom had cried maybe two times I could remember. Mom was the one who stayed up way too late to make sure all of us ate and bathed and got ready for the next day. Mom was the one who took the weight of all our pain and comforted us when we were upset or sad or angry.

She was the strength, and Dad was her support.

"Okay," she said, running to the back door in the kitchen. "I'm unlocking the doors now. Just come in when you get here." She paused again, then pressed the phone to her chest, her gaze flicking between us again. "You guys need to go upstairs, hide."

Ana straightened. "But—"

"Coño, Ana. Now."

I ran around the table, grabbed my sister's hand, and pulled.

"Go, go," Mom urged.

"Mami, what's going—"

Mom grabbed Ana's other hand. "Ana, mi amor, please. Take Marcelo, and hide."

Ana clenched her jaw next to me, but squeezed my hand and limped away from the kitchen.

As soon as our backs were turned, Mom continued on the phone. "I knocked him out, but—but I know he'll wake up soon." We hobbled up the carpeted stairs, Ana's single red footprint *leaving a trail on the beige rug. I remember turning around, at that final moment, and my mother's eyes were on me. I hadn't called my parents* mami *and* papi *in years. I thought it was lame. At that moment, as her brown eyes met mine, urging me to continue, I wanted to scream out to her. I wanted to yell, "Mami, Mami, Mami, I'm scared!"*

But I didn't. And that was the last time I saw my mother's eyes so vivid, so . . . alive.

Ana hauled me onward, moving through the hall as we passed my room, our shared bathroom, and finally got to her room. Just as we walked through the doorway, Mom's voice rang out from downstairs. "No! Leave my husband alone!"

Ana kept pulling me into her room, she didn't let me stop and turn around, she didn't let me run down to help Mom. Not as we heard another loud thud, glass shattering, or Mom's screams.

Pausing in the center of the room, Ana looked all around. Her bed had drawers underneath, and the door opened outward so we weren't able to hide behind. She looked down at the carpet, surely seeing the red footprints. Her gaze met mine and something behind her eyes hardened.

I was fourteen, but puberty hadn't hit in full-stride just yet. I was still short and skinny. Ana grabbed my shoulders and shoved me back, toward her wardrobe.

"Hide in there," she demanded, and without another word, dashed into her closet. I followed her command, opening the wardrobe and climbing into it, tucking myself behind her cardigans and jackets she kept in there. The drawers underneath me groaned at my weight, but the whole thing held sturdy as I watched Ana hide within her clothes in the closet and slide the door shut, just as I closed mine.

I sat still, barely breathing, as I listened. The house was deathly quiet, still, just as it had been right after the power went out. Whatever was happening downstairs isn't happening any-more, and the only sound I can hear is my heart pounding in my chest, between my ears. It's so loud, I don't hear the footsteps up the stairs, down the hall, I don't hear the ragged breath, the hag-gard walk—I don't hear any of it until the thing wearing my father's skin is in the doorway.

I'd seen enough movies—movies my real father *had shown us—to know what was happening, no matter how crazy it sounded. My mom and I had a pact. While Ana didn't believe in ghosts and Dad was a full on skeptic, my mother and I were diehard believers. We made a deal, if either one of us ever saw a demon or ghost, we would believe each other, no questions asked, no "well, let's see."*

And after hearing my mom on the phone with our priest, Father Rodrigo, and after she said "that isn't your father," I knew *what my mom was saying. Ghost, demon, Hell, were-wolf—whatever this thing was, it meant I had to believe her. It meant she wasn't lying.*

It meant this wasn't my dad.

I stayed absolutely still, not even breathing, as I watched the shape scan the room. I prayed Ana did the same, prayed the thing would turn around and walk away, prayed my real dad would take the pistol he kept in his nightstand and come and shoot the fucker to oblivion. But once again, time seemed to slow. Dad didn't appear out of the shadows, and the thing wearing his face continued to survey the room. Its eyes were a sickly, vibrant yel-low. Like the Emperor in Return of the Jedi. *Its skin was pale and clammy, sweat making his short brown hair stick to his fore-head and the neckline of his shirt soaked through.*

A low, breathy snicker came from its lips as its eyes caught on something in the dead center of the room. Through the small crack between the doors, I tracked his line of sight and—

And my stomach dropped.

She knew. Ana knew, *and I felt like such an idiot, such a horrible brother—Ana knew her footprints would lead the shape right to her, her footprint bright crimson against the light beige carpet in the center of the room.*

"Come out, come out, Little Ana," the shape said, and if I still had any reservations about this being my dad, which I hadn't, they would've all disappeared. The voice that came out of the shape was so unlike my dad, it felt like my brain couldn't keep up with the words as he said them. It was just too . . . wrong. It broke the code my brain had been hardwired with for so long. I knew Dad's voice came out of Dad. Not . . . whatever this was.

The shape hobbled into the room, up to the footprint. Slowly, it crouched down, pressing its face into the stain. I heard a long and deep inhale and had to bite my lips as it slowly licked the print. The shape crawled forward, following the path of the prints till it stopped just before the sliding doors.

I didn't think, didn't even process that my body was moving—it just reacted, moved into motion at its own will. I leaped out of the wardrobe, stumbling to my feet.

"H—Hey!" I said.

The shape slowly turned around, a wide, unnatural smile already spread across my dad's face. My dad never smiled like that. Not even in his happiest moments, not even his widest grins. My dad was an eye smiler—and this smile didn't meet his eyes.

"Well if it isn't Little Serrano, how I've heard so much about you. Your papi *thinks you're a pussy, you know. He's scared you take after him too much." The shape snickered again, but before it could react, Ana jumped out of the closet and onto its back.*

"Stay the fuck away from him!" she yelled, punching and kicking as her arms tightened around the shape's throat. But it only kept cackling before it flung itself back, hard.

Ana smashed into the wooden doors behind her, and as her

hold loosened, the shape simply stepped away from her. Ana slumped to the ground but tried to push herself up, screaming, "Marcelo, run!"

The shape's cackle grew louder, louder, deafening. And suddenly — Ana was floating. Her limbs were stretched as far as they would go, her long dark hair coalescing around her as though she were underwater. She hovered there, in the middle of her room, her eyes locked on mine, wide and frozen.

And as quickly as she'd been lifted into the air, her head started turning.

And turning.

And turning.

"Ana!" I screamed, but just after I did, I heard the loud CRACK!

Yet, her head kept turning.

The shape was doubled over now, laughing hysterically as Ana's head twisted fully around, her neck bunching up as it continued to turn, making another rotation.

My heart broke, and I couldn't process what I was looking at.

Dead, *my mind told me.* She's dead.

And you will be too.

I ran. I heard the thud of Ana's body hit the carpet, but I didn't turn around. I followed her bloody footsteps back down the stairs. I needed my mom.

I ran so fast down the stairs, I tripped halfway, my foot totally missing a step, and tumbled the rest of the way down, landing on the hard tiles on the first floor.

"Mami!" I called to the empty room and pushed myself up to go to the kitchen.

"Marcelo!" My mother's voice rang through the living room, emerging from her bedroom. I stepped to follow when I heard a second voice — no. The same voice, but coming from somewhere else.

"No! Marcelo, don't go to my room. It's not me, it's the demon." It was coming from the kitchen.

"I'm not the demon, she is!"

"Puta mierda," my mom cursed. My mother never cursed. Unless it was really worth it.

And this was definitely a time it was worth it.

I dashed to the kitchen, hearing heavy foot falls bound toward me at an alarming rate. It was like the sound of my heart beat, only I felt it getting closer and closer and closer.

Just as I turned around the dividing wall and threw myself into the kitchen, a taloned hand grabbed my arm, nails immediately piercing skin, the force so strong it felt like breaking bones.

"No!" my mother yelled on the floor in front of me. I heard her before I saw her, but when my eyes landed on her, I wanted nothing more than to reverse time. She was pinned to the kitchen floor, literally. The shape cackled in my ear, its fingers tightening on my arm as it made me watch my mother in a mock of the crucifixion. Her palms were nailed down, another nail thrust into her feet, her body was bloody with lashes I couldn't begin to explain, and upon her head sat a crown of thorns. Yet, still, she fought as she saw me in the demon's clutches. She tried to push herself up, drenching the kitchen in her own blood. "Let him go! Take me!"

It all happened so fast, the moment the words were out her mouth, the backdoor flew open.

"Blessed Michael, archangel, defend us in the hour of conflict." Father Rodrigo burst through the door, Bible open and crucifix gripped firmly in his hand. "Be our safeguard against the wickedness and snares of the devil (may God restrain him, we humbly pray): and do thou, O Prince of the heavenly host." The shape let me go, and I scurried to my mother's side. "By the power of God thrust Satan down to Hell and with him those other wicked spirits who wander through the world for the ruin of souls."

The shape hissed and bucked, but then continued to cackle at Father Rodrigo, even as its skin sizzled. The priest had been about my dad's age, and though I attended church weekly, I didn't really know him. Not well. I went to Mass, but that didn't mean I paid attention or cared. But right now, Father Rodrigo was my Goddamn hero.

He frowned at the demon, as if it were nothing more than a cockroach too stubborn to die. But all it needed was one more good whack with the chancleta. *"Amen!" he shouted, pushing the cross into the demon's face. And then he repeated the prayer again, pushing the demon farther back, and again, the demon became less and less.*

"God, help me!" It yelled, but this time—it sounded like Dad. "Ayudame!"

"Fight it, Javier, fight it!" Father Rodrigo yelled.

And Dad did. Second by second, I could see the shape shifting, weakening, becoming more and more of my dad—his stance, his breathing. Everything that had been other *before was now back to normal.*

Rodrigo was still praying when my Dad's warm brown eyes found mine. When the taloned hand that still wasn't totally his reached up, resting at his throat. When he said, "Marcelo, I promise—it wasn't me."

And then the hand tore through my father's neck, one more cackle breaking from lips that were no longer his, before his body slumped down, blood pooling all around him.

I held my mom's hand, frozen. First Ana, now Dad. The demon got both of them.

Rodrigo stopped praying. The power in the house flickers back to life slowly, the George Lopez ending credits playing quietly from the TV.

"I—Is it over?"

Rodrigo nodded. "It—" he stopped as he turned to look at me.

His eyes widened, and only then did I realize they were on my mother, not me. As I turn to follow his gaze, I hear police sirens begin to blare down the street. Red and blue lights shining through the windows. As they got closer, they shimmered in my mother's unblinking eyes, as her gaze stared past me, into nothing.

"Marcelo," Father Rodrigo said softly.

But I couldn't look away. Looking away meant this was real. Looking away meant it'd be the last time I'd see my mother, the last time I'd hold her hand.

"Marcelo, please." His hand was on my shoulder, his voice soft and gentle, though choked up.

My mom's gorgeous curly hair lay in a pool around her, and she looked so serene despite the gashes marring her skin, despite the blood she lay in. I remember the hot liquid touching my bare toes, and with it came the haunting realization that the demon had taken her too.

43

JUNE

I started crying from the moment he realized his dad wasn't really his dad at all. From the words of adoration he spoke about his sister, the love he had for his mother. And by the time he got to Ana's death, I had to hold back gross sobs. The thought of this man, this . . . wonderful, amazing, loving man, going through anything like that breaks my heart. He didn't cry as he told his story, his hand just gripped mine harder at the rough parts, his arm wrapped around me a little snugger. So I cried for him. And cried, and cried.

When he tells me about the demon grabbing him, I notice the scars on his arm, beautifully hidden beneath the faces of Rosa and Ana and Javier. A face for the three claw-like marks that ultimately tore him apart.

My finger grazes the marks now, over and over, as he finishes telling me.

"After that, the deaths were ruled murder suicide. The media said my dad snapped and killed my mom and sister, tried to kill me too, but killed himself instead. Only Rodrigo and I knew what really happened that night. Only we knew my dad was innocent."

I swallow hard. I can't even imagine what that feels like, for his father's name to be sullied while dealing with the loss.

"I was moved around in foster care for a bit after that, but it didn't even last two months before Rodrigo worked it so I could live with him. That's when I got closer to Willow and Rowan. We had already been friends from Mass, but the two were always at the church, spending time in the little playground, helping Rodrigo with his gardening. After he took me in, the three of us became inseparable." I can see Marcelo's in a different place. He's not in this car with me right now, but maybe on that playground from his memories, maybe in the halls of the church in Miami.

"Of course, everything came back to me. By the time I was sixteen, I was a full blown ass. I rebelled and fought and partied. But one night, Willow and I got into trouble. We got into a fight and the guys tried to grab her. One fucker had a knife and used it on me before I could stop them. Thankfully, Rowan, the snitch that he was, told Rodrigo where we were going that night. The bastard showed up, exactly when I needed him—just like that night in August."

Marcelo twirls his finger around a lock of my hair, focusing on it. "Thankfully, seeing a bishop in full Catholic garb emerge from the darkness at three in the morning is terrifying as shit. He scared off the little twats and took Willow and I home. Willow put the party life behind her, and I shoved my demons as far down as they were willing to go. The next morning, Rowan convinced me to work toward priesthood and . . . at the time it sounded like a really good idea."

He chuckles as his eyes meet mine. "Now? Not so much. I think if I would've met you then, songbird, I would've dropped everything to be with you."

I giggle. "Well then maybe it's for the best you've found me now. What happened after that?"

He shrugs. "Rodrigo helped me get my GED, then I went to seminary school and double majored in psychology. I knew I wanted to be an exorcist. I knew I wanted to be to others what Rodrigo was to me. Only, I hoped I'd be quicker. It made sense to learn about the human brain, to decipher what was mental illness and what was demonic influence. I knew I wouldn't be able to sense the same kind of 'otherness' I sensed from my dad that night with just any random stranger. I only sensed it because I knew him. So instead, I studied the brain."

"And that's how you became an exorcist?" I ask.

Marcelo shakes his head. "Rodrigo had been secretly teaching me from the day he adopted me. He thought it would help comfort me if I could protect myself. And maybe I abused his guilt a little bit, because it more than protected me. It filled me with purpose. I knew from that first night of learning with him what I wanted to do. I just didn't know how to get there. And, for a while, I didn't think I *deserved* to get there. But Rowan talked me out of that. And now, years later, I'm here. With you."

"Not part of the plan?" I smirk.

"Not really. But a more than welcome addition." Marcelo pinches my nose and then leans forward to kiss my forehead.

I huff out a long breath and finally sit up, stretching my back as Marcelo follows. His chest touches me as he wraps his arms around my waist again. Leaning his cheek against the top of my head, he mumbles, "I think that's why I got so mad earlier. I . . . I hate to see you treated that way, by people who are supposed to love you."

Marcelo's parents seemed like saints compared to mine, they were so loving and close and supportive. It feels like the polar opposite of my mother and Daren.

"I just want you to feel loved and adored and cared for, songbird. And if I have to make up for your fucked up parents, I will." His hands tighten on my stomach, and he places another kiss on my head.

I turn in his arms, facing him, and place my palm on his cheek. "Thank you for telling me your story, Marcelo. I know it was hard, and I only wish I could've been there to support you then. But . . . I'm here now. Just as much for you as you are for me." I lean up and kiss his lips. "I love you."

He tucks hair behind my ear, which I'm slowly discovering may just be a new comfort to him. "I love you, June." He pulls me against him, and kisses me soft and sweetly.

After we got home—and after he fingerfucked me with soapy hands in the shower ("Let me clean you up, little songbird, you're absolutely filthy")—Marcelo wanted to have a proper movie night. We ordered pizza, again, and he ran out to get some M&M's and popcorn as I put on my pjs. By the time he was back, I made our little living room into a nest of blankets and pillows, Diablo already perched on the tallest pillow he could find.

Marcelo's eyes dazzle as he takes in the room, and I

grab the ingredients for movie goodness from his hands, heating up the popcorn and melting butter on it just as he described his dad would do.

"Who picks the movie tonight?" I ask as I carry the bowl into the room. He's already lounged on the pillow nest, his head resting on the cushions of the couch.

"Mmm, you pick," he grins, and my God, does it make me want to melt into his arms.

I bite my lip, thinking about the movies he mentioned in his story. His dad loved horror. Ana loved John Carpenter. And just like that, I have it. "How about *The Fog*. It's my favorite Carpenter movie."

He raised an eyebrow, but that grin threatens to end world hunger again as he nods and pulls me down onto his lap.

"Great choice, my little horror queen." He chuckles and opens his mouth to be fed popcorn. I happily oblige.

44

JUNE

My fingers run along the keys as though they were made to create the hymns blowing from the pipes of all sizes behind the organ. It's only been a few days away from my baby, but it feels like a lifetime of untuned repression and creative buildup. Though, Marcelo has been a great outlet in its place.

We got maybe five minutes into the movie last night before his hands began to wander, before I started to trail soft kisses along his neck, and then, the rest was history. It didn't matter that my body was still sore all over, he'd made love to me on that couch, then again in his bed, slow and steady, his eyes never leaving mine as he drove into me, deeper and deeper with each thrust.

This morning, there was a plastic bag on the kitchen counter when I woke up.

"I ran out and got this for you," he said. "But . . . only

if you want it." It was the morning-after pill. Catholics aren't supposed to believe in contraceptives of any kind, but—screw that. I didn't even need to think it through, I picked it up and swallowed the little pill dry.

Now, Marcelo stands below my little perch, assisting with Mass next to Father Callum as I play a closing hymn before the final prayer. During the liturgy, I peeked over the side of the banister and saw my mother and Daren, who has been sporting a nasty bruise on his chin.

I couldn't help the grin on my face every time I thought of that punch, Daren's head being thrown back as Marcelo's fist made impact, repeating in a constant loop in my mind.

My fingers play the final notes, and as Father Callum says the final blessing, I stand and stretch, my back tight from hunching over for the last hour and a half.

I reorganize the sheet music, smooth out the wrinkles on my dress, and go to meet Marcelo downstairs just as Father Callum booms, "Go in peace."

A cacophony of everyone in the building echoes the same words, "Thanks be to God." The voices boom through the wooden door at the bottom of the spiral stairs, drowning out the patter of my steps.

But as the voices end, the spiral becomes . . . heavy. Almost as if now there is an *absence* of all sound rather than the abundance of it from just a moment ago. Gone are the sounds of the parish, of the shuffling of people shimmying out of the aisles, of the congregation moving down the center to say goodbye, of . . . everything.

Suddenly, the stairwell is too dark. The doors above and below me are shut, and the journey down is so short, I didn't bother flicking on the only light to illuminate the space. I don't notice how shallow my breath is until I feel the ache in my lungs, the heaviness on my chest.

Something isn't right.

Trapped, trapped, trapped in the dark, my head screams.

I try to take a few steps down, but my legs won't move save for the slight tremor in my knees. I've felt this before. I recognize this fear, this . . . oppression.

I think of small, sharp teeth on baby faces. Of hooved feet and goat-like eyes.

Demons.

I hurriedly scan the room, ready to see the tall black shape with horns I've come to expect. Only . . . this heaviness doesn't feel the same as when the shadow man is around. With him, it's definitely eerie, but not hostile. Not malicious.

Right now, I feel like a fly caught in a spider's web.

Like death is just around the corner. Like a hand is already wrapped around my throat, it's just waiting to squeeze.

"*Junia.*"

I feel the tickle of air against my neck before I hear the voice, and it makes me want to leap from my skin. But my body doesn't move, it's frozen in time and space—the web finally tangling me within, the spider finally approaching.

"*My pretty little heathen, how sweet you are.*" The voice is cracked, husky. Not quite like that of a smoker's but something close. But every word is said *too* slow, drawn out, as if this . . . thing . . . is taking its sweet time purposefully.

Suddenly, a pair of hands grab my arms from behind, too rough, too painful, with skin like leather covered in sandpaper and nails sharp enough to pierce skin—one of which slides under the seam of my sleeve at my bicep. It's so simple, yet it feels like such an invasion.

The hands keep me rooted in place, absolutely petri-fied. It chuckles behind me, against my neck. The heat from its breath is searing, burning me with each huff. Fi-nally, I try to move, try to fight out of the creature's grasp, but it only tightens its grip and pulls me against it.

"No!" I manage to let out, but it only makes the thing laugh more.

"*Mmm*," it hums. "*Say that again. It drives us* wild."

All at once, I feel so much more around me. The stair-well had just been like a deprivation room, and now was a sauna, dungeon, and Hell all in one. The room heats like an oven, my skirt is torn up the length of my thigh, and three terrifying imps just *appear* on my legs, holding me back from taking another step. As if they'd been the reason I couldn't move all along.

The imps smile up at me, those tiny teeth gleaming white as their light blue eyes grow wide in ecstasy as they hump against my legs.

"*You've no idea how long we've wanted you, Junia. How long we've waited.*" The hands at my arms pull me in close and wrap around my front, circling my waist. The body pressed against my back feels like black concrete on a summer day. It burns my back through my clothes everywhere it touches, and I fight to get away from it. "*I've been preparing you for me. Preparing your body to accept me.*" Its hands begin to wander, slowly trailing up my sternum. I feel the creature's hard erection press into my ass, sharp and hungry. But just as it's about to take what it wants, the creature hisses and draws back as if burned. Thank the Heavens Marcelo's rosary is tucked under my shirt, the cross resting between my breasts.

But the reprieve only lasts a moment. The creature grabs my hips, yanking me into him once more. "*I wanted to be your first,*" it snarls against my neck. The demonic hand slides between the slit in my skirt, rubbing my upper thigh with its sandpaper skin.

"Let me go," I whisper, pleading, my voice too shaky to come out any louder.

"Beg me. Fight me. I don't want your consent. In fact, I prefer to do without it. You'll be so much prettier as you cry, so much sweeter as you scre—"

The imps stop humping, the figure behind me freezes, and the heavy energy shifts into something so much more. The air feels thin, as if I were on top of a mountain, and my vision begins to swim, darkening in the corners.

"Let her go." I know this voice. It's gruff and ungodly deep, with a timber strong enough to knock the entire cathedral into the dirt. It's the same as the horned demon in my dream, the same from the convent.

Though he is still just a shadow, the demon grabs the creature behind me, yanking the hand at my thigh away. The imps flee, or try to—the moment they turn to run, their entire bodies burst into a plume of smoke, as if an invisible fire had already overtaken them, burning them through and leaving nothing but the scent of charred flesh and hair. They scream in an agonized cry that rattles through my ears, finally freeing me from the spider web.

A large hand finds my shoulder and pulls me forward, down the stairs, and behind the shadow.

"Boston. Find Marina Morales," the shadow demanded. I don't know why, but I lock the name to memory, and do as he says, hurrying down the steps.

"I knew you'd come back." The shadow chuckles just as I reach the door. And though my back is to the pair of demons, I can practically feel the creature with sandpaper skin smile against the back of my neck. I hear the laugh in his tone, the smirk in his eyes.

"I never left."

45
MARCELO

"Thanks be to God," I say along with the rest of the parish. As Callum follows the procession down the nave, I turn toward the little door behind me, where I know June will come out of any moment. I want to steal her away from here *before* her rotten parents cause any more chaos. More than once I caught their eyes on me during Mass. Daren's black eye continued to bring a smile to my face for the entire hour and a half.

My phone buzzes in my pocket, and I quickly pull it out. As I'd hoped, it's the text from Rowan I've been waiting for.

Rowan: You owe me big. Took all night to find.
Also, thank Willow cause she's

the one who actually found anything.
Here's an article from Belmouth about the convent and the fire. Seems like there were a ton of deaths and disappearances, only a handful of survivors.

Me: Deaths? Belmouth is a small town. The kind that'd memorialize a big event like that.

Rowan sent back a shrug emoji.

Me: Well, thanks. Anything else?

Rowan: I saw mention of a survivor in Boston. Marina Morales. She was a nun in the convent when it burned down.

I take a deep breath. *Finally*, a lead.

Me: Thanks, Row. Really.

Rowan: Thank Willow too before she flies there and kicks your ass.

I huff a breath.

Me: Priests don't curse, fuckface.

Now he sends an emoji of a donkey. Hell, I didn't even know they had an emoji for that.

I slide my phone back in my pocket and go to find June just as she bursts through the door and into my arms.

"We have to go," she pants in a panicky voice. "We have to go *now*." Before I know it, she's grabbing my hand and pulling me toward the back hallway. I follow her without restraint, but it is only now that I see the tear in her skirt, the shuddering in her shoulders.

I squeeze her hand just after we pass through the door and pull her into me. Her doe eyes are wide, pupils dilated.

"What happened?" I demand more than ask. Cupping her cheeks, I take in her expression. She's terrified. "Daren?"

June feverishly shakes her head. "No, not him. But we have to *go*. Now, Marcelo."

I curse under my breath but run down the hall to our room. She quickly kicks off her skirt, replacing it with a new one.

"Where are we going?" I ask, following her lead and replacing the priest uniform with a fitted black tee, jeans, and boots.

"Boston."

I turn to her and stare. "Boston." I don't have to ask her what's there—Rowan just told me.

June moves into action again, huddling Diablo into her arms. "I—I don't want to leave him here," she mumbles.

I place my hand on her back as I shove my mask and knife in my pocket. "Bring him. Fucker'll have to deal with it if he doesn't like car rides." I grab my hoodie and follow June out the door.

"How long does it take to get from here to Boston?" I ask.

She shrugs. "I've only done the trip a few times. I think about two and a half hours."

June slides into the car the moment I open the door for her, Diablo putting up no fight as he's jostled along with her. As I peel out of the parking lot, I light a cigarette and lower the window. "All right, what happened?" I demand.

Scratching the cat's chin, June bites her lip. "I was coming downstairs and . . ." She hesitates, searching for the words. "And what happened in the hallway with the imps—the day I found out you were my masked man—happened again."

My head snaps to her. "You saw the shadow figure again?"

"Well, yes. But . . ." she huffs a breath, "This wasn't him."

Before I can ask what she means, she straightens in the bench and scooches closer to me, her thigh touching mine as Diablo jumps into the back seat. June grips my upper thigh as if she's holding on for dear life.

"I had a dream the other night. When you left the room and I found you in the confessional. The horned shadow demon was in the convent, and he said something. He . . . didn't feel scary. Not like those freaky imps that day, and definitely not like what I faced today."

"Demons lie," I interrupt.

"I know," she sighs. "But, Marcelo, it was different. He said some things I didn't understand. But, today . . . today there was another demon. A demon leading the imps. The horned one saved me. He stopped the other demon from . . ."

June trails off, and my mind immediately goes to the slit in her skirt.

My grip tightens on the wheel, knuckles going white. "Did it hurt you?"

A corner of her lip lifts. "It tried to. But" —June pulls out the rosary from beneath her shirt—"this also saved me. Right after the demon burned himself, the horned one came and stopped him. He told me to leave. To go—"

"To Boston."

June nods. "And to find—"

"Let me guess. Marina Morales."

Her head snaps back as her eyebrows scrunch together. "Ho—How do you know?"

I grab the wheel with the hand holding my cigarette and pull out my phone. "Rowan texted me with the same name. Apparently, Miss Morales is one of the sole survivors of the convent burning."

June shifts, facing the front again, but still pressed against me. "How do we find her?"

I take a puff of my cigarette and throw it out, not wanting to get anymore of the smoke on my precious little songbird. "Rowan was the one who texted me, but Willow was the one who found the information. Maybe she can find us an address too."

I dial Willow, but—of course—she doesn't pick up. In fact, it goes so quickly to voicemail, I'm pretty sure she's got her phone on "do not disturb." Which means—I can break through it. I call her over and over again, until a frazzled, raspy voice yells, "God dammit, what?!"

June flinches at the volume.

"Willow, I need you to find something."

"*Coño carajo*, do you know what time it is?" she screams.

I keep my voice level, knowing it'll piss her off even more. Which I find incredibly fun. "Yes. Eleven a.m."

"You know *never* to call me before one! It's the rules!" I hear ruffling in the background, the tossing of sheets, the smacking of pillows. "Wasn't the article and the lady's name enough?"

"Well . . . no," I say matter-of-factly. From the corner of my eye, I see June bite back a laugh. "I need her address, Will. June and I are going now."

"You and June, ay?" I practically see her eyebrows wiggling. "Weird fucking date, but okay." The sound of keyboard clicking takes over the phone for a moment before she blurts, "By the way, I'm a video editor. Not a hacker. You could find this lady's address just as easily as I can."

I know she's lying. The girl took IT classes for four years in high school, worked in the field during college, and only later realized her true passion was for editing. She also is an avid true crime fan, considering herself an internet sleuth, and lives on the internet so . . . I *know* she knows her way around a computer way better than me.

"Anyway, I found it." Bingo. "I'll text it over to you now."

"Thank you," I coo.

"Don't call me early again," she hisses, and then, in a brighter tone, "Bye, June!"

June's doe-eyes widen. "Ah, b—bye!" she stutters. So fucking cute.

Willow hangs up and, not even a second later, I get the address to an apartment in the heart of Boston. On the drive, I make June tell me every single detail of the encounters she's had with the demons. I rack my brain trying to figure out what the demon meant in her dream but come up short.

With my hand now braced on her up thigh, I gently squeeze her skin. *Something* touched *my* songbird, and I have every intention of reclaiming what's mine.

My fingers graze her inner thigh, running over the jagged little stretch marks, and something about her soft, textured skin immediately calms me. June shivers next to me, her thighs pressing around my fingers.

"What . . ." she begins, "What demon is affecting us?"

I squeeze her thigh, pausing. "How do we know there

has ever been a demon affecting us?" I turn to look at her briefly. "I know what I feel for you is real. There's never been a doubt that *you* are the reason I've become feral. How do we know the visions and the bouts haven't just been . . . *us* the entire time?"

She grabs my wrist, pulling it from her thigh. "I'm not saying it isn't us," she breathes. I half expect her to place my hand on the wheel and slide to the far end of the bench. But instead, she gently guides my hand to the center of her thighs. With her hand over mine, she presses my fingers against her panties, feeling the heat emanate from her pussy, the damp, slippery wetness already present. "Look what you do to me with just a caress. I *know* it's you doing this to my body—not the demons. But . . ." she says, letting go of my wrist, but leaving my hand free to wander. "The bouts started before you came. And they're different. They're dirty and wrong and nearly painful from how bad it demands something from me." June slowly lifts her skirt over her knees, then raises it to her waist so I can see the dark teal lacy panties she's wearing. "With you, it just feels right. Dark and needy, yes. Sometimes a little depraved." She smirks shyly, and it lights a fire in my chest. "But *right*. With the demon . . . it *always* feels wrong. I don't—It's not like I'm consenting to it. I'm forced into it."

I remove my hand from her thighs and throw my arm around her instead, pulling her flush to me and hugging her. "It feels right with you too. The fantasies I have of you . . . they don't feel evil. As you said, they're definitely depraved. But . . . you make me feel that way."

She curls her legs to the side, tucking her skirt around them. "Is it possible," she starts, leaning her head on my shoulder, "we're being affected by different demons?"

I sigh. "With two, I guess anything is possible."

We're both silent for the rest of the drive, and I'm pretty sure June falls asleep at some point on my shoulder, her breaths growing heavy. Diablo hops back over the bench and curls around June's other side, sandwiching her between us.

I don't want this to end, I realize. I want to stay here, in my car, with my girl and our devilish cat, for as long as possible. I want to take her from Belmouth and find what her heart desires. I want to give both of them a home, a place to call their own. Something I haven't had in a really, really long time. Something I haven't *wanted* since the night Ana and my parents were murdered.

By the time we finally reach Boston, June's rubbing Diablo's little ear, the cat sitting on her lap, but alert. The small tuft of white fur on his chest catches the light, and it once again reminds me how much he does look like a little feline priest.

Traffic is a nightmare, but I would sit through hours of bumper to bumper if only to see the absolute wonder in June's eyes as she takes in the sights around us.

It's a brisk seventy-three degrees out, the sun is shining, and the leaves are a gorgeous array of reds, oranges, and yellows. I roll the windows down, breathing in the fresh city air. It's just about lunchtime, and we see all the people walking the streets to and from offices and homes, colleges and stores. And June's eyes take in all of it.

Once we find our address, we spend nearly twenty minutes driving in circles just to find parking. Diablo hops out of the car, meowing softly as he looks back at June and waits for her.

I shove my arms into my hoodie as we walk, tucking the mask deep into my back pocket.

"We don't know what's going to happen," I say to June.

"So stay close. For all we know, this lady's part of the cult. Or part of the reason the convent burned down."

June grabs my hand, quickening her step to keep up with me as Diablo trots along next to us.

We weave around people in the street, following my phone's map till we make it back outside the apartment building. It's tall and fully made of red brick with black-painted fire escapes. The neighborhood itself isn't too shabby but not necessarily rich either. I take the small set of steps of the stoop two at a time and immediately find *Morales* on the call box at the top. Unit 4B.

"Here it is," I say, pointing at the button. "Wanna do the honors?"

June presses her lips together and steps forward, pressing the call button. It rings once, twice, and then we finally hear the answer tone.

After a moment, an older, accented voice comes through, "Hello?"

"Hola, señora. I'm Father Marcelo Serrano and this is Junia Forester. We're here from St. Mar—"

"Ah," she interrupts. "I wondered when you'd be coming. Come, come."

The door buzzes, and I feel myself hesitate. *I wondered when you'd be coming.* What the Hell does that mean?

June pushes past the entry, holding the door for Diablo to follow in after her before her eyes meet mine.

"I don't like this," I admit, entering behind her.

"It's the only lead we have," she sighs. Her doe eyes meet mine again, and they're full of worry.

"Just . . . stay behind me."

We take the small elevator up to the fourth floor, and quickly find the apartment in question. Partially because there are only five doors, but mostly because the door to 4B is already propped open.

A small, thin woman leans against the door frame, her arms crossed around her. Her long, straight hair has silvered with age, creating a stunning image of tanned skin and glowing hair. Her eyes are dark brown, and a sharp eyebrow raises as she takes us both in. The woman, Marina, doesn't look like a nun. She's dressed in a fuzzy dark cardigan, a black turtleneck, and jeans rolled to her ankles. I do spot a rosary around her neck, in a red so dark it nearly looks black.

"*Hola*," she calls as she straightens. Her eyes fall to Diablo and her hard facade melts away. "Ay, what a cute baby!" Marina makes kissing noises and Diablo runs to her, rubbing himself against her leg. Unfaithful tool.

"Marina Morales, yes?" I ask, squeezing June's hand.

She nods and opens the door wider. "And Marcelo *y* Junia. Come in."

She pads into her apartment, her feet bare on the hardwood, and June and I look at each other once more before following in behind her.

The apartment is small and quaint, with artwork all around the walls. The paintings range from gorgeous fields of flowers to shadowy abysses, with no rhyme or reason as to where they're placed.

Marina walks to her small kitchen and pours some *café* she clearly made only minutes ago into three tiny cups. Then, she pulls a can of tuna from her cabinet, dumps it into a small bowl and places it on the floor for Diablo.

"Marcelo, will you help me carry these to the living room?" she asks.

I grab two of the small cups, and together we follow her into the next room where she sits her cup on a glass coffee table and flops back onto a bright yellow couch. June and I sit on the matching love seat next to it.

"H—how did you know we were coming?" June asks, fiddling with her fingers in her lap. The moment she plucks the skin around her thumb, I entwine my hand with hers.

Marina's eyes follow the movement, lingering on our fingers for a moment, before meeting our eyes again. "You two are in love." It isn't a question but a statement. A fact. Taking a deep breath, she nods. "The church says it's a sin for a priest to break his vows. Well, they say the same about nuns. We're supposed to be married to God. Married to the church. And to live our entire lives in that devotion, and nothing more."

It isn't till she mentions marriage that I see the black band on her ring finger. It's simple, thin, but something about it captures my eyes in that moment, and I find it hard to look away. The black is so dark and deep, so . . . I don't know. It looks like a void, like the true absence of light.

Once again, Marina's eyes track mine, and she waves her hand, turning to her ring.

"I believe this will be easier if you both tell me what you know first," she says, picking up her coffee and sipping slowly.

"No. It won't," I say, leaning back in the chair. "Tell us how you're involved, then we'll tell you what we know."

Marina smirks, slowly nodding. "Fair enough." She sits up straighter, placing the cup back on the glass table with a loud *clack*. "My husband sent you to me. He told me you were coming."

I scowl, but June just tilts her head. "Your . . . husband?"

Marina, once again, nods.

I watch June from the corner of my eye, her eyes darting

around Marina. From her face, to her rings. "Your husband—how long have you been married?"

"Since 1978." Marina smiles, watching the two of us connect the pieces—the small pieces—she gives to us.

That year . . . 1978. That was the same year the convent burned down.

"If I'm wrong," June starts, "this is going to sound *really*, really stupid, but . . ." She pauses, looks at me, then back to Marina, squeezing my hand. "Is your husband the horned demon?"

46

JUNE

Marina smiles at me, her teeth a stunning pearly white.

"He is. Az told me he's had a very difficult time keeping you safe in that hellhole."

My mouth falls open. This woman, once a nun, is married . . . to a demon. An actual horned, shadow demon.

Her grin widens, and she turns to Marcelo. "I told you how I'm involved, now tell me what you know."

Marcelo clenches his jaw and runs his free hand through his already-mused hair. "Fine," he grunts. "I'm an exorcist for the Catholic Church. I was called in to find a demon and eliminate it, but it's been . . . complicated.

"I'm going to assume you know all about demons, being married to one. Upon arrival at St. Mary's, I found . . . your husband. And other creatures. A number of imps, signs of a cult, and now, June has encountered a second demon."

"In which my *husband* saved her from," Marina quipped.

"What Marcelo has said is pretty much all we know. We found the burned convent by following the cult's trail, and your husband was there."

"The cult was also there. Or, about to be—" Marina explains. "He was getting you both out of there before they came."

We're both stunned into silence for a moment. All along, he's been . . . helping us?

"Tell me about this cult," Marcelo pleads, sighing again. I feel the frustration oozing off of him, and I can't help but feel like it's frustration at himself. "I specialize in searching for the occult. I put a stop to cultists practicing and stop them from summoning more into our world. But this—I can't figure out anything about it. Nothing. I know one person who *may* be involved, and that's it."

The mention of Daren sends shivers down my spine. Marcelo wraps his arm around me again, like he had in the car, and pulls me into him. The weight of his arm, the warmth of his skin—it grounds me like nothing else, comforts me like a toasty blanket in a cold room, like fuzzy socks on chilly toes, like my favorite movie on a rainy day. I immediately feel at ease.

"Tell me, exorcist, do you know of the hierarchy of Hell?" Marina questions.

"Sure. Devil, demons, lesser demons, imps."

Marina nods. "There is one, small, subcategory between Devil and demons."

"The princes of Hell?"

"The closest companions to the Devil himself, yes." Marina grabs her coffee again, and this time, I follow her, taking up mine. "The Devil and his princes, Leviathan,

Asmodeus, and Bael. Together, they make for the most powerful combination the nine rings have ever seen. But because of it, their power is often questioned. Namely, by a demon so close in power to the four, he became greedy for more. Valac was condemned to earth, tethered to a mortal body, after trying to usurp the four. He's the leader of your cult."

Marcelo abruptly stands, pacing the room. "Wait. So you're telling me the cult leader is a demon himself?"

Marina nods. "He was when he had his followers overtake the convent too. Asmodeus was the first demon he tried to tether to the earth, and"—she lifts her hand, flashing her ring to us—"he was successful. Az hasn't been able to return to Hell since."

"Not that I mind." A voice, deeper than I've ever heard, but smooth—familiar—rings behind us. Marcelo halts in his tracks and I quickly turn to look as well. Walking from what I only assume is the bedroom comes a massive man decked in a three-piece black suit. He's larger than large, with shoulders the width of a doorway, and more than a few inches taller than Marcelo. His tan skin is darkened by black, wavy hair reaching his waist, and his eyes—his eyes are a brilliant amber, like that of molten gold.

The man saunters across the room casually, and plops on the yellow couch next to Marina. He smiles at her before grabbing her chin between his forefinger and thumb, pulling her lips to his. As they kiss, I see a matching black ring on his finger, and instantly know—this . . . *man* isn't a man at all. He's the demon, Asmodeus.

Marcelo falls onto the couch next to me, stunned. "What the fuck does he want with June and I?"

Asmodeus leans back on the couch, his arm draped around Marina. He looks like he's in his mid-thirties,

Marina twice his age if not more—yet, it's so obvious the two are still madly in love with each other.

The demon pulls Marina back against him. "With you? I have no clue. With her . . ." Those amber eyes lock onto me. "He's wanted her for a long time. He's been . . . grooming her. Getting her ready."

Marcelo's entire body goes rigid. His fists clench, his teeth grind against each other. "For what?" he barks out.

"Valac has had a long, *long* time to plan. I know he wants to tether us to mortals, to get us out of Hell, but somehow, he plans on breaking *his* tether to get back in. And my guess, he plans on doing that through her." He raises a long, thick finger. I hadn't noticed before, but his nails are long and sharp, the entire tips of his fingers a dark charcoal, as if dipped in soot.

"Is he possessing someone in the church?" Marcelo asks, but the words are beginning to sound fuzzy. Far away.

All I can think of are the demon's words. *Grooming her. Getting her ready.* And then, the other demon. *You've no idea how long we've wanted you, Junia. How long we've waited. I've been preparing you for me. Preparing your body to accept me.*

I'm a target. No. *The* target.

I know who the demon is. I should've known a long time ago.

Asmodeus slowly nods. "Valac—"

Just as he says the name again, my entire body convulses forward. Suddenly, it's too hot in the apartment, too hot in my clothes, too hot in my skin. My cheeks flush, and my skin feels like it's on fire.

"June, what's wrong?" Marcelo grabs my shoulders, his touch rocking through my body, shooting straight to my core. I'm already so wet in just a matter of seconds, my pussy throbbing for . . . something, anything. I grab Marcelo's arm to steady myself, digging my nails into him.

"We have to go," he says, more to me than to Marina and Asmodeus. "Thank you for your help." Marcelo helps me stand, holding me to him the entire time. His hard body rubbing against mine sends another wave of euphoria through me.

Marina stands, taking a step toward me before Asmodeus catches her wrist, his dark voice booming. "You know what's happening to her, love. You can't help her."

Marina's eyes harden, her lip sticking out as if she's not ready to give up. "Have him help you, June." She nods her head at Marcelo. "Until it ends, have him help you." Her eyes shift to Marcelo. "I'm sorry to ask this of you, Father, but continue to break your vows for her. Save her. Stop Valac."

Marcelo pulls me to him again as I stumble over my own feet. He lifts me into his chest, hugging his hands under my ass as he positions my thighs around his waist. "I will," he tells her. Then, louder, "Diablo!"

Marcelo turns toward the door, my head swirling to face the room, Marina, Asmodeus, and Diablo trotting up to us. For a brief moment, Diablo turns to Asmodeus, and the demon looks back. A smile tilts the demon's lips, a wink of a golden eye.

And then, the door to apartment 4B closes, with me draped in Marcelo's arms and Diablo running under our feet.

Marcelo dashes into the elevator, and as soon as the door closes behind us, I can't help but grind against him, hiking my skirt high enough to feel his jeans press against me, to feel the rough texture against my skin. I'm moaning before I even realize it, pressing my face into the crook of his neck. His leathery scent fused with the frankincense from the church is enough to make me drunk, I can never have enough of this—of him, of his scent, his body, his touch.

Marcelo takes a few shuffling steps back, leaning against the elevator wall.

"June," he groans. "June, tell me what you need." I feel his cock hardening against me, reacting to my neediness. And, my God, does that not turn me on even more.

I can't help but kiss his neck, licking his Adam's apple, hungrily searching for his lips. "You," I say against his skin. "I *need* you."

He cups my ass, squeezing hard as he pulls me into him again, grinding his hips in time with mine. His cock is so hard now, pressing against my lace panties, and I want nothing more than to rip all the fabric between us so our skin can be touching.

Marcelo chuckles, a deep sound that reverberates through his chest to mine, sparking my nipples to life as they rub against him. "The demon can't have you, June," he grunts into my hair. His hands tighten around me, forcing another moan to slip free.

"I'm all yours," I breathe. The demon may be the reason this is happening to my body, and it may even be a way for it to try to claim me—but it can't have something that is already taken. "You are my Salvation, my freedom, and I want to make this demon regret it ever tried to stake a claim on my body." I grind against him more, more. Desperate for him, needy, and wanting. I kiss him, mixing the hunger I feel for him with the lust the demon has embedded in me. I'll make the demon regret making me want for anything, but I will *never* want for *it*. I will only ever want for my masked man, my priest, my Salvation. I will only ever want for Marcelo.

47

MARCELO

The moment the elevator doors open, Diablo knows to get as far fucking away as the little devil can. I'd fuck June in this lobby if I didn't think someone would interrupt us. I kiss her, cupping her perfect fucking ass, and carrying her back out to the Boston roads. Her legs clamp tighter around me as I walk, and each step is like a new training in torture as my hard cock rubs against her soaked pussy.

Part of me feels bad about running out on Marina and the demon. The other part of me has already forgotten everything they told me.

All I can focus on is this perfect fucking woman wrapped around me, with her teeth nibbling my bottom lip, her hands digging into my hair, her tight ass filling my palms.

I dip into the nearest alleyway—and while it may be

the middle of the day, it's dark and secluded enough that I really couldn't give a fuck if anyone walks past us. When deeper into the alley, I spin and slam June against the brick wall. She moans as my cock rubs against her, and before she can focus her eyes to the darkness, I'm hiking her skirt to her waist and shoving some of the fabric into her mouth.

June looks up at me with those stunning eyes through her long lashes, and it takes everything in me not to drop her to her knees and fuck her mouth as she keeps those doe eyes on me.

Instead, I smirk. "Pinned against a wall, songbird, just like that night in your room." It was the first time June tried to be a little brat with me. She fought so hard to deny that her body wanted me, but in the end—I knew. I always knew. Her body craved me like I craved her.

"Now, use that pretty mouth and bite down on your skirt so I can fuck you nice and hard."

June throws her head back and nods, grinding into me more and more. I can feel how soaked she is as it seeps through her panties onto my jeans, and a part of me hopes she leaves a mark on them if only to show everyone what I do to her.

My fingers at her ass move, trailing the backs of her thighs before inching up to her slippery cunt. I move in to kiss her neck as I pull her panties to the side and slide my fingers between her wet lips. She immediately groans at my touch and it reminds me once again that I'll never get enough of hearing her sing.

I don't have to ask her if she wants this—I *know* she does. She's become greedy for my cock, wanting it more and more, and now is no exception.

Sliding my index and middle finger inside of her, I unzip my jeans and pull myself free. I'm already rock hard from her sweet little sounds and desperate hips from the elevator, I don't need any kind of preparation.

"So fucking hot," I breathe, watching the cross tattooed on my finger disappear into her cunt over and over again. June bucks her hips, begging for more.

Leaning into her, I bite her neck, my teeth sending goosebumps along her skin, just as I pull my fingers out and replace them with my cock. June screams around her skirt as I thrust fully inside of her, not waiting for her tight cunt to adjust to my size. I feel her hot inner walls flutter around me and I feel like I'm about to pass out from how fucking tight she is, how squeezed my dick feels inside of her.

I want June to see the same stars I am, so I pull all the way out before slamming back into her. She screams again, her legs bucking as her nails dig into my shoulders.

"You wanted hard, didn't you?" I huff a laugh. There are tears in the corner of June's eyes, but she nods feverishly, moaning around her skirt. I'm suddenly desperate to hear her sing, desperate to feel those fast, short breaths from her pants against my skin.

Shrugging the hoodie off, I let it fall to the ground and wrap my arms around her. Her eyes fall to the veins under my skin connecting all my tattoos, and I feel her cunt clamp around me. Fuck, she's so naughty, lusting after me. And so fucking hot.

"Eyes up here, baby." I chuckle and pull the skirt from her lips, letting it fall between us. "I wanna hear you sing. Fuck if anyone walks by, let them hear you too."

June's mouth falls open as if she's about to say something, but I don't wait for her. I pull out once more and slam into her, her ass slapping against the bricks behind her.

"Ah, Marcelo!" she screams, and then softly moans my name again. "More—please!"

I do as my goddess commands. I fuck into her harder, faster, not slowing my pace. June pulls my shirt to my waist, watching my abs contour and move as I lift her, as I grind into her. She watches the thrust and dip of my hips as I fuck her, and it drives her wild. June's eyes have never looked more heady; her cheeks are a shade of red I don't think I've seen before. She moans loudly, not caring that we're in public—in fact, I know she does it *because* we're in public and I find it so incredibly hot, it fuels each thrust of my hips into her.

I smash my lips into hers, feeling how tight she is around me, how she clenches her pussy around my cock as though she's begging me to stay.

Mi amor knows I'll never leave her.

I won't. I can't.

I may be her Salvation, but Junia Forester is my *every-thing*.

I walk a few steps behind June, watching her waddle. She came hard, covering her thighs in her sweet come as she dripped down my cock. I offered to lick her clean, but June could barely catch her breath by the time I finally pulled out of her and set her back on her feet. I didn't think it'd be fair to her lungs.

Plus, now it just gives me an excuse to *clean her up* in the shower when we get back.

"You feelin' okay, love?" I tease, knowing fully well how sore she must be. I haven't fucked her that hard. Not even as the masked man. But I *know* she loved every second of it.

June turns around and raises a brow. "I don't know. I think I'm still sick." She shrugged. "I think I need a little more *medicine*."

I laugh and sprint up to her, smacking her ass and feeling the bounce of it on my palm. June gasps, tensing the entire lower half of her body. "Really?" Now I raise a brow. "Is that what the doctor ordered?"

"The doctor said to take as needed, and I'm still needing."

I can't wait to get home.

As we finally round the final corner to the car, I see Diablo sitting on the hood of the Mustang, licking his front paw. The moment his golden eyes find us, he jumps from the hood and waits by the door.

Damned smart cat.

The car ride back is uneventful—save for the mind-blowing head June gives me the moment we pull away from Boston and onto lesser-known roads. Diablo hides in the back, and I couldn't be more thankful to the little fucker to give us our privacy—even if we're in a contained metal box.

Her tongue slides over my cock, and her hot mouth feels just as delicious as her cunt did in the alley, it isn't long before I'm gripping her hair and coming down her throat.

Fuck. My angel.

Part of me knows why she's so needy for me right now, why she needs more, more, more—it's why I'm desperate too.

As I carry her through the threshold of the apartment, my tongue sucking on hers, I know it's because everything will change tonight. As I lay her down on our living room floor, and slide the skirt back to her waist, ripping her panties off, I know it's because she knows it too. As I feast on her till she's screaming my name, her back arching and fingers digging into my hair, I know it's because we're already planning to face the cult tonight, to face the demon. As I fuck her slow and steady under the hot steam of the shower, her ass pressed against the cold wall, I know it's because there's a chance we won't get to be like this again.

As I hold June in my arms, her naked body cuddling into mine, her damp hair on my shoulder, her arms tracing the tattoos on my chest, her legs wrapped around me—I know I'm desperate to show her how much I love her, how much I want her, and how much I need her—

Because, after tonight, we might not get another chance.

I kiss her head, and then push back onto the bed, hiking her legs on my shoulders, ready to make love to her again.

48

JUNE

I've begun to lose count of the times Marcelo has brought me to absolute euphoria when the bedroom finally shifts from the radiant pinks and oranges of the sunset to the full darkness of a Belmouth night. I cling to him, limbs wrapped around his neck and waist, and I've determined that it would be completely fine if I decided to never let go.

What's one demon in Belmouth going to do about it?

What'll two demons do about it?

I sigh into his chest, where the wings of an angel are scarred into his skin. Marcelo's fingers twist into my hair, twirling a lock round and round as his other hand rubs my back.

"We can stay," he says to the room. "We can stay here tonight. Pretend we learned nothing."

I want nothing more. *What's one night to a demon?*

But I know we can't. The demon showed itself to me today. And if the raging horny-fest was any indicator earlier, it *knows* we know.

And worse, *I* know the demon is Daren. The bouts only started *after* he moved in with us. Not to mention, he's basically told me himself. *He said if I wait till the time is right, I can have you.* Now, it makes sense—the *he* Daren mentioned is the demon, Valac.

"What do you normally do at this point?" I ask, looking up at him; his brown eyes look black in the darkness.

Marcelo sighs and cups my cheek. "I'd follow the lead."

I press my lips together and sit up. "Then that's what we have to do."

Marcelo follows me, and I can't help but watch his abs tighten as he sits up. I'd be drooling over this man all day if I could.

Note to self: remember to burn all his clothes when this is over. I want to see him like this every day for the rest of our lives.

I know it's wishful thinking. But . . . it's what I need to be brave enough for tonight.

"But this is different, *mi amor*. Nothing about this follows my normal routine. Not since you became the center of . . . of everything. Of *my* everything." He grabs my shoulders and turns me to him. My breasts press against his chest, his heartbeat in sync with my own. "You heard the demon today. *You* are the target."

"And I'm sure it'll find a way to use me whether we face them tonight or not." I cup his face in my hands and force him to look into my eyes. "That . . . *thing* showed itself to me today. It paralyzed me, and I could do absolutely nothing to fight against it. You didn't even realize it was happening, but it felt like I was trapped for hours, yet it was only a few minutes."

Taking my hands, Marcelo entwines our fingers and brings them to his lap. "So, what are you proposing we do?"

I take a deep breath. "We follow Daren. Let him lead us to the convent, confirm there is in fact a full-fledged cult, and then—"

"And then, what? Take on a group of who knows how many men? Take on a demon? Songbird, I don't know if you'd be able to throw a punch without breaking your finger."

"We call the cops."

He chuckles, and while my immediate reaction is to feel like he's patronizing me, I know he's not. He knows so much more about this than I do, it must be like explaining Demon 101 to a toddler.

"One, cops aren't necessarily equipped for demon combat. Two, in half the towns I visit like this, the entire police force is part of the group."

I straighten. "Okay. No cops."

"A better idea would be to get you as far away from here as possible. I could send you to Miami. Rodrgio will know what to do—and you could stay with Willow. Then I'll have Rowan call in back up. Until they get here, I'll follow the cult members, one by one, and pick them off."

"I'm *not* leaving. You promised you'd never let me out of your sight."

"*Mi amor*, this is the only way I can think to do that." His fingers tighten on mine and he pulls our hands to his chest. "I have exorcised a lot of demons. I have hunted much of the occult. Never, once in my fifteen years of doing this, have I encountered anything close to dealing with the Devil. If this demon—" He pauses and takes a deep breath. "If Valac is trying to face the Devil, trying to overpower and outsmart him, if he already *has* tethered one of the princes of Hell to Earth, then he is stronger than anything I have ever faced. And he wants *you*."

I bite my lip, not wanting to give in.

"Songbird, *please*. Please do this for me. If you got hurt—" He stops himself just as his voice breaks. There are unshed tears in his eyes, worry and fear pouring out of him. "Please," he begs quietly, squeezing my hands once more.

I've never seen fear in this man. Not when he faced down a league of demons, not when he snuck into the heart of a cult, not when he punched my stepfather in the face and confronted my mother. And especially not when he broke his vows of priesthood—for me. Marcelo is rough around the edges; he's hard, strong and courageous and uses his trauma to his advantage.

But now, the fear is breaking, cracking the hard facade he's built after so many years. Fissures grow rapidly, and I see the fear in his eyes. The image of his sister, bent and broken, of his father, lost and bloodied. Of his mother, crucified.

I see that fear and know he is imagining me as they were. Battered, murdered, and no more.

This is more than me, I tell myself. If Valac is able to un-tether himself to the mortal realm *through me*, what would that mean for humanity? Would it go unnoticed? Would the literal Devil walking amongst us, stuck here instead of in Hell where he belongs, be any different?

Would the world simply end? Armageddon and all that?

"Okay," I mumble. Marcelo doesn't ask twice. He grabs my face and kisses me, over and over, my lips, my cheeks, my jaw, my forehead, my neck, all the while murmuring against my skin, "Thank you, I love you."

Sliding out from under the covers, his warmth now a visceral absence, Marcelo slides into the pair of jeans he'd thrown to the floor hours ago and grabs his phone from the nightstand.

"I'm gonna go call Rodrigo. We'll get you the soonest flight out of her so get dressed and pack a bag if you can."

I nod, starting the crawl out of bed. "And Diablo?"

Marcelo is already scrolling through his phone. "You can take him with you." His eyes find me in the dark of the room, and he steps toward me. His lips are on mine before I even clock that he's leaning down, and he presses me back into the bed, his body atop mine.

"I fucking love you, June. Please, please know that." I feel his bare chest heave against my nipples, the rough fabric of his jeans between my legs. "I'm going to fucking kill Daren for you. I'll make him regret ever laying a hand on you, ever seeking you out." More kisses, his tongue sliding between my lips.

"When you get back," I breathe against his lips, "I want you to spank me so hard, you leave your mark on me forever."

Marcelo bites my lips and pulls till it's almost painful. "I'll spank your pussy till you're coming all over my hand." My lips are swollen, but I want more. More of him. Always. Forever. "And I'll do it where anyone can hear us, where anyone can walk in and see the mess you make all over me." He licks the shell of my ear, sending shivers all over my body, heating between my thighs. And I know he feels the heat through his jeans as I feel his cock harden against my stomach. My eyes flutter closed, imagining each and every thing he whispers to me. "And then I'll lick you all clean, my little songbird."

There's a weight on the bed around me, heavier at first—before it's completely gone. Gone is the leg between my thighs, gone is the length of him on my stomach, gone is the heat of his chest teasing my nipples.

My eyes snap open, and Marcelo is just . . . gone.

His phone is resting by my head; there's no sound in the apartment to tell me he's walked outside.

It's like he's just vanished.

All that's left to prove he was just here is the warmth spreading in my core, the scent of frankincense and leather, and—

And the circle of black soot marring the carpet where he had just been.

49

MARCELO

One minute, I'm ready to give June a little taste of what I plan to do to her once we reunite, and the next, all I see is black smoke and the familiar smell of sulfur. The smell of demons.

I'm shirtless, shoeless, Bibleless, and rosaryless, but fuck if I'm not going to adjust to whatever the Hell is happening. The smoke starts to dissipate around me, and I'm immediately hit by the chill under my feet. Cold, wet stone, and the smell of damp moss. I know where I am before I see it.

The burned convent.

As the black smoke falls around me, I find myself standing in the center of a massive, painted sigil on the stone floor. It isn't the typical, rudimentary upside down pentagram. It's . . . more. It's advanced. Sharp, jagged lines fused with swirling symbols, four-pointed stars, interlocked triangles—so much my eyes can't take it all in at once. Lit red candles sit on the circumference of the circle, wax dripping down and spilling through the lines, ignoring gravity all together. But what's more daunting than the clear dismissal of physics are the fifteen or so hooded figures all standing around the circle.

Each figure is shrouded in a long black cloak—typical, yes, but on their faces are masks similar to that of the imps I've faced in the time since I've been in Belmouth. Horrifying, unnatural, cherub-like faces with big blue eyes and sculpted-on blond curls stare back at me and I can't help but chuckle as I face them all.

"So, the imps were yours, huh, Valac?"

I slowly spin, trying to pin which one the leader could be—which one the demon is hiding behind. If my hunch is right, it's Daren. And as I told June earlier, I will get such sweet satisfaction in ending his life and sending the demon within him back to oblivion. I try to clock any differences in attire, any sign that shows one of these babies might truly be *el jefe*.

But, there's nothing.

They are all dressed the same, staring at me with those bright, dead eyes.

"This is the game you wanna play?" I open my arms, taking a deep breath. "All right," I grunt, steeling myself. "Blessed Michael, archangel, defend us in the hour of conflict—"

"Shut him up," a voice says behind one of the masks.

But I don't stop, even as steps scurry toward me. "Be our safeguard against the wickedness"—the first pair of hands grab for me, and I blindly swing, punching a cultist in its baby face—"and snares of the devil, may God restrain him, we humbly pray."

Another pair of arms, and I'm spinning out the way, yanking on fabric as I go. One of the bodies trips and the other clumsily falls over their taut cloak. As expected, these are just townsfolk coerced into something dark. Something promising. If they're allowing themselves to be led by filth like Daren, maybe I worried for nothing. "And do thou, O Prince of the heavenly host, by the power of God thrust Satan down to Hell and with him those other wicked spirits." The fools finally stop coming at me one at a time and rush me together. Four bodies collide with mine as I crash to the floor, hard. I feel scraps on my shoulder blades and they drag me against the stone, but I don't let up. If I can only finish the prayer—"Who wander through the world for the ruin of souls! Amen."

The bodies stop. All is silent.

And then, a cackle.

The hands around me suddenly melt, flesh oozing onto my skin like the wax from the red candles. "What the fuck?" I yell as the cloaks quickly deflate, more of that wax melting onto my skin, hardening all too quickly.

Suddenly, it's not wax at all but more like cement.

A husky yet booming voice reverberates through the convent. "Father Marcelo, exorcist of the church—I must thank you. The prayer of Michael is always one of my favorites."

Fuck, this is bad. I can't move my arms or legs. They're plastered to the stone below me. New shadowy figures emerge from the darkness in the corners. More cloaks, but now the cultists don't hide their faces behind plastic masks—instead they're painted stark white with red haphazardly dragged over their eyes.

"My favorite part," says the voice again, his voice morphing into something recognizable—losing the rasp and shifting into something almost human. "Is when you little priests say, 'Thrust Satan down to Hell and with him those other wicked spirits who wander through the world for the ruin of souls.'" He cackles again. "Don't you know, my dear boy? That's exactly what I'm trying to do."

One of the cloaked figures walks up to me and just as they breach the circle, all the candles extinguish, bathing us in pure darkness.

I can't see the person's face, but someone grabs hold of my hair, yanking my head up.

"Now, I've been planning exactly what I want to do to you, and I just had the most wonderful idea," he coos. The hard wax pinning me down feels like it's ripping at my skin the more the figure pulls me, like my limbs are preparing themselves to be torn away.

"Any guesses?" he teases.

But I don't give the fucker any satisfaction.

"Our Father, who art in Heaven," I spew, and for a moment, I hear the sizzling of flesh, smell the burning of skin.

The figure yanks my scalp again. "That's right. *Your* father. I think it's time we paid an homage to him, whaddya say? Your mother did such an excellent job filling the role, it'll be hard to fill her shoes—but I think you've got it."

My blood runs cold at the mention of my mother, memories of her lifeless body on my kitchen floor, limbs strung out to mimic the cross, her blood everywhere.

Let him go! Take me, she said.

"Let him go!" the demon mimics. "Take me!" The figure pats my chest before finally releasing my hair and standing straight. "Oh, honey. I'll never let you go."

It all happens way too fast. The faceless cloaked figure lets me go and the hardened wax around me quickly heats, melting onto me like a faux layer of armor, red and bright as it coats me in a burning hot casket of a second skin.

The new, real cultist figures circling me step in closer, blurring my vision in a flurry of darkness as hands grab at me everywhere. I feel hot, sharp slashes against my arms, my chest, and then the hands wrap around me, lifting me from the floor and raising me up high.

"What are you doing?" I grunt out.

A hand jabs into my ribs hard. "Shut up!" This voice . . . it's different from the one before. It's gruff and harsh, and just a little bit slurred.

Daren.

50

JUNE

hat the fuck, is all can think. The words play on repeat in my mind like a broken radio.

Marcelo's gone—no, taken. I jump out of bed, careful not to damage the summoning circle that wisped Marcelo away from me, and get dressed as quickly as possible. I'm on autopilot or . . . protect-boyfriend-pilot, as I slide one of Marcelo's hoodies over the simple black dress, and lace-up boots over my tights, making sure to put on his rosary. On the nightstand sits his mask, knife, and car keys. I pocket them all, grab his phone abandoned on the bed, and run from the bedroom.

Diablo stayed outside when we got back home, running into the backyard of the cathedral as he hunted after a bug or a bird—but now the black feline trots up to me the moment I open the back door of the apartment. He follows me as I hurry to Marcelo's car, and leaps into the bench the

348

moment I open the door. The little devil is as smart as I knew him to be.

My body is still simply reacting to Marcelo's disappearance. I haven't *thought* about following him, I just simply am. I haven't *thought* of where this drive will take me, I just know.

I put the car in reverse and step a little too hard on the accelerator. It has been such a long time since I've been behind the wheel, but I refuse to let it stop me.

As I feel the thrum of the engine roll through me, I can't stop my mind from spiraling. Daren took Marcelo. He *took* him. Stole him right from my arms. I know Marcelo wanted me to be safe, to get as far away from here as possible . . . but that just wasn't going to happen anymore. Not with him in danger. Not when I could maybe do something about it.

I speed down Belmouth roads, not even checking the speedometer. I lift Marcelo's phone and thank God he keeps it unlocked as I call the contact already pulled up.

"*Oye, papo, qué bolá?*" a gruff but joyous voice says through the phone. Based on everything Marcelo has told me about the man, Father Rodrigo's voice matches him perfectly.

"H—Hi," I squeak. "I'm calling on behalf of Father Marcelo. My name is—"

"Ah, June, *si?* Marcelo told me about you. How can I help you, *señorita?*"

I don't know if it's the years of being terrified of my mother but delivering bad news has *never* been my strong suit.

"Um," I stutter, "this is a lot. But . . . Marcelo has been kidnapped."

"What?" Father Rodrigo says dumbfounded.

"By a demon," I continue.

"*Ay, Dios mío,*" he sighs, and I can practically imagine the man crossing himself. "Tell me everything."

So I do—of course, I leave the part out that we were naked in bed, about to go to bone town, when he was abducted by the evil powers that be. I don't think Father Rodrigo needs that part. But I do tell him of our earlier visit to Marina and Asmodeus, of everything they told us, and of my suspicions about Daren.

"You met Sister Marina?" he asks, his voice in shock.

"Yes."

"And did she tell you? What the demon wants?"

I huff a breath. "More or less."

"So you know you should be turning the car around right now and start driving in the opposite direction as fast as you can?"

I should. But I won't.

"I'm going to save Marcelo. I'm *going* to get him out of there."

Father Rodrigo blows out an exasperated breath.

"Figured. Can I convince you to wait?" he asks, uncertain. But if he's asking, it already means he knows the answer. When I don't answer, he mumbles something under his breath in Spanish. "Don't trust anyone, *mija.* Only Marcelo. And . . ." The priest pauses, and I can hear hesitation in his voice. "And Asmodeus, if he returns to assist you—if any of the four appear. I know it is outlandish to hear, but the Devil and his princes are not our enemies."

I do a quick double take at the phone before returning my eyes to the road. "You want me to . . . trust the demons?"

"Not all of them. Just the four."

I think of the ex-nun, of her demon husband. I think of that same husband saving me from the clutches of darkness, from the terrifying imps threatening to devour us.

Nothing makes sense, but nothing has ever made sense in my life.

"Okay, I will."

"I'll call every contact I have in the east. Don't lose faith, *mija*. It's your strongest ally right now."

I nod even though he can't see through the phone and hangup, not wanting him to hear how reckless I'm being.

Because no matter how much I don't want to admit it, I *do* have a plan.

It's not a very good one.

In fact, it's downright awful and I fully believe it *won't* work.

But it's the only thing I can do for Marcelo.

I'm going to give the demon exactly what he wants— me.

51

JUNE

No, stay here!" I hiss at Diablo, but the little fur ball leaps from the car, already running across the street where I parked the Mustang, and into the woods.

Dammit.

Cars line the side of the woods, Diablo disappearing between them. I recognize a lot of these cars. There's Mark Winston's—he's at church every Sunday. And there's Jeremy Rodrick's—my math teacher in the seventh grade.

And of course, there's my mother's car—which Daren has a habit of borrowing without permission on late nights.

I zip Marcelo's hoodie up to my neck and grab his mask still hanging from the pocket. I know my identity being hidden won't make a difference, but . . . Marcelo always finds strength from this piece of painted leather. So maybe I will too.

Sliding the mask over my face, I pull the ties on the back of it till it conforms to my cheeks, my chin, my eyes. The material is tough and the small, hidden eye holes darken my vision—but something about wearing it also invigorates me. I will be Marcelo's Salvation, just as much as he is mine. I'm ready for whatever the Hell this demon is about to throw at me.

Patting the rosary still around my neck, I sprint across the street and into the woods. Diablo matches my pace next to me and together we run to where Marcelo and I had found the hatch just days ago.

The moon is bright, not quite full but definitely close, and the early fall wind is in full bloom as it rushes against me. Trees rustle, leaves dance, and while I am absolutely terrified of what's about to happen, of what *is currently* happening to Marcelo, a part of me is also . . . happy.

With the wind rushing through my hair like this, it reminds me of driving with Marcelo, the windows down. It reminds me of running from Daren that night, of running from my mother's house and all I've ever known. It reminds me of letting myself give in to my desires and fucking Marcelo in that confessional.

It reminds me of being free, and in a sad, twisted way, this decision I've made here, tonight, is the first real decision I've ever made for myself. No one else contributing or telling me what I should do, no one else stopping me, no matter how reckless I may be. Tonight, I break the final pieces of the shell Marcelo has been hacking away at.

Tonight, I am Junia Forester, a woman free to make her own choices, to live her own life, to write her own song.

My boots skid along the leafy ground when I finally spot the hatch. It's not covered like it had been the other day, the leaves clearly misplaced when people had used it earlier, I guess.

I heave it open. A gust of stale air hits my legs as I stand above the opening. It looks so much different than it had when the sun was up. Now, the ladder leading into the hole completely disappears before reaching the bottom, as if begging me to climb into a fathomless abyss. I take a deep breath, steeling myself for my recklessness, sending a prayer to protect Marcelo.

"Okay, now you have to stay *here,*" I tell Diablo, scratching between his ears. But the cat only continues to look at me with those golden eyes. His pupils are huge and so freaking cute, but no matter how much it might make me want to cuddle and squeeze him, I won't bring him into demonic affairs.

However, Diablo seems to have other plans. The moment I begin my descent, the cat leaps onto my shoulders, digging its claws into my hood and climbing till, somehow, he's resting between the back of my head and the fold of the hood. Diablo meows into my ear, clearly annoyed, but makes no further movement.

I pause in my descent, ready to throw the cat back up if I have to, when I hear a guttural, agonizing yell. Immediately, I know it's Marcelo.

"Fine," I grunt at the cat, not wanting to waste a moment more as I hurry down the ladder.

It's pitch black as I climb down, down, down. I don't remember the ladder being this long, nor the tunnel's ground being this far away from the surface. With each step, I'm more and more sure the next peg just won't exist, and I'll slip all together and fall into the nothingness below me.

Finally, my boot hits something, and it takes more than a moment to realize it's solid ground. I don't know how

I'm going to navigate the rest of the tunnel in the dark, but—that fear doesn't matter.

Because right when I plant both of my feet in the tunnel, the entire path illuminates with red wax candles.

Just like the other day, the path curves, making it seem endless—just like the ladder. I step into the tunnel, slowly making my way to the door leading to the convent.

It's so much eerier now than it had been the other day, when Marcelo was with me. Now, it feels like something is walking right behind me—on top of me almost. It's different from feeling eyes on the back of my head—I can feel the warmth, *almost* hear the sound of footsteps, the hair on my neck reacting to the static of something *else*. But every time I look over my shoulder, nothing is there.

The candles continue to drip with wax, overflowing the sconces and spilling onto the floor. They look like they've been burning for hours, which can't be since they only turned on when I got here, but the red wax leaves trails like blood on the ground, my instincts screaming at me to *run away*.

I shiver, so glad now to have the warm fuzzball at my neck comforting me.

And it is exactly when I have this thought that all comfort shatters.

Because, shit—every horror movie has trained me for this moment, trained me to *know* that *shit is about to go down.*

At that moment, down the winding corridor, an organ strikes its first note.

It's somber than anything I've ever played, eliciting even more fear within me. The notes match each of my footsteps, drawing me closer and closer to the door awaiting me at the end of the tunnel. The music from the organ reverberates through the dirt around me, the candle lights flickering as if an unfelt wind were blasting through, surrounding me.

Diablo's nails dig through the hoodie, poking at my skin, and the slight sting reminds me *this* is real. Not a horror movie. Not a nightmare. Not a vision.

I'm really here—in the tunnel leading me to a *real* cult, worshiping and summoning and doing Heaven knows what with a *real* demon. All to save my *real*, incredibly hot, incredibly scandalous, *priest, exorcist, boyfriend*—three words that sound so fictional, the idea of them together makes even less sense.

But somehow, it's real and I'm here, and the haunting symphony only an organ can make is pulling me deeper and deeper into this warped reality.

Finally, the familiar wooden door with black iron designs stands before me. The door almost seems to . . . to breathe, growing slowly as if it's been waiting for me for a very, very long time. I now realize the symbol on the door had been carved and weathered into it. The style just doesn't match the gothic slopes of iron, not with its fast and jagged lines.

I take a deep breath, finding the mask oddly breathable as the warm air against my cheeks steadies me. As I approach the door, the music begins to speed, the player clearly laying on the keys with fast fingers. Once again, I feel the draw to go within as I near, the symbol almost begging me.

Staring at it, I notice it starts to look like overlapped letters. I see two *X*s, and *L* and a *C*. I know *CLXX* is 170 in roman numerals but . . . the number doesn't mean anything to me. I reach my hand up, ready to trace the symbol, when the music slams into an eruption of sound. I jump out of my skin, yelping as I feel my heart burst from my chest.

Like an explosion, everything is *too* silent the moment the notes fade—the music stops, the violent scream from earlier doesn't repeat, and all I can hear is my own rapid pulse thrum in my ears.

My mother's words from what feels like a lifetime ago slither into my mind. *"We need to fight off his influence. You don't want to be his puppet, do you?"* She was talking about the Devil then. How everything I thought I knew has changed since she said that to me. How *she* was the puppet controlling my strings all along, influencing me to retreat, to hide, to obey.

But . . . if Marina and her husband, if Father Rodrigo, if *Marcelo* are all right . . . if the Devil is not one to fear, then maybe I've been just afraid for nothing all along. Maybe the "Devil" hasn't been the evil lingering over my life that my mother always warned about—maybe it's not the pitchfork-wielding red guy in Hell, but more the devils we know, the person sitting next to you in a pew.

And if that's true, the devil *I* know has always been her. She's brought the danger to me, brought her flock of demons in the men she dated. She beat me like I was a seducer in Dante's eighth circle, a demon in her own right.

Compared to her, compared to what I've lived through, this demon—Valac—will be nothing. And maybe . . . just maybe . . . she's been influenced all along. Maybe the daggers in her eyes have been caused by the demon—like my bouts. Maybe those daggers aren't *really* her.

That's when I realize the sigil on the door isn't roman numerals—those aren't Xs, but a *V* and *A*.

The sigil is spelling Valac.

I take another deep breath and push myself through the marked door and into the stone basement of the convent.

52

MARCELO

*F*uck, *I can't feel my hands, my feet.* I lost feeling in them minutes ago, hot blood dripping down from where I'm hung, down my forehead and into my eyes.

There's music encompassing the room—so loud it feels like it's coming from directly inside my head. The notes are dark and ominous but the sound . . . it reminds me of my songbird, her fingers playing over the keys of the organ during Mass.

I smile to myself, thinking of her . . . thinking of her soft brown hair twirled in my fingers. Thinking of her lips as she kisses me. Thinking of her plump ass hanging off the back of the bench when she feels the music encompass her as she plays for a church that doesn't deserve her.

And as I smile, I finally start to feel . . . everything.

I don't know when I blacked out—I can't even remember it happening. But one moment I was being dragged across the room, and slammed onto a wooden slab, as my limbs were yanked and pinned by the hands and knees of others. It had been like a nightmare—until they flashed the metal nails they planned to use to permanently pin me to what I only now realized is a cross.

They crucified me then, just like the demon from my childhood had done to my mother, nailing my palms to the wood, my feet together. I screamed myself hoarse, my throat raw, and at some point, everything must've gone black.

Now, I've been thrust at the front of the convent, just behind the altar at the head of the church.

Stabbing pain mars my scalp, as I feel a crown of thorns jabbing into my forehead. Yet, through the blood dripping from my brow into my eyes, I can see the floor below me. The hooded figures are all crouched in a half circle, their heads bowed toward the altar. The organ music continues to rise, notes blaring in a tumultuous dumpster fire filling every sliver of space in this decrepit room.

What follows is silence. Cold, eerie silence for prolonged minutes, hours—I can't tell anymore. The pain in my hands buzzes up through my arms, the stabs into my scalp rendering me incoherent. Confused. All I hear are the sounds of my own blood dripping from my toes to the stone below me.

Drip.

Drip.

Drip.

The faceless cloaks still bow.

The space is unmoving, like a photo.

I am nothing but an ornament in a room of evil.

I want for the notes to coalesce around me once more. For the damage to be done.

How easily I can give up, after all these years. After all

the demons, after all the cultists. After my parents. After June.

I'm not ready to give up.

Drip.

Drip.

Step.

Faintly, I hear small footsteps against stone. Nothing in the room moves, and yet . . . the footsteps sound like they're coming from the stairwell leading to the basement.

Drip.

Step.

Step.

Drip.

And then . . . she's here. My beautiful little angel. My . . . Salvation.

I pray and pray it's a delusion—the blood loss has gotten to my head, making me see what I so desperately want to see. I pray the stabbing crown is making me lose my mind. I pray the demon is influencing me with more visions of what I desire.

But I know this isn't a vision. I know June is really here, wearing my mask, my hoodie. She flinches when her eyes finally land on me, and I can feel her taking me in as though I were truly her God being crucified.

"Marcelo?" she whimpers. "What have they . . . are you . . ."

"J—June." I try but even the movement of my lips pulls the dregs of pain through me once more. I grunt, my throat on fire, but I don't stop. "June, get out of here."

She stands at the top of the stairs, her palm clasped around my silver rosary, and Diablo is curled around her neck, somehow propped within the hood at her neck. Those green eyes land on me, and I swear I almost see something like anger flash through them. June steps forward, the white cross on my mask catching the small flickers of candlelight.

"June," I beg. "Please. Run."

But she doesn't. My girl pulls Diablo from her neck, yanking him as he digs his claws into the fabric in objection, and gently places him on the floor. With a final scratch between his ears, she stands straight, her shoulders moving as though she's taking a deep inhale, and then she struts forward—toward the cloaked figures.

"Valac!" she calls and every part of me wants to yell, beg, plead, *something* to just make her go the other way. To get out of here and as far from the cloaked figures as she can. "Let him go!" she screams as I ignore every instinct in me telling me not to move, every ounce of pain that nearly blinds me as I attempt to *pull* myself free.

My hands move along the thick nails, metal through flesh and muscle, but—I have to get to June.

I have to get—

53

JUNE

Marcelo's head falls forward as his shoulders sag, his hands once again sliding back to the base of the cross behind him.

"Marcelo!" I scream, running to him.

The cloaked figures haven't moved since I've entered, and I'm half-convinced they may not even be real. But the moment I try to yank the nail pinning his feet free, the cloaks—as one—flick up.

"My sweet, darlin' Junia," a voice coos, and as my eyes track it, it comes from a hooded figure slowly rising in the center of the semi-circle.

"Daren," I say, just as he slides his hood down and removes an all-white mask with the same symbol from the door painted on the forehead. "How long have you been worshipping demons? Did that happen before or after you met my mother?"

The bastard smiles. And it fills me with just enough rage to fully pull the nail free.

Marcelo's legs fall free, the wounds bleeding immensely. Quickly, with my eyes still trained on Daren, and the rest of the circle, I slip out of Marcelo's hood and wrap both sleeves around each of his feet. Hopefully, that'll be enough for now.

Enough until he wakes up or until someone comes for him.

"I've never seen this side of you." Daren licks his teeth, his eyes drifting to Marcelo's slumped form before falling back on me. "I liked how submissive you were. How easily I could dominate you. It made me think, maybe when I finally fucked you, I could make you do whatever I wanted. I liked the idea of you suckin' my cock with my hand around your throat or the idea of fucking you while I had your momma gagged in the corner, watching. I wanted to show her just what she was missin' all these months. Bitch never put out." His serpentine smile sent shivers down my spine as he slowly got closer, climbing up the steps to the altar toward me.

"But she was never the prize, so it didn't really matter, anyway. I never wanted her. If I fucked her, it would've only made me want the younger, *suppler* model. Your momma's all skin and bones, darlin'. But you? Fuck, look at you!"

I took a step back, flinching as Daren climbed the final step.

"I wanted you to be my little doll, Junia. I wanted to dress you up, fuck you silly, then leave you tied to my bed as I went out for a drink. I imagined you waiting, all hot and bothered and begging for me when I got home."

I kept my eyes on Daren, even as my hand fell to my thigh. Even as my hand dips just under the hemline of my dress. Even as my fingers pull free the knife I have tucked between the seam of my undershorts and my thigh.

Daren steps closer, but I don't move. I have one chance at this. One. And I need the fucker closer.

"But," he grunts. "This fucker here took you from me. He had you before I could. I saw how flushed your face was as you stumbled out of the confessional. I know what he was doing to you in there." Another step. "I was so fuckin' jealous then, I nearly killed him." Another step. "I could've, you know. Killed him. I could've summoned the demons to hold him down while I slit is filthy fuckin' throat." As he says the word, his hand darts out and wraps around my neck. He doesn't squeeze hard, but I know his touch is meant to rattle me. I force another flinch, feeding his ego as he steps in.

"But you know what? Maybe this is for the best." Daren closes the distance between us, and I thank God for the mask filtering out his hot, gross breath. "Now, I can fuck you as I make you watch him die. Now, I can beat that little brat out of you. It'll be so much more fun to spank you when you misbehave than to spank you when you were just a pathetic little puppet to your whore of a mother."

Just then, blood splatters on Daren's face. The red jewels spat onto his sandy hair, his pale face.

There's a chuckle above our heads. "You didn't answer her question, fucker." My eyes dart up to meet Marcelo's. Blood drips down his face, his chin, but it doesn't stop him from smirking at me. It doesn't stop him from seeing the knife.

Daren scowls up at Marcelo, his face contorting into something almost demonic. He opens his mouth, ready to spew whatever venom he has left—but he doesn't get the chance.

The moment his lips part, I thrust the knife up between us, stabbing it into the space behind his chin and up through his mouth. I watch as the blade pierces through his tongue, finally silencing him. Daren's eyes fall to me, his mouth still gaped, and now I can't tell if it's from shock or from the blade pinning him there.

He staggers back, grasping for the blade. But he staggers too far and trips on his own feet—right over the few stone steps. Daren crashes to the floor, his body writhing as he gasps for breath, as he twitches and spasms, as the gurgles become the only thing I hear.

I straighten, readying myself for whatever comes next. Marcelo braces his feet on the cross behind me, still trying to lift himself off the nails after regaining consciousness, after he spit his own blood on Daren's face.

Daren may be down, and while it's satisfying as Hell, there still is no way out of here. Not with the rest of the faceless cult. Not with Marcelo still pinned to a cross too high for me to reach.

Not with a demon still waiting to reveal himself.

"Let Valac out," I say, my shoulders back. "And be the coward you always have been."

The room is silent save for the continued gurgling. I lost sight of Diablo a long time ago. And the faceless figures are still crouched in a semicircle—watching. Waiting.

A huff of breath breaks the silence like an earthquake as one lone figure rises.

"For the record," it says as it walks forward, the other figures hurriedly scooting out of its way and dropping into even lower bows. "This piece of shit joined *after* he met your mother. He didn't join until she brought him along to church one Sunday."

My eyebrows furrow, and my entire body stiffens. I

know this voice. I know this voice as comfort, as hope. I know this voice as guidance and teachings. I know this voice as love and sometimes solace.

"He didn't join," it continues, and I can practically see the warm smile spreading over the familiar face. All too suddenly, the air is pulled out of me as I race to catch up to what my mind has already realized. As my eyes process what I already knew I'd see. As the hood falls from his head, as the same mask Daren wore is pulled aside, Father Callum grins. "Until he met me."

Father fucking Callum.

Callum is—

"He came to me one day for confessions." He saunters up to June, and the fight in me is once again rejuvenated. I struggle to pull my hands off these nails, but my limbs are weak from blood loss, my strength depleted. "Told me how badly he wanted you. How he'd sometimes peek in on you at night. How'd he go through your room when you weren't home. How he dreamed of forcing himself on you when your mother was asleep in the next room," Callum says to June. "And it brought a smile to my face. Like him, I always knew there was more to you, June. I knew there was a little demon ready to break free from her mother's overbearing gaze. It's part of the reason I forced those little bouts of horniness on you—just to see what'd you do."

June is frozen below me, the mask obscuring her expression. I can't tell if she's more shocked or afraid right now, but both are bad—both will slow her reaction time.

"Saint Michael, defend us in battle that we might not perish at the dreadful judgment," I pray quickly, my lips moving as I've trained them to, as if it is second nature rather than practiced effort.

A sharp stab erupts in my chest, and I swear there is a knife carving me open. My yell echoes around the convent as Callum tuts. "Oh, Marcelo, you're quite the eager one!" He chuckles. "Though, I didn't think it'd take you this long to figure everything out. I guess you were busy falling under this one's spell." Callum flicks his hand toward June, smirking. "You heathens really took advantage of the little lust spell I put on her. Fucking in the confessional booth? Licking her pussy between the pews where anyone could see you? Down right satanic if you ask me. And you—you're supposed to be a priest." He tuts again, and I feel the invisible knife twist.

Fuck!

"I was told you were the best exorcist, and then I waited and waited. But you never found me."

He wanted me here. He still wants me to exorcise him—to send him back to Hell.

"I was always going to use June to get home. The moment I met her, I knew she'd be the one—like I'd been drawn to this godforsaken town because of *her*. But once you came"—he grins again, raising an eyebrow—"once I saw the look in your eyes as you fell for her, I *knew* it was . . . ah—you'd call it *divine intervention*, I believe."

As one, the hooded figures begin to hum. It's quiet at first, but grows louder and louder too fast.

"I have to admit," Callum continues, ignoring them, "it

upsets me that you thought I was possessing Daren." He walks up to the body still squirming on the floor. Daren grabs Callum's leg, pulling himself up and gurgling something incomprehensible. "This filth unfortunately is just that rotten, dear." He looks up at June, flashing her what is supposed to be a comforting smile. "Your mother too. I've never had to influence her. She's always just been that vile. For that, I am truly sorry. Before I was condemned to be stuck here, I had forgotten just how evil humanity can be. How, often, they outshine even the nastiest of demons." He shrugs nonchalantly, as if he didn't just confirm every hard truth June has ever felt. She didn't say so earlier, but I knew there was a level of hope in her that maybe Jill and Daren weren't actually that bad. Maybe they were just being made worse by the demon's influence or by a demonic possession.

But, no. Jill was just Jill—a rotten mother through and through. And Daren was just Daren—a pig of a human, evil in heart, soul, and body.

"What do you want?" June demands, and I'm so fucking proud of her as she stands her ground, as her voice doesn't stutter.

Callum smirks. "Tell me what you want, dear, and then I'll tell you what I want. Deal?"

June clenches and unclenches her fist. "I want you to let him go. You said you wanted me. So take me and leave him."

Let him go! Take me.

"No!" I yell, jerking against the wood. "No, don't."

Callum smiles up at me. "Damn, Marcelo. How do you do it? You've got two for two ladies sacrificing themselves for you." He clicks his tongue and continues to pace in front of the altar, kicking Daren's hands away from him and leaving him in the center of the circle as no one helps him. "See, I would. But, unfortunately, June, you *both* are part of my equation to get the *Hell* out of here." He runs his hand through his hair, like the bastard doesn't have a care in the damned world. "See, I take you, then Father over here does everything he can to save you—exorcising me and sending me right back down to Hell."

"I can exorcise you without her. Just let her go," I grunt.

"Unfortunately," Callum huffs. "Ya can't. I'm tethered from body to body. So, I need to *un*tether myself from this guy and go into little June's body."

"What did you do to the real Father Callum?" she asks.

"Oh, this guy?" Callum points at himself before shrugging. "He was some bum two towns over. He was a no one."

June startles and Callum chuckles again, pausing in front of the altar.

"Little June, you're still not getting it. Your Father Callum isn't *possessed* by the demon Valac. I *am* Valac. I have been, all along.

"Anyway. That's enough yapping. I'm tired of this damned place, and I'm ready to see exactly how this lovely little lady feels inside. Grab her," he commands, and immediately the humming intensifies, and the shapes move. Figures dash around Valac and Daren, running at June in full force.

So many things happen at once.

So much, I can barely see any of it.

A flurry of velvet black brushes past my body. A large, slender pair of hands wrap around one of wrists, pulling a nail free. The humming crescendos as ritual blades are pulled from hidden pockets, from billowing sleeves. A scream erupts from June's lips as her arms are grabbed. Valac chuckles loud and clear through the chaos. The ghostly organ music picks up once more, the soundtrack for the horrific scene.

Then, my body is falling till I slam on the stone below me. Every bone feels like it's shattered on impact, and I curse as I try to lift myself. This is going to fucking hurt tomorrow.

"Marcelo!" June calls, and her voice is like Heaven to my ears as her soft hands wrap around my arm.

"Get up," another voice says—a new voice. A hand firmly grabs my other arm, lifting me to my feet and as I stagger to regain my footing, I'm forced to look up. And up. And up.

A *third* demon stands before me, grasping my arm with long fingers and even sharper nails. As my eyes slowly take in the figure, I realize his skin is pitch black with a velvety soft texture all over. He's incredibly tall with an inhumanely thin waist and a vibrant white tattoo on his chest in the shape of another sigil.

But what makes me pause isn't the fact that there is yet another demon here, nor the fact that this one seemed to have gotten me down.

No, it's his eyes.

They're a golden yellow, with a hint of distaste.

"Diablo . . ." I mutter, and the demon grins, flashing sharp, white fangs.

"Bael, actually. But yeah."

June stands next to me, her hands still propped on my arm as though she's helping me stay upright. "Our Diablo?" she asks, complete confusion in her tone.

This demon's features are more catlike than Asmodeus. His eyes are sharp, his nose is small and buttoned, and his jaw is incredibly pointed. But more than that, atop his head are short, thick horns shaped like what appear to be two large cat ears.

Fuck. My cat is *actually* from Hell.

How many times have I fucked June in his presence?

"Bael!" Valac calls. "There you are. I'd been wondering when you'd show up."

The cat demon grabs my hand and yanks it toward his mouth. "Save June," he demands. And then I feel my soul leave my body as he *licks* my wound, his tongue just as rough and dry as an actual cat's. "Yuck," Bael spits, but as I pull my hand away, I notice the stigmata hole in my hand is knitting itself back together. Actually, they all are. Each of the wounds on my back, the knife-like wound in my chest, the stigmata on my feet—all of it, healed.

And with it, so is my energy.

"For the record," Bael snarls, "I like June more." Bael dashes into the crowd of figures, pulling them apart.

That makes two of us.

I turn to June and grab her hands. "We need to get you out of here."

But the moment I start to pull her along toward an exit, our hands are pulled apart. I'm pushed back by an unseen force.

"Not so fast, the party hasn't even begun."

Valac stands between us—but he isn't in the familiar facade of Father Callum. It is the demon from the painting at the forefront of the sanctuary. He's as tall as Bael, but his skin is a brutally vibrant crimson. Huge, spiraling horns protrude from his head, as he currently hovers over June, cupping her cheeks and forcing their faces so close to each other.

"Get the fuck away from her," I grit out, throwing myself at them. I'm grabbed from behind, but Bael is there to rip the cultists hands away from me, to continue challenging them as I focus on June and Valac. But just as I reach them, Valac grins, his smile unnaturally wide as black ooze slips between the millions of small, sharp teeth—just like the imps had—and drips from black lips onto June.

The moment the black touches her, June screams, her entire body going so taut, it looks like a simple breeze might break every bone in her body.

"June!" I yell, trying to pull the demon away from her, but it's useless. Valac is literally *melting* onto June, just like the candles from earlier. In a matter of seconds, the demon is completely gone, and all that's left is the black substance covering my songbird, like oil caught in her wings.

"Marcelo," she chokes out.

And then her spine audibly snaps as her back bends to be parallel to the floor.

I freeze, Ana's death playing over June's, an overlay of my past colliding with my present.

But I won't let June go. I won't let him take her. I won't let her end up like my family.

I carefully grab her, pulling her body into my arms as I kneel to the floor. Her chest is moving rapidly, and I see the slightest trail of steam coming off the rosary resting atop it as it actively works to fight what's inside of her.

"June," I whisper as I untie my mask from the back of her head and slide it off her. Her stunning doe eyes are wide and vacant. "June, stay with me. Fight him." I caress her cheek, rubbing my thumb along her lip.

She fidgets in my arms, and I can feel her fighting. Her will battling that of Valac's. I grab her hand and place it over the rosary. Immediately, her fingers tighten around the cross, and she turns her head into my chest, taking deep breaths.

Carefully, I choose my prayer, and begin in a hushed whisper. "Let God arise, and let His enemies be scattered,"

I pray, my fingers tightening around her hand, pulling her cold body in closer. "And let them that hate Him flee from before His face."

June whimpers, her body convulsing in my arms. "No, no!" she screams—but I know it's at Valac.

"As smoke vanishes, so let them vanish away. As wax melts before the fire, so let the wicked perish—"

June screams again, her eyes rolling to the back of her head as her back arches against me. But I don't let up, I can't.

"So let the wicked perish at the presence of God."

She convulses again, coughing hard.

"So let the wicked perish at the presence of God," I repeat, and June's coughing turns into choking as she spits up the black ooze. I quickly turn her on her side, rubbing her back as she chokes out more.

"So let the wicked perish at the presence of God!"

June gags, and a final stream of what's left of Valac finally spills out onto the convent floor.

55

JUNE

My throat hurts. My lungs are on fire. And I can hardly remember anything from the last five minutes.

I remember the demon standing before me as Marcelo ran for me. I remember before that, my cat turned into a literal demon, who saved my boyfriend, and then went to attack the rest of the cultists. I remember my priest had been the villain all along. And I remember stabbing my stepfather through the mouth.

But there was a gap. A gap in time, in memory, in vision—and as I see the black gore dripping from my lips, I think I'm glad for it.

"June?"

Marcelo is here, rubbing my back in slow circles, and the moment I sit up, he's pulling me into his arms.

I don't even clock when the tears start streaming, but

the moment his arms are around me, I'm throwing myself at him.

"You're okay," he breathes, petting the back of my head. "You're okay."

"Is—is he gone?" I whimper, too afraid to look and see if the black puddle becomes anything more.

"Gone. For now," says Dia—*Bael*. The demon pads up to us, a number of cloaked men laying at his feet, but it's clear most had run away. "That was smart, Marcelo. You exorcised him from June alone. He's still stuck here." Bael crouches down, as though he really were a cat, and watches the black puddle.

"But he got away?"

Bael nods. "The coward always was good at running away."

There's silence for what feels like a long time. I feel like I'm still catching my breath and Marcelo holds me just as tight.

"You're the *he* Asmodeus wanted me to keep safe?" I ask.

Bael sniffs. "I didn't mean to deceive you both. I have been more cat than man for as long as I can remember. I prefer it. I do not like this long and cumbersome body."

I shuffle, turning to face the demon. "So be a cat. Be our cat, if you like."

His head perks, almost as if his ears are at attention—just like when he was simply Diablo. He turns those gold eyes to Marcelo.

"Are you going to try to steal June away from me?"

I can't help but bite back a chuckle.

Bael turns his head to the side. "Yes." Then his eyes fall to me. "But, not like that. I don't . . . feel romantic feelings like that. June is simply my human. And you are the spare human."

Now Marcelo chuckles. "Fair enough. You can stay."

In the blink of an eye, the demon is gone and now only stands the large black cat with gold eyes and the white tuft of fur at his chest.

Bael blinks at us, long and slow, before prancing up to us and rubbing his head along my hand.

"I feel like I need a three-day-long nap," I groan.

Chuckling, Marcelo slowly stands with me still embraced in his arms. "Fucking ditto. We're not leaving bed until at least seventy-two hours pass."

"Well." I bite my lip. "Actually, we *may* have some phone calls to make. I sort of called Father Rodrigo on the way here and let him know everything that was going on."

Marcelo pauses midstep. "Oh, fuck."

"And he may or may not be sending every available exorcist *here*."

"*Fuck*. There goes our next three days, *princesa*."

As we descend the steps from the altar, a groan has me nearly jumping from Marcelo's arms.

Daren still squirms, grabbing Marcelo's pants.

"This fucker is *still* alive?"

Marcelo gently places me on my feet and then crouches down. "A promise is a promise, fucker."

He pulls his knife from Daren's chin, watching as the blood splatters from the hole. Daren convulses, but it doesn't matter—he wasn't trying to save him. As Daren finally bleeds out, I feel a rush of relief. Of freedom. And of safety. He's finally *gone*.

Marcelo then takes his blade and carves a large cross, from Daren's forehead to upper lip, and then across his eye lids. "And lead us not into temptation," he mumbles, "but deliver us from evil. Amen."

It has been days since the convent—days of speaking to Rodrigo's officials, letting them sleuth out the rest of the cult members, days of finding a replacement for Callum, and days of rest. But Marcelo and I are finally packing up the Mustang, Bael in tow, and leaving Belmouth all together. I have no clue where we're going. Maybe New York—he's mentioned taking me to see Tisch in case I'd like to try applying again. He's also mentioned Miami, to visit Rowan, Willow, and Rodrigo.

But, truthfully, I will happily go anywhere with him.

There's just one thing left to do here in Belmouth.

"Ready?" Marcelo asks, closing the trunk and facing me. Bael already jumps into the back seat, curling atop a blanket specially laid out for him.

I sigh deeply. "As ready for this as I'll ever be."

Coming up to me, Marcelo takes my hands. "I'll be right here. You can yell and I'll come running. Okay?"

I nod.

"You sure? 'Cause you also don't *have* to do this if you don't want to."

"No," I say, pressing my lips together. "I think I do have to."

Marcelo squeezes once more before letting go.

Mass is just ending, people are streaming out in the sunlight, and there, with no one around her, is my mother.

Taking another deep breath, I walk up to her.

My mother's eyes dart up to me, as if she sensed I was here. Her blond hair looks nearly white in the sunlight, and no amount of concealer can hide the bags under her eyes. Yet still, somehow, she manages to look at me with those daggers.

"Hi," I say.

"What do you want?" She straightens, raising a brow.

"I'm sorry about Daren," I lie. She doesn't know about the cult. The official report is that he skipped town, leaving her behind.

"No, you're not."

She's right.

"I'm not." I meet her eyes, my back straight. "I'm leaving Belmouth with Marcelo. I wanted to say goodbye."

"Skipping town with the priest," she scoffs, rolling her eyes. "How did I raise a such a whore?"

I smirk at her. "Monkey see, monkey do, I guess."

My mother scowls.

As I watch her, I realize something. My mother has always been so violently angry—and it took me twenty-five years, three demons, and a hot priest to realize that anger was never my fault. Jill Forester is a miserable person, through and through. She has no life save for what I gave her—and without me, she will be nothing. She *is* nothing.

I don't need her. I've never needed her.

She's the one who's needed me.

"Look. I don't know when or if I'll ever come back here. But if you ever need me . . ." I pull the small slip of paper I had tucked into my pocket with my new phone number scrawled on it. It took me about four tries to get it just right, as my hand shook each time I tried.

Now, I held that little paper up steady.

"This is my number. You can call."

My mother's daggers drop to the little paper, and I'm thoroughly convinced she won't take it. Or worse, she'll snatch it and stomp on it.

But she does. She tentatively grabs the paper, almost as if she's afraid it might poison her on contact. But she takes it. She reads it, and then she tucks it in her purse.

I could spend all my life hoping my mother would wake up one morning, wishing she'd been better. I could hope she'd try to be different, try to fix things, finally apologize.

But my expectations aren't high, and I know the simplicity of that alone would be asking too much of her. So I will continue my life, knowing my mother's daggers are really meant for her. I will spend my life slowly forgetting the tiny house we lived in, letting the scars along my back fade into nothingness, and forgive how little she cared for me.

She will become a piece of my history instead of my revolving present. And that's okay.

I look at her once more, those daggers a shade so similar to my own eyes.

"Get home safely," I say in way of goodbye, and after giving her one final moment to say something—she doesn't—I turn from my mother and finally walk away.

I'm cuddled in the crook of Marcelo's arm as Bael loafs on one of my thighs and Marcelo's hand grips the other. The cat has been asleep for the greater part of an hour as Marcelo drives through the winding dark streets of Massachusetts at night.

We've taken turns picking songs to play as he tells me stories of his past exorcisms, as though they were only horror movies he'd seen and not atrocities he's lived. He tells me of ridiculous times he spent in his youth with the twins and all the trouble they'd gotten in with Rodrigo.

"Look," Marcelo gasps.

Now leaving Massachusetts.

"We're in New York state," he tells me.

"Is that where we're going?" I ask.

Marcelo shrugs. "I honestly have no idea where we're going, songbird. I figured we could decide when the sun rises."

I smile at him, kissing his cheek.

"That sounds perfectly good to me."

ACKNOWLEDGMENTS

This book was a monster to write—in both the monster fucker sense—because, my god, was it hot—and in a general "oh shit, this thing is gonna kill me" kind of way. A *lot* was going on in my life while writing this book, between switching jobs and adjusting to a new lifestyle and routine, and I think that affected my process more than usual. Not to mention, this genre is vastly different from what I've written before, and yet still totally me. It was so fun, and also incredibly terrifying to make sure I not only did the story and characters justice, but the genre too.

I truly don't know if this book would've gotten to the light of day without my amazing support system encouraging me on.

First and foremost, I need to thank my wonderful fiancé, Mike. If it weren't for you telling me, "You need to write," on an almost daily basis, I don't know if this book would've been finished, let alone written at all. Thank you for always supporting me, and for always carrying my boxes of books. Of course, I can't thank you without thanking our beautiful baby, Maki. She inspired so much of my writing for Diablo, but in truth, Maki was an actual menace this time around. I am convinced she was actively trying to *stop* me from writing as she nudged my hand away from the keyboard and mouse, or stood with her butt in my face to block my view. Who knows. But she did get a lot of pets during the writing of this, so she better be happy.

Next, I'd like to thank my mom. She wanted me to put, in writing, that Jill was *not* based on her *at all*. Which is true—Marcelo's mom was based on her. Minus her horrible death. Oops. Sorry, Mom! Thank you for all the wild support you give me, thank you for being my biggest cheerleader forever and always, thank you for supporting this weird and dark brain of mine, and thank you for being nothing like June's mom.

My partner in crime, Anto—you already know I couldn't do any of this without you. Literally, because you made this stunning cover and all the gorgeous book elements for me. Thank you for being the other half of my brain, I love you to death and back.

Thank you to Larissa, Sara, Maddie, and Slasher for being such an amazing team of supporters throughout the process of this book. Whether it was editing or making content so I could focus on writing, your help has meant the world! Also, thank you to all my little birds for always supporting me and reading my books!

Finally, thank *you*, dear reader, for joining me on this journey. I hope you love Marcelo and June as much as I do. We may just be seeing more of them soon.

Love always,
Julie

ABOUT THE AUTHOR

J. M. Failde (fah-eel-deh) spent just over one hundred fortnights rigorously studying the complexities of the English language at Florida International University. While she is not conjuring up stories, she can be found searching for *el chupacabra*, befriending the ghost in her house, or dying her hair a new color. Failde currently resides in her gothic manor on the outskirts of Atlanta, Georgia, with her fiancé, Mike, and her familiar—the round but feisty calico cat, Maki.

Follow her on Instagram @jmfailde or go to her website, jmfailde.com, for more.

www.ingramcontent.com/pod-product-compliance
Lightning Source LLC
Chambersburg PA
CBHW030734310726
48969CB00005B/1214